characters are only part of her appeal. The winning combination of toughness and tenderness is what enthralls readers."
—RT Book Reviews

"This first-rate tale easily measures up to its predecessors and will make readers eager for their next visit to Bitter Springs."
—*Publishers Weekly* (starred review)

"A tender, engaging romance and a dash of risk in a totally compelling read. . . . Gritty, realistic, and laced with humor."
—*Library Journal* (starred review)

"Jo Goodman is a master storyteller and one of the reasons I love historical romance so much."
—The Romance Dish

"Fans of Western romance will be thrilled with this delightful addition to Goodman's strong list."
—*Booklist*

"A wonderfully intense romance. . . . A captivating read."
—Romance Junkies

"Exquisitely written. Rich in detail, the characters are passionately drawn. . . . An excellent read."
—*The Oakland Press*

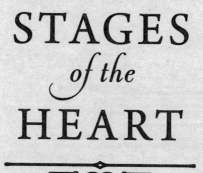

STAGES *of the* HEART

Jo Goodman

JOVE
New York

A JOVE BOOK
Published by Berkley
An imprint of Penguin Random House LLC
penguinrandomhouse.com

A JOVE BOOK, BERKLEY, and the BERKLEY & B colophon
are registered trademarks of Penguin Random House LLC.

ISBN: 9780440000679

First Edition: May 2020

Printed in the United States of America
1   3   5   7   9   10   8   6   4   2

Cover photo by Claudio Marinesco
Cover design by Sarah Oberrender
Book design by George Towne

For Pam Hopkins—agent and fan.

1

Cabin Creek Trail, Colorado Territory

May 1872

There was no room to stretch. Of all the discomforts one experienced traveling by stagecoach, the lack of leg and elbow room was at the forefront of McCall Landry's mind. He imagined extending his long legs to the opposite bench seat and resting his bootheels between the corpulent assemblyman on the left and the snake oil drummer in the center. If the drummer would only press himself closer to the heavily bearded miner on his right, Call figured there'd be about enough room to affect the semi-prone posture that suited him. Call believed in never standing when you could lean, never leaning when you could sit, and never sitting when you could be lying flat on your back staring at the clouds in daylight or stars in the night sky. Call thought a man should have beliefs, and if he stood by anything, he stood by this one.

There was no chance of putting his belief to the test now, as he was wedged between a dandy who breathed behind a handkerchief to avoid the road dust that seeped into the stage and a flatulent minister who had been white-knuckling a Bible since boarding the stage in Denver. Given the narrow route, much of it mountain on one side and gulley on the other, clutching the Bible was understandable. The flatulence, though, was a trespass. A slim smile changed the shape of Call's mouth as he considered taking the dandy's handkerchief and using it to cover his own nose and mouth. It had been at least twenty minutes since the minister passed gas. Surely he was about to blow.

Although introductions were made soon after the stage left Denver, Call was more interested in each man's trade than his given name. The minister was identifiable by his collar. The assemblyman identified himself as an attorney, newly elected to his position on a platform of achieving statehood for the territory. The snake oil salesman opened the black leather case he kept on his lap to show his wares and generously offered a sample of his liver-purifying tonic. No one took him up on it, and he simply shrugged and closed the case. The miner was an itinerant job seeker, moving between mines that were played out and ones reputed to hold promise. The dandy claimed to be a reporter for a New York paper, but since he'd never come out from behind his handkerchief to pose a question and showed little interest in the view outside the coach, Call harbored doubts.

When it was Call's turn to say something, he smiled briefly, let his gaze drop to the holstered Colt at his side, and told them he was a gun for hire. He wasn't, but he could have been, so that's what he told them. No one said anything for a long time after that, which suited Call just fine. He had learned enough to know that what they had in common was their destination. They were all headed to Stonechurch.

After forty-five miles and three brief stops at swing stations, where the tired horses were exchanged for fresh ones and a new driver took over at one of the stations, Call regarded the vaguely queasy features of his companions and concluded they had something else in common. They were all feeling wretched.

Call slid down in his seat as much as he was able, rolled his shoulders, and tipped his broad-brimmed hat forward so that it shaded his eyes before he closed them. "Misery acquaints a man with strange bedfellows."

"What's that you say?" asked the miner.

Call didn't open his eyes. The swaying coach was hardly a cradle, but traveling by this method provoked in Call a desire to sleep, which was preferable to staying awake and becoming increasingly nauseated. At the last station, Call had inquired about riding shotgun since the new driver had no companion for the next leg and Call's own shotgun was packed on the roof beside his bag, but the driver was suspicious of his motives and he was summarily dismissed.

"I said, 'Misery acquaints a man with strange bedfellows.'"

"That something from the Good Book?" asked the miner, his eyes dropping to the minister's hands, which were once again folded tightly around the Bible.

"Shakespeare," said Call. "*The Tempest*. Also a good book. Well, a play."

"Huh." The miner nodded, looked around, and nodded again, more emphatically this time. "I reckon we are strange bedfellows. No question that we're miserable. Not you so much. Looks like you're aiming to sleep."

"That's the plan."

The minister turned his head sideways and stared at Call's slanted hat. "Are you likely to snore?"

"Less likely than you are to fart." Call thought the dandy reporter might have sniggered behind his handkerchief, but he was opposed to opening his eyes to confirm. Call touched the brim of his hat, lowered it another notch, and smiled ever so slightly under the cover of shadow. He was asleep in mere minutes.

The Henderson Express Stage Line was the sole provider of coach services along the Cabin Creek Trail from Denver to the mining town of Stonechurch. It was a lucrative route, funded in part by government grants because of Stonechurch's value as a gold and silver mining operation. The coach carried payroll, mail, passengers, and occasionally gold and silver bricks. Transportation of the precious metals was naturally a secretive affair and not necessarily accompanied by armed guards, whose presence would have raised suspicions. Payroll for the miners was scheduled randomly to make robbery less likely, though the coaches and the living stations were still targets.

Stonechurch was a popular destination for men looking for work, for journalists looking for a story, for preachers looking for souls to save, for drummers looking to hawk their potions, and for politicians looking to make deals with the powerful Ramsey "Ramses" Stonechurch, but it wasn't the end of the line nor was it the only town growing up northwest of Denver. The home stations, those sites chosen by the line to offer meals, accommodations, sell tickets, provide a fresh team and sometimes a fresh driver, were points along the route that served as living magnets to attract people and build a sense of community.

The home station at Frost Falls was an important addition to the cattle town that was encouraging settlement, business, and law. Forty-five miles distant was another home station at Falls Hollow, where the station was the hub for the outlying farm families. With each business that was successfully established, the town drew more settlers and more entrepreneurs. Stonechurch Mining was vital to the financial health of Henderson Express and the home stations dotting the Cabin Creek Trail, but the mining operation's success was also going to spell the end of the stage line and the home stations. It was inevitable. The railroad was coming.

And Laurel Beth Morrison was ready.

Laurel had operated the Falls Hollow home station since her father and two brothers were murdered when the rebel Grant clan attacked and robbed the stage while the horses were being exchanged. She had been inside the farmhouse when the renegade rebels struck, and she was the only one with enough time to grab a shotgun. She made good use of it, killing one of the Grant boys and wounding another, but her effort was not enough to save her father and brothers or the stagecoach driver. The man riding shotgun was one of the renegades, so the gang had the advantage at the outset. That was seven years ago, not long after Lee's surrender. She had been twenty then, old enough to take on the responsibility of the home station but grieving so deeply that she had almost no recollection of doing it.

Now she employed four men to assist with managing the horses, keeping the grounds, house, and outbuildings in good repair, as well as help with the milking, egg gathering, tossing slops to the pigs, gardening, butchering, and smoking. She employed one woman to do the cooking and housekeeping. On her own, Laurel took care of the account books, purchasing, hosting, and telegraphy. She was also the one who maintained relations with Ramsey Stonechurch, Samuel Henderson, and just recently, Alexander Berry, the government's man in charge of establishing the route and rails from Denver to Stonechurch. It was Laurel's mission to make certain that Falls Hollow was a stop along that route and that she secured the contract to operate the station.

It made all kinds of sense for Alexander Berry to use the existing Cabin Creek Trail, which was already well worn and even widened in some places by the regular passing of the Henderson Express stages. But it was Laurel's opinion that people who depended on a government man to do what made sense were more foolish than the government and the man. She had been doing her research. Money exchanged hands as often as a tired team of horses was exchanged for a fresh one. She didn't know Mr. (please call me Alex) Berry well so she was reserving judgment as to his commitment to corruption, but in the event he was like so many others with a hand out, Laurel was saving her money.

It was late in the afternoon when Laurel stepped outside and onto the wide, freshly whitewashed porch. There was a swing on her right, a pair of rockers and a hip-high stool on her left, all of them painted in cheery sunshine yellow. It was a welcoming entrance, and it often elicited comments from the stage passengers, especially the women, who were relieved to discover that niceties existed in the rocky enclaves beyond Denver.

The farmhouse was stone that her father had quarried out of the mountainside. It had taken years. Laurel had no memory of living in the tidy shack that was the family's home until the house was ready, but her brothers did and liked to tease her about how she slept in a basket with a ham their mother was curing because there wasn't much room for her and God forbid they find another place for the ham. Laurel had always liked it when the teasing circled round to stories about their mother because years of miscarriages and early childhood deaths separated her birth from her brothers. The baby that came after her was stillborn and the death of their mother quickly followed. Her brothers had had cherished happy memories while Laurel's memories were elusive, occasionally triggered by the scent of lavender or someone's tuneless humming.

"Dillon! Hank!" Laurel called to the two young men loitering beside the barn. "If the stage is running true, it'll be here inside of ten minutes. You'd be doing yourselves and me a service by looking sharp." She watched the brothers exchange sheepish glances, lift their hats to run a hand through their flaxen hair, and then snap their suspenders into place. The boys—and that's how Laurel thought of them because they were not yet twenty—came to attention, bracing their shoulders and straightening their spines. They looked enough alike that it was not unusual for them to be mistaken for twins. At a distance, Laurel knew them apart because Dillon typically wore red suspenders and Hank preferred dark blue. "At ease," she said when they were standing like Praetorian guards. She simply shook her head when they took that as a cue to simultaneously deflate and collapse backward against the barn wall, looking as if they were depending on it to keep them upright. They probably were.

Laurel had hired the pair as a favor to their mother, who owned the mercantile. Mrs. Booker despaired of her younger boys amounting to more than a pond of frogs and said so frequently. Sometimes she feared aloud that they would amount to significantly less. Edna Booker had all the help she needed with her firstborn son loading and unloading freight and her two married daughters alternating days behind the counter while Edna saw to the accounts and assisted customers. Mr. Booker sat outside the store except in the most disagreeable weather. He invariably had an open book resting on the arm of his chair, but few people had ever seen him read. Mostly he chatted with passersby or slept and was content to do either. Mrs. Booker went into hand-wringing spasms when she thought about Dillon and Hank going the way of their father.

So Laurel had taken them under her wing, removing them from under their mother's feet. All in all it was a satisfactory arrangement. They were quick learners, hard workers, and enjoyed being outdoors. Early on, Dillon showed an interest in tending the garden while Hank had a deft touch with the horses. Rooster Keller, her handyman and right hand, who had arrived in the wake of the massacre and helped her bury the bodies and mark the graves, mentored the boys. She couldn't recall hiring Rooster. He simply showed up and never left, and now she couldn't imagine not having him around. If Rooster put her in mind of her father, then Dillon and Hank reminded Laurel of her brothers when she was yet a child. She had a place in her heart for all three of them.

Her fourth hire was a different story. Josiah Pye was a recent addition brought on after Laurel noticed that Rooster was favoring his right hip and walking with a pronounced limp if he didn't think she was watching. Mr. Pye had been on his way to Stonechurch in expectation of employment and lingered in the yard smoking a cheroot when the other passengers went into the house for a hasty meal. It was mere happenstance that during the team exchange one of the mares began bucking and kicking and rearing back in such a fierce fashion that Hank and Rooster were in danger of getting caught by a hoof. It was Mr. Pye who took the horse in hand, flinging his cheroot to the ground and swinging himself onto the mare's bare back. It was a wild ride, attracting Laurel's attention at the window. She saw the stage driver was staying well clear of the animals as he should, but his riding companion had his shotgun raised in anticipation of putting the mare down.

Mr. Pye made that unnecessary. He rode the mare until she calmed, and when he dismounted, he had words with the man riding shotgun. That confrontation ended with him delivering a blow that put the man on his backside in the dirt. Laurel had no problem with that. She only wished she had delivered the blow.

Over the meal that Mrs. Lancaster served to the passengers in the dining room, Laurel learned that Mr. Pye had honed his horse sense during his service as a Confederate cavalry officer. That lasted until his horse was shot out from under him, and with no replacement available, he became a foot soldier. Officers did not matter so much toward the end of the war.

Without consulting Rooster and with uncharacteristic impulsiveness, Laurel offered Josiah Pye a job before he boarded the stage. If he was surprised by the offer, he gave no indication of it, while she experienced the first frisson of unease as he looked her over in a manner that was more carnal than considering. In Laurel's mind, there was no reneging on the offer, so when he accepted, that was that.

Mr. Pye proved his worth taking care of the horses. He had a calming influence on the animals and possessed some healing skills as well. He made his own poultices and balms and was able to apply them to even the most recalcitrant animal, and while he was an asset in the horse stalls and the corral, he was, if not quite a liability with miscellaneous chores, certainly a reluctant participant. Laurel had overheard the boys remarking that it was easier to get chores done outside of Josiah's presence than it was with him hanging around. Depending on the task at hand, Mr. Pye practiced incompetence as if it were an art form, pulling up plants instead of weeds, hammering his thumb instead of the roof tiles, setting fence posts at an angle so they were sure to fall, and spilling more whitewash than he applied. His horse skills would not have been enough to keep him employed, but he didn't mind milking, retrieving eggs, or butchering the pigs and did those things capably. He was also an excellent cook, which they discovered by accident when Mrs. Lancaster took ill for three days and required her daughter to tend her at home. Mr. Pye volunteered his services in the kitchen but Laurel never seriously considered replacing Mrs. Lancaster. The cook was family.

Rooster and the boys called him Josey, but Laurel maintained a more formal boundary with him by always addressing him as Mr. Pye. She deemed it necessary after that initial sense of discomfort. At first he pointed out that they were of an age as though it should be reason enough to drop the convention, but after a number of attempts to get her to call him Josiah or Josey without success, he finally gave up. It was what Laurel wanted, or thought she did. The fact that he looked secretly amused by her formality made her question the wisdom of her decision.

She did not want to amuse him. If Laurel had her druthers, she would avoid him altogether. It was just not possible. He looked after the horses as if they were his own and made apple fritters that melted on the tongue.

Laurel forgot all about that as she heard the stage approaching and saw a dust cloud rising in the distance. She stepped off the porch and felt the ground vibrate under her feet. Out of the corner of her eye she saw that Dillon and Hank had pushed away from the barn and were walking toward her. Rooster and Mr. Pye came from the backyard, where they had been filling the water trough, just as the coach came to a full stop thirty feet from the porch. Laurel waved a hand in front of her face to waft away the accompanying dust.

The business of the Morrison home station was underway.

2

Now that the stagecoach was no longer in motion, the minister removed his hat and poked his head out the window to take in the still view. Like a turtle ducking into its shell, he quickly pulled back. "I thought one of you said Morrison Station was operated by a woman and that she would be greeting us." His eyes darted to the other occupants as he tried to remember who'd shared that nugget.

Call touched his forefinger to the brim of his hat and levered it upward. Without apology to the minister, he leaned sideways until the window served as a frame for his face. He took measure of the person standing at the foot of the porch steps, chuckled, and drew back, squeezing his shoulders between the minister and the dandy. "That *is* a woman," he said dryly, "and I can't say that it doesn't pain me some that you didn't know." Maybe if she offered the Bible-clutching minister an apple, he'd recognize her for what she was. It shouldn't have mattered that her attire wasn't traditionally female. Call had required only a glance at the chambray shirt tucked into a pair of denim trousers to identify a trim waist and hips with a definite feminine curve. She wore a buff leather vest and belted the trousers. Suspenders would have hugged her breasts like parentheses, drawing attention to them in a manner he supposed she wanted to avoid. The sleeves of her shirt were neatly folded to her elbows, revealing freckle-dusted forearms and delicate wrists. A slender neck rose above the open collar of her shirt and supported an oval-shaped face. Her hat, like his, shaded her features and hid her hair, but Call suspected when she removed it, he'd see another sprinkling of freckles across her nose.

"Someone open the goddamn door," said the dandy, coming out from behind his handkerchief. "Sorry, Parson, for the language, but not much."

The assemblyman reached for the handle at the same time the stagecoach driver pulled the door open. The politician nearly spilled out of the opening, narrowly saving himself at the last moment from going ass over teakettle by clutching either side of the door frame. He lowered his robust physique delicately to the ground, and the weight of the coach shifted noticeably.

"Miss Morrison," he said, stepping up to greet Laurel. He put out both hands to take hers as if they were dear friends. It was a tactic he used to affect familiarity and warmth. He had met Laurel Beth Morrison on only three occasions, but he knew she wanted to curry his favor as he did hers, so he was in full expectation that she would take up his greeting.

Laurel did. It would have been awkward to do otherwise, but she couldn't help wishing she were wearing riding gloves. The assemblyman's palms were hot and damp, and she had never gotten used to the way he drew his thumbs across the backs of her hands. She smiled, nodded, and slid out of his grasp as soon as she was able to manage it politely.

"Mr. Abrams. It's a pleasure to see you again. I didn't know you would be on the stage. Business in Stonechurch, I imagine."

"Indeed. I shall have news for you on my return."

Laurel smiled, nodded, and then swept her hand toward the house. "You know the way, Mr. Abrams. Please. Make yourself at home. Mrs. Lancaster is putting the spread on the table now and the coffee's hot."

Abrams nodded genially and walked confidently past

her with every indication he meant to avail himself of the home station's hospitality.

Laurel looked to the team of horses and saw that Mr. Pye and Hank had their work well in hand. Dillon was headed back to the barn to bring out the fresh team. Another passenger alighted from the stage, but Laurel spoke to the driver first.

"Hey, Brady. It looks as if you ran your team hard. Was there some reason you were in more of a hurry than usual?"

Brady swept his hat off and slapped it against his thigh. Dust motes collected in a beam of sunlight. "For no good reason that I know, Holloway was running late so I wanted to make up some time. Plus, I have me a passenger that asked to ride shotgun. For all kinds of good reasons, I didn't trust that."

Laurel nodded. Brady—she'd never known him to say whether it was his first or last name—was an experienced driver and a little full of himself as so many of the whips were. He'd been with Henderson Express since its earliest days. She remembered him from when she was a young girl and her father had gotten the contract for the home station. Sometimes he let her clamber up the stage to sit with him on the bench. He always had a bag of sugar treats for her. He reached inside a pocket in his duster and drew out a bag now. She grinned when he flicked his wrist and tossed it to her. Laurel caught the paper poke and peeked inside. "Lemon drops. My favorite."

The creases in Brady's weathered face deepened as he flashed a grin in return. "You only have favorites. I learned that a long time ago. Enjoy." He was all business again as he slapped his hat on his head, covering the salt-and-pepper hair that was still as thick and full as it had been in his youth. "Did I hear you say Mrs. Lancaster's got a spread for us?"

"Doesn't she always?" Laurel would have pointed him to the house, but he was already on his way, pausing just long enough to call out admonishments to Mr. Pye and Hank to have a care for his animals.

Amused, Laurel let him go on and then stepped to greet the next pair of passengers to alight from the carriage. At a glance she knew that neither of these men was guilty of asking to ride shotgun. The minister had his hands full of his Bible and the drummer wouldn't part with his case. They introduced themselves as Reverend Marshall, the newly appointed minister for Stonechurch's Presbyterian flock, and Samuel Littlejohn, a supplier of the finest tonics for a variety of ailments.

Laurel welcomed them and sent them toward the house, mentioning in a quiet aside to the vaguely malodorous minister that the privy was out back.

The heavily bearded John Spellman came next. Laurel recognized him as a miner from his faintly stooped posture and wiry frame. He was indeed looking for work in Stonechurch and she wished him well. As he headed toward the house in search of sustenance that she thought he desperately needed, the fifth passenger alighted from the stage and introduced himself as Thomas Brandywine, reporter for the *New York World*. She waited until he'd neatly folded and carefully tucked his handkerchief into a pocket before she held out a hand. He took it lightly in his, squeezing it with such gentle pressure that Laurel was tempted to wrestle him to the ground just because she could. He was a little worse for the wear from the tight confines of the stage, but his stiff collar was still in place and most of the creases in his suit were meant to be there. Sunlight glanced off his spectacles so she couldn't make out his eyes immediately, but when he tilted his head to the side and made a rather calculating assessment of her person, Laurel concluded he was as narrow-minded as he was narrow-eyed. If she figured at all into whatever story he was preparing to write, she did not expect to fare well in the telling.

"Will you require the telegraph while you're here? The office is inside the station." She waited him out while he considered whether or not to avail himself of the service.

"No," he said finally. "The drive from Denver has been uneventful. I intend to interview the Pharaoh in Stonechurch."

Laurel frowned slightly. "I hope you don't mean to use that rather disrespectful moniker for Ramsey Stonechurch in your reporting. He's Ramsey, not Ramses, no matter what you've heard. And you definitely should not mention it in his presence."

"Surely he knows people refer to him as Pharaoh."

"He knows. He doesn't particularly like it."

"I see."

Laurel wasn't sure he did, and she didn't trouble herself to hide her skepticism.

"You know him, I take it."

"Yes."

"Then perhaps I can interview you. Background for my piece."

"I don't think so."

Thomas Brandywine shrugged as if it were neither here nor there. "If you change your mind, let me know. I believe Mr. Pulitzer's readers would be interested in your story."

"You mean Mr. Stonechurch's story."

"Yes," he said carelessly. "That's what I mean."

Laurel stepped aside so Brandywine had a clear path to the farmhouse and waited for the last passenger to step down from the stage. She was curious about the man who had asked if he could ride shotgun. He was obviously a stranger to the line and didn't know Brady's history with Henderson Express or he would have known better than to make the inquiry. It was Brady's cousin who had been driving the stage when the rebel gang attacked the home station. It was Brady's cousin who had accepted a last-minute substitute to ride shotgun and found himself sitting next to one of the Grant rebel gang. It was Brady's cousin who was knifed before he had a chance to draw his weapon. From the window, Laurel had been a witness to the carnage and had a clear view of Brady's cousin falling from his perch and Ollie Grant grinning down at him before he stood and sheathed his bloody knife and took aim with his shotgun.

Laurel observed the final passenger step out of the coach with an ease that surprised her. It was not unusual to see men lumber clumsily as they alighted, many of them shaking out the bones of their arms and legs, rolling their shoulders, and stretching their necks. Perhaps this man had done that all while he was waiting his turn, or perhaps he was one of the fortunate who could sleep comfortably in the cramped, swaying coach and awake refreshed.

He was taller than any of his companions had been, at least six feet in Laurel's estimation. Slim and easy on his feet, he walked toward her in no particular hurry. He wore a black oilcloth duster with a caped shoulder similar to what Brady wore, and when it parted as he approached, she saw his gun belt. Frowning, she waved Rooster over.

When he was at her side, she spoke to the visitor. "You'll have to leave your gun with Rooster before you can go inside. Morrison Station rules, Mr.—"

"Landry," he said. "McCall Landry."

Laurel thought he might voice an objection to surrendering his weapon, but he unfastened the gun belt without a murmur and handed it over to Rooster with considerable respect, though whether that was for her, for Rooster, or for his gun, Laurel didn't know.

Rooster held the belt in two hands and stared down at the butt of the weapon. "I know this model," he said. "Colt Army issue."

"That's right," said Call. "Cavalry."

"Yankee, then."

"Northern side of the Mason-Dixon, about halfway between Pittsburgh and Philadelphia. Little town called Chambersburg, about a hard stone's throw from Gettysburg."

"You fought there?" asked Laurel.

"No. I was . . . elsewhere by then."

The pause in his answer left Laurel wanting to know more and certain that questions would be unwelcome even if they were answered politely. "Welcome, Mr. Landry."

"Call," he said. "That's what I answer to."

Laurel smiled but gave no indication as to how she would address him. She held out a hand. "I'm Laurel Beth Morrison." She liked that he grasped her hand firmly. He shook it once and then released her, looking expectantly toward the farmhouse but without taking a step in that direction.

"There's no ceremony here," she told him. "Go on. There'll be plenty of room for you at the table. Money jar's on the mantel. Everyone pays what they can."

"If it's all the same, I'd like to wash up." He held up his hands.

Rooster chuckled. "I guess your mama raised you right."

"My mother and all of my aunts. I don't aim to disappoint them now." He used a forefinger to raise the broad brim of his hat. "And I wouldn't mind washing the grit from my eyes."

Laurel blinked, struck by what fine eyes they were. Gunmetal gray, with a touch of silver glinting in the sunlight, they were direct, without cunning, but not without cleverness. His eyes had tiny creases at the corners, possibly from years outdoors, squinting in the daylight, but his affection for his hat made her suspect that the creases were laugh lines.

Laurel drew back from staring into his eyes to take in the whole of his face. His features had been chiseled by a careful hand, the jawline marked by a neatly trimmed beard, his upper lip made more distinct by the mustache that followed its curve. She was still regarding him with uncharacteristic interest when he grinned at her. It was an easy grin, like his walk. Untroubled. Unhurried. Relaxed. It also revealed a perfect set of pearlies that had probably never seen a dentist. That just wasn't fair. She had nearly had her jaw broken by the traveling dentist who removed two of her wisdom teeth. She'd looked like a nut-hoarding

chipmunk for weeks following the operation, and sometimes if she sneezed too hard, her jaw would still lock.

To Laurel's way of thinking, McCall Landry's teeth
were just one flawless feature too many. She was grateful
when Rooster pointedly cleared his throat and drew her
attention away from that grin, those eyes, and that jawline.

"Pump's around back. You can wash up there. Rooster
will show you." Laurel turned abruptly and headed to the
house.

Rooster watched her for a few seconds, shaking his
head, frowning as he scratched behind one of his ears.
"Strange, that."

"How so?"

Rooster didn't realize he'd spoken aloud or that he was
frowning at Laurel's back. His frown was more quizzical
than disapproving, but he hadn't meant to be an open
book to anyone, certainly not someone who had no business with Morrison Station except washing up and getting
a decent meal.

"Nothing," he said and started off to the pump. "This
way."

Call shrugged. He hadn't really expected an explanation. Laurel Beth Morrison struck him as unaffected,
straightforward, and possibly naïve about her attractive-
ness. Of course, the preacher hadn't recognized her for a
woman, so perhaps she was more self-aware and her manner of dress was as much a disguise as it was a practical
consideration.

He fell in step beside the man called Rooster. He was
curious about the name but let it go. "You'll be careful
with my gun?"

"Just going to put it up in the smokehouse till you're
ready to go. No one will touch it."

Call nodded, satisfied. He observed that Rooster was
still carrying the belt in two hands, palms up, as if it were
an offering. That was the kind of respect the weapon deserved. Rooster was correct that it was Army issue; it just

hadn't been issued to him. The Colt had saved his life, though, or more accurately its previous owner had, so he had a certain attachment to the weapon and the man who willed it to him with his final words.

At the pump, Call removed his hat, sluiced fresh cold water on his face and neck, and made runnels in his cinnamon-colored hair with damp fingers. There was no towel and Rooster didn't offer to get him one, so Call shook out his hands and rubbed his face dry. When he was finished, he put on his hat and at Rooster's direction went around to the front of the farmhouse while Rooster went off to secure the gun.

Following the tantalizing scent of hot bacon, Call found his fellow passengers and their driver sitting around a large oaken table in the station's generously sized dining room. They were helping themselves to equally generous portions of the cook's fare. In the case of the portly attorney, a second generous helping seemed to be finding its way to his plate.

Call saw that there was indeed room for him at the table. He doubted it was planned, but the empty chair put him between the driver and the station's owner. Miss Morrison was the only person at the table who did not have a plate in front of her, but she participated in passing food and in the lively conversation. Call was glad she hadn't been on the stage. He'd have never had a moment's sleep for all the chatter.

He dropped a dollar and two bits in the money jar and took his place at the table. Platters of food made their way to him. The fare was still warm. Fried eggs. Crisp bacon. There was honey and sweet cream butter for the biscuits. Brown Apple Betty also made the rounds. No one saved it for dessert. The meal was eaten as a whole and washed down with coffee or green tea. Morrison Station did not serve beer or liquor but the drummer spoke in favor of Miss Morrison adding a bar or at least a sideboard and offering thirsty travelers another choice. The good reverend, his Bible lying beside his plate as he had a utensil in each hand, spoke to the opposing view. Call was not surprised when Laurel ended it diplomatically with the promise to take it all under advisement. She did point out that there was a saloon in town if anyone wanted to imbibe and risk missing the stage. Brady spoke up and warned them he waited for no man, but in the event that wasn't a consideration, Miss Morrison did sell tickets for the next available coach to Stonechurch.

Everyone stayed seated.

Brady was the first to excuse himself. He pushed his plate away, patted his belly, and stood. "Easy, gentlemen. I have the mailbag to fetch. There's time yet. I'll give you fair warning when I'm ready to leave. There'll be slow going ahead of us. Inclines as steep as any you're likely to encounter. Some of you will prefer walking to riding."

By Call's estimation, the stopover was not yet forty-five minutes long. Still, that was an eternity compared to the brief rests at the living stations, where the teams were exchanged with such efficiency the passengers barely had time to get out and stretch.

When Brady started to go, Laurel held up a hand to get his attention. "Where's your shotgun, Brady? You never said what happened to him."

"Drunk." He shrugged. "Suppose Digger's sober by now but he'll reek for days. I reckon you know where I stand on you serving liquor. There's no help for a man who can't hold his own."

Laurel nodded and let him leave without comment.

One by one the men excused themselves to answer calls of nature before Brady reappeared and announced he was ready to go. As the last at the table, Call lingered a bit longer while Laurel got up and helped Mrs. Lancaster begin to clear the plates and utensils. The platters, he noticed, had been laid bare except for a single biscuit. He snatched it when the sturdily built cook deliberately tempted him by passing it under his nose. She chuckled as he swept it away.

"Good for you. Don't be afraid of putting some meat

on your bones." She winked at him. "A gal doesn't mind having something to squeeze."

"Mrs. Lancaster!" Laurel wasn't sure why she was blushing, but she was and wasn't happy about it.

"Oh, go on with you, girl." To Call she said, "You don't mind a bit of flirting, do you?"

"If your husband doesn't mind, then I don't." He winked back at her and she dramatically held the empty platter up to her heart and sighed. "I imagine that means he doesn't."

"It means I'm not saying a word about it. Not a word, you devil." She looked at Laurel, who was standing at the head of the table slack-jawed and pink-cheeked. "That's how it's done. I hope you were paying attention." With that as her parting shot, she left the room swinging her wide hips so that her skirt fluttered about her legs.

3

Call sat back in his chair and eased his long legs under the table as he split the biscuit. "Well," he said, grinning, "that was unexpected."

"I apologize for that."

"Why?"

"Because . . ." Laurel searched for a reason. Lamely, she repeated, "Because."

"Yes, then," he said easily, tongue in cheek. "Understandable."

Laurel watched him bite into one half of his biscuit and chew it with evident enjoyment, though whether it was the biscuit he was actually enjoying or her embarrassment was not at all clear. She decided to move the conversation to firmer ground. "Why did you ask Brady if you could ride shotgun?"

Call finished off half of the biscuit before he answered. "The stage is uncomfortably crowded. I was the last to board and had to wedge myself between the flatulent preacher and the dandy."

"The dandy? Oh, you mean the reporter."

"Mm."

Laurel did not question him further on that account. The reporter was a bit of an odd duck, but she didn't doubt he was what he said he was. Since the discovery of silver at Stonechurch and the resurgence of the mine after the gold veins had played out, Ramsey Stonechurch had attracted the interest of newspapers across the country. A reporter on the trail was nothing unusual.

She said, "So you wanted to join Brady on the box because you were cramped."

"That was the least of it. You heard me mention the preacher's flatulence."

A hint of a smile lifted one corner of Laurel's mouth. "I did."

"So there was that," Call said. "Worse, I was starting to feel a little green."

"Jealous, you mean?"

"No. I mean sick. Sitting inside a swaying carriage turns my stomach. The window shades were drawn to combat the dust so looking out was not possible. I find that helps a little. What helps the most is riding in the box. When the driver dismissed my request, I relied on the second means of dealing with the motion. I slept."

"Ah. I hadn't considered that. Your sensitivity is not an unusual condition. I've been told it's similar to being on a ship."

"That doesn't make me feel better."

"You got out and walked when you were able, didn't you?"

"I did. The driver said there would be an opportunity to walk during the next leg. I'm probably the only man looking forward to it." Call decided he didn't want the second half of his biscuit after all. With a self-deprecating grin, he laid it on his empty plate and pushed the plate away.

"Let me talk to Brady," Laurel said. "No promises that he'll change his mind. You're a stranger. He might not want your company."

"Understood. When I made my request, it wasn't my intention to merely sit beside him, but perhaps I wasn't clear. The Colt your man took from me isn't my only weapon. My twelve-gauge is with my bag. I have some experience riding shotgun. I worked for Overland after the war."

"I take it you didn't mention that to Brady."

"No. He turned me down so fast I didn't see the point in explaining."

"And after Overland went belly up when the railroad took their mail route?"

"Odd jobs mostly."

"That's all?" she asked.

Call shrugged. "I took up with some of the smaller stage lines that haven't felt the impact of the railroad."

"Like Henderson Express."

"Not Henderson. I'm not auditioning for a position, if that's what you're thinking."

"It occurred to me. And now you're unemployed?"

"I am. I heard Mr. Stonechurch is hiring security at the mine. Rumor is that he doesn't want to use Pinkertons. Thought I'd give that a try."

"Before you came to the table, Mr. Abrams said you told everyone you were a gun for hire. I wasn't sure you weren't pulling someone's leg, but it appears that you were telling the truth."

"In a manner of speaking. I carry for protection. Mine and those I'm hired to protect. I'm not a gunfighter."

"Seems like a narrow distinction."

"Not to me."

Laurel picked up more plates and balanced them on her forearm. "I'll speak to Brady. The things you told me, I only have your word for them."

"That's right," he said, holding her frankly assessing gaze with his own direct one. He waited to see if she would call him a liar. She didn't. Her eyes eventually dropped away, a hint of pink returned to her cheeks, and she turned and headed for the kitchen.

He was still watching her so he saw her glance backward at him before she disappeared. He couldn't tell if she was annoyed with herself for giving in to the urge to look over her shoulder or because he caught her at it. She didn't strike him as someone who'd admit her interest, and there was always the possibility that he was mistaken to believe it was there, but the deepening flush to her cheeks was a promising sign.

Call did not see her again until Brady invited him to take a seat on the box. The invitation was offered churlishly, but Call did not let that stop him from accepting it. Laurel appeared from around the side of the house to return his gun belt and weapon. There was something in the way she handed them over that made him think she was trying to avoid touching him. He wanted to grin, but she was so serious that he simply thanked her and had to hope she understood that he was grateful for more than getting his gun back. He strapped on the belt and climbed aboard. Call noticed that Brady took his seat on both sides of the center, not leaving much room on the box for a partner. Figuring the jouncing of the stage would move Brady better than he could, Call let it go and seated himself on Brady's right.

"You gonna get that twelve-gauge of yours or are you thinking that drawing your sidearm will be enough to stop a holdup?"

Call turned around and reached for his bag and shotgun, which had been strapped to the roof. Because he arrived late, there wasn't room in the carryall at the rear of the stage for his belongings. They could have fit under the driver's box, but for reasons Call only suspected, Brady never suggested putting them there. Call grabbed the butt of the shotgun and wiggled it free from under the straps. He carefully brought it forward so he didn't hit Brady with it. It wouldn't take much for the driver to send him back inside the stage, Call thought, and he did not want to provoke that action. He stood the shotgun barrel up beside him and nodded in Brady's direction to indicate he was ready.

Brady scowled, deepening every crease in his weather-lined face. "If you think you're gonna lose that good meal you just had, make sure you don't spit it in the wind. That clear enough for you, Mr. Landry?"

"Clear."

"All right, then. We're off." Brady snapped the reins and called out encouragement to the team in his particular manner. "Yee-ha! Hi-yah!"

Call had taken the precaution of holding on to the box with his free hand. The stage's jerk from stationary to moving would have unseated him otherwise, and it wasn't beyond all possibility that that had been Brady's intent. Once they were rolling forward in a smoother fashion, Call released his grip, looked back at the home station, and found Laurel standing with her hands and stage tenders. He raised his hand in a salute and farewell. She did not reciprocate in a similar fashion.

As the station disappeared from view, Call set himself to considering the problem of how he might return.

Laurel turned back to the house once the stage was out of sight. She had no instructions for her men. They knew what was expected and separated to go about their tasks. Mr. Pye and Hank went to the barn to finish wiping down the horses, check their shoes for wear and their legs for injuries. Hank always had dried apples in his pockets for treats. Dillon returned to the garden to pick tender herbs for Mrs. Lancaster and then stayed in the kitchen to help clean up. Rooster got out a ladder and set it up against the barn to make repairs on the weather side. Laurel sat at her desk in her study, which was also the post and telegraph office. She looked over the mail that Brady had delivered and slid the letters into individual slots to wait for town folk to wander in and collect them. If a letter remained in a slot for two weeks, Laurel had Dillon or Hank deliver it to the addressee's home, usually a farm well outside of town. She offered the service primarily as a way to check on isolated families and be certain they had come to no harm. Even seven years after the war, farms were particularly vulnerable to raiders looking for livestock, food, moonshine stills, and the money farmers hid

under floorboards or in their fruit cellars. Falls Hollow
had recently added a bank to its main street, but there
were folks who didn't trust turning over what little cash
they had and receiving a Jones Prescott savings book in
return. It didn't seem equitable. A barter economy was
still preferred by many, but the railroad would eventually
put an end to that. Railroad agents couldn't accept chickens or eggs or flour or feed. The stage company didn't like
it either, but Laurel had managed to work around that to
help people who needed to visit Denver.

Laurel sat at her desk, her chin propped on the back of
her hands, long after she had finished sorting the mail. At
first she simply stared out the window. The stage was
gone but it did not require much imagination to see it
there. She had seen hundreds, all of them more or less
uniform in design, color, and markings. More difficult to
see in her mind's eye was an engine, a mighty black work-
horse with steam and smoke rising from its stacks, throwing ash to the rear as it snorted and squealed to a stop so
passengers could disembark.

What would it be like? she wondered. Whole families
could travel together. There would be individuals, of
course, but also couples and kin and more settlers. Stonechurch would call to them, but some would find Falls Hollow more to their liking, and seek out opportunities to
start businesses or farm. The grasslands that existed on
either side of the hollow were more suited to raising sheep
than grazing cattle, but that was also a good living. The
town already had a saloon. Sweeny's was a popular meeting place for drink and conversation. Mrs. Fry's brothel
was another. She supposed the railroad would bring more
of both, though she personally thought the town was better off with only one of each.

She wondered about Brady. What would he do when
the railroad replaced the stage line? He knew how to command a team, but an engine didn't respond to yee-ha or
hi-yah. It didn't respond to a whip.

It was natural that her thoughts would wander in the

direction of McCall Landry and his very fine eyes. There
was no room in the engine's cab for a shotgun rider, but
she wasn't as concerned for his welfare as she was for
Brady's. Mr. Landry would find his way easily enough.
Skill with a gun was always marketable in these parts.
Ramsey Stonechurch would be foolish if he didn't hire
Mr. Landry, and no one had ever thought the Pharaoh was
a fool.

She didn't think McCall Landry was either. Maybe he
would think twice about working for Stonechurch Mining
and decide that he was better suited for stagecoaching for
as long as it lasted. Riding on the box apparently did not
affect his delicate constitution.

It was impolite, but no one was around to see Laurel
smile when she thought of Call's constitution as delicate,
so her smile broadened until amusement bubbled on her
lips.

She lifted her head and dropped her hands to the desktop and folded them. Her smile and laughter faded. She
closed her eyes, and when she opened them, the engine
and all of the cars behind it vanished. The stage did not
reappear. A few red-comb chickens wandered into the
yard, pecking the ground out of habit more than in a
search for food.

Laurel rose, pushed herself upright from the desk, and
went in search of Mrs. Lancaster to see what help was
needed to prepare for the next stage.

The trail to Stonechurch was every bit as arduous as
Brady had warned it would be. It was made tolerable
only by the fact that there was no rain and no indication
that any was on the way. Mud could suck the coach's
wheels like quicksand, and every man aboard would be
expected to haul and heave to keep the stage moving.
They were expected to get out and walk, even when they
were against it in principle. Assemblyman Abrams and
the reporter were the last to exit the coach and did not do

so until the mountain grade became precipitously steep. The Reverend Marshall and John Spellman walked in front of the stage while Samuel Littlejohn and the others followed it. The reverend had his Bible. Littlejohn carried his case.

The route was hardly wider than the stage, and to a man, they marveled at Brady's calm and skill in negotiating the ascent. Call Landry, too, stayed in his seat. The animals strained and snorted but never faltered. They were released at the next living station and the new team took them another fifteen miles. The passengers returned to the coach each time the trail leveled off and walked again when it rose or took a hard curve.

It was well on dark when the Henderson Express reached the home station in Stonechurch. The passengers alighted and were shown into a large log structure that was the passenger eating house. In spite of the hour, they readily devoured the spread laid out for them for the nominal cost of one dollar and fifty cents each. The fare was similar to what they had enjoyed at Morrison Station but to a man they were of the opinion that Mrs. Lancaster's fare was tastier. Abrams and Thomas Brandywine left for the hotel after eating. John Spellman was directed to a wayside home where he could rest for the night and register for work at the mining office in the morning. After reviewing his options, the salesman elected to try the boardinghouse where he could rent a room a few days at a time cheaper than at the hotel. Reverend Marshall was told how to find his church and carried his bag to the small parsonage that shared a yard with the church and the cemetery.

Brady and Call did not follow the passengers into the station. Though Brady never complained, it was clear to Call that the driver was exhausted. He should have been relieved at some point on the trail by a fresh driver just as he had relieved one earlier. For reasons that Call wasn't sure he understood, Brady had elected to stay with the coach. They were both stiff when they finally stood while the horses were being released and cared for. Call's bones ached some. He didn't want to think about how much Brady was hurting.

Call stretched, shook out his legs, and breathed deeply. The drive had been harrowing in places but uneventful. Not to say that it was boring. It wasn't that by any stretch. The view had figuratively taken his breath away when he was casting his eyes around to absorb the vista and literally stolen his breath when the panorama included a sheer vertical drop over the side of a mountain. Brady, he observed, was enjoying himself, and that made Call vow to keep his silence and remain steady on.

Besides, in the less harrowing moments, he'd been able to think about Laurel Beth Morrison. He was tempted to ask Brady about her, starting with how she'd come to be operating the station, but he wasn't hopeful the driver would supply particulars so he allowed his imagination to wander.

It occurred to him that she was a widow and took up managing the home station after her husband died. He didn't like that scenario much, didn't like contemplating her with another man, especially when he couldn't settle on the sort of man who was good enough for her to marry and then stupidly up and died. He moved on to other thoughts, like the way she looked walking toward him, and then, just as intriguing, the way she looked walking away. It wasn't often he saw a woman in trousers or had an opportunity to observe the sweet sway of the female form without the exaggerated artifice of a bustle. He could have spent an entire afternoon in one of those rockers on her porch doing nothing but watching her coming and going.

He recalled clearly how she had turned her head to look back at him. She hadn't wanted him to see her interest. Surprise that he was watching her quickly turned to annoyance. Even annoyed, she was pretty, though he allowed that "pretty" was too insipid a description to do her justice. He only glimpsed her curled upper lip before she turned away, but it was still a splendid mouth. Curled or not, it was definitely worth kissing.

Call thought about that for a while until thinking made him uncomfortably tight in the groin. After that, he welcomed the steep pitch of the mountain trail to keep him straight until they reached Stonechurch.

"I'll empty the carryall," Call said, reaching for his own bag, which was still tied down. He stopped when Brady shook his head.

"Leave it. Mack is the station agent. He'll take care of the passengers' cases. There's something you can help me with, if you don't mind. Your bag will be here when we get back."

"Sure. What can I do?"

"I have a delivery for Mr. Stonechurch. No one will be in the office at this time of night, but he and his wife and daughter live above the office while their home is being built. By all accounts it will be a grand domicile when it's done, but for now we'll find him in his modest quarters."

"And you need me for . . . ?"

"Your gun. Keep it close. I've got the payroll."

Call knew then that he had been sitting on a fortune. The payroll for the miners had to be substantial. "Is it in a strongbox? Maybe you want me to carry it."

"Not in this lifetime, Mr. Landry. I'll get it. You keep an eye out for whatever doesn't look right. I aim to get this safely to the Pharaoh."

Call nodded. "As you wish." He hefted his shotgun and climbed down from the box. The stage tenders carried lanterns and there was sufficient moonlight for Call to watch Brady raise the lid on their perch and lift the strongbox out. The driver held the strongbox under one arm and made an awkward descent. Call suggested that Brady toss it to him, but the man was having none of that. When the driver was on terra firma, he started off in the direction of town. After a moment's hesitation, Call strode forward until they were walking abreast.

"You ever been robbed before carrying that thing?" asked Call.

"Nope, and it's my sincere wish that this trip is no exception."

Call smiled to himself. It was the longest sentence Brady had spoken to him since leaving Morrison Station. The man was becoming downright loquacious. "Big responsibility."

"Yup."

There wasn't anything Call could think of to extend the conversation so he fell silent and remained watchful. The town's main thoroughfare wasn't far from the station, perhaps no more than a quarter of a mile. The street had no lamps and there were only a few windows above businesses that were lit with the activity of the occupants.

"You thought about where you're going to stay tonight?" asked Brady.

"Figured there'd be a wayside home or a rooming house."

"I take a room at the Jameson place. Boardinghouse. No meals, so if you want to get a bite before you turn in, you'll have to head back to the station. They'll feed you at all hours."

"Is that what you're going to do?"

"I'm straight for bed. Dreaming about it now. Mrs. Jameson keeps a room for us drivers. Can't promise that there's room for you, but the station has a cot in their tack room that will do you at no cost since you rode with me."

That sounded fine to Call. "Thanks."

Brady slowed his steps as they neared the saloon. "Have a care," he told Call. There were several men loitering on the boardwalk outside the barroom. One was sitting on a barrel, another was leaning heavily against the saloon's outer wall, and the third had his hands deep in his pockets and was swaying slightly on his feet.

"You want to cross the street?" Call asked.

"You got second thoughts about using that gun?"

"No."

"Then hell no. Not gonna raise any suspicions by making a detour. The mining office is just up ahead."

Call thought precaution was wiser than being forced to shoot up the town, but Brady was in charge, and Call kept pace with him. Lamplight spilled out of the saloon's swinging doors, briefly illuminating their approach. Call supposed they were all miners, though his reasoning was simply that most men in the town worked in the mine and that they bore a resemblance to John Spellman, his traveling companion on the first few legs of his journey. Like Spellman, they wore dungarees, flannel shirts, and sported untrimmed beards that lay against their chests.

Call was aware of how closely he and Brady were being watched. He kept his eyes most particularly on the miner with his hands in his pockets. The man didn't move, nor did his companions. Call nodded to them as he passed, his shotgun in clear view. Brady grunted at them. It might have been a greeting, Call thought, or a curse. Whatever it was, the miners didn't return the sentiment and Brady and Call kept walking.

Call looked over his shoulder once, but the men remained as they were. The smell of liquor had been strong on them. Call figured they were pickled in place and no real threat even if they foolishly decided to try a holdup.

"This is it," said Brady, hefting the strongbox once again under his arm.

Call couldn't make out any sign to indicate they'd reached the mining office, but he had no reason to doubt Brady. The upper floor of the frame building was dark. Call would have hesitated to disturb Ramsey Stonechurch at this late hour. Brady showed no such reluctance, he noticed, but then the driver had experience dealing with the man some called Ramses or the Pharaoh with an unpleasantness mostly born of envy. It was said that Ramsey Stonechurch did not merely run the mining operation. He ruled it.

Call followed Brady up the outside stairs to the second

story and lowered his shotgun while he waited behind the driver for someone to open the door. He expected to get his first look at Ramsey Stonechurch when the door finally opened. Instead, it was a woman in a nightgown and robe and she was bouncing a child in the crook of one arm and holding an oil lamp in the other.

"Brady!" She greeted him warmly as she stepped back and invited the driver in. She thrust the lamp at him. "Take this. Put the box over there." She nodded toward the table and then turned her attention to the man still standing on the landing. "You must be Brady's shotgun for the drive. You're new."

"Just a substitute, ma'am. McCall Landry."

"Come in, Mr. Landry, but please rest your shotgun in the corner. I'm Maud Stonechurch. Ramsey's wife." She looked down at the child in her arms. "This is our daughter Ann. She's fussing tonight. Another tooth coming in, I think."

Call nodded politely. He'd had some experience with teething babies in his youth, but it had been a long time since he'd been around one. "Have you tried dipping a washcloth in cold water and rubbing it against her gums? She might chew on it, but that will relieve the pressure."

"A cold washcloth," Maud repeated thoughtfully. "No. The women I asked suggested a whiskey finger rubbed against her gums would do the trick, but right now I'm thinking two fingers of whiskey might serve me better."

Call set his shotgun in the corner of the kitchen as directed and held out his hands, palms up. "May I?"

Maud Stonechurch did not hesitate. Relieved, she gave over her daughter to a man who, for all intents and purposes, was a stranger. She was feeling that desperate. "I'll soak a cloth."

Call cradled the child in one arm and bounced her gently while he made little clicking noises that caught her attention so that she stared at him wide-eyed.

Watching this as he set the strongbox and lamp on the

table, Brady made his opinion clear. "Christ," he said under his breath. More loudly he said, "What next?"

Call shrugged. The movement jostled Ann enough to cause her discomfort, and she opened her mouth to howl just as her mother arrived with a damp, cold washcloth that had one corner twisted into a cone. Maud slipped a bit of it into her daughter's mouth and Ann clamped down hard and began to suck.

"How old is she?" asked Call.

"A year this month. She usually sleeps through the night but the new tooth has been troublesome."

Brady cleared his throat.

Maud didn't look at him, but she did respond to the pointed bid for attention. "I haven't forgotten you, Brady. I'm going to wake my husband now since you're here on his business and Ann is in capable hands."

"I'd appreciate it, ma'am."

"Sit," she said in a tone that brooked no argument. "You look dead on your feet. You, too, Mr. Landry, not because you look as if you're about to fold like Brady here, but because Ann might sleep if you're down." She thrust her delicate chin in the direction of a rocker that was situated near the stove.

"If it's all the same, Mrs. Stonechurch, I've had my fill of sitting and rocking on the stage. I'm fine standing."

"As you like," she said. She bent to kiss her daughter's forehead before she left the room.

Brady shook his head again. "You're something else, Landry."

"Call. Not Landry."

"All right. You're some piece of work, Call."

"Why? Because there's a baby in my arms?" He spoke softly and directed his words to Ann, not Brady.

The driver raised his eyes to the ceiling, seeking a power beyond the room.

Ramsey Stonechurch had been following his wife, but when they reached the kitchen, he stopped cold on the threshold while she went straightaway to the stranger cradling his daughter.

"What the hell?" he asked, placing his big, square-cut palms on either side of the door frame.

"Language," Maud admonished. "I know you're tired, but you have to start minding your language."

Ramsey sighed, nodded, and dropped his hands so that he filled the doorway. "Brady." His eyes dropped to the strongbox. "I thought this was coming tomorrow."

Out of respect, Brady rose to his feet, though with some effort. "Change of plans. Mr. Henderson got some hints that the Miller boys were sniffing around. Nothing definite. Moved the money to the first living station out of Denver. I took the box when I relieved Jed Holloway and didn't let anyone take it over."

"You drove the stage all that way?" When Brady nodded, Stonechurch was visibly impressed. "There aren't many like you, Brady." He turned his head to Brady's shotgun, who was shifting a little awkwardly, arms hanging at his sides now that Maud had relieved him of the baby. "Who's this?"

"McCall Landry," said Brady. "Goes by Call. Rode shotgun with Overland, but he was a passenger until Morrison Station. Digger was drunk when I took over. I did two legs alone, but when Laurel Beth put in a good word for this feller, I let him up in the box."

Stonechurch raised a dark eyebrow and knuckled his chin thoughtfully. "Not like you to trust a stranger, especially with payroll on board."

"Needs must," said Brady. He lowered himself stiffly into the chair behind him.

"Drink?" asked Stonechurch.

Brady nodded. "Don't mind if I do."

Stonechurch turned to Call. "You?"

"Nothing for me, thank you."

Maud said, "I'm pleased to have met you, Mr. Landry. Brady, it's always a pleasure to see you. Husband, I'm going to bed now. Do you see that Ann is sleeping? That's

Mr. Landry's doing. Keep that in mind." Her smile encompassed all of them before she left the room.

Stonechurch watched her go; a smile lifted his meticulously groomed mustache. "She's a wonder," he said quietly in case his guests had any doubts. When she was gone, he poured a generous portion of whiskey for Brady and let the man have a full swallow before he joined him at the table and drew the strongbox toward him.

Call was curious about how full the box was, but he kept his distance, figuring that too much interest wouldn't speak well of him. He was going to see Mr. Stonechurch again in the morning to inquire about a job after all. Better that the man was left with a good impression.

Stonechurch released the catch on the metal box and threw open the lid. He clenched his teeth; his complexion turned ruddy. "Is this a joke, Brady?"

Brady sat up and leaned forward to examine the contents. Neat stacks of newspaper clippings the size of bills filled the box. He watched Stonechurch pick up the coin pouch, open the neck, and turn it over. Pebbles and small rocks scattered on the table. Brady stared at the pebbles until they were still and then he stared at Stonechurch. "I don't know what it is, but it's no joke of mine."

In unison, the two men swiveled in their chairs to stare at McCall Landry.

4

When the hammering began at her bedroom door, Laurel sat straight up in bed and reached in the nightstand drawer for her revolver. She did this without thought, having rehearsed the very same in her mind every night for the first three years after she buried her family. The motions came as naturally to her as breathing.

She threw off the bedcovers and padded barefoot to the door in her nightgown. She stood to one side as she called out, "Who's there?"

"It's me!" And then, in case she didn't recognize the voice, he added lamely, "Hank." For good measure, he said, "Hank Booker."

Laurel opened the door. "In the future, announce yourself at the same time you're pounding on my door." She showed him her gun. "I might have shot you."

Hank's pronounced Adam's apple rose and fell as he swallowed hard. "Beggin' your pardon, Miss Laurel, but I thought you'd want to know that one of the mares is gone. I woke up, don't know exactly why, maybe 'cause I had an urge to visit the outhouse, but it's good that I did since I noticed that Penelope's stall is empty. She didn't wander into the corral because the barn door was shut." Hank's blue suspenders were hanging from his waistband. He pulled them up, snapped them into place, wincing as he did so.

"Were you sleeping in the barn?" She didn't know why

she asked. It was perfectly obvious that he had been. He had bits of hay in his hair. There was a bunkhouse that could accommodate eight, which it sometimes had to when a driver and shotgun and a couple of male passengers swelled their number. Hank should have been there, but she could hardly scold him for sleeping elsewhere.

"Thought I'd bed down there to keep an eye on Willow. It seemed she was feeling poorly so I figured I should stay close."

"All right. So you woke and noticed Penelope was gone."

"Yes, but Willow's fine. Couldn't tell that anything was ever ailing her."

"Good to know. Did you wake Rooster? Mr. Pye?"

He nodded hard. "My brother, too. Rooster said I was to get you. He's saddling up now."

"And Mr. Pye?"

"Well, about that, Miss Laurel, Josey Pye's plum disappeared. Suspicion is that he took Penelope. Horse thief like that, he's surely gonna hang."

Laurel's cheeks puffed as she blew out a long breath and considered her options. They couldn't completely abandon the station to look for Mr. Pye. She didn't say so, but she wasn't entirely unhappy that he was gone, only irritated that he had made off with Penelope, one of the sturdiest and most reliable mares.

"Go and tell Rooster that I'm coming with him. You and Dillon will stay here in case we're late returning for the morning stage. Mrs. Lancaster knows what to do. You do your regular work and follow her instructions. We'll let the sheriff know that Mr. Pye and Penelope are missing and let the law determine if it's theft or something we haven't thought of."

"Theft," said Hank. "It's theft."

Laurel didn't argue the point. She couldn't. The boy was probably right. It bothered her that she'd not suspected that Mr. Pye was planning to leave. He'd given them no indication and now she'd have to find another stage tender, which was aggravating in its own right.

Laurel shooed Hank away, closed the door, and began dressing, pulling on the clothes she had worn the previous day after she shook them out. She fashioned a loose braid, secured it with a leather tie, and took her hat and coat when she reached the front door. She was shrugging into the coat as Rooster came out of the barn leading his mount and hers.

"Any ideas?" she asked, stroking her mare's neck before she swung into the saddle.

Rooster shook his head. "Not a one." He grunted softly as he seated himself in the saddle. There was no hiding the effort it took to set his hips right.

Laurel pretended she didn't notice Rooster's discomfort. He wouldn't thank her for calling attention to it. If she asked him if he needed help, he'd deny it. "Did you suspect he was planning to leave?"

"Nope. The boys didn't either. Seemed like he was content enough. Not content, you understand, just content enough."

She nodded. "Makes sense that he could follow the Cabin Creek Trail, or at least not wander too far away from it. Trouble is, southeast to Denver or northwest toward Stonechurch?"

"I vote Denver."

"Glad we're of a similar mind." Laurel saw that Rooster had placed her rifle in the leather scabbard. He was carrying, too, and he was a good shot, at least as good as she was. That eased her mind some. "Town first. To let the sheriff know what's happened." She snapped Abby's reins and pressed her heels into the mare's flanks. "Let's go."

Sheriff Rayleigh Carter was sleeping in one of his cells at the back of the jail. He roused himself enough to sit up and take notice of his visitors. The other cell was occupied by Magnus Clutterbuck, a frequent guest of the sheriff's, who never stirred once while Laurel and Rooster were telling their tale. They didn't expect the sheriff to get a posse together in the middle of the night, but he did tell them he'd have men out at first light. He understood why they didn't want to wait but cautioned them about going out at night. "You don't even know how long ago he left."

That was true, but Laurel would not be deterred, and Rooster would not let her go unaccompanied. They left the jail and headed southeast on the Cabin Creek Trail, hoping for a piece of luck that would put Josiah Pye in their sights.

When the two men turned to stare at him, Call stood his ground, not even raising his hands in a gesture of innocence. Their stares were more accusing than questioning and that bothered him some but not enough to start protesting. He simply stared back, mostly in Brady's direction. It might take the driver some time to realize Call couldn't have had anything to do with the missing payroll, but Call was confident the man would come around.

Brady slumped back in his chair, shaking his head. "It's not him," he told Ramsey Stonechurch. "Wish it was on account of that being easy since we got him right here, but he had no opportunity."

Stonechurch gestured to a chair at the table. "I don't like a man standing over me. Come over here and sit."

Call took a seat across from Stonechurch and at a right angle to Brady. He folded his hands and set them on the table. Stonechurch might not realize he had a gun belt under his duster, but Brady did. There was nothing to be gained by setting Stonechurch on tenterhooks when he needed to think clearly about what had gone wrong.

Satisfied when Call was down, Stonechurch eyed the stagecoach driver. "What about you, Brady? I don't think you did it, but I'd be the worst kind of fool not to ask."

Brady didn't flinch from Stonechurch's hard dark gaze. "I reckon you're going to have to decide if you can take me at my word. I got no idea what happened to your money. I checked the box myself when I relieved Holloway. I didn't count it, but it was real bills. The coins were real. No paper. No rocks and pebbles. Secured your box under the stage box and sat on it all the way to Morrison Station. Got up then to stretch, have a bite of Mrs. Lancaster's fine cooking, deliver the mail, and relieve myself. Wasn't away from the box above an hour, and I went back to the stage once to get the mailbag. You've been to Laurel Beth's place. The dining room is at the front of the house. I sat at the table where I could see the stage. Kept an eye on it, more or less. No one climbed up there while I was watching."

Stonechurch looked across the table at Call. "You see anything?"

"I had my back to the window. Didn't see a thing."

"You were last off the stage," said Brady. "I was already in the house by the time you got out."

Call nodded. "And Miss Morrison called Rooster over to take my gun. Then Rooster escorted me to the pump, where I washed up and went straightaway from there into the house, took a seat at the table. I was either accompanied by someone or in your sights, Brady. I'd appreciate it if you'd stop bringing me into this."

Brady grunted, but he didn't apologize.

Stonechurch said, "You have a gun under your coat?"

Call nodded. Without being asked, he stood, parted his duster, and unfastened the gun belt. He hung it over the back of the empty chair. "That's my shotgun in the corner," he said in case Stonechurch hadn't noticed it.

"My wife told me. She doesn't like guns in the house though she tolerates my collection of old firearms." He eyed the butt of Call's gun, recognizing it as Army issue, but didn't comment. Instead, he turned back to Brady. "What about your other stops?"

"Just two other living stations between there and here. Got down when the tenders changed the team but I never left the stage. Pissed in the yard." Seeing Stonechurch's lips twist in disapproval, he said, "Too much detail? Seemed to me I should mention it to let you know how serious I was about keeping the payload safe."

"I appreciate that you thought you did everything you

could, but you have to acknowledge that it wasn't enough." He waved his hand over the stones still scattered across the table. "Otherwise . . ." It wasn't necessary to finish the sentence. The evidence of Brady's failure was in front of them.

The driver nodded heavily. "Had to have happened at Laurel Beth's place. Maybe I wasn't watching as closely as I thought I was. Can't think of how it could have happened anywhere else." He picked up one of the pebbles, examined it between his thumb and forefinger. "Hurts me more than a little to think Laurel Beth is somehow involved."

Call had never considered that, not for a moment, but now he had to because Brady had put it out there. He had nothing but his gut telling him that she was innocent so he remained quiet rather than try to defend her. He waited to see what Stonechurch would say.

"Not Miss Morrison," said Stonechurch. "Not in this lifetime or the next. I'm putting that out of my mind. But one of her tenders? You know them. What do you think?"

"Rooster's been with her for years. The way I heard it, he helped her bury her father and brothers and stuck around. He'd do anything for her is my guess, but if we agree she's not behind the theft, then he didn't do it. Dillon Booker and his brother—can't bring the name to mind right off—are still whelps, but they've been with her for a couple years. Can't say I know them, not like I do Rooster. Maybe they could pull off a robbery, there being two of them and all. Brothers, like I said, working together."

"All right. We can look into that. Send her a telegram. She runs the office so no one will get wind of it."

"Good idea. Can't even let the sheriff know without Miss Laurel getting the message first."

"Right. Just as well she's not on our suspect list."

Brady nodded, swallowed, and regarded Stonechurch frankly. "Am I off it? The suspect list, I mean."

Stonechurch was not giving quarter just yet. "Let's see how things go. If it sets your mind at ease, you're off it for now."

Call didn't notice that Brady breathed any easier. In the driver's shoes, he wouldn't either. "What about that other fellow?"

"What other fellow?" Stonechurch wanted to know.

"Oh," said Brady. "Yeah. He's talking about—" He stopped, searching for a name. "Damn. Dye. Fry. Rye. Pye! That's it. Pye. Not like pie you eat. P-Y-E. Don't know why that sticks in my mind when I couldn't think of his name right off. Laurel Beth always calls him Mr. Pye, like Mister is his Christian name. Struck me funny. Rooster. Dillon. Hank—*now* I recollect it. But always Mr. Pye."

Ramsey Stonechurch didn't ask if Mr. Pye had a first name. It was certain that he did, but it wasn't important and Brady had already strained the outer limits of his brain. "What about Mr. Pye?"

Brady shrugged. "Can't say much about him. Laurel Beth told me she hired him when she saw that Rooster was favoring his hip. That's all I know. He hasn't been around long. Maybe a year. Maybe not quite that long. Don't know if he's a local or someone who was passing through and seized an opportunity. That's something worth learning."

Stonechurch knuckled his chin, thoughtful. "I'm going to get dressed and walk over to the station. No point waiting until morning to send the news to her."

"I'll walk with you," said Call. "I'm headed back that way for a bite to eat and a cot."

"There's a rooming house."

"I'm not exactly flush." He said this without embarrassment. It was simply a fact. "Brady says I can sleep in the tack room at no cost because I rode with him."

"Are you looking for a job?"

"Yes, sir."

"With the stage line?"

"No. At least I wasn't thinking that. I told Brady I wasn't auditioning for a job when I climbed onto the box, not that I'd turn one down out of hand if it was offered, but I'm in Stonechurch because I had an idea your operation might need security, leastways I heard rumblings about that in Denver."

"I see."

Call was aware that Stonechurch did not confirm the rumblings. Neither did he say they were rumors without foundation. "I'm thinking now that maybe they'll need another hand or two at Morrison Station so I'm keeping my mind open to other possibilities."

"There's nothing wrong with that." Stonechurch stood. "Give me a couple of minutes to change out of these night-clothes. We'll walk together. Brady, you get yourself to Mrs. Jameson's before you fall asleep at my table. Come back for breakfast."

Brady nodded. "Breakfast sounds good. Thank you." His chair scraped the floor as he pushed away from the table. "I'm real sorry about the men's wages. Real sorry."

Stonechurch left the kitchen without a word.

Brady closed his eyes and rubbed his forehead with his palm. "Damn me if I know what happened. Didn't see a blessed thing." He lowered his hand and tugged at the brim of his hat, fitting it snugly on his head. "I shoulda checked the strongbox before we left Laurel Beth's place."

Call didn't argue the point, though he understood why Brady hadn't felt the need. "Are you relieving a driver tomorrow?"

"Yeah. Afternoon most likely. I'll be headed back to Denver eventually."

"Then I'll probably see you."

Brady looked Call over. "You serious about picking up work at Morrison's?"

"If there's a position to be had, then sure. It's hard to fathom that if someone there made off with Mr. Stone-church's payroll, he'd still be hanging around the station."

"You could be right. Then again, he or they might stay put and sit on the money for a while. Hide it. Bury it. Fill a mattress with it. Bide their time until Mr. Stonechurch moves on."

"Is he likely to do that?"

"Hell, no. But they don't know that."

Laurel and Rooster rode until daybreak without sighting Josiah Pye. They passed one of the living stations and stopped long enough to make inquiries, but the stage tenders weren't helpful and all their cattle were accounted for. If Pye had come this way, he hadn't stopped to steal a fresh mount. "He's going to run Penelope into the ground," she told Rooster when they turned to head back. "I could string him up myself for that."

"Hard to figure him out," said Rooster. "Bothers me more than a little that he left under cover of night. Can't see the point when he could have announced he wanted to leave and taken the stage or bought a horse from you if he was set on riding out."

Laurel let Rooster go on. They'd already discussed this earlier and he was repeating himself, but he obviously needed to mull it over, get it right in his mind.

"When we get back," he said, "you'll do an inventory."

"Yes. I said I would. Mail. Money. I don't have many valuables. Penelope is the real loss."

"You ever think about not giving the animals names?"

"No. And this won't change my mind. I like naming them and they appreciate it."

Rooster chuckled. "You know that, do you?"

"I do." She looked at him sideways, saw that one corner of his mouth had kicked up, and repeated herself, this time more emphatically. "I *do*."

They rode the rest of the way back to the station in silence, together but with their own thoughts.

5

The morning stage arrived not long after Laurel and
Rooster returned. The boys did the work of exchanging the team. Mrs. Lancaster had prepared the usual fare
for the passengers—four men and two women this time—
and collected the dollar and a half fee for the privilege of
sitting at the table. Although Rooster felt it necessary to
grumble mightily about being sent to the bunkhouse for
some shut-eye, he did not gainsay Laurel's order. Laurel
went straight to her study to examine the mail she had
sorted the previous afternoon. As far as she could tell, it
was all there. No one had tampered with her safe. Since
the arrival of the bank, she'd never kept much money
there. She could account for what she'd put in. A quick
inventory of those few valuables she had were also still in
the house: her mother's gold filigree framed cameo and
her pearl earrings, her father's timepiece and the fob it
hung from, and the Springfield rifles and revolvers her
brothers had been issued during the war but weren't carrying when the renegades swarmed the station. They all
had sentimental value, but on the whole they wouldn't
fetch much. She couldn't say that Mr. Pye even knew she
had the items. She never wore the pearls or the cameo.
The timepiece lost minutes every hour so she kept it in a
drawer in her office desk and hardly ever took it out. The
revolvers and rifles were maintained in good working order, cleaned with hot, soapy water to keep them from

clogging, and greased with bear fat if oil wasn't handy. Mr. Pye had no doubt seen her cleaning the weapons because she often sat on the front porch to do it, but he'd never commented, and he didn't know where she kept them. They were still there.

It wasn't until Laurel swiveled in her chair that she saw the telegraph had produced a ribbon of paper in her absence. Since it was unusual to receive any messages late at night, she had never thought to look. Now she stood, walked over to the machine, and carefully threaded the ribbon through her fingers. After tearing it off at the end of the series of dots and dashes, she returned to her chair and began to translate the code.

The message was short and to the point, but then the sender was not known for wasting words. She read the message twice before she put pen to paper and wrote it out. Somehow seeing the words made it real. Still fantastic, certainly, but real.

When she was finished, Laurel set the pen and paper down, removed the spectacles she used for close work, and closed her eyes. She pressed a thumb and forefinger to her eyelids and released a slow breath. A wave of fatigue suddenly washed over her, and her shoulders slumped. Her eyes remained dry though she felt like wailing.

Damn Josiah Pye! Hanging was too good for him. Did anyone still draw and quarter criminals? At the moment she could embrace that notion. Mr. Pye had to be responsible for the theft. He was missing. The payroll was missing. In her mind, the connection between the two events was straightforward.

Laurel swore under her breath and finally opened her eyes. Nothing had changed. That was still her handwriting on the paper, still the same message. Did Mr. Stonechurch blame her? Laurel felt selfish for asking the question, even if she didn't say it aloud. The miners were out the money they'd earned, money they depended on to feed themselves and their families, to buy goods and services, to drink themselves unconscious if they had a mind to, and she was wondering if Ramsey Stonechurch held her responsible. Worse, did he suspect her? His message gave no indication of what he was thinking. The theft had happened, and it had happened at her station. The Pharaoh knew that much. Laurel reasoned that Brady must have been able to account for the contents of the box before that and had convinced Mr. Stonechurch that he was not the thief.

Could it be a mere coincidence that Mr. Pye chose to leave the very same night that the robbery was discovered? If he hadn't absented himself from the station, she would have cast about for another suspect. It was true that Mr. Pye made her uneasy, but for all of that, it didn't make him a thief. His disappearance pointed to guilt, but she still had to consider other possibilities before she sent a reply to Ramsey Stonechurch.

So what *were* the other possibilities? First, there was Brady. He had the easiest access to the strongbox. He knew what he was carrying. How many other people actually knew that the mining payroll was on the stage? She certainly hadn't. Brady hadn't hinted at it, and it was not something she ever asked about. The fact that he had no one riding shotgun would seem to indicate that he *wasn't* carrying a strongbox. Perhaps that was why he had been reluctant to allow McCall Landry to join him on the box. Brady had wanted to maintain the deception that he had nothing on the stage worth stealing. That made sense to Laurel, and she dismissed Brady as a suspect. It would have broken her heart if she hadn't come to that conclusion.

She considered Rooster and the boys and simply couldn't see her way clear to considering them suspects. She could understand that Mr. Stonechurch might want to question them, but she'd never gone wrong by depending on them and she'd stake her reputation on their innocence. To continue the exercise, Laurel even considered Mrs. Lancaster for all of two seconds. Not only had the cook not had the opportunity, but her aching knees would have prevented her from hauling herself up to the box.

Laurel did not dismiss the passengers out of turn, but she couldn't recall that any one of them had returned to the stagecoach alone, and the salesman was the only person with the means of hiding the money. His case would have served the purpose, but there was no evidence of discarded medicine bottles on the property. It just wasn't practical.

How had Mr. Pye done it? How had he known that Brady's stage was carrying the payroll? What opportunity had he found that no one had seen him in the commission of the robbery?

Laurel stood, returned to the telegraph machine, and composed the message in her mind before she tapped it out, then she went to the dining room to say farewell to the guests she had neglected since their arrival.

McCall Landry heard the tapping at the door but didn't recognize it as a bid for his attention until someone shouted his name. He stirred, rolled over, and pulled a blanket over his head. It didn't matter to him that sunlight was slipping through the cracks in the boards of the tack room. He was owed a full night's sleep even if night for him ended at noon. "Go away!"

"Can't!" came the voice. "Mr. Stonechurch is asking for you."

"Yeah? What's he asking?"

"Not my business, but he wants you straightaway at the mining office."

Hoping the voice would leave, Call didn't respond. There was a long pause and then the voice came again, this time with an edge of pleading.

"You gotta get up. I'm expected to wait until you do."

"I'm up." Call buried his shoulder into the bunk's thin mattress.

"No you're not. You're lying."

"Jesus." Groaning, he flopped onto his back and lowered the blanket. He was thirty and his bones felt as if they were on the wrong side of sixty. Riding on the box had taken a toll after so long an absence from that work. He was surprised he didn't rattle on his way to the door. Opening it, he pointed to himself and said, "I'm up." He closed the door in the kid's face—he couldn't have been more than twelve—and then sat down on the bunk to pull on his boots. He tucked in his shirt, buttoned his vest, and fastened his gun belt. After he put on his jacket and hat, Call slung his duster over his shoulder, picked up his shotgun and valise, and walked out of the tack room. It wasn't a complete surprise to find the kid still standing at his post. He'd known soldiers with less commitment to duty. "I'm not going anywhere until I wash up," Call said. "Show me."

Call followed the boy to the pump and privy and relieved himself before he washed his face and hands. Afterward, he ran damp fingers through his hair and reset his hat at the angle he preferred. The kid lingered nearby. Call ignored him, taking his time to comb out his mustache and beard. He was particular about some things, not so much about others.

"Can I get some breakfast?" he asked, repacking his bag and tossing it to the kid.

"Don't you think you should get yourself over to the mining office?"

"I do and I will. After I've had something to eat. I'll be human after I'm fed." His stomach growled loudly enough for the kid to hear it, supporting Call's claim. "See?"

"Yes, sir. Follow me. The cook will rustle you up something. We're between stages so it'll be potluck."

"Suits me fine."

As it turned out, it was better than leftovers from the previous meal, and after a short stack of flapjacks dripping in maple syrup, a couple of crisp strips of bacon, half a can of peaches, and two cups of black coffee, Call was ready to answer the Pharaoh's summons. He left his shotgun, bag, and duster in the safekeeping of the station owner with the understanding that he'd collect his belongings if he stayed in Stonechurch. Whether or not he remained in town was still a question in his mind even if Ramsey Stonechurch offered him a job.

It was going on noon when Call arrived at the mining office. A man sitting behind a desk covered in open ledgers greeted Call and introduced himself as Frank Fordham, the bookkeeper for Stonechurch Mining. Frank had a pencil behind his ear and one in his hand, which he hastily dropped to greet Call. His spectacles rested against his forehead, but he patted down the desktop looking for them before he returned to his seat. Call touched his own forehead to give Frank a hint, which the bookkeeper accepted sheepishly.

"You go on in," said Frank. He took the pencil from behind his ear and used it to point to the door to an adjoining room. "Mr. Stonechurch has been expecting you."

Call was already opening the door when he realized he hadn't actually given Mr. Fordham his name. He looked back over his shoulder, one eyebrow raised in question, but the bookkeeper waved him on.

"Close the door," Stonechurch said and pointed to a spindly straight back on the opposite side of his desk.

Call looked suspiciously at the chair he was offered, wondering if it was sturdy enough to hold him. He chose the green-painted companion chair instead because it had thicker, more substantial legs. He sat and the chair wobbled on those sturdy but uneven legs.

Stonechurch chuckled, enjoying himself. "There's a lesson there, Mr. Landry. If you're going to work for me, it's better if you trust me."

Call nodded and switched chairs. "Got it. Am I going to work for you?"

"Still thinking on it. You?"

"Still thinking on it."

Stonechurch sat back in his wide armchair and regarded Call with a calculating gaze. He pressed his lips together and tilted his head to one side. "My brother was supposed to join us. He was here for a while but he couldn't wait any longer. A situation in the number one mine required his attention. Leo is our problem solver. He's also a better judge of character than I am." One corner of his mouth turned up. "Do you believe that?"

"About your brother being the problem solver? Sure. A better judge of character? I doubt it."

"Good. He's not. Sees the best in everyone. Optimistic to a fault. That's Leo."

"That's probably what makes him good at solving problems. You have to believe there's a solution to find one."

"I like that, Mr. Landry."

"Call."

"Yes. All right. Call." Stonechurch folded his thickly knuckled hands on the desktop when he leaned forward. "I'm estimating that I sent for you a little over an hour ago. You took your time coming."

"Waking up. Washing up. That takes time. Had a bite to eat, too. Also arranged for the station to hold on to my belongings. Came here straightaway after that."

"I appreciate your honesty, but I expect less attending to your needs and more attending to mine."

"You mean if I work for you."

"Yes."

"But I don't," said Call. "And here's more honesty you might or might not appreciate. Even if I draw down pay from you, my needs will pretty much always come first. There could be situations where our needs are one and the same. In those cases, we won't have any conflict."

"I see. For a man who told me last night that he wasn't exactly flush, you don't seem eager to ingratiate yourself to a potential employer."

Call shrugged. "I lean toward optimism, like your brother. Something will turn up."

"Maybe it will." Stonechurch unfolded his hands and placed them on the arms of his chair. He tapped the calloused pads of his fingers against the curved wooden arms. "I received a reply from Miss Morrison."

"Oh?" Call had considered several reasons that would

prompt Stonechurch to command his presence. A reply
from Morrison Station had been the most likely. It seemed
to him that whatever the news, Brady should have been
invited to hear it. Last night the driver had been marginally successful at concealing his fear, but Call figured
he'd been sick with it. "And she told you . . ."

"Seems one of her stage tenders ran off last night.
Took a mare that didn't belong to him and disappeared.
You'll likely know that horse thievery is a serious offense
in these parts."

"In other parts, too."

Stonechurch nodded. "Just so. Her message was short
on detail, but it was clear that she made an attempt to find
him, which is likely why she was so long responding to
me. She thought she was looking for a horse thief and that
would have kept her on the trail most of the night. Miss
Morrison isn't one to give up easily."

Call hadn't been around her long enough to share that
judgment, but he was glad to hear that Stonechurch
thought so. "Brady mentioned something last night about
her burying her father and brothers. What was that about?"

"Not the most important thing right now, but I understand your curiosity and I'm going to indulge it because it
will be important." Stonechurch stopped drumming his
fingers and for several long moments the silence was por-
tentous. "Laurel's father and her two brothers were murdered in a raid on the station. This was seven years ago, not
long after Lee surrendered at Appomattox. There were
rebel stragglers, deserters, and even men who served with
honor traveling through here. Some looking for work.
Others looking for trouble. It was inevitable that they
found each other, united by their defeat and their hunger
and their need to keep on fighting.

"They roamed around, taking what they wanted at the
point of their swords and guns, and there wasn't much
resistance because they perfected the ambush. In the raid
at Morrison Station, the fellow riding shotgun was one of
the raiders. The driver never had a chance. Mr. Morrison

and his sons were unsuspecting and unarmed. There was no reason to gun them down except that it's what the rebels wanted to do. Miss Morrison's never spoken to me about what happened. What I know is from a couple of the passengers who were robbed but not killed and eventually ended up here in Stonechurch. Their stories were similar, and the way they told it is that Miss Morrison returned fire from inside the house. She must have witnessed all of it. She killed one of the men and wounded another. All but the man she killed got away and she was left to bury her family. When Brady said she had help, that's the first I knew of it."

"Rooster."

Stonechurch nodded. "Telegraph lines hadn't come out this way yet. She was on her own. Folks put together a posse but nothing came of it. Several of the raiders were from the same family. Everyone got to calling them the Grant clan, but that didn't aid in the search. It's been seven years now and no one's heard from them in almost that long. There were more raids with no consequences to the clan so I'm not sure how or why they disappeared. One day they were a scourge and then they weren't."

Stonechurch's cheeks plumped and then deflated as he blew out a breath. "Not that I believe we've heard the last of them. Their kind doesn't change their ways. They've probably just moved on and I'll wager Miss Morrison thinks about that each day."

"You don't think they're responsible for your payroll theft, do you?"

"No, but only because no one died. Death was their calling card."

There was nothing to say to that. Call let the statement settle before he asked, "Who is Miss Morrison's missing stage tender?"

"Josiah Pye."

"And he's in the wind," said Call.

"Seems to be. At least Miss Morrison wasn't able to run him to ground."

"What do you think?"

"The same. Miss Morrison already sent a wire to the sheriff in Denver and she's alerted the law in Falls Hollow and Frost Falls. Passed on a description. I'm not hopeful it will be much help, but I appreciate her effort."

"Have you spoken to Brady? He has a stake in this."

"He does, and no, I haven't sent for him yet. Thought he'd turn up here on his own."

From Stonechurch's tone, Call could tell that it was a black mark in the mental book he kept on Brady. He didn't make excuses for the driver although several occurred to him. Brady's absence had likely put him back on the list of suspects. Josiah Pye had disappeared, but that wasn't proof that he had the strongbox in his possession. As far as they knew, he was guilty of stealing a horse. That was it.

Call said, "I'm guessing you've realized that Pye had an accomplice."

Nodding, Stonechurch said, "At least one. He couldn't have known the payroll was on that stage without help. Hell, *I* didn't know it was coming early."

Call remembered Stonechurch had said the same last night. "You move the payroll on a random schedule?"

"We do." He pointed to the door of his office to indicate the room and the man on the other side. "Mr. Fordham is in charge of choosing days and times and the stage that will carry it. Sometimes he doesn't inform me until the money's left Denver. Sometimes he forgets to mention it altogether, but he's never failed me. He's a cautious man. I trust him absolutely."

"All right. Take Mr. Fordham off the table."

"He was never on it. I want you to start at Morrison Station. Talk to everyone. Put your ear to the ground and listen for the rumbling."

Call's right eyebrow lifted in a skeptical arch. "That's what you want, huh?"

"Yes, it is, but I'll bite. What is it you want?"

"I sure would like to understand why you've decided that I'm the man to do this."

Stonechurch chuckled. "And I was so sure you'd ask about money, but I suppose that will come." He waited for Call to confirm, and when nothing was said, he went on. "You're an outsider, and that's in your favor. You've ridden for Overland, so if this assignment means you have to take up a job with Henderson Express, you'll know what to do. Sam Henderson owes me after losing my payroll, but I won't be putting in a good word for you unless you need the job and can't get it on your own. I judge you're a decent shot, maybe better than merely decent, and you survived the war so you're lucky or skilled and probably a little of both. Does that reasoning do it for you, Call?"

"It does."

"Then let's talk money and get you out of here."

6

Rooster was just about finished loading dry goods from Booker's mercantile onto the wagon when he happened to glance up and see Call Landry coming toward him. It took him a moment to place Landry. Seeing the fellow riding on horseback and not on or in a stagecoach made Rooster question himself. Turned out that his eyes and his memory were better than either of his hips. He raised a hand to greet Landry when the man came abreast of the wagon.

"Rooster, is it?" said Call, though he remembered perfectly well that it was.

"That's right."

Call pointed to his chest. "McCall Landry. I was here a few days back."

"Yeah. Thought it was you. You here on particular business or passing through?"

"Stonechurch business."

Rooster blinked owlishly. "He sent *you*? We knew he was sending someone, but never had word that it was going to be you."

"It's me." He patted his jacket pocket. "Have a letter right here."

"Well, don't show it to me. I never did read so good, and anyway, I reckon it's business between Miss Laurel and Mr. Stonechurch. You're just the messenger."

A little bit more than the messenger, Call thought, but

he kept that to himself. "Are you heading back to the station?"

Rooster grabbed a twenty-pound burlap sack of flour by the ears and hefted it onto the wagon. "Am now."

"I'll ride with you, if you don't mind."

Rooster didn't object. He climbed onto the buckboard's bench and guided the horse in a wide turn on Main Street and then started for home. Call Landry's mount kept the same easy pace. "Does that horse belong to Mr. Stonechurch?"

"Uh-huh. On loan to me for as long as I need her."

Rooster looked the cinnamon mare over with a keen and practiced eye. She had a pretty head, refined lines, and big, soft brown eyes, which she fluttered like a flirt. Her neck was in good proportion to her body. The shape was perfect and balanced. She held a saddle well and her hindquarters were strong, her gait stable. She had good bones. "I didn't think Mr. Stonechurch knew much about horseflesh. I guess I was wrong."

"I'm not sure you were. I picked this animal out from the livery. I had my choice of half a dozen. She was the best. The others didn't compare."

"Huh. She have a name?"

"If she does, she hasn't told me."

Rooster cocked a wiry eyebrow and gave Call a considering glance. "Well, you better name her or Miss Laurel will, and she's partial to names that'll set a man's teeth on edge. We got a Willow, a Sylvia, a Henrietta, a Mary Sue, and her sister, Mary Ann. Miss Laurel calls her mare Abby. I probably shouldn't go on. You get the idea. Oh, and we had a Penelope until Josiah Pye took her."

"I see. Well, this mare's a sweet girl with a good heart and stamina to spare. She took the steep grades with hardly a break in her stride. And she's pretty, too. She should have a name that suits her." Call fell silent, thinking on it. "I'm partial to Artemis." The mare swung her head. "Guess she agrees."

"Artemis?" asked Rooster. "That's one we don't have."

"She's the Greek goddess of the hunt, the moon, and nature."

"Huh. I like that. Can't speak for Miss Laurel, but since your girl has a name, I don't think she'll call her anything else."

Laurel was sweeping off the porch when she heard the noisy approach of the buckboard. Its creaks and squeaks were at lower pitch this afternoon, a sign that the wagon bed was heavily laden. She turned to greet Rooster, leaning comfortably on the broom handle until she saw he had picked up a companion. Straightening, Laurel set the broom against the porch rail and lowered her hands to her sides. She was struck by an urge to smooth her hair and finger her braid and didn't much like herself for what she thought of as simpering, girlish urges. What did it matter if strands of hairs were flying away from her face or her braid was no longer neatly plaited? Mrs. Lancaster was not around to tell her that it mattered very much indeed, and Laurel wasn't sure that she believed her anyway.

"Mr. Landry," she said. "This is a surprise."

Call tipped his hat, inordinately pleased she had arrived at his name without hesitation. In this particular instance, it was gratifying to be remembered. "Miss Morrison."

Rooster said, "I'm going to unload around back."

"Need help?" asked Call.

"Sure, but I'll get the boys. You can stable your horse in the barn. Grooming brushes, blankets, everything you need is in there. I'll leave you to explain yourself."

"Appreciate that." Call waited for Rooster to move out of earshot. When he turned to look at Laurel, it was clear from her expression that she thought his explanation was already too long in coming. He dismounted, held the reins loosely in one gloved hand, and set his feet in the at-ease position. "Mr. Stonechurch sent me. Rooster indicated you were expecting someone."

"Not you."

"I'm afraid if you have a problem with me, you'll have to take it up with Mr. Stonechurch."

"I will—if I have a problem with you. I don't. Not yet, but it's early days."

Call considered it a minor victory that she hadn't pointed to the trail and told him to leave, though why she would do that, he didn't know. He hadn't done anything to give her cause. On his only other visit to the station, he'd been polite, careful, respectful, and probably made himself an object of amusement admitting that traveling in the coach caused him no end of upset.

Call kept his eyes on hers. She wasn't wearing a hat on this occasion. Her hair was as burnished as a chestnut, brown with hints of copper and fire, and there was a light dusting of freckles across her nose and cheeks. Her ivory complexion was slowly turning pink the longer he stared. He thought he should look away, but then he thought she could do the same. Neither of them did. Her lips parted. He waited, but she didn't speak. He did instead.

"I understand that you might need another hand, or have you already replaced Josiah Pye?"

"Not yet. There's been some interest, but I haven't made a decision. I don't want to make another mistake."

"Understandable."

"Why do you ask? You have a job."

"It doesn't mean I can't help out here. I mean to make this station home while I conduct my investigation."

"Home?"

"In a manner of speaking. It's about halfway between Denver and Stonechurch so it suits. I can also board in Frost Falls when I have to. They're building a hotel there that'll be done soon. Can't imagine I won't be able to get a room when I need it."

"But home will be here." It wasn't exactly a question, but it was filled with doubt.

"Unless you tell me different. If money's a concern, Mr. Stonechurch is paying."

"If you help around here, your room and board is taken care of." Laurel's eyebrows puckered and twin vertical creases appeared between them. "I'm not sure how you're going to do what he expects of you while you're doing what I expect of you."

"That's a fair point. Why don't we see how it goes? You've been managing so far without Mr. Pye."

"It's only been a few days."

"And I'll only be absent a few days here and there."

Laurel fell silent, mulling it over. Finally, "Mr. Stonechurch is set on this?"

"He is." In truth, Stonechurch didn't care how the work was carried out. He wanted the payroll back, and if he couldn't have that, he wanted Josiah Pye. Call wanted to begin the inquiry at Morrison Station, and Stonechurch hadn't objected.

It seemed to Call that it was an endorsement of his methods. "Mr. Stonechurch is depending on your cooperation."

Laurel pressed her lips together, nodded. "Very well," she said after a moment. "You can stay. I'll eventually have to hire someone to take up your slack."

"Your prerogative."

"You can stable your horse and set yourself up in the bunkhouse. The stage isn't due here for several hours. That's when the next meal will be put out. We eat after the passengers leave. Talk to Rooster about where he needs you most and make yourself useful. The boys are around somewhere. Introduce yourself and don't let them get underfoot. They're good workers but easily distracted and they'll dog your steps if you let them."

Call nodded. "Appreciate it, Miss Morrison." He had it in his mind to shake hands on their arrangement and started to remove a glove, but if she understood his intentions, she wasn't having any part of it. She took a step back from the lip of the porch, picked up the broom, and resumed sweeping. He'd had plenty of experience in the army being dismissed so he recognized this for what it was. He was tempted to salute. Thinking better of it, he turned sharply instead and led his newly christened mare to the barn.

Laurel had second thoughts about what she'd agreed to while he was still in her sights, and third thoughts when he disappeared into the barn. She certainly understood Ramsey Stonechurch hiring someone to get his money back, but why he would put his trust in McCall Landry, a virtual stranger, was more difficult to comprehend. Perhaps Mr. Landry had skills and experience she knew nothing about. Mr. Stonechurch would have made a better study of the man than she had, and probably hadn't noticed or cared that he had as fine a pair of gray eyes as she had ever seen. The fact that they glinted silver in the sunlight was unlikely to have been a consideration.

Sighing, Laurel made a final pass with the broom and carried it into the house. Those eyes shouldn't have been a factor for her either when she agreed to take him on, but she couldn't honestly say they hadn't been. She had to cast her mind back years to remember the last time she'd felt something for a man with fine eyes. It was her recollection that she'd been a silly girl and the fine eyes had belonged to a boy who thought he was a man at fifteen. She'd thought so, too, back then. Her father caught her coming out of the barn with straw in her hair, and Johnny Turner appeared too soon after her exit for there to have been any doubt in her father's mind as to what had been going on in the loft. The straw clinging to Johnny's narrow shoulders and the back of his head was evidence her father didn't need and would have rather not seen. Johnny elected to leave with his tail between his legs rather than take a thrashing for the girl he'd professed to love only minutes earlier.

Johnny-fine-eyes married his second cousin a few years later, and had a child on the way when he went off to war. He never came back. Laurel didn't presume he was dead. She figured him for a deserter.

Laurel had put Johnny Turner out of her mind by the time she reached the kitchen. She set the broom in a corner and sidled up to Mrs. Lancaster, who was kneading dough on the table. She breathed deeply of the yeast aroma rising from the dough. "Are all the dry goods put away?" Laurel asked.

"In the pantry. Rooster took care of it. That's a man with something to prove to himself. He wouldn't let me help." She shook her head and used a forearm to brush back strands of dark brown hair and threads of gray. "Hefting those heavy bags. He's got no sense."

"I know. There's no point in trying to go easy on him. He won't allow it."

Mrs. Lancaster nodded. She folded the dough, folded it again, and pushed down with the heels of her hands. "Rooster says we have a new fella helping out. Was he pulling my leg?"

"No. His name is McCall Landry. Mr. Stonechurch hired him to find Mr. Pye. Well, to find the money Mr. Pye took. Mr. Landry was a passenger on the stage that was robbed. You flirted with him when you were clearing the table. Remember that?"

"Flirted with—" A new thought interrupted her. "Ah, yes. I *do* remember. Landry, did you say? I don't believe I caught his name then, not that it's what I would have recollected anyway. Fine-looking man. *That* I remember."

"McCall Landry," Laurel said. "I believe he prefers Call."

"That so? I bet you never called him that. Bet you called him Mr. Landry."

"What if I did? There's nothing wrong with that. It's his name."

Mrs. Lancaster lifted her flour-dusted hands out of the dough and held them up to profess her innocence. Her dark brown eyes, though, were shrewd. "Just an observation. I meant nothing by it."'

"Uh-huh."

The cook offset her exaggerated shrug with a glimmer of a smile and went back to kneading. "You have somewhere else you need to be?" she asked. "Or is it your intention to hide out here?"

"I'm not hiding out."

"Sure, and you always prefer the kitchen to the outdoors."

"Sometimes I do."

"Then you can peel the taters and cut up some onions. We're having stew. I've got the beef stock simmering."

Peeling and chopping were hardly Laurel's preferred tasks, but she couldn't very well back away from them now without proving the cook's point. Mrs. Lancaster's quiet chuckle followed her into the pantry. She ignored it. By the time she returned with the vegetables, the cook had sobered and Laurel was on even footing.

7

Call introduced himself to Dillon and Hank Booker in the barn, where they were tending the horses. They stopped what they were doing to pepper him with questions. He answered enough to temporarily satisfy them while he cared for Artemis. After she was watered and fed, he left the boys so he could take his belongings to the bunkhouse. They would have followed if he'd given them the least encouragement, but he remembered Laurel's caution about not letting them get underfoot and recognized the wisdom of it.

He put his clothes in the trunk at the foot of the bunk he judged to be the most comfortable out of the ones that were available. It was close to the door, which he preferred. After spending almost two years in confinement, exits were important to him.

Rooster was struggling to set a ladder against the back of the house when Call came across him. "I can help you with that," he said and started forward.

"I got it."

Call stopped. He recognized stubbornness in a man who refused to give ground. Call let him have his way, prepared to step in if the ladder proved too unwieldy, and was glad that he waited when Rooster managed on his own.

"There." Rooster gave the ladder a shake to be sure it was grounded and steady. "You can hand me that box with the hammer and nails," he said, pointing to the wooden box close to Call's feet. "And that roll of tar paper."

"Why don't you go on up and I'll carry it to you? Miss Morrison said I should make myself useful. Seems this is as good a way as any to start." Call waited to see if Rooster would take his suggestion as an insult, but it seemed that invoking their employer's name into the offer made it palatable.

"All right. That'd be fine."

Call picked up the box by its handle and put the short roll of roofing felt under an arm. He waited until Rooster had transferred from the ladder to the roof before he began to climb. The rungs were sturdier than he'd thought and he was climbing with more confidence by the time he reached the top. He stepped onto the roof and followed Rooster up the incline. He stopped when Rooster did but stayed standing when Rooster dropped to his haunches.

"I'm figuring the leak is about here. We're above the kitchen. Mrs. Lancaster had a conniption last time it rained and her hot cinnamon buns took a drubbing. Not something I want to see or hear again." Studying the wooden shingles, he held out his hand.

Clearly Rooster expected him to know what he wanted. Call gave him the hammer and took Rooster's grunt to mean he had chosen correctly. Rooster pulled up half a dozen oiled shingles and set them to the side. He didn't make Call guess that he needed the tar paper next; he asked for it. He unrolled it, eyeballed the size he needed, and took a knife from his back pocket to score and cut it.

"Tacks," said Rooster.

Call handed them over one by one, studying Rooster as he secured the felt to the roof, laying it over the weathered tar paper that had been put down years earlier. The man had a steady hand, deftly and accurately tapping the tacks in. It didn't take him long to put the shingles back, setting them in place with roofing nails. When he was done, he looked up at Call.

"Reckon you can do that?"

"I've never done it before but I think so."

"You were watching, weren't you?"

"Yes."

"Then I reckon you can do it." He held out his knife to Call. "Go on up three feet higher and four feet to the left. Pull up the shingles and add new felt. That should take care of the other damp spot I noticed. Always hard to tell about leaks so that's my best guess."

There was no possibility of Call refusing. "I have a knife," he said, patting his boot as he stooped to pick up the toolbox. "Three up and four to the left."

"Right."

Call went five feet on the diagonal to reach the point. On his own, the incline seemed steeper than it had when he was standing beside Rooster. He tried hunkering as Rooster had but learned quickly he was better off kneeling. Removing the shingles was more difficult than Rooster had made it seem. He struggled enough with the hammer's claw that Rooster felt compelled to warn him not to crack the shingles. Call eased up on pulling and worked the shingles loose by twisting the claw and tugging at the same time.

Call estimated that it took him twice as long to accomplish the same work that Rooster had done, and he couldn't help but think Rooster had been showing off a little, proving once again that he had a lot of years to work left in him.

Call picked up the box and paper and straightened, shaking out his legs before he started down the roof. Now that he was standing and facing a descent, he took note that the ground seemed quite a distance away. He also took note of Laurel Morrison watching him, hands on her hips, her head tilted back. He wondered how long she had been there and how much she had seen of his clumsy efforts to repair the roof. His gaze shifted to Rooster, who was grinning at him, obviously appreciating the moment.

His lips set in a wry twist, Call said, "Enjoying yourself, Rooster?"

There was no point in denying it. "Sure am. You gonna be able to get down all right or do you need me to hold your hand?"

"I'll manage."

Rooster's grin faded when Laurel called to him. "Uh-oh," he said only loud enough for Call to hear him. "I'm in for it now."

"Rooster!" Laurel called again, cupping her hands around her mouth this time.

"Yes, ma'am. I hear you."

Laurel dropped her hands to her sides. "You told me Mr. Pye fixed those leaks."

"I told you Mr. Pye was *gonna* fix the leaks. It was likely the prospect of climbing up here that sent him running. The man had a fierce fear of heights. Leastways he said he did." Rooster shrugged. "I allow it could have been a lie. Always hard to tell with Josey."

Laurel had no patience for hearing it now. Seeing Rooster up on the roof made her want to wring her hands and quite possibly his neck. Still, she tempered her frustration. "Would you please come down?"

"Coming. Thought I'd have to steady the greenhorn here, but he says he can do it on his own."

Laurel's gaze shifted to Call just as if she hadn't been watching him all along. "Can you?" she asked.

"I'll be fine," said Call and hoped it was true. He saw Laurel was taking him at his word because her attention returned to Rooster as the man stepped from the roof and onto the ladder. Once again, Rooster made it look easy. Call wasn't so sure that it was.

"Give me the paper and the box," Rooster said. "You'll want to have both hands free."

Call believed him. He gave over both and watched Rooster disappear over the lip of the roof. When Rooster was standing beside Laurel, Call grasped the side rails and stepped sideways onto a rung. He hesitated and Laurel called to him not to look down. It was humiliating, but he reasoned that the feeling would pass when he did.

He stepped down and turned to face his audience. Rooster was grinning again, and Call noticed the man had a gap between his front teeth. It wasn't big enough for Call to drive his fist through it, but he would have considered it if the gap didn't make the man look so plainly ridiculous. Call found himself grinning, too. Laurel, in contrast, was shaking her head and dividing her disapproval equally between the two of them.

"Do not make me regret taking you on, Mr. Landry."

Call sobered. Rooster did not.

"And, Rooster, show some sense."

Now Rooster sobered.

Laurel left them staring at her back as she entered the house through the kitchen.

"Is that it?" Call asked out of the side of his mouth.

"That's it," said Rooster in a like manner. "You know she's watching us from the window. Don't hint that you're amused."

"I'm not."

"Good fellow. You'll do just fine. Get the ladder and take it to the barn. I'll get the rest."

When the stagecoach arrived a few hours later, Call helped Rooster unhitch the team of four and lead them to the barn while the brothers brought out the fresh team. Once that was accomplished, they each tended to one of the spent animals. Call pointed out that the mare he was caring for needed a new shoe before she could go out again. He was more diverted than insulted when Hank checked the animal's hoof to verify it was true. He didn't point out that he had far more experience than the boy did. Call simply did not have a need to assert himself in a way that might make Hank Booker feel small.

After the stage had departed, they all sat down in the dining room for a hearty meal of beef stew, which they sopped up with warm chunks of crusty bread. Mrs. Lancaster sat with them and served up big squares of berry cobbler for dessert. They cleaned their plates of everything but the floral design.

It was not until the coffee was poured that Laurel finally posed the question to Call that had been on her mind since his arrival. By the attention it received as others leaned forward to hear his answer, she realized she had not been carrying the question alone.

"So when do you begin?" she asked, folding her hands around her cup. And in the event he didn't understand, she added, "Your interrogation, I mean. It's why you've come here first, isn't it?"

Call was the only one still sitting back in his chair. He blew out a short breath. "Are any of you going anywhere?" he asked, looking around. When they all shook their heads, he said, "Then there's no hurry and no point ruining a good meal with unpleasant conversation."

Mrs. Lancaster beamed at him. "True words."

Call patted his stomach and shook his head when she offered him a second piece of cobbler. "Mr. Pye is long gone. Stonechurch knows that. I'm not going to find him following a cold trail already trampled by a succession of stagecoaches. I thought I'd learn more about the man starting tomorrow. Further, I want to speak to each of you alone. If you haven't already been comparing stories, don't start now. It will just muddy the waters."

Hank said, "Dillon and me ain't talked about much else since it happened so those waters are already stirred some."

It was what Call had expected. "Who else have you spoken to about what happened?"

Hank held up a hand and began ticking off a list on his fingers. "Ma. My other brother. My sisters. Pa, of course." He closed his fist and opened it again, one finger at a time. "The sheriff and Bobber Jordan. Bobber got sworn in as a deputy on account of him running up a bill at Sweeny's and facing jail or working it off. I guess that's it." He looked at the two fingers he was holding up and remembered the five that had come before. "Seven. That's all."

Call looked at Dillon. "Anyone you want to add?"

"I'm thinkin' our sisters probably told their husbands

and I guess Mr. Abernathy knows. He's the druggist. He was jawin' with Pa outside the mercantile when we told Pa all about it."

"Oh, and Mrs. Scott," said Hank, unfolding another finger. "I plum forgot that she came by."

Sighing, Call's gaze wandered around the table. "Perhaps a better question would be is there anyone in town who *hasn't* heard what happened here?" He was met with silence. "I see."

"It's a small town," said Rooster. "Can't be more than a couple hundred or so people hereabouts. Word was bound to get around."

"Why is it important?" asked Laurel.

"Because Josiah Pye had help. It'd be a good thing to know if that person is one of your own or someone down the line. Just makes my job harder if there's more than one version of the story making the rounds."

Mrs. Lancaster chuckled. "By my count, the boys told at least eleven people. I can promise there are now eleven slightly different versions of the story, maybe more since they probably never told it the same way twice."

Call nodded. "That is an excellent point."

Laurel said, "No one from town was here the day the strongbox disappeared. I don't see how Mr. Pye's help could have come from anyone there."

"And maybe it didn't. I'm trying to keep my mind open to all possibilities." He raised his eyebrows a fraction as he regarded the cook. "You don't live here, do you, Mrs. Lancaster?"

"Oh, no. Seems as if I do sometimes, but no, I have a house in town and a grown daughter and son-in-law who live with me. Three grandchildren. Two girls and a boy, all of them little devils." She said this last with an affectionate smile. The little devils were her pride and joy.

"Your husband is . . . ?"

"Dead. I've been a widow these six years past."

"I'm sorry."

"So am I. He survived the fighting and died two years later in his sleep. No rhyme or reason for it."

Laurel said gently, "Mrs. Lancaster's husband was a doctor. Since he died, the town's had to go without. There are plenty of folks who still miss him."

Mrs. Lancaster pressed her lips together, nodded at Laurel in appreciation of the sentiment. Aware that the turn in conversation had cast a pall over the table, she took a breath and released it with purpose. "Hank, I'm recollecting it's your turn to help clear and wash." She stood, gathered a few plates, and thrust them at Hank. "Let's go and get this done."

"I'll help," said Call, getting to his feet.

The cook shook her head. "Sit back down. It'll be your turn soon enough. We do a rotation here. Everybody lends a hand."

Call sat. His coffee was lukewarm now but he took a swallow anyway. "I stepped into that, didn't I?"

Rooster said, "It would have come up sooner or later. Sometimes sooner is best."

Dillon rested an elbow on the table and propped his head against his palm. "Just so you know, Hank and me sometimes stay here, sometimes we stay with our parents. Not always at the same time. Depends on what's going on here. Ma likes to know we're close by but not so close that she's tripping over us. And you might as well know this, too. We ain't had nothing to do with the robbery. Until we learned different, we thought Josey was a horse thief, and that made him no-account in our eyes. Sure, it bothers us that he robbed the stage, but it bothers us worse that he took Penelope. She was our responsibility so we take that personal."

"Penelope?"

"The mare," said Laurel.

Rooster gave Call a knowing look. "Told you."

Laurel frowned. "What? Penelope is perfectly suited to her name."

"Uh-huh," said Rooster.

Not for anything was Call going to involve himself in what appeared to be a long-standing difference of opinion. "I'm going to go outside. Maybe take a walk into town. I didn't look around much when I came through." When no one offered him a reason to stay at the table, he stood. "Will there be another stage tonight?"

Laurel shook her head. "There's nothing on the schedule. Take your time."

Call did. There were not many people out after dusk, but he talked to folks closing up their shops or sitting out in chairs on the boardwalk. He met Dillon and Hank's father, who invited him to play a game of checkers. Call accepted, was roundly beaten both times, and learned more than he ever wanted to know about Falls Hollow. Mr. Booker roused himself enough to leave his chair and accompany Call to Sweeny's, where Call bought him two shots, one for each of his victories.

Call asked casually after Josiah Pye to get a sense of how well the man was known. The answer appeared to be not well at all. Pye mostly kept to himself, drank alone, and if he did sit down for a couple of rounds of poker, he was a quiet sort, good with a bluff, but seemed to lose as often as he won. They agreed he wasn't particularly upset when he lost or excited when he won. Even-tempered, they said. Someone mentioned Pye was a more regular visitor to the brothel than he was to the saloon, and Call let that pass while making a mental note of it.

Laurel was sitting in one of the rockers on the porch when Call returned to the station. Night was coming on quickly, and she was as much shadow as she was substance. Her head rested against the back of the rocker; her eyes were closed. The only indication he had that she was awake was the slow, steady lift and fall of her heels as she pushed the rocker with her toes.

"You can say something," she said, her eyes still closed. "I know you're there."

"I didn't mean to disturb you."

"No? Then you should have gone straight to the bunk-house."

Call could not remember being set in his place so neatly. "I guess what I meant was that I didn't want to frighten you by speaking up."

"Then you should have said that."

"Maybe so. May I join you?"

"Suit yourself."

A slim smile lifted one corner of Call's mouth. If she thought he would be deterred by her lack of a genuine invitation, she was about to learn differently. He eyed the rocker on her left and the swing on her right and chose the swing, which was some distance away. He sat at the end farthest from her so he could stretch his legs on the seat and still be facing her. It took a few moments for him to find the spot for his maximum comfort, and when he did, only a hammock could have offered better.

"You're prickly this evening," he said. "That's an observation, not a conversational gambit."

She snorted lightly and continued rocking.

"I met Mr. Booker when I was in town," said Call. "He beat me at checkers. Twice. Also gave me a history of Falls Hollow. Did you know he was an early settler? I didn't realize there was mining around here."

"For about a minute," she said. "The mine played out quickly. A lot of men moved on, most to Stonechurch, some to Leadville. This valley is better suited to farming."

"That's what your family did?"

"Early on. I don't really remember that. The success of Stonechurch Mining brought the stage line, and my father got a contract to operate the farmhouse as a home station."

"You've got a nice spread here."

"Mm."

"And what appears to be a successful operation."

"We do all right." She stopped rocking. "For now."

Call waited for her to resume the gentle back-and-forth rhythm of the rocker. If he watched her for too long, he thought he might fall asleep. Except for the chance that he could fall off the swing, he would have given into the urge. "You have a plan for when the railroad comes?"

Laurel opened her eyes, turned her head, and stared at him. "You know about that?"

His eyebrows lifted a notch. "The railroad coming or your plan?"

"The railroad."

"It's not a secret that the railroad will lay rail to Stonechurch. There's eventual profit for them in the investment. The telegraph ended the pony express. The railroad is taking over the stagecoach routes. Until something better, something more efficient, comes along, there's no stopping it."

Laurel sighed softly but audibly. "I know. It's hard to think about much else these days." Her short laugh was humorless. "Mr. Pye's activities were almost a welcome distraction. Not really, but you get the idea."

"I do. So you have a plan?"

"I'm trying to secure an agreement with the railroad that they'll keep to the Cabin Creek Trail and make Falls Hollow a station on the line. At the moment, it's still not clear which railroad line is going to win the bid to put down tracks between Denver and Stonechurch. I've had conversations with Alexander Berry about it. He's Federal; at least I've been given to understand that. He's an agreeable sort, always watchful, though, as if he expects to catch someone doing something wrong." She shrugged. "But he's the man in charge of the bidding process so I endeavor to be pleasant and not act as if he holds our livelihood in his hands. He'll also establish the route, and I aim to see that he chooses the one I've laid out for him."

"So he's been here already."

"Twice. I've written to him a few times, promoting this route, this station. Falls Hollow will live or die by the railroad."

"You feel responsible for that?"

Laurel rested her head back again and closed her eyes.

She nodded because she couldn't speak for the catch in her throat.

Aware of her distress, Call gave her time to recover but not so much time that she might suspect she was being coddled. She would not appreciate that in the least.

"You have competition?" he asked.

"There's a spread some fifteen miles from here. Ephraim Hammersmith and his brothers own the land. It's well north of the living station that's on the trail now, but if the railroad decided to take that detour—and there's an argument that can be made for it—the track could bypass Falls Hollow altogether."

"What's the argument?"

"The grade is more gradual than the incline leading in and out of Falls Hollow. That weighs heavily with the railroad."

"Is that the only factor in its favor?"

"As far as land goes, yes, but it's generally believed that the Hammersmiths come from money. Mrs. Ephraim Hammersmith anyway. I can't say that it's true, but I don't know that it isn't. You understand what I mean about the money, don't you? Why it's important?"

"From what you're saying, I'm thinking bribery."

"Keep thinking that."

"Do you suspect—what's the government man's name again?"

"Alexander Berry."

"Right. So do you suspect Mr. Berry is likely to be persuaded by a bribe?"

"I'd like to believe he isn't, but that would be foolish on my part."

Call was inclined to agree. He was formulating his next question when Laurel sat forward in the rocker and turned sharply in his direction.

"If you're thinking that I had a part in the robbery to manage a bribe of my own, you're—"

Call threw up his hands as though he could ward her off. "Never crossed my mind. Swear."

It took a couple of moments, but she finally relaxed, slumping back into the rocker. "I don't know why not. In your place, I'd wonder about it."

"I'm not going to win this, am I?"

"No."

He dropped his hands. "Just so we're clear, even though you've planted the idea full bloom in my head, I'm still not wondering about it."

"You think you know me that well?"

"Probably not, but Mr. Stonechurch thinks he does. He and Brady are both confident you had nothing to do with the theft. Without evidence to the contrary, I'd be hard pressed to convince either one of them otherwise. Without evidence, I'm hard pressed to convince myself."

"Is that the truth?"

"Gospel."

"Hmm. That eases me some."

"You were concerned what Mr. Stonechurch thought?"

"His good opinion is important. He has a lot of influence in these parts, not just in Stonechurch. If he thinks this station is a liability, it won't matter if I offer a bribe to Mr. Berry. The rails will detour over Hammersmith land. That's a given."

Call didn't doubt that she was right. "I don't think you have to worry about Stonechurch's good opinion. You have it."

"I'm not sure what I've done to earn it."

"The expression 'don't look a gift horse in the mouth' comes to mind."

Laurel chuckled quietly.

"What's your opinion of him?" asked Call.

"He's intelligent, works at least as hard as anyone working for him, and knows his own mind."

"Do you know his brother?"

"Leo? We've met. They work well together, depend on each other. You know that town isn't named after the man who hired you. It's named after his grandfather. Mr. Stonechurch is *not* a Pharaoh in spite of what people think."

"Ramsey. Ramses. I assumed that's how he acquired the nickname."

"I imagine it is."

Call hesitated, wondering if he should say anything about what he'd learned. He decided in favor of letting her know. "He told me about you," Call said. "About what happened here after the war."

Laurel nodded.

"You're not surprised."

She shrugged. "People talk. I'm used to it. If you told folks in town that you're working here, I imagine you heard it again."

"I did tell them, and I didn't hear it."

"Now *that* surprises me."

"Do you mind talking about it?" She was so long in answering that Call thought silence was her answer.

"Do you know, Mr. Landry, you're the first person in a long, long time to ask me if I minded and only the second person ever to take my feelings into consideration. In case you're wondering, Rooster was the first. Plenty of people talk around me, about me, but rarely to me. I believe they think they're taking my feelings into account because these are good people doing the talking, but the opposite is true. It's uncomfortable. It feels pitying. I don't want that. I don't need it. So, no, I don't mind talking about what happened. What do you want to know?"

Call wasn't sure. He wasn't expecting the question to be put to him so bluntly. At last he asked, "How did you survive?"

"I didn't realize it was a choice. I'm not being glib. My father—his name was Thomas—was dead. My brothers, George and Martin, were dead. I was alive and I had to go on. It was that simple and that awful. Rooster showed up and never left. That helped. Folks trickled in from town after the shooting. A few stayed on to help me run the station. I've had different stage tenders over the years. Hired as many as six at one time, but four or five seems about right. We get by."

"I think you do better than that."

"Maybe."

"What about the raiders? Mr. Stonechurch didn't think they were ever caught."

"I don't think they were. I had it in my mind to go after them. Foolish, of course. Rooster threatened to hog-tie me. I took him at his word and stayed right here."

"Do you regret listening to him?"

"No. Well, sometimes. I know he was right. I knew he was right then. You and I wouldn't be talking now if I had tried following them."

"You followed Josey Pye."

"That was different. I'm a better shot now, a better tracker, and I had Rooster with me. It made me feel a little more settled to know I was doing something instead of waiting around for Sheriff Carter, who, by the way, barely roused himself to name a deputy and begin searching. When I gave him Mr. Stonechurch's message about the robbery, he and his deputy went out again, but they've already given up. I let Mr. Stonechurch know, and here you are."

"Here I am."

"I have a feeling you won't give up so easily."

"Mr. Stonechurch shares your feeling."

"Are we right?"

"Yes."

Laurel nodded, satisfied. "Do you remember Mr. Abrams, the portly gentleman who was one of your fellow passengers?"

"Your description helped. Yes, I remember him. Why?"

"I don't know if he mentioned that he is an assembly-man, but he is. He advocates for the territory's admission to the Union. He will also have some influence with the route the railroad takes, which he reminded me when he came through this last time. It's not important to the robbery, but I thought you should be aware."

"At this juncture I don't know what's important and what's not. All information is helpful to the investigation."

"Do you suspect someone on the coach of helping Mr. Pye?"

Call tapped his temple with a forefinger. "Open mind."

"Probably for the best. I'm trying to do the same. I was taken completely by surprise when I received Mr. Stonechurch's message that the payroll was missing. Mr. Pye is the obvious culprit because he disappeared that night, but that's hardly proof."

"But you agree the coincidence is hard to swallow," said Call.

"I do."

Call removed his hat and set it on his outstretched legs. He pushed his fingers through his thick hair. "If he hadn't taken off with Penelope, where would you have put him on your list of suspects?"

"I've already thought of that. There really wouldn't be a list. Mr. Pye would be the only name."

"Why?"

"Mostly because I don't know him as well as I know Rooster and the boys. He hasn't worked here as long as the others. I hired him after I noticed Rooster was slowing down a bit, favoring his hips, the right one especially. I thought he should rest it some." She paused, and then said urgently, "Please don't repeat that. It would be humiliating for him."

"Not a word."

"Thank you." Laurel was silent for several long seconds. She stopped rocking, stretched, and crossed her legs at the ankle. "I was not comfortable around Mr. Pye," she said at last. "Never warmed to him, I'd guess you'd say. That's not a requirement to work here, but it seems to make the work less demanding if we're easy with each other."

"Yet you kept him on."

"He was good with the animals. Surprised us all when we discovered he was also a decent cook. So, yes, I kept him on for what he could do and ignored all the things he tried to get out of doing."

"He was a shirker."

"Yes, he was that."

"Where did he come from?"

"He arrived on the stage, same as you, but he's from some town I never heard of in Illinois. Like a lot of folks who pass this way, he was looking for work in Stonechurch. During the team exchange, one of the horses proved too difficult for Hank to handle. Before I could get there, Mr. Pye stepped in, gentled her, and led her away."

"And you offered him a job."

"Not right then, but yes, before he got back on the stage."

"So about forty-five minutes later."

Laurel was reluctant to admit it. "Yes. Impulsive, wasn't it?"

"Not a sin," said Call. "Out of character, perhaps."

"I'd like to think so."

"How long before you regretted the offer?"

"Days, but it was at least a month before I admitted it to myself."

"Do you know why you were uncomfortable around him?"

"Yes."

When she did not elaborate, Call asked, "Are you going to tell me?"

"No. I don't think I will."

Her refusal told him quite a bit, he decided. It was personal, not work related. Call didn't press for more information. "I was in Sweeny's tonight. I asked after him while I was there. It seems he mostly kept to himself."

"I'd agree with that."

"I learned he spent a fair amount of time at the brothel."

"Mrs. Fry's place. I don't know about that. The boys might. Maybe Rooster."

"I'll ask."

Laurel drew her braid forward over her shoulder and fingered it. Up and down. Up and down. Working up to asking the question that had been uppermost in her mind.

He seemed to know it, too, because he let her sit there in silence and didn't feel a need to fill it. "Why are you doing this?" she finally asked. "Why did you accept the job?"

"There are a few different answers to that, all of them true, some of them truer than others. Are you sure you want to know?"

"I asked," she said. "Yes, I want to know. I want to know the truest answer."

"All right, but don't make me sorry I told you. Don't suddenly get up like you forgot something you have to do and disappear on me."

"I don't run."

"Mm. Let's see. Here it is: I took Mr. Stonechurch up on his offer because it was an opportunity to see you again." Call waited to see if she would say something. She didn't. She didn't move either. She was so still that she might have been stone. "Are you breathing? Doesn't seem as if you're breathing."

"Yes, I'm breathing." In fact, her breath had caught for a moment and the next breath she captured was shallow. There was no reason to tell him that. "You must think a lot of yourself if you believe I'd be so flattered that I'd cease to breathe."

Call shrugged. "I've seen it happen."

"You're either a liar or a braggart. Neither quality recommends your character."

He chuckled low in his throat. "True. What about your heart? Did it skip a beat?"

Laurel smirked. "Uh-huh. Tripped right over itself."

"You're mocking me, aren't you? I hear mocking."

"I'm smirking, too."

"Can't see that. Not sure smirking is an attractive expression for you."

"That's unfortunate. I do it a lot."

"Doesn't put me off, though. I'm still glad I took the job."

"That's ridiculous, you know."

"So you say. I'm satisfied."

Laurel simply shook her head. "What are the other, slightly less true reasons you took the job?"

"So we're moving on, are we?"

"Yes." She was firm on that.

"Well, you know I was looking for a job with Stone-church Mining when this came along. I needed money, and I figured a job was a better way of getting it than thievery. Maybe I can rise a little in your estimation by telling you that stealing never occurred to me." He waited to see if she would comment. She didn't so he went on. "I didn't have enough capital to buy into a poker game. Didn't want to start riding shotgun again if I could avoid it. And I figured my prospects were limited for what the army trained me to do."

Laurel peered through the darkness, trying to make out his features and gauge the truth of what he was telling her. "And what was that?"

"Kill."

"Oh."

"Yeah," he said flatly. "You probably don't want to know if I was any good at it."

"No, Mr. Landry, I don't. Your presence is testament enough to your talent for it."

"Call," he said.

"What?"

"My name. You keep calling me Mr. Landry, I'm going to stop answering to it."

"I'll think about it. Maybe I won't say your name at all."

"That'd be better than the other."

"I'm not sure I understand your objection."

He shrugged. "Isn't it enough that I have one?"

Laurel considered that. "All right," she said at last.

"Thank you."

The silence that followed was surprisingly companionable. Laurel resumed pushing the rocker, slowly and rhythmically. Call watched the movement. It was restful and he closed his eyes. It had been a long day in the saddle, yet he was reluctant to retire as long as he could spend time in Laurel's company. He didn't think too hard about the attraction he felt. It was just there. There was no reason that he could think of to deny it.

"It's not really a talent," he said as much to himself as to her.

"Pardon?"

"I told you the army trained me to kill, and you said I had a talent for it. I'm saying it's not a talent. It was hard learned. I knew a few men who came to it naturally, maybe even enjoyed it. I wasn't one of them."

Laurel considered what he was telling her and wondered that he cared enough for her opinion that he would explain himself. When she spoke, her voice was quiet, grave. "I should have chosen my words more carefully. I admit that you shocked me. I wish I hadn't responded so dismissively. I apologize."

"I wasn't looking for that. I don't know, maybe I meant to shock you. The army trained me to do lots of things. I could have answered differently."

She refrained from asking what those things were. "Were you a volunteer or a draft recruit?"

"Volunteer. Joined up as soon as the local company was formed. Marched off with my eyes wide shut. I didn't know a damn thing and thought I knew it all. The army's good for waking a soldier up. Fighting does that."

"How old were you?"

"Old enough." He heard her make a sound that indicated she wasn't satisfied with that answer. "Twenty. I was twenty. There were lots of boys younger than me, all of us looking for adventure and glory. Like I said, fighting woke us up."

"My brothers were older, but I don't think that matters. Is anyone ever prepared?"

"Not in my experience."

"George enlisted first. When he came back, Martin went. Couldn't be talked out of it, so my father went, too. He had some idea that he could watch Martin's back. It didn't work out that way. Martin saw fighting. My father saw the aftermath. He worked in the medical tent, collecting sawn-off limbs and mopping up blood. None of them talked much about it. My father said the worst part for him was waiting for the wagons to bring the wounded in and living with the dread that he'd see his son among the bodies."

"Hard to bear," said Call. "Nothing about the war was ever easy, but some things were harder to bear than others."

"Mm-hmm." Laurel didn't trust herself to do more than murmur agreement.

Call judged it was the right moment to leave. She deserved privacy for her thoughts. The truth was that he wanted the same. He dropped his legs over the side of the swing and sat up. It rocked gently in response to his movement and he dug in his heels to stop it. "It's been a pleasure, Miss Morrison." He caught his hat as he stood and returned it to his head. "Good night."

Laurel nodded. She continued staring straight ahead and didn't spare him a glance. She did not trust the darkness to keep him from seeing that her eyes were damp.

8

The morning stage came from Stonechurch. Call thought Brady might be driving, but it seemed he was still holed up in the mining town waiting for the Pharaoh to give him leave to go. Mr. Stonechurch did not appear to be entirely confident in Brady's innocence because after that first night he kept finding excuses for the driver to stay. It was a reminder to Call that he had a job to do for Stonechurch and couldn't linger at Morrison Station without talking to Rooster and the Booker boys.

After breakfast, Call had an opportunity to question Rooster alone while the man was fitting one of the mares with a new shoe. Call made himself useful grooming and feeding the animals while Rooster worked so conversation was more natural than a sit-down interrogation.

"Can't say that I knew the man all that well," said Rooster as he examined the available shoes for one that would fit the mare. He tried several before he found the right one. "Josey talked but didn't say much if you know what I mean."

"I do," said Call. "Was he friendly?"

"He wasn't unfriendly. He was real good with the animals. Spoke to them more than he did to me. Found them more interesting, I suspect."

"Would you say he was close to anyone here?"

"No."

"Anyone in town?"

"Never heard that he was. You looking for someone who might have helped rob the stage?"

"Helped him or knew something about his plans."

"Well, I can tell you that someone ain't one of us. Mrs. Booker would lay her boys out flat if she even thought they were involved. She's a real gentle woman until her back's up then you gotta back up. Far."

A glimmer of a smile crossed Call's face at this description of a fierce mother. He was not unfamiliar with the type. "You're telling me Dillon and Hank wouldn't dare."

"That's right."

"And you?"

"I guess you had to ask outright, but it's still an insult." Rooster tapped a nail into the shoe and the mare's hoof. The animal didn't stir. "I got a conscience I have to live with. Listening to it has served me just fine all these years. So, no, I didn't have anything to do with the robbery in the planning or in the doing. Whether or not you're inclined to believe me, that's up to you."

Call was so inclined and he told Rooster that. "A couple of men at Sweeny's told me Pye spent more of his free time at the brothel than the saloon. Does that sound about right?"

"Can't say. I wasn't with him and he didn't talk about it."

"So you don't know if there was a particular woman he saw there, someone he might have talked to more than anyone else."

Rooster shook his head. He finished shoeing the mare and dropped the animal's hoof. Straightening, he put a hand at the small of his back and stretched. "Like I said, wasn't with him and he didn't talk about it. Did you ask the boys?"

"Not yet."

Rooster chuckled. "There's a better chance you'll learn something from them than me. They've been known to visit the Fry house. Can't keep young'uns away from the place."

Call raised an eyebrow. "Does Mrs. Booker know?"

"Don't know how she couldn't. Dillon and Hank aren't exactly what you'd call discreet. Words kinda spill out of them, especially when she's giving them that gimlet eye."

Laughing, Call finished brushing the mare Laurel had named Sylvia. He was beginning to think the name suited the animal. Leastways, she responded to it. He set aside the brush. "Where are the boys this morning?"

"Dillon's tending the garden. He might have roped his brother into helping him."

"All right. You need me to do anything right now?"

"I'm good. You go on. Send Hank here when you're done with him."

Call nodded. "Thanks."

The brothers were indeed in the garden. Dillon was bent over, pulling weeds as he moved slowly down a row. Hank was leaning on a rake, content to watch Dillon work.

Call stood at the perimeter of the garden and waited to be noticed. Hank saw him first and suddenly stood at attention, though Call couldn't imagine why he did. Dillon stopped weeding, brushed off his hands, but stayed hunkered down.

"You two mind answering some questions?" When they shook their heads in unison, Call started right in. He didn't vary his questions much from what he had asked Rooster, but he lobbed the questions at the brothers separately. Dillon took one. Hank took the next. The only time the boys hedged or hesitated was when Call asked about Mrs. Fry's place.

Hank finally said, "Yeah, I guess we've been there some."

"Did you know Josey went there?"

Dillon said, "Saw him once. You gotta understand that me and Josey Pye having the same time to get away didn't happen often."

"What about you, Hank? Did you see him?"

"Never saw him, but I knew he'd been there."

"Because Dillon told you?"

"Dillon never said a word about Pye, but I heard his

name mentioned while I was there so I asked after him. Mainly I wanted to know who he was bedding because it bothered me some to ask for the same girl. Not sure why. I know they're whores and all, but it just made me—I don't know—kinda unsettled. Same with Dillon. He goes with Marie. I usually ask for Alice Mae." He shrugged. "Sometimes Liz if Alice Mae's busy."

Call took this all in, primarily because he couldn't figure out how to stop Hank once he got started. "Do you know if Josey Pye had a favorite?"

"Not sure she was his favorite," said Hank, "but I heard he mostly went upstairs with Desi. Desiree."

Dillon said, "That's who was draped all over him the night I saw him there."

"Is she still there?" asked Call.

Hank shrugged. "Couldn't say. I ain't been there in a while."

Dillon nodded. "Same here. You can ask Miss Laurel, but I'm pretty sure Desi's never bought a ticket to leave town. We'd have seen if she took a coach, and it's hard for me to imagine her leaving on horseback or taking off on foot. Maybe she'd take Mrs. Fry's carriage, but that'd be stealing and I don't see Desi being good for that. She's a decent sort."

"For a whore," said Hank.

"For anyone," Dillon said, objecting. His eyes narrowed as he studied Call. "You keep things to yourself?"

"I can."

Dillon took his time taking Call's measure before he spoke. "I never even told Hank this." Here, he looked sharply at his brother with a clear threat of violence if a word of what he was about to say was repeated. "I never figured it out exactly but Desi sometimes puts me in mind of Miss Laurel."

Hank's jaw slid sideways as it fell open. "Me, too!"

"Huh," was Call's only comment.

"Took me back some to see her on Josey Pye's lap.

Desi, I mean. Not Miss Laurel. Seemed wrong somehow. They don't really look much alike. You think so, Hank?"

"Not much. Not like you and me. Their hair ain't even the same color."

"Still, there's something." Dillon regarded Call. "I reckon you're going to talk to Desi. Maybe you'll see the same thing we do."

"Maybe," said Call. He wondered if Josiah Pye had seen the same resemblance that the boys had. That alone made Desiree worth seeking out. He remembered Laurel saying that she felt uncomfortable around Pye. Was this why? It wasn't out of the question that Pye had shown an interest in Laurel and she put him off. He could have found that Desiree was an adequate substitute. He hardly would have been rejected there. "If Pye's responsible for the theft, have you come up with how it was done?"

"If?" asked Hank. "No question about it."

Dillon's brow furrowed. "Has something changed your opinion? You seemed pretty set on his guilt yesterday."

"Trying to keep an open mind."

Hank shook his head. "I guess you gotta do that, but Dillon and me already made up our minds. It wasn't us. Rooster doesn't move quick enough to have done the deed. Miss Laurel's got more to lose than gain, and Mrs. Lancaster couldn't have climbed up on the box. So I suppose you can keep that mind of yours open, but ain't nothing gonna come of it."

"Maybe not. Still, I'd like to know how it was done. Any ideas? You must have talked about it."

"Sure," said Dillon, "we talked. Didn't much come of it. Our best guess is magic. Nothing else explains it."

"Magic," Call said dryly.

Hank shrugged. "You asked. That's what we come up with."

"Well, that's enlightening, but I don't think I'll be sharing that with Mr. Stonechurch."

"Probably better if you didn't," said Dillon. "We know

how it sounds. You don't want him thinking you're a knucklehead. Hank and me don't care so much."

Call chuckled. "All right. I appreciate your help. One last thing, which bunk was Pye's? It wasn't obvious to me."

"That's cause Rooster stripped it," said Hank. "Josey didn't have much and he took it all with him, but since you want to know, it was the last one on the left, farthest from the door."

Call nodded and thanked them again. "I'll still have a look around if you don't mind."

The brothers shook their towheads in unison. Dillon said, "Suit yourself."

9

Call stood on the right side of the bunk that Josiah Pye used to occupy. He had no idea what he'd hoped to find, but he thought he should look. It would have been too much to expect that Pye had left a note behind claiming responsibility. Something like a joke's-on-you confession. Apparently Pye did not possess Call's own dark sense of humor.

There was a small chest at the foot of the bed that Pye would have used to store his belongings. Every bunk had a similar chest. Call opened Pye's. As expected, it was empty. Still, it was hard not to be disappointed. Call closed the lid with the toe of his boot and considered his next steps. He knelt beside the bunk, looked under it, picked up the mattress, and swept his arm beneath it. Nothing. It was as if Josiah Pye had never existed.

As he stepped back into the aisle between the two rows of bunks, Call's gaze moved from one identical chest to the next, and it occurred to him that just because a particular bed wasn't in use did not mean its chest was necessarily empty.

He was prepared to examine the one nearest to him when the bunkhouse door swung open. He straightened as Laurel appeared on the threshold and wondered why he felt like a child caught with one hand in the cookie jar.

Her head tilted to the side. She wasn't frowning, although she seemed to be leaning toward that expression. "What are you doing?"

"Satisfying my curiosity."

She stepped into the bunkhouse. "That's not a helpful answer."

"I thought I'd have a look in these empty chests to see if Mr. Pye might have left anything behind."

"That chest you were about to open wasn't his."

"I know, or at least it isn't where you'd expect his to be. Doesn't mean that he didn't use it. It was just a thought." He paused, studied her. "Why are *you* here? Do you need me for something?"

"I just sent Hank to help Rooster muck out stalls. I thought you'd be doing that."

Call frowned. "I asked him if he needed me for anything before I left."

"Rooster's not one for saying he needs help."

"Clearly. I'm on my way."

Laurel put out a hand. "No. Do your search first. Hank needed to be put to work. He was leaning on a rake watching Dillon work when I found him. I'm afraid he picked up some bad habits from Mr. Pye."

Call didn't mention that Hank had been friendly with that rake for a while now. "You want to observe? It's probably not a bad idea to have a witness in the event I find anything."

"What are you looking for?"

"Don't know. Just looking seemed like a good enough idea on its own." He cocked an eyebrow at her. "Interested?"

She was. "All right. I have some time before I sort the mail." Laurel propped open the door to let in more sunlight and then she came to stand beside Call. "He borrowed a book from me that he never returned. Maybe we'll find that. It's hard to believe he would have taken it with him." She huffed a quiet laugh. "Then again, everything about this has been hard to believe."

Call nodded. He bent, lifted the chest's lid, and dropped it back so Laurel had a view. "Nothing."

She nodded and moved on while Call closed the lid. They went through the same process with the same result two more times. They expected nothing more on the fourth try.

They were wrong.

Sitting squarely on the floor of the chest was a strongbox similar in size to the one Brady had carried from the stage to Mr. Stonechurch's kitchen. It may have been more than similar. Call thought it might have been exact.

Laurel stared at the box. "You don't think the mining payroll is in there, do you?"

"I'm fairly certain it's not, but there's only one way to know." He picked it up and set it on the bed. "You want to open it?"

Laurel stepped back as if she expected the box to bite. She shook her head. "No. I don't want to touch it."

Amused, Call's mouth lifted in a half smile. "Very well." He ran his fingers along the latch, found the lever, and sprung it. Before he lifted the lid, he asked, "Should I draw my gun?"

"Not funny. And you aren't wearing it anyway."

"Right. I forgot."

"Go on." She didn't move forward but curiosity had her leaning in.

Call lifted the lid and dropped it back. "Well?" he asked, turning his head to look at her.

"It's empty."

Call heard her disappointment. She had actually been hopeful. He was careful not to smile, but for her sake he wished he'd been wrong about the contents. "There's something," he said, peering closer. He picked up the box and cradled it in one arm, tilting it so she could also see. "Here. In the corner. A scrap of something."

"I see it," she said. "It looks like paper."

"Maybe." Call tried to pull it out but his fingers were too large and his nails too short to grip it. He shook his head. "It's wedged. You try."

Laurel examined her neatly clipped nails. "Maybe this

one," she said, holding up the little finger of her right hand. She took the box, cradled it similarly, and scraped at the corner with her pinkie. "It's so small. I can't pull it free. Maybe tweezers."

"Of course. I have a pair in my kit. Give me a minute."

Laurel followed him to the chest at the foot of his bed, where he retrieved tweezers from his grooming kit. The light was better here closer to the door, and when she tilted the box toward it, she had a clearer view of what was lodged so tightly in the corner as long as she squinted. "I think it's a remnant of a legal tender note. A greenback. I can just make out a thread in the paper." She turned it so Call could examine it.

Call peered closely, nodded. "I think you're right." He held up the tweezers. Do you want to try?"

"No. You do it. Mr. Stonechurch hired you."

"All right. But you hold the box." Call caught the scrap on his first attempt and gently tugged. What he extracted was slightly bigger than what they had been able to see. He held it up so they could both look at it.

"Don't drop it," said Laurel. "We'll never find it again."

Call agreed. "It's exactly what you thought it was."

"I have a magnifying glass in the house. Why don't you bring that in and examine it under the glass? Then there won't be any doubt, and we can find something to put it in so it won't be lost."

Call didn't have any doubt about what he was holding, but Laurel's idea was still a good one and he followed her across the yard and into the house through the kitchen. Mrs. Lancaster looked as if she had questions but refrained from asking a single one. Call could have kissed her.

Laurel invited Call to sit at her desk. The magnifying glass was lying between a paperweight and a letter opener. She handed it to him and peered over his shoulder as he studied what he had found. "Well?" she asked.

"Look for yourself." He gave her the glass and held up his prize.

Laurel examined the scrap. The coloring was clear now. "It's from a greenback."

"Yes." Call lowered the tweezers. "Where can we put this?"

Laurel looked around. "What about between the pages of a book?"

Call was doubtful. "What about under the paperweight?"

"I'll forget and move it and then it will just disappear." She paused, thinking. "I have an idea. I'll be back in a moment." She was as good as her word, returning with a shot glass from a cabinet in the parlor. "Put the paper on one of the bookshelves and I'll put this glass on top of it. The glass is out of place so I won't forget why it's here and I won't move it. Don't worry. I'll tell Mrs. Lancaster it's not to be touched."

It sounded reasonable to Call. He stood and carried the tweezers to the bookshelves at the far side of her office. Choosing a shelf at Laurel's eye level, he held the tweezers closed until she turned the shot glass over and captured the remnant of legal tender under it, then he carefully opened the tweezers and pulled them out from under the glass.

"That's proof, isn't it?" Laurel said.

"It's something."

Laurel turned away from looking at the glass to look at Call. She frowned. "That didn't sound convincing."

"Because I'm not convinced. What do you think we have here?"

"Evidence that Mr. Pye switched strongboxes and that he had the mining payroll in his possession until he stuffed it in a saddlebag and took off with it in the middle of the night. What do you think we have?"

"A bit of a greenback found in a strongbox in a chest next to a bed that was not Mr. Pye's. Do I think that box was the one Brady brought here? Yes. And do I think that bit of greenback was part of the payroll? Yes again. Do I think that Mr. Pye had a box in his possession that he switched out? I do. But can I prove it? No. Not yet."

"But—"

Call shook his head. "Hank and Dillon told me the theft must have been the result of magic. It was amusing at the time; now I'm thinking they weren't far off the mark. It only required some sort of distraction to manage the switch. The newspaper clippings that Brady and I discovered in the box that went to Stonechurch, the bag of pebbles and stones that gave the box heft and substituted for coin, point to intention and planning. This was carefully thought out. Not without risk but definitely well considered."

Call studied Laurel's upturned face, the troubled brown eyes, the crease between her eyebrows. He shouldn't have been thinking it, but what he wanted to do right then was kiss her. Deep trouble, he thought. He was in deep trouble. "Is that the Josey Pye you knew?"

"Maybe." She shook her head, an infinitesimal movement that caused a wispy thread of hair to brush her cheek. She impatiently pushed it out of the way and was aware of Call's eyes following the movement. A tingle tripped lightly down her spine. Bent on ignoring it, she said, "I don't know. Maybe planning is what he was doing when we all thought he was merely trying to get out of work. There's a lot of thinking to be done leaning on a rake. Ask Hank."

"Right."

"So what happens now?"

"More questions. How did you pay your employees?"

Laurel sighed as she grasped the whole of the problem before them. "Legal tender notes."

"Greenbacks."

"Yes."

"Did you know if Pye kept money in a strongbox?"

"No."

"What about the others?"

"No. I didn't ask after what they did with their pay. The strongbox is a surprise. I'm not sure who occupied that bunk before Mr. Pye. Rooster would know. We have drivers who stay here to rest after a hard leg. One of them could have used it."

Call blew out a breath. "Complications. I guess I should get started with those questions." He hesitated. "Unless there's something you need me to do?"

"I noticed when I was sweeping yesterday that a few boards on the front porch are lifting. They need replacing. Is that something you can do? Because if you can't, I can."

"I have enough carpentry skills for that."

"All right. Go ask your questions and then take care of the porch."

"Yes, ma'am."

Laurel simply shook her head, waved him off, and waited until his back was turned before she grinned.

10

Another stage arrived while Call was cutting replacement boards for the porch. He set down the saw and went to join the others as they made the exchange of horses. The stage was headed to Stonechurch and beyond with six passengers and a carryall heavy with their luggage. This coach was carrying freight on top as well and the horses were visibly tired. There was no time for Call to catch the name of the driver when he climbed down the box. The man was familiar with the station and hurried off to the outhouse at the back to relieve himself. Call was more interested in the shotgun rider, a man about his own age, ten years or so younger than the driver. He carried a coach gun, a twelve-gauge double-barrel. It was the shotgun Call also preferred. He wanted to strike up a conversation, but the station work came first for now. He followed Rooster to the watering trough and then into the barn, where he began wiping the animals down while the brothers took out the fresh team.

"Who's the shotgun?" asked Call.

"That's Digger Leary."

"Digger. Why is that familiar?"

"Probably on account of him being late to his post when Brady took over the box. You were a passenger then. Remember? You rode shotgun in his place."

That nudged Call's memory. "Right. Digger. Brady said something later about him being drunk."

Rooster showed no surprise. "Probably."

"What about this driver? What's his name?"

"That's Jed Holloway. He's been a driver for the Express for years. One of the first hires." Rooster looked at Call over the back of the mare he was wiping down. "You have some special interest in them?"

"No. Not special. Just regular interest."

"Uh-huh." Unconvinced, Rooster continued working.

Hank and Dillon appeared, arriving a little out of breath after an unnecessary footrace to the barn. They argued about who won until Rooster gave them a sharp look.

"You two have something worth saying?" Rooster asked when there was quiet.

Dillon spoke up after Hank elbowed him. "Jed and Digger are bunking with us tonight. Miss Laurel wanted you to know. We needed to get back on the schedule with exchanging drivers and shotguns. Danny Shea and John Waterman were passengers so the plan was for them to take over. Looks like we'll have regular relief going forward."

Rooster scowled. "Jed snores. Digger drinks. It's a blessing it won't be for long. Tell me there's another stage soon."

"Morning," said Hank. "We got the rest of the day and night with them."

"I like Digger," said Dillon. "He's got good stories."

Rooster grunted something unintelligible. Call interpreted it as a difference of opinion. Rooster said, "Go and make sure there are linens and blankets for the beds. Mrs. Lancaster is always fussing with those things like we ain't just grateful to have a mattress under us." He waved the boys away. "Go on. Git."

They took off at a run, another impulsive footrace.

"I have it in mind that they're twelve and just big for their age."

Call chuckled. It had occurred to him as well. "I was surprised you weren't boarding drivers and shotguns when I first arrived. You're a home station after all."

Rooster shrugged. "Happens from time to time that

someone leaves, someone doesn't make the trade, someone takes ill. Puts the schedule off. You heard the boys. We're righting it now. More's the pity."

"You don't like hosting them?"

"Doesn't matter what I like. Miss Laurel's got the contract and the stage line pays for boarding the drivers. She accepted the terms and likes to keep them. Me? I wish we had separate lodgings for them, but you know what they say about wishes."

"If they were horses, beggars would ride?"

"Huh? If they were fishes, we'd all cast our nets."

Call huffed a soft laugh. "That's true, too."

Rooster changed the subject. "What's that you were doing for Miss Laurel when the stage came in?"

Call told him about the porch. "It won't require much of my time if you need me for something else."

"No. I got this. You go on."

Call didn't ask again. He wanted to get back to the porch work, but it was more important that he made sure Hank and Dillon didn't give one of the overnight boarders the bed where the strongbox was once again concealed in the chest paired with it. As it happened, he didn't have to say anything. The brothers were setting out blankets on other beds. They both looked up when he entered the bunkhouse.

"Just needed to get something," said Call. He rummaged through his belongings and randomly chose a comb out of his kit. Aware of their curiosity, he held up the comb before he pocketed it and said the first thing that came to his mind. "Grooming. Not only for horses."

Wearing identical expressions of bemusement, Hank and Dillon stared at Call then at each other until laughter broke through. Call could hear them laughing long after he left the bunkhouse. "Grooming," he repeated under his breath. "Not only for horses." It was a sure bet that the brothers thought he was a cartridge shy of a full load. It had been that kind of laughter. Shaking his head, Call picked up the saw and resumed the work he'd been asked to do before the arrival of the stage.

Laurel came outside when the passengers were leaving. If she was aware of him pausing to watch her, she paid him no mind. Jed Holloway and Digger Leary stood on either side of her and had words with their replacements, who were already taking their positions on the box. The three of them remained there until the stage moved on and then Jed turned in the direction of the bunkhouse, Digger started walking toward town, and Laurel set her path on the diagonal and was coming to him.

Without preamble, she asked, "What did you learn?"

Call required a moment to get oriented to the question. Her long-legged and unhurried approach had held his attention for a little too long. By the time she'd reached him, he was holding the saw so loosely it fell from his hand. He bent, picked it up, and laid it over the board he was preparing to cut. He offered a brief apologetic smile though it did not seem to be expected.

"No one knew anything about a strongbox," he said. "I didn't mention that we'd found one. I gave them an opportunity to mention that they'd seen a box around or owned one. No one did. I asked about Josey Pye and anyone who came before him. They were sure they'd never known anyone to have so many valuables or money to squirrel it away in a strongbox."

"Did you inquire about what they do with their pay?"

"Hmm. I eased into that one. Truth is, I needed advice about it. I've been wondering what to do with the money that Mr. Stonechurch gave me for miscellaneous expenses. It's making my boots a tad tight."

Laurel's eyebrows lifted. "You're keeping notes in your boots?"

"For now. Legal tenderfoot."

She groaned softly. "That was horrible."

"Sorry." He shrugged, grinning. "Anyway, Rooster has an account at the bank. Dillon and Hank turn over most of their wages to their mother and she gives it back in the form of an allowance. It seems to work for them. They agreed that Josey Pye spent his money almost as fast as he earned it on those visits to Mrs. Fry's and less often at Sweeny's."

Laurel took this in, nodded slowly. "How confident are you that Mr. Pye owned that strongbox?"

"He owned *a* strongbox, not *that* strongbox. The one we found likely belongs to Henderson Express or Stonechurch or the bank that released the payroll."

"Yes," she said. "Of course. I understand that. But tell me how confident you are that Mr. Pye had it in his possession."

"Close to one hundred percent."

"Even though Rooster and the boys never saw him with a strongbox?"

"Oh, I don't think he kept his in the bunkhouse, at least not until he was prepared to use it."

Laurel stared at him. Her mouth twisted to one side as she tried to work what he was telling her. "Then . . . oh." Her puzzled expression cleared. "Mrs. Fry's."

"I think so. I'll know more after I visit the house." He waited to see if she would comment. She didn't. She didn't even look troubled by the thought of him going to the brothel. It was discouraging. "Are you familiar with a woman named Desiree? You might know her as Desi."

"I know her as Desiree. I think I've met all of Mrs. Fry's ladies at one time or another." She said this matter-of-fact. "You're surprised."

"I guess I am."

"Falls Hollow simply isn't big enough for people to be strangers. Desiree came to this station on the arm of a fancy gambler about four years ago. She spent a night here on her own until the gambler got a room in one of the wayside homes and then she joined him. He wasn't in Falls Hollow long. I don't even remember his name, but I do recall he was run out for cheating and had luck enough

not to be shot at the table. Desiree stayed behind and settled in at Mrs. Fry's. I think she was familiar with the
work when she met the gambler."

"Huh. Well, it seems she was Josey Pye's favorite."

"Did I need to know that?"

"Maybe not. I figured you'd want to know why I asked
after her."

Laurel conceded that he was probably right. "So you're
going to speak to her."

"I am. Only makes sense that she might know something." Call also wanted to see if Desiree put him in mind
of Laurel as she did the Booker brothers. "Do you know
her last name?"

"I'm not sure I know her first name. 'Desiree' always
struck me as her working name."

Call nodded. This was not unexpected. "It very well
might be. True names are personal, too revealing for
some, and there are girls who guard them as closely as a
card sharp guards his hand."

Laurel looked at him oddly.

Call interpreted her expression as wanting to know
something she couldn't quite bring herself to ask. "My
mother was a whore." He said this in a straightforward
manner without a trace of discomfort. When she merely
blinked, he added, "You were wondering how I knew
about the names, weren't you?"

"I—I was, um . . . Yes. Yes, I was."

He nodded again. "That's how."

Laurel did not shy away from staring at him. "I haven't
met the like of you before, Mr. Landry."

It was difficult to know what to make of that so Call
asked, "Do you count making my acquaintance as a good
thing or something you wish you could have avoided?"

"I'm not attaching any judgment to it."

"Probably better that way. And I'm Call, by the way.
We agreed last night that there'd be no more Mr. Landry."

"Right."

Call lifted his chin in the direction of the porch to indicate the work he'd done. "What do you think? Satisfactory?"

Laurel looked at the boards he'd already laid down and nodded. "There's more whitewash in the barn you can apply when you're done."

"All right. I have this one last board to cut and set."

"Good." Laurel turned and hopped up on the porch. Without looking back, she disappeared into the house. What would he think, she wondered, if she asked to accompany him to Mrs. Fry's?

11

With no stages scheduled for Sunday, Call figured that he'd visit the brothel in the afternoon. It was his experience that Sundays were generally quiet and the whores were not in demand. Men who frequented brothels on Saturday night were likely to be in church in the morning and sitting with their families for an afternoon meal. Unmarried men often avoided the place in favor of courting their sweethearts.

Mrs. Fry's house was as anticipated. Three women were quietly playing cards at a small oval table in the parlor. Two wore white chemises and petticoats; the other wore an afternoon dress printed with dainty flowers and trimmed with a flounce. He presumed Mrs. Fry was wearing the modest print dress. The madam looked to be in her late thirties, while the petticoat ladies were at least fifteen years her junior. Mrs. Fry didn't leap to her feet to welcome him, which he figured was by design. It gave him time to look around a little longer, perhaps make a selection. She couldn't know he had a specific purpose that had nothing at all to do with the business of the house.

The parlor was a slightly rougher version of the sumptuous parlors Call had seen in the East. Every effort had been made to make it an easy, comforting room. The flocked wallpaper was a deep shade of red, the de rigueur color for a whorehouse, and the furniture was large, overstuffed, and upholstered in red-and-cream-striped damask. There were straight-back chairs with crewel-worked seat covers. He saw lots of roses, another familiar favorite.

There was a young woman occupying one corner of the sofa. Her bare legs were drawn up and to the side. She was reading what looked to be a well-worn copy of the Bible, not an unheard-of choice, especially on a Sunday. She never looked up once while he stood on the parlor's threshold.

Two women shared the piano bench. Neither was poised to play. Instead, they were sorting through sheet music quietly arguing about a selection. Call walked up to the piano, placed an arm on the upright's polished top, and leaned against it. Both whores looked up. He suspected immediately that the one on the right was Desiree, but his easy smile did not single her out. It encompassed both of them.

"Do you know 'Mollie Darling'?" he asked.

"I have the sheet music right here," said the one who was not Desiree. She pulled it out from among the others and held it up.

"Good. Play that."

She set it on the piano and opened it up, but it was Desiree who put her hands to the keys and began to play.

Call watched her hands nimbly move over the ivories before he lifted his eyes to study her features. It was the shape of her face and the set of her mouth, perhaps the directness of her gaze, that bore the most marked resemblance to Laurel Beth Morrison. He couldn't say if she had long legs and a no-nonsense stride, but her coloring was not at all similar to Laurel's. Desiree's carefully coiled hair was almost too pale to be considered blond. Without powder and rouge, her complexion would have been alabaster. Not a single freckle dared make an appearance. For all that was different, there was still something that made the likeness to Laurel seem reasonable. Something intangible, he thought. Confidence? Independence? He couldn't put his finger on it and stopped trying. Hank and Dillon had found it elusive as well. Call decided it might be better if it stayed that way.

Mrs. Fry left the card game but not her cards. She introduced herself to Call and invited him to have a drink. When he politely turned down the offer, she asked him if he'd made a selection. "If you'd like to wait, a couple of girls are busy right now, but they'll be down soon. You might prefer one of them."

"That's kind of you, but I'm already partial to 'Mollie Darling.'" Still leaning against the piano case, he pointed casually to Desiree.

"Ah, that's Desiree."

Desiree's fingers paused.

"No," said Call. "Don't stop. Finish."

Mrs. Fry said, "Why don't you step over here and we can discuss particulars."

"In a moment. When she's done."

Mrs. Fry was too successful a businesswoman to show annoyance at a customer's request, although she did pointedly glance at her cards and then back at the table, where the girls were waiting for her.

It was not five minutes later that Call concluded the transaction with the madam and Desiree was leading him up the stairs. She paused once on the steps to make sure he was following. He wondered if he did not seem eager for her company and made an effort to affect some measure of excitement.

Desiree's room was also not unfamiliar with its mixed scents of perfume and sex and tobacco. Call wondered if she smoked or if the odor lingered from the parade of men before him. Both things could be true. Her mirrored vanity was crowded with pots of cream and rouge, lotions, atomizers, hairpins, and combs. One of the wardrobe doors was open, revealing a space crowded with undergarments and several afternoon dresses and gowns. One white stocking was draped over the lip of a partially open drawer in the highboy. He had an urge to roll it up and stuff it inside. It was a reminder that old habits die hard.

Call realized he hadn't precisely hidden the urge when Desiree walked over to the chest of drawers, shoved the stocking inside. She turned on him, one pale eyebrow raised as she closed the drawer. A smile played about her mouth.

"Better?" she asked. "If your pleasure is tidying up, sugar, I don't mind letting you have your way."

It was the first time he clearly heard her accented voice. The lilt was Deep South. His ear recognized Georgia. He knew it well enough. His jaw tightened. He felt a muscle twitch in his cheek.

"You all right?" she asked. "I can't tell if you're sick that you got snake bit or angry about it. Sit down. Something's got you feeling crossways."

Call took a breath, steadied himself, and sat on the edge of the bed.

"Well, look at that. You're right where you need to be. How about I get you out of those boots?"

Call put out a hand, stopping her before she dropped to her knees. "I'll keep them on."

"Not in my bed you won't."

"I have something else in mind."

Desiree's frank gaze went to his groin. "Sure, you can leave your boots on for that. Toss me a pillow, sugar. For my knees."

Call held out a hand again. "No. Not that." His lips quirked when she revealed her confusion. He pointed to the wing chair next to the cast-iron stove. "Sit there," he told her. "Or I can, and you can sit here. I want to talk."

Desiree didn't move. "You're an odd duck, aren't you, sugar? No, don't answer. It was rhetorical." Shrugging, she turned and went to the chair. Before she could sit down, she had to remove several petticoats, a horsehair bustle, two towels, and a pair of red kid slippers. She dropped the bundle on the floor and took her seat. "I know you're itchin' to put that all away."

Call chuckled. "You know how to tempt a man."

"Honey, you're a disappointment. A handsome fellow like you just wanting to make order of my particulars, well, that's all wrong." She looked him over, shook her head sorrowfully, and said, "You wanted to talk. Talk. But you have to tell me if I'm supposed to listen. You didn't say anything about that."

"Listen *and* respond."

She sighed. "Are you certain you don't want to get out of those boots?"

"Certain. Tell me about Josiah Pye." He'd caught her by surprise, which was precisely what he'd hoped for. The smile that had been playing about her mouth faded and she raised her chin, losing the flirtatious tilt to her head. Her blue eyes lacked the warmth and amusement they had shown earlier when she was teasing.

"Why do you want to know about Josey? Who are you?"

"McCall Landry. Josey's disappeared. I aim to find him."

"Why? Is he someone to you?"

"He's of interest to me. Do you know him?"

"You already know I do," she said flatly, "or you wouldn't be here asking about him."

"True. So what can you tell me?"

"He worked at Morrison Station. Something to do with the horses. He didn't talk about his work."

"What did he talk about?"

"He wasn't a talker. He'd ask if I wanted to be on top or bottom and that was often the extent of our conversation."

Call smiled thinly. "I don't believe you."

Desiree shrugged.

"You said 'often,' not 'always.' What did you talk about when he was feeling loquacious?"

"I'm having a drink," she said, getting up. "Are you sure you don't—"

"Sit. Down." Call didn't flinch as she turned her sharp, narrow-eyed stare on him. He merely lifted an eyebrow and waited. She sat.

"Josey never spoke to me the way you just did," she said. "I can tell you that. He was a gentleman through and through. Decent."

Call watched her make a show of crossing her legs and

carefully tugging on the hem of her shift so that her bare knees were uncovered. If she'd hoped to gain some advantage by the display, she was sadly out of it. He glanced at her shapely legs just long enough to appreciate them and then returned his gaze to her face.

"I'm not sure why you're being protective of him," he said. "Did he make promises?" When she blinked out of rhythm, he knew he had touched a nerve. "Were you expecting to go with him when he left Falls Hollow?"

"You're talking out of your head. I don't know what you've heard about me, but I do all right on my own." Desiree pushed the hem of the shift back over her knees and leaned forward. "Look. I'd have to be deaf, dumb, and blind not to know what folks are saying about Josey and the Stonechurch payroll. They're both missing so they must be together. That's the kind of thing that makes sense to men lacking imagination. Well, I'm telling you that Josey never expressed the least interest in money except when it came to giving me my due. Is that clear enough for you?"

"Clear."

"Then . . . ?"

"Does he know you're in love with him?"

Desiree sat back as though pushed. She tried to recover by staring him down, but in the end she was the one who looked away. "You're talking out of your head again," she said quietly.

"I don't think so."

She closed her eyes, shook her head.

"Where is he from?" asked Call.

"Evanston."

"And that's in Illinois?"

She nodded. "Outside of Chicago, he says."

"Family?"

Desiree opened her eyes. "There was a brother. Killed at Shiloh. He never mentioned anyone else."

"What did he ask you to do for him?"

Her lips parted as if she were about to speak. Nothing came of it.

Call repeated his question and was met with the same nonresponse. "I know you think you're not saying a word, but your silence is telling." When she remained quiet, he switched tacks. "Who else did he see when you weren't available?"

"I don't think I like that question, sugar."

The way she lifted her chin and tilted her head reminded Call of Laurel Morrison. The similarity faded as soon as Desiree spoke. He put the question to her a second time.

"There was no one else," she said finally. "You can ask Mrs. Fry if you like. He always asked for me, and why wouldn't he? I treated him like the gentleman he was, and you know what?"

"Hmm?"

"He treated me like a lady."

"Which you certainly are."

Desiree cast her eyes at her folded hands and spoke on a breath of air. "Which I certainly used to be."

In that moment, Call clearly saw what she had been and what she had become. She represented the demise of the Old South. She was both a victim and a survivor, a daughter of the plantations, privileged and mannered, fallen on hard times and making her way as best she could. He doubted the gambler who'd brought her to Falls Hollow had been the first of his ilk to seduce her with promises. All these long years since the end of the war, she'd been robbed of what had been the best of her. Almost. She still had the memory of that other life.

Call asked again, "What did he promise you?"

"A new beginning."

"Where?"

"Anywhere that wasn't here. I didn't care."

"When is it supposed to happen?"

Desiree said nothing.

Call thought he understood the reason for her silence. "The new beginning was supposed to have already begun, is that it?" He didn't wait for her response. "You believed he was going to take you with him."

"He made me believe it," she said quietly. "They always make me believe."

She wasn't looking at him, but Call nodded his understanding anyway. "I'm not the law," he said. "I work for Mr. Stonechurch. What you tell me about the robbery is for my use, no one else's. I'm not going to march you to the sheriff's office."

She smiled crookedly, without humor. "You won't have to. It's possible you'll see Rayleigh Carter when you're leaving. He's here most Sundays."

"You'd have to point him out. I haven't met him yet."

"He wears a tin star. That should help."

"Right." Call took a breath and released it slowly. "Has he spoken to you about Josiah Pye?"

"No. I don't think he'll be interested in tracking Josey until a reward has been posted. Has it?"

"Not yet. Maybe not ever. That'd be up to Mr. Stonechurch. Would you be motivated by a reward?"

"Motivated to do what?"

"Tell me how Josey did it. You got the strongbox for him—I know that—and you kept it until he asked for it. I saw some broadsheets in the parlor. Looks like you read the *Rocky Mountain News.*"

"Yes. So?"

"So you made a pattern using a legal tender note and cut hundreds of them out of the paper. You stuffed the strongbox with them. I'm betting that you probably cut more than you needed. I might even find some still here if I look around. Maybe under that pile of clothes you dropped on the floor."

Desiree stood and gestured toward the door. "You know so much, Mr. Landry, what do you need me for? I take it that our time is up. I'd like you to leave."

12

So you left?" asked Laurel. "Gave up just like that?" She stared across the wide expanse of her desk at Call. He'd made himself comfortable in one of the chairs she kept for visitors, which was something she'd always thought was impossible. It wasn't that she didn't want visitors to be at ease in her office; it was simply that she didn't want them to overstay their welcome. McCall Landry demonstrated no awareness that the chair he was in was straight-back and armless. He lounged in it as if it were one of the plump armchairs in her parlor.

"So I left," he said. "I learned what I needed. I thought she was probably telling the truth about your sheriff being a regular Sunday visitor."

"He isn't *my* sheriff."

"Maybe not, but Mrs. Fry probably has him in her pocket. I didn't want to risk an arrest if Desiree decided to make a scene."

"Hmm. Did you actually see some of those broadsheet clippings in her room?"

"No. She cares for her room and her belongings as though she expects someone to pick up after her. Someone probably did at one time. It's one of the ways she hasn't changed." Call told Laurel what he suspected about Desiree's background.

Laurel sat back, gripping the arms of her chair. "I don't

think I know anyone who wasn't wounded by that war. We all bear scars, some deeper than others."

Call didn't disagree.

"What about you?" she asked. "You know about my wounds. They're practically public fodder, but you keep yours well hidden."

"Do I?"

"You know you do."

Call said nothing.

"I didn't truly expect you to tell me," Laurel said after a moment. She moved on. "You're satisfied that she helped Mr. Pye even though she didn't confess to it?"

"She didn't deny it either. I'm satisfied. She showed me the door when I laid out my suspicions and she never answered my question about being motivated by a reward. I think she's hoping against all evidence to the contrary that he's coming back for her."

Laurel frowned. "Really?"

He nodded. "She wants to believe. She's vulnerable to hope."

"It's sad, isn't it?"

"Mm."

"You're not going to expose her in this?"

Call heard the slight inflection at the end that made it a question. "No, I told her I wouldn't, and I won't. As you pointed out, there's been no confession. If there was evidence anywhere in that room of the newspaper cutouts, I think she's motivated now to tidy up and find them. It's a warm day, but I wouldn't be surprised if she's already built a fire in her stove to destroy them."

"That's why you showed her your cards," said Laurel. "You wanted her to get rid of them."

Call merely shrugged.

Laurel chuckled at the back of her throat and sat up. She placed her hands on the desk and folded them. "What is to be done now?"

"There's still the matter of how Pye knew that the payroll was arriving on that particular stage. He would have had a general idea of when it was going to be sent out from Denver, and he likely had the strongbox in his possession by then, but knowing that the payroll was on Brady's stage-coach, well, I haven't figured that out yet."

"You're right that he had to have known. He didn't take a lot of time to make the exchange. Anyone should have been able to see him do it and somehow no one did."

"Seems that way."

Laurel nodded slowly, musing. "Unless . . ."

"Unless?"

"Unless someone did see and is not speaking up." Laurel regarded Call openly. "You're not surprised. It's already occurred to you."

"It's occurred."

"Not one of my employees," she said, making it clear she would not entertain a different opinion.

"That is precisely why I kept my thoughts to myself. I have a fairly good idea of what you're willing and not willing to explore."

"Maybe you do. I am not going to apologize for defending Rooster and the boys."

"They're not the only people who work for you."

Laurel actually gaped at him. "Mrs. Lancaster? You would accuse Mrs. Lancaster?"

"I didn't accuse her of anything. I'm merely pointing out that you keep forgetting her."

"Well, I don't mention myself either. Perhaps you think I should."

"I've already eliminated you from consideration."

Strangely, this did not mollify Laurel. "Maybe I wish I *had* seen something and was keeping it all to myself."

"All right," he said. "I'll bite. Why would you wish that?"

"To prove you wrong."

Call watched her for a long moment, saying nothing. Had he ever known anyone quite like her? Maddeningly attractive and then simply maddening? "You're annoyed because I *don't* suspect you? I'm not even going to try to understand that."

Laurel realized she had been puffed up with an unwarranted sense of righteousness and now felt deflated. She stared at her hands and wondered if she could have possibly made herself more foolish in his eyes. She sighed inaudibly, reminding herself they were really very lovely eyes. "Good," she said quietly, in the manner of a confession. "I don't think I can explain it to myself."

Call was grateful for her downcast eyes. There was no chance of her seeing his amusement. He sobered quickly, thinking her loyalty to the men who worked for her—her friends—was admirable. He said, "There are passengers to consider. And Brady."

"Brady?"

"I keep going back and forth about Brady. So does Mr. Stonechurch."

"Does Brady know?"

"I don't know how he couldn't."

"He'd been driving for years. I think he would have found a way to take the payroll without bringing suspicion down on himself."

"A fair point."

Laurel was preparing to ask about the passengers when Mrs. Lancaster appeared in the doorway and announced that Sunday supper was ready. Mrs. Lancaster cocked an ear toward the kitchen. "Hear that?" she asked, referring to the thunder of footsteps and elbow jostling that was occurring out of her sight. "Troops have arrived."

Call did not have to be told twice. He managed to launch himself out of his chair in spite of its being armless. A childhood deferring to women was all that kept him from cutting in front of Laurel on his way to the dining room. The heady aroma of roasting chicken had been teasing him since he'd entered the farmhouse. He found it was a vast improvement over the fragrances that permeated the brothel.

Jed Holloway, by the virtue of there being no Sunday stage, was enjoying the additional day of rest. He had asked to be awakened for church services but slept through them. He had been up for several hours already but still managed to come to the table looking sleepy-eyed and disheveled. He held out a chair for Laurel before he set his lean, loose-limbed frame into one beside her. Rooster made grumbling noises as he took his seat and gave Jed an eyeful for occupying what was normally his chair.

When everyone was at the table, Dillon Booker folded his hands, bowed his head, and said grace. The young man wasted no time after that, taking the platter closest to him and dropping two biscuits on his plate.

Laurel looked around as the food was being passed. "Where is Digger? This is not a meal he'll want to miss."

Hank pretended to be holding a mug in his hand and tipped it back as though he were drinking.

"He's at Sweeny's?" she asked. "Still?"

"Can't say for sure," said Dillon. "I think he stumbled in last night and then left again. His bunk ain't really been slept in. Anyone else hear him?"

Hank shook his head. "Hard to hear anything over the racket Jed makes. How do you sleep through that, Jed?"

Rooster muttered, "Was wondering the same thing myself."

Call had no comment. He thought of himself as a light sleeper, but he hadn't heard Digger Leary come in. When he woke this morning, he retained a vivid memory of a dream involving Miss Laurel Beth Morrison, a picnic basket that never got opened, and a blue-and-white-checkered quilted blanket that they sat on, then lay down on, and finally made love on. With very little effort, he could have retrieved that dream. In other circumstances, he might have done so, but Sunday supper was hardly the time and place.

Stealing a glance at her now, Call decided that his imagination had not done her justice. He hadn't pictured her as she was now with her chestnut hair smoothly coiled at the back of her head. The wisps of hair that escaped the ivory combs framed her face and added a softening effect. He also hadn't visualized her in a gown. She was still wearing the daffodil-yellow dress she had worn to church.

This morning he'd watched her walk off to services flanked by the Booker brothers. Her skirt swayed. He had a glimpse of petticoat that was infinitely more intriguing than anything he had seen at Mrs. Fry's.

Jed Holloway ignored the comments about his snoring and turned sideways to address Laurel. "I hope you don't mind me saying, but you are looking as fine as sunshine, Miss Laurel. I don't know that there's a color in the rainbow that doesn't suit you, but you're particularly fetching in yellow."

"Thank you, Jed. I don't mind you saying so at all."

Although she accepted the compliment graciously, Call noticed that a pale wash of pink touched her cheeks and the light dusting of freckles vanished. Damn, but he liked those freckles, though he had to grudgingly admit that the translucent pink was fetching, too. He just wished he'd been the one to put the color in her complexion. Call had some regret about not accompanying her to the tent church at the far end of town. He wasn't one for attending services and hadn't been for a long time. It seemed a mite hypocritical to make an appearance in the Lord's house when he had carnal thoughts on his mind and he wasn't looking for redemption. He still had just enough of the Good Book's beliefs left in him to consider the possibility that he'd be struck down for carrying those thoughts inside the tent.

So he'd stayed back while the others went to church and rode out a ways on Artemis, following the Morrison property perimeter that Rooster had described. A fence line made it relatively easy to get an estimate of the size of the spread. He found evidence of long-abandoned mine shafts and recalled that Laurel told him there had been mining in and around Falls Hollow for a time.

"Have you thought about boarding up those entrances to the old mines on your property?" he asked, raising both eyebrows when everyone stopped eating and turned to look at him. "What?"

"I think you must have been a hundred miles away,"

Laurel said. Her smile was gentle but left no doubt that she was amused. "We were discussing Dillon's interpretation of this morning's sermon."

"Oh. Sorry." He waved his fork at Dillon. "Go on."

Dillon returned to his favorite theme of questioning the preacher's every tenet while his brother challenged him just to see his face turn red. Laurel leaned toward Call and whispered, "Talk to me later about what you're thinking." And then she leaned into the conversation and never looked Call's way again.

It was dusk when Call saw Digger Leary returning. For a man who had allegedly spent his time away from the station drinking at Sweeny's, he was walking upright in a mostly straight line. Call watched from where he was standing at the entrance to the barn to determine if Digger needed help to reach the bunkhouse. He didn't move until the man stumbled, dropped to one knee, and struggled to rise.

"Need a hand?" asked Call, extending his.

Drink made Digger's smile loose and sloppy. His rheumy eyes were vaguely unfocused. He still managed to regard Call warily. "Who are you?"

"McCall Landry. We met yesterday." Call kept his hand out.

"Did we? Suppose that's good."

"Yes. Do you need help?"

Digger's hand wavered until it found Call's. "Thanks." He didn't help much as Call pulled him to his feet. "That's better."

Call didn't release his grip until he thought Digger could stand on his own. "It seemed like you were steadier when I first saw you."

"Don't know. Might've been. It's a long walk from there to here, wherever there was."

"Right. You good now?"

"Yep." Digger took two steps before his legs started to

fold. "Whoa." He managed to straighten, weaved a bit, and then looked back. "Maybe I could use some help."

Nodding, Call gave Digger his shoulder for support and was careful not to breathe too deeply. The man was ripe with the scent of sweat and spirits. Digger Leary had been stewing in his own juices for too long. Call was tempted to pitch him in the watering trough on their way to the bunkhouse. He didn't, but only because he caught a glimpse of Mrs. Lancaster coming out the back door carrying a bucket. That good Christian woman would probably cheer him on if he were to dump Digger in the trough, but Call doubted the same could be said of Laurel when she heard about it.

Call released Digger as soon as they reached the man's bunk. He stepped back and let Digger find his own way onto the bed. He wasn't surprised when the man simply pitched forward. Call picked up his feet and swiveled him lengthwise onto the mattress. Digger groaned softly, turned on his side, and mumbled something that might have been thank you or go to hell. Call left him to his own devices and removed himself from the stink.

Rooster met him crossing the yard. "The boys and Jed and me are gonna play cards. You want to join us?"

Call glanced back at the bunkhouse and then looked doubtfully at Rooster. "You'll want to give the place a chance to air out. That's why I left the door open."

"Oh, that. Yeah, well, Hank saw you with Digger and knew what was what. He asked Laurel if we could play in the dining room and she said sure. You interested? Ain't none of us with money to waste. We play with matchsticks."

"All right. I can afford that."

When Call agreed to playing, it was with the hope that Laurel would be joining them. She didn't, though she did come in from time to time when the game grew too quiet or too raucous. He wondered what she was doing in between visits, but on one occasion she came in carrying a book with her finger pressed between the pages to mark her place and then he knew. He tried to make out the title and couldn't, but his effort must have been obvious because she told him it was *Wuthering Heights* and that the book, a prized possession, had belonged to her mother.

Call finally played out his hand in response to some pointed throat clearing from Dillon and then Hank. He stayed in the game for a few rounds after Laurel walked out to the porch before he excused himself.

"About damn time," Rooster said under his breath.

Hank grinned. Dillon chuckled.

Jed Holloway winked at him.

Call cast a sheepish look over his shoulder. Their laughter followed him out the door. So much for not being obvious.

Laurel was sitting on the porch swing, but it wasn't moving. She'd made herself comfortable sitting with her legs curled sideways under her dress. She looked up when he stepped out of the house.

"You're out of the game?" she asked. "No more matchsticks?"

"Something like that." He approached and took up a seat on one of the rockers when she invited him to sit.

"I heard the laughter before you came out. Are you the butt of their amusement?"

"Something like that," he said again. "I guess it's no secret that I quit the game because I wanted to be out here with you. At least that's what they figure."

"Are they right?"

"Mm-hmm."

She chuckled. "You are unexpectedly straightforward."

Call shrugged. "I told you I took the Stonechurch job because I wanted an opportunity to see you again. Can't see the point in denying it now."

"Are you courting me, Call?" There was an undertone of teasing in the question.

He liked the fact that she finally said his name without prompting, but her question, even said lightly, deserved to be answered thoughtfully. Was he courting her? It hadn't occurred to him to think of his interest in those terms. Now he was forced to. He said, "I don't know what my intentions are."

"Oh, now I'm disappointed. I think you do know." When he didn't reply, Laurel said, "It's all right. I appreciate that being straightforward has its limits. I know you're not courting me. That's a serious business. You have to declare yourself. Apply for permission. Occasionally show up with flowers. Invite me to walk with you."

"That's a lot to consider," he said wryly.

She responded in the same vein. "It can take months. Even years."

"Years?"

"Uh-huh. Ben Shipley courted Ellen Wanamaker for two and a half years before she agreed to marry him."

"Marry," he said, deadpan.

Laurel laughed. "You know that's generally how a courtship is concluded."

Call said nothing.

"Your silence is telling," she said.

"Hmm."

"I suppose I can admit that I am just this much flattered by your attention if not your intention."

The dimly lit lamps in the dining room were still sufficiently bright for him to make out that she was holding up one hand with her thumb and forefinger pinched together. "That much, eh?"

"Yes."

"You know, Miss Morrison, you are unexpectedly straightforward yourself."

"Am I? I believe I would prefer that it's not unexpected. I'm twenty-seven, and I've been managing this station more or less on my own for the last seven years. I favor saying what's on my mind. I think it's the same for you."

"It helps that we're having this conversation mostly in the dark."

Laurel considered that. "You might be right."

"Did Josiah Pye try to court you?"

The question disconcerted Laurel. She flinched.

Call reached over and steadied the swing. "And we were getting on so well," he said. "You don't have to answer if you'd rather not."

Laurel drew in a breath, collecting herself. She was disappointed in her reaction. "No, I'd rather answer actually. Mr. Pye never courted me. Like you, it didn't occur to him. I told you I was uneasy around him so I'm not sure why you put the question to me."

"I was wondering how his plans might have changed if you had reciprocated his interest."

"Oh, so we're discussing the robbery now."

"Yes. Do you mind?"

She shook her head. "Whatever you like. How do you think his plans might have changed?"

"It's possible he would have tried to gain your cooperation."

"You mean he might have asked me to help him with the theft?"

"I only said it was possible. He managed to convince Desiree."

"She's not me."

"No, but I think in Josiah Pye's mind she was."

13

Laurel spoke carefully. "That's absurd. I hope you mean to tell me you're not serious."

"I can't do that. Take some comfort from the fact that I might be wrong."

"I'm taking comfort from believing one of the animals kicked you in the head."

Call cocked an eyebrow. "Do you want to hear me out?"

She looked through the window into the dining room. The poker game showed no signs that it was drawing to a close. The conversation in the house was animated, punctuated by bursts of laughter. "Please," she said, turning back to him. "Tell me."

"It seems unlikely that anyone's ever told you that you and Desiree bear an odd resemblance to each other, but there's a general, though very small, consensus that you do." He paused, waiting for a reaction. When there was none, he asked, "Are you offended? I can't tell."

"Offended? No, but I'm intrigued. In what way are we similar?"

"Age. Height. Frame. Those are obvious. The likeness is more about the way in which you carry yourselves. I didn't see it at first, but then Desiree tilted her head, pinned me back with her candid stare, set her shoulders, and would not be moved off her feet."

"In that case, I think she must be a kindred spirit."

"It's in the gestures, yes, but also an attitude, a manner.

Some vestige of what was once an authentic lady still exists. It was bred in the bone."

"I'm not sure that's true of me."

"Evidently there are those who think so."

"Hmm. That's interesting. Who says that?" Almost immediately upon asking the question, she put out a hand to stay the answer. "No, don't tell me. I don't want to know."

Call had had no intention of telling her so he was relieved when she decided against finding out. "My point in saying any of this is—"

She interrupted him, shaking her head. "You think Mr. Pye's affections turned to Desiree when I spurned him."

"See? You expressed that in a proper fashion. I don't know that I would have termed his interest as affection or your avoidance of him as spurning."

"I'm sure you wouldn't have," she said primly. Call's chuckle rumbled pleasantly in her ears. He had a soft laugh that struck her as vaguely wicked. She thought she should not like it as much as she did.

"What do you make of what I've told you?"

"Honestly? If you're right, it's disturbing. I prefer to believe you're wrong."

"Or that I've been kicked in the head."

"Or that, yes. Have you figured out how Mr. Pye knew the payroll was on that stage?"

"Not yet. I have some ideas."

"Are you sharing?"

"No."

Laurel didn't press. "Tell me about the abandoned mines. When did you see them?"

"When you were at church. I took Artemis out and explored your property. It's more extensive than I realized. Rooster gave me landmarks to follow."

She nodded. "So you think the entrances should be boarded?"

"Yes. You don't have a lot of livestock, but I don't think you want one of your cows disappearing into the mountainside."

"The cows don't go that far. The grazing is too poor."

"Then that was the ugliest horse I saw wandering near one of the openings."

"No. You didn't. Truly?"

He crossed his heart and raised his right hand. "I swear."

She sighed. "Then by all means, board them up."

"First thing tomorrow."

"After the stage comes and goes."

"Right."

"Will Digger be ready to ride shotgun? I saw you helping him to the bunkhouse. He was looking rather worse for wear."

"He was. Hard to know if he'll recover by morning. Where were you? I didn't see you."

"At the kitchen window."

"Hmm. You don't miss much that goes on here, do you?"

"With that stray cow being an exception, I hope I don't. The station is my responsibility."

"How well do you know Jed and Digger?"

"Well enough, I suppose. Jed's like a pair of old boots. Comfortable. He's been around longer than Brady. Digger is, well, he's a bit of a mess, isn't he? He's been around for maybe five years, but I wouldn't say that we're acquainted. The drinking is a relatively new development. He wasn't always stupid drunk when he came back from town. The first time he came back that way, Mr. Pye half carried him to the bunkhouse the same as you did. I was surprised when he showed up yesterday with Jed."

"Probably for the same reason I was. I didn't think he'd still have a job, not after failing to accompany Brady on the Stonechurch payroll drive."

Laurel nodded. "Yes. It's out of character for Sam Henderson to keep a man on when he's shown himself to be unreliable. I doubt Digger will get a second chance so I hope he's up on the box tomorrow."

"Any idea what brought on the heavy drinking?"

"None. I asked Mr. Pye if he knew because it seemed

he made it his business to look out for Digger. He told me that Digger kept his demons to himself."

"Or maybe he just kept them a secret from Josey Pye," said Call. "I'll ask around."

"Why?"

"Just curious."

Laurel was doubtful and said so. "I don't think I believe you."

Call pushed himself out of the rocker. "I'm for bed."

"That's it? You're not going to comment on my skepticism?"

"No."

Disconcerted, it was a moment before Laurel spoke. "Very well. Good night, then."

"G'night."

The late morning stage left with Jed Holloway and Digger Leary in the box. Call observed that the near endless poker game took a bigger toll on Jed than the drinking had taken on Digger. The shotgun rider woke bleary-eyed but almost unnaturally cheerful while Jed started grumbling the moment his feet hit the floor. No one seemed to find anything remarkable about their behavior so Call kept his thoughts to himself.

Hank helped Call cut enough planks to board up the entrances to two mines. They tossed the planks on the bed of the buckboard and Dillon harnessed the sure-footed Sylvia to the wagon. Both boys offered to go along, but Rooster had other ideas and they shuffled off behind the older man, heads hanging with exaggerated disappointment.

Call kept the hammer and box of nails beside him on the bench seat and laid the saw in the back. He waved to Mrs. Lancaster as he set off. There was no clear route to follow so the going was slow. Sylvia was a good choice to pull the buckboard. The mare showed no reluctance to make the shallow water crossing, and she was intuitive about picking her way around the rocky outcroppings.

He pulled her up outside the first entrance and began unloading the planks. The entrance was wide enough that another pair of hands would have been helpful to hold the board while he secured one side. He got as far as thinking it when he heard someone approaching from behind. Sylvia whinnied and tossed her head, recognizing the newcomer.

"Could you use some help?" Laurel asked as she dismounted. "I brought my work gloves." She reached into her saddlebag and pulled them out.

"You read my mind," said Call. "You want to hold one end of this while I nail the other end into the supports?"

Laurel slipped on her gloves and joined him at the entrance. She hefted her end and held it up. "Why didn't you ask me to come out with you when everyone else was busy?"

"Truthfully? I didn't think of it."

"Because I'm a woman?"

He laughed, shaking his head. "Lord, no. Because you're the boss."

"Oh. Well, I suppose that's understandable." She stepped back when he'd finished securing his side and took over her end. They repeated the work with a second plank, hammering it in crossways so an X barred the entrance.

"That'll keep the cows out and give a human being pause before entering. At least a human being with some sense."

"You're right about the sense. My brothers used to dare me to go in."

"And you did."

"Of course. I wasn't going to let them get the better of me. The shaft isn't very deep and it's mostly horizontal. As I told you, the mine played out early. There might still be something worth digging out, but that takes machinery that I can't afford or dynamite that I don't want to handle. I have no desire to be Morrison Mining. I have smaller ambitions."

"Oh, I don't know. Operating a station for the railroad and managing the post office and telegraph service seems rather ambitious to me. Especially since you still have to get that route established."

She sighed. "It sits on my brain every day. Sometimes it's hard not to be overwhelmed by it. Operating the station is what I know, but getting the government and the railroad to agree on the route that benefits us, that's been more difficult. It's not a pleasure talking to the politicians. And the thought that I might have to put money in their pockets to see my way clear, well, that just rubs me wrong."

Call felt the full effect of Laurel's frank stare and held his own.

"And now," she said, "there's this robbery. I know word's gotten around. Mr. Abrams will have heard. And the government man, Mr. Berry, surely knows. It wouldn't surprise me if it occurred to them that I had a part in the theft. I'm not certain if they'll hold it against me or assume that some of that money will find its way to them."

"That's why I'm going to clear you. There will be no doubt when I've finished that you're not involved."

"You sound very sure."

"Because I am. It would help my investigation if you'd stop harboring guilt for something you had no part in."

"I hired Mr. Pye. It's not unnatural to feel a measure of responsibility for his crime."

"If you say so."

"Wouldn't you?"

"No," he said flatly. "I'd say I was responsible for hiring him and that's all. What he made of the opportunity is his blame to bear."

"But I presented him with the opportunity."

"And you've given the same one to Rooster and Dillon and Hank and probably a dozen others and none of them used it for criminal purposes. You can't be sure that Josey Pye didn't arrive with a plan."

"If he did, he was a long time in executing it." Laurel

considered that possibility a moment longer and then shook her head. "No. Too many coincidences in that event. He couldn't have known that I would hire him or much about the stations between Denver and the end of the line. I'm confident the idea for the theft was born here."

"And not your responsibility," said Call. "There's no need for you to martyr yourself."

She stiffened. "I am not martyring myself."

"Uh-huh. If you say so," he said again. Rather than debate the point as she seemed poised to do, Call turned and headed for the buckboard. He climbed aboard and took up the reins. "There's still another entrance to close if you want to come along. I could use your help."

Laurel didn't move. "Can we agree not to have this conversation again?"

Relieved, Call said, "You have my word."

"All right." She walked over to Abby and swung herself onto the mare's back. "Do you want to lead the way or shall I?"

"It's probably better if you do." He waited until she was out in front before he snapped the reins and followed.

The second mine had an entrance about two hundred yards from the first. Laurel had a much smoother ride than Call. The buckboard bounced so hard and high across the uneven and rocky ground that he was almost unseated twice.

Laurel helped him unload the lumber and carry it to the entrance. It didn't take long for them to put the boards in place and they accomplished the task without any conversation at all. It struck Laurel that they worked well together, but because she was unsure of what he would make of that, she refrained from saying so.

Call stood back to admire their work. "I think we did that tolerably well."

"It's not precisely skilled carpentry."

"No, but I didn't hammer my thumb and you didn't drop a board and it looks as if it's going to hold."

"Uh-huh." She gave him a wry look. "The test will be repeating our success. There's one more entrance to board."

"What? I only found the two we've done."

"The other one might have collapsed, but we should look. Besides, you brought enough wood to build a cabin."

"I wasn't sure how much it would take, and Hank kept cutting and I kept loading."

"I think Hank was having you on. You're a little out of your depth with this kind of work, aren't you?" She added quickly, "That's not a criticism. Merely an observation."

Call saw no point objecting when what she said was so obviously true. He wiggled his uninjured thumb. "I'm learning."

She grinned. "And so quickly, too."

It was the grin that decided him. Call thought that sassy smile required some kind of answer and his response was swift and certain. He kissed her full on that mocking mouth. It was not a kiss meant to linger. He thought of it more as punctuation, like an exclamation point at the end of a particularly good retort. Call had no idea if she would view it in that light.

He lifted his head and met her startled gaze with calm. Her gloved hands remained at her sides. Mildly curious, he asked, "You aren't going to slap me?"

The question grounded Laurel. "I'm still deciding."

He nodded. "I understand."

"Why did you do it?"

"I doubt explaining will be helpful."

"Let me decide that."

"All right. In the moment, it simply seemed that I should."

"That's it? That's all you have to say?"

"I told you I doubted it would be helpful."

Laurel said, "You can do better."

"You were giving me a smile full of sass. I thought you should answer for it."

"So, just to be clear, kissing me was retaliation."

"It was a response, not retaliation."

"Hmm." Her cheeks puffed slightly as she released a breath. "We should get going." She left him staring after her and went to mount her horse. "You can probably get the buckboard within fifty yards of the last entrance. We'll have to carry the wood from there."

It turned out that Laurel's estimation of their walking distance was off by another fifty yards. They had to find the entrance first on foot and then return to the wagon for the lumber. Call was prepared to take two planks on his shoulder, but Laurel decided they should share the burden and walk in tandem, each of them supporting an end. They boarded the entrance quickly and neither of them paused to comment on their work. Travel back passed silently until the station was in sight and the path widened so they were able to ride side by side.

"Do you want me to apologize?" asked Call.

"Do you think you should?"

"No. I'll apologize if you like, but you should know I'm not sorry."

"I didn't think you were. Perhaps you should save it for something you truly regret."

"All right. In case you're wondering, I'm not going to seize the moment every time you flash a sassy grin my way." He paused then added, "No matter how much it's called for."

"Yes," she said dryly. "That was uppermost in my mind."

"See? You can't help yourself. One would think you wanted to be kissed again."

"I wasn't grinning."

"I'm not sure that entirely matters. It's more of an attitude, I'm thinking now."

"An attitude," she repeated. "In that case, I hope you can restrain yourself because I surely cannot."

Now it was Call who grinned. "Duly noted."

When they reached the station, they were on even footing. Laurel accepted Call's offer to look after both horses and went to her office to sort the post and respond to messages. It was not until she was sitting behind her desk and certain that she was alone that she allowed herself to think about Call's kiss. It had been unexpected, but it was not unwelcome. If he stayed past a few weeks, she would tell him that. Maybe. In the meantime, it was for her alone to know.

14

Call posted a letter to Ramsey Stonechurch detailing his progress and the lack of the same. He visited Sweeny's again, this time with Dillon, to see if there was anything more to be learned from the locals. He was curious about Digger Leary's drinking habits, and while the information he gleaned was edifying, he learned considerably more watching Dillon match his father shot for shot at the bar.

He had a chance to return to town some two weeks later. The Booker brothers were once again escorting Laurel to church and this time Call caught up and joined them. The boys expressed surprise at his sudden appearance, but Laurel took it in stride.

Services were held beneath a large tent that could easily accommodate a quarter of the town's three hundred people. Still, it was standing room only on the sides and at the back after the benches were filled. Call and Hank gave up their seats to a young mother with a child gripping each hand. Hank grumbled under his breath, but Call was happy enough to surrender the hard bench and lean comfortably against one of the supporting tent poles. It was one of the few times that Call could remember when standing was preferable to sitting. In addition to being at his ease, he was able to survey the congregation.

He didn't expect to recognize many people, but he counted eighteen faces he'd seen at Sweeny's, a few others that he'd seen on his walk through town, and three of the women he'd seen at Mrs. Fry's, along with the madam herself. Desiree was sitting toward the back of the tent, bearing little resemblance to the woman he'd met sitting at the piano or spoken to in her room. She sat on the backless bench with a straight spine and a lifted chin, and when her gaze happened upon him, there was a moment's recognition but no acknowledgment before her eyes moved on.

Call studied Laurel's profile until her head swiveled in his direction and she caught him out. Shameless, he grinned at her. He swallowed his laughter when she pursed her lips and turned away, lifting her chin at precisely the same angle as Desiree.

When the service was over, the majority of the congregation did not leave immediately. Folks lingered to greet their friends and neighbors and share stories. Laurel and the Bookers were no exception. Call did not mingle. Neither did Mrs. Fry or any of her entourage. He gave them ten minutes before he slipped out the side and followed.

Call was standing at the corral, ostensibly watching the horses as they moved listlessly inside the fencing, when Laurel came upon him. She was no longer confined by her Sunday-go-to-meeting dress, and she climbed the rails so she could perch on top. Call's forearms rested on the rail beside her as he leaned in. He looked up at her when she was still.

"Yes?" he asked.

"You hardly spoke at dinner."

"I didn't have anything to say."

"Is something wrong?"

"No."

"Should I leave?"

"Not unless you want to."

"I don't."

Call nodded and resumed looking over the horses.

"You're not really watching the animals, are you?"

"No. I was thinking." He removed his hat and hung it on a post, then he shoved his fingers through his hair. "Hard business, thinking."

"It seems so, at least the way you do it."

Call's eyebrows lifted and fell as though in agreement. "Why do suppose he took Penelope?"

"Ah. So that's what you have on your mind."

He slid her a sideways glance. "Only the part that you don't occupy."

Laurel wished she could pretend she hadn't heard, but her face was already registering the opposite. Her mouth curled to one side and her eyes went heavenward. She shook her head. "You're not even sorry you said that."

"I rarely am. So what do you think?" He lifted a finger, cautioning her. "Be careful what you say. I'm asking about Penelope."

"I knew that."

"Uh-huh."

"Very well. I never gave Mr. Pye's choice any thought."

"Think about it now."

She did. "Penelope has strength and stamina, maybe more than others that were available that night, but not as much as my Abby. The only good sense he showed was not taking her. I believe I would still be hunting him."

"Hmm. Anything else about Penelope?"

"She doesn't have any special markings. We would know her on sight, but to describe her, well, she looks like a lot of others. You worked for Overland. You understand the stage animals don't belong to me. I care for them as part of my agreement with Henderson Express."

"I see some of them have the HE brand but not all. What about Penelope?"

Laurel closed her eyes and tried to form an image of the horse. "No," she said finally. "No brand. She hasn't been on the trail very long. If anyone even noticed, I suppose one station was deferring to the next."

"So no brand makes her even harder to identify," said

Call. "Worse, she can be branded with someone else's marking."

Laurel nodded. "Perhaps that's why Mr. Pye took her. He can hide her anywhere. That stops his trail cold."

"His trail has been cold for a long while, but you're right. Pye's made it as difficult as he possibly could."

"I never thought of him as this clever."

"I still have doubts that he is."

"You want to tell me about that?"

"Not yet."

Laurel lifted a hand to acknowledge Rooster as he walked out of the bunkhouse and headed toward the kitchen. "Where did you go after services this morning?"

"I think you know, or at least that you have your suspicions, else you would have asked me in front of everyone while we were at dinner."

"Mrs. Fry's."

"Yes. I wanted to see Desiree again, and I would have done it the same evening that I went to Sweeny's with Dillon. That didn't work out. I didn't have any purpose other than my investigation."

"I didn't ask."

"I'm very aware."

"Did you learn anything from her?"

"No. She didn't want to talk to me. Mrs. Fry made her take me to her room because I paid for her time. She read. I napped."

"Oh." Laurel thought she should not feel relieved to hear that. It was foolish. "What were you hoping to learn?"

"How much time Digger Leary spent with her when he was here the last time. I know he was there because I learned that from someone at the saloon who saw him go in, and one of the younger women confirmed it when I asked about Desiree and Digger. Mrs. Fry shooed her out of the parlor before I could ask anything else, and the madam was as tight-lipped as Desiree turned out to be."

Laurel was sure that she didn't want to think about

Desiree and Digger. She shifted uncomfortably on the rail.

"I'm sorry." He meant it. "I've said too much. I should have never told you about the resemblance between you and Desiree. That's it, isn't it? It's what's bothering you now."

"A little. I'd rather not think about it, if you don't mind."

"It's a comparison without foundation. You don't look anything at all like her."

Dark humor edged Laurel's short laugh. "I saw her in church, Call. Now that I know what to look for, even I found the similarities. It's no good backing away from what you spent time convincing me. Can we agree to be done with Mrs. Fry's house?"

He nodded. "I really am sorry."

She smiled. "I believe you. I think I'm learning how to separate the wheat from the chaff."

That made Call grin. "Good for you." One of the mares wandered over. She nudged Laurel first, nearly unseating her. Call pushed her nose aside and began stroking it, giving her the attention she wanted. "Hey," he said softly. "Hey there, girl. You only had to ask. No pushing." He looked up at Laurel. "Are you all right? Steady up there?"

"I'm fine." She reached out and patted the mare's neck. "I've occupied too much of your time. I think she's jealous."

"Are you, girl?" asked Call. "Are you jealous?"

The mare tossed her head as though she understood.

"I think you're right, Laurel." His hand stilled on the mare's nose. He'd spoken without thinking, spoken her name in the manner he always thought of it when he thought of her. "Miss Morrison."

Laurel lowered her hand to the rail to steady herself for the second time in the matter of a minute. She'd come closer to being unseated by hearing her name than when the mare had nudged her. It would amuse her later, in private, but just now it was too important to let it go without comment.

"I don't mind if you call me Laurel when we're alone," she said. "But it would set a poor example if you were to do it in front of the others. I gave Rooster leave to use it a long time ago and he rarely does. That's his way. Brady sometimes calls me Laurel Beth because that's how he first knew me. I still feel twelve when he says it. Hank and Dillon call me Miss Laurel. That's acceptable, too, but I don't think I'd like that when it's just you and me. You're Call. I'm Laurel. That seems right."

Call appreciated that there was nothing in her tone that suggested she was conferring a privilege, but he didn't miss the gravity with which she spoke. This was significant to her. He wondered how many men she'd ever invited to call her Laurel.

"It does seem right," he said. He gave the mare a final pat and sent her on her way. Call decided against dwelling on the moment when what it called for was kissing her, and not the swift buss on her mouth that he'd managed at the old mine. No, this time he wanted to linger. This kiss should be long and warm and tempting. It should leave her wanting more. He'd whisper her name against her ear and she'd hear the promise in it.

Except for the occasional glance, he had avoided looking at her. It was unexpected that she'd join him at the corral, and not just join him, but climb up the rails and settle contentedly beside him. She only would have been closer if she'd perched on his shoulder. It was just this morning on the way to services that he had been thinking how fine she looked in her mint green gown and how the simplicity of the dress suited her. There were no flounces, no ruffles, no lace trim, and yet the lack of those furbelows did not make it seem less fashionable than what every other woman was wearing. She did not carry a parasol or wear elbow-length gloves. She'd wound a ribbon the same shade as her dress in her coiled hair and was one of the few women in church who did not wear a hat.

He remembered how she pursed her lips in disapproval when she caught him staring at her. It made him smile now. He didn't have to study her any longer to bring her image easily to mind.

Laurel tapped Call's shoulder. When he looked up at her, she asked quite sincerely, "Where do you go?"

"Hmm?"

"You're a thousand miles away. I wonder where you go."

"Nowhere. That is, nowhere far. Mostly inside my head, I suppose."

"Inside your head," she repeated softly. "Do I want to know what goes on in there?"

Call chuckled. "You don't even want to visit."

Laurel accepted that, though she didn't agree. "Since we're speaking of going places, what about Mr. Pye? I imagine he quite literally could be a thousand miles away."

"Possibly. If he's smart, he will be. I'm going to recommend that Mr. Stonechurch put a bounty on him."

Laurel's eyebrows lifted. "Why now?"

"Because I'm convinced that he's the right man."

"Weren't you before? It seemed that you were."

"I came here believing it, but it's no good if I only find evidence that fits my belief. I realized early on that I had to cast a wider net." One corner of his mouth lifted in a self-mocking smile. "I'm not much of a fisherman. It took me a while."

"But you're charged with finding him. Does that mean you're giving up?"

"No. Not at all, but I could use some help. Bringing in Josey Pye isn't the same as finding the payroll. The payroll is what is important to Ramsey Stonechurch."

"Won't the one lead you to the other?"

"Maybe."

"What if he's spent the money?"

Call shrugged. "If he's spent that much, then he's already called attention to himself. It's hard to imagine a place he could hide throwing around that much money. It would be a good outcome for Mr. Stonechurch if Pye was smarter than that."

"When will you be leaving?" she asked.

"What makes you think—" He stopped because she was shaking her head.

"Don't pretend you don't already have plans to go," said Laurel. "I'm surprised you've stayed this long. What has it been? Almost a month now?"

It had been twenty-six days exactly, but Call did not tell her that. "I have to visit the other stations on the line, make some inquiries. My last stop will be Denver. I'll be there for a few days, maybe a week, then I'll be back."

"You're coming back?"

He frowned because the question was unexpected. "Of course. I thought you understood. I thought I made that clear from the first."

After a moment's reflection, she said quietly, "You did."

"Oh, I see. You didn't believe me."

"I didn't *know* you. I still don't, not really."

"Morrison Station is my *home* station, Laurel. And you're the reason I decided that. I haven't changed my mind. If anything, I'm firmer on it." He paused a beat, then, "In fact, I might just be courting you."

A slip of a smile lifted the corners of Laurel's mouth. She'd heard the thread of humor in his voice. It would not do to take him more seriously than he took himself. She asked again, "So when are you leaving?"

"I'm waiting for Digger Leary to return. I figure he'll make an exchange here, spend a night, and be riding shotgun the following day. I'm leaving when he does. I'll take Artemis and ride alongside or follow. I'm not riding in the coach."

He said this last with such vehemence that Laurel had to laugh. "I'm recalling that you looked rather sickly at our introduction."

"Sickly? That was earlier. I slept the last leg to keep from being sick. I was just waking up when I met you."

"That's what you look like waking up?"

Call immediately saw a problem with that assessment. He was quick to defend himself. "Not always. Not usually. Not when—"

Laurel laughed. "I get the idea," she said. "And I was teasing. I can do that, you know."

"I'm learning. Maybe if you did it more often."

His forearm was still resting on the top rail. She nudged his elbow with her thigh. "Maybe I will."

Call looked down at where her leg brushed his arm and then looked up at her. "Are you flirting with me?"

"Why? Does it seem as if I might be?"

"It does."

"I figure lots of women have flirted with you. You're probably better than a fair judge. I must not be doing something right since you're raising the question."

"Oh, no. You're holding your own. I was just trying to clarify your intent. With very little provocation I could be moved to kiss you breathless out here in front of God and everybody."

Laurel knew God was there, but she'd forgotten about everybody else. She looked around. Dillon and Hank were walking toward the station from town, where they'd been visiting their mother, Rooster was whittling something on the back stoop, and the driver and shotgun boarding in the bunkhouse for the night were occupying the rockers on the front porch. Mrs. Lancaster was the only one she couldn't see, but the reverse was probably not true.

Laurel drew herself up and pulled her leg away. "Do you have eyes in the back of your head? You're facing the wrong direction. You can't possibly see that—"

"Doesn't matter if I can see them or not," he said. "Better to act as if someone's always watching."

He was right. She had forgotten herself. "It's good of you to protect me from myself."

"You think that's what I was doing?"

"Weren't you?"

"I was looking after my own neck. Rooster would string me up if he thought I was treating you poorly and Mrs. Lancaster would kick out the stool from under me."

Laurel was intrigued. "And Hank and Dillon? What would they be doing?"

"Knitting."

Laurel gave a short shout of laughter before she covered her mouth with a hand and muffled her mirth. When she could speak, she said, "Like Madame Defarge at the guillotine. Oh, that's an image."

Call massaged the back of his neck as if he could feel the blade or the hitch of the rope.

Watching him, Laurel said, "Maybe too clear an image."

"Uh-huh."

"Let's walk."

"All right." He pushed away from the corral and held out a hand to help her down. She shook her head at the offer and executed a nimble jump to the ground. "Which way?" he asked.

"The same way we went this morning. Toward town. There's still plenty of light. We'll be back before dark settles."

Call fell in step beside her. Laurel stopped as they were about to pass Hank and Dillon and inquired about their mother even though she had seen Mrs. Booker only that morning. They didn't act as if there was anything odd about her going for a walk with Call, but when Call looked back over his shoulder, they were both looking back over theirs, and they were grinning.

"They're a pair," he said.

"They're good boys. Young men, really. I have to keep reminding myself."

They walked in silence after that. The pace was leisurely, suited to the warm evening. Pink and purple wildflowers, early risers in May, appeared in grassy spreads and rocky crevices. They walked on the edge of the trail, careful to stay away from the ruts made by the stagecoaches and the plodding of the horses.

"Have you seen the falls?" she asked suddenly.

"The falls? No. I didn't know there were any."

"It's Falls Hollow."

"Lots of places have names that have nothing to do with their geography."

"Well, Falls Hollow does. It'll take us away from town, but it's not far. Would you like to see?"

"Sure."

"I'm not taking you there for my own nefarious purposes, if that's what you're thinking." She stepped off the trail onto a narrow path that was only obvious if you knew where to look.

"I wasn't thinking that," he said. It wasn't exactly a lie, but he had been hopeful.

Laurel paused, eyeing him narrowly. His gaze was steady in return. His gunmetal gray eyes were as seductive as moonlight. She blinked. "This way," she said. "You should follow me. The path isn't wide enough to walk beside me."

Walking behind Laurel was not exactly a hardship. She didn't have to be wearing a bustle to bring a man's attention to her, well, to her bustle. She didn't swing her hips. The movement was subtler than that, more suited to her character. There was an easy sway, a roll in her step that was visible because she wore trousers. Not for the first time, Call thought there was a lot to recommend trousers on a woman, most particularly this woman.

Occasionally she glanced back to make sure he was following. She never caught him staring at her behind, and he didn't dwell on what she would have done if she had.

By Call's estimation, they walked three-quarters of a mile, most of it uphill, before he heard the rush of water that signaled they were approaching the falls. Their destination was another half mile beyond that. He caught glimpses of the falls between thick nests of pine trees but didn't have the full view until they broke into a clearing at the foot. He'd wondered why they hadn't been following a stream and now the answer was obvious. The path of the water coming off the falls veered sharply in the direction opposite of the one they had taken. The pool at the base churned and bubbled with the force of the falling water.

Laurel led him to the pool, picked her way across some flat boulders, and stood perilously close to the edge. A fine spray of water touched her upturned face. She licked her lips and waved him over. "C'mon. It's better here."

"I'm fine where I am, thank you."

"Suit yourself."

"Is the water in the pool deep?" Which was his way of asking if she'd ever been swimming in it.

"About fifteen feet deep, I'd say. Maybe twenty in places." Laurel dropped to her knees and then pushed herself onto her stomach so that she lay flat against the warm stone. She inched forward until her head and shoulders were over the water and reached down so that her hand skimmed the surface.

Call felt some trepidation watching her but he stayed his ground. "What are you doing?"

She turned her head to look at him at the same time she cupped her hand in the water. "This!" She scooped a handful of water and tossed it in his direction. Very little found its target, but it was enough to satisfy her. Water droplets glistened in his neatly trimmed beard. For just a moment they looked like diamonds. She grinned because the sparkle did not suit him at all.

Call swiped at his face. "Nice. You probably are feeling confident that I won't retaliate. I will. You just won't know when."

Laurel grinned. "Come over here. I promise I won't push you in. That would be cruel." When he hesitated, she added, "And I'm not going to throw more water at you. Come. Lie down here."

Call moved closer, stopped when he reached the level of her knees. If he leaned forward, he could see over the lip of the stone he was standing on. "I believe it is incumbent upon me to tell you that I can't swim. I'm saying that in the event you go back on your word not to toss me in the drink."

"Really? You can't swim?"

"I really can't."

"Now that is a shame."

"Is it?"

She raised herself up on her elbows and patted the stone slab. "Come down here and put your hand in the water. You'll see."

Call regarded her doubtfully. After another moment's hesitation, he hunkered beside her.

"Almost there," she said. "Stretch out."

He took off his hat and set it between them then he assumed a position identical to hers.

Laurel dropped off her elbows and reached for the water again with one arm. "Like this," she told him. She stirred the water with her hand. "Put your oar in."

Call slipped an arm over the lip of the stone. There was no point in dipping his fingers to get a feel for it so he thrust his hand under. And pulled it out immediately. "Jesus. That's cold."

She laughed. "Well, yes. I know it looks a little as if it's simmering but it's mountain spring water. What did you expect?"

"Not that it would freeze my arm up to the elbow."

"Hardly. Go on. Do it again. You'll get used to it."

"I'll be numb to it." He put in his hand again and moved it back and forth as she was doing. "You swam in this?"

"Mostly splashed around with my brothers, but yes, swimming was required. The water is marginally warmer in July and August."

Call turned his head to look up at where the water spilled over the rocky ledge above them. He made it to be about one hundred feet. "You've been up there?"

"Not recently, but yes, when I was young and foolish. It's a difficult climb. My brothers dared me to jump. They swore they both had done it so naturally I had to try."

"Did you jump?"

"I didn't have to. They got scared when I reached the top and hollered at me to come down. They admitted that they'd lied."

"Do you think you would have done it if they hadn't said anything?"

Laurel shook her head. "I know I wouldn't have. I was never that young or that foolish. From up there, this pool of water looks awfully small. I thought jumping in from that height would be like threading a needle and I'm not much of a seamstress."

Call's eyes followed the swift descent of the water. That she had even made the climb contemplating that jump was alarming. He wondered at what point her brothers had regretted their dare. Withdrawing his hand from the water, Call shook it out and sat up. He crossed his legs tailor-fashion. "Did your father find out?"

"Of course." Laurel sat up as well. She raised her knees toward her chest and hugged them. "But not because I told on them. George and Martin told on themselves because they didn't trust me to keep quiet and it would have been worse for them if I tattled."

"Did they often do things like that to you?"

"Tease me, you mean?"

"I suppose, if that's what you call it."

Laurel gave a throaty chuckle. "I'm fairly certain I did worse to them. In their eyes I was their bratty little sister, and I did a better than fair job of proving them right." Her head tilted to one side as she studied him. "What about you? Brothers? Sisters?"

"Neither."

"Oh, that is too bad. You missed out."

"Well, I didn't have anyone daring me to kill myself."

"It wasn't like that."

"Uh-huh." He looked up at the falls again and shook his head. "Maybe not, but that was the likely outcome if you had jumped."

Laurel frowned. "I don't suppose you can understand, you being without brothers or sisters of your own, but George and Martin weren't deliberately mean. They were young, too. Thoughtless. They didn't see as far as the consequences until I was almost at the top. George had already started up after me. See? They wanted to make it right. To protect me. It was always that way. That's what brothers do. Sisters, too, I reckon."

"Hmm. You're right. I don't know about that, but I had a lot of women around me growing up. Not sisters exactly.

More like aunts. No blood relations except for my mother, but every one of them looked out for me."

"Then you know about family."

"Of a particular kind, yes."

"Your aunts . . . were they . . . ?" She hesitated, reluctant to finish what she'd started.

"Whores? Yes. Like my mother. I grew up in a house very much like Mrs. Fry's establishment."

"A brothel," she said flatly.

He nodded. "A brothel. My mother's parents tried to take me away when I was an infant and again when I was seven, but my mother wasn't amenable to that arrangement. They hired lawyers. She hired better ones. Her parents didn't want her in their home again. Everything hinged on that. When they learned she was pregnant, they turned their backs on her, called her a whore. She always maintained that's why she became one. For a lot of years, I believed her, but later I began to understand that it helped her to blame them for her choices."

"So they only wanted you."

"That's right. Bastard or not, I was my grandfather's heir. The only child of his only child. I have no doubt he loved my mother, but it wasn't reason enough to forgive her."

"May I ask about your father?"

"There's nothing to tell you. I don't know who he is because my mother would never say. She never told her parents either, which is part of what infuriated them. I suspect he was married. I have no proof of it, but it makes sense that it would be motivation for her silence."

"She was protecting him," said Laurel.

"If I'm right, it's more likely that she was protecting his wife. The town was already scandalized by my mother's behavior. Knowing her, she would not have wanted to destroy another family."

"I don't know if I could be so magnanimous."

"There's that," he said, "but Mother is also a bit of a martyr."

"Are your grandparents still living?"

"No. They died within a few months of each other not long after my grandfather's factory was burned to the ground. The last time Confederate soldiers came to Chambersburg, they left a lot of ash and rubble in their wake. My grandfather didn't have the will to rebuild."

Laurel nodded her understanding but said nothing.

Call said, "I didn't know any of this when it happened. I was deep in the South by then. I learned all of it when I returned home. That was years later and the town was still recovering."

"What about your mother?"

"A survivor. By the time Johnny Reb came calling, my mother was the owner of the house. She says she paid a ransom to keep the soldiers from setting fire to the house, but I think she may have offered more than that. I heard other families paid ransom and had their homes destroyed anyway. The fact that her place was left standing did not endear her to her neighbors, but she redeemed herself to a large extent by taking in whole families, feeding and clothing them, giving them medical care if they needed it and sometimes money if they needed it more. She kept her home open for that purpose until families rebuilt or found shelter with relatives."

"I'm not sure your mother could be more interesting. What is her name?"

"Edwina. After her father. Edwina Mae Landry." Call's lips formed a half smile. "Everyone calls her Eddy. She prefers it."

"Eddy," said Laurel, returning his smile. "And just like that she's already more interesting. I bet you called her Eddy, too."

He laughed. "She didn't like it, but what was she to do when everyone around me called her that? I understood she was my mother, but Eddy stuck."

Laurel looked up at the sky and saw shades of orange and rose on the underside of distant clouds. "Sun's setting," she said. "We should leave now."

Call hopped to his feet and scooped up his hat. He put it on and then held out a hand to Laurel, who was slower to rise because she was watching him. When she didn't take his hand, he lowered it to his side. "What?" he asked.

"There's a halo over your head."

"Water spray and sunlight," he said.

"I know, but it's still a very nice effect. No, don't try to wave it away. It'll disappear soon enough with the lowering sun."

He stood there in spite of feeling awkward. "I don't deserve a halo."

"Maybe not, but it's there anyway." Her smile faded as slowly as the light. "And now it's gone." She held out her hand for him to take, and when he pulled her up, it was with enough strength to bring her flush against him. Oh, yes, she thought, the halo had definitely disappeared. She raised her face to his slightly lowered one and used her free hand to nudge the brim of his hat upward. His features were no longer shadowed and his eyes, hinting of silver and blue, were clear and cautious. She offered no objection, and the moment he understood that, his mouth covered hers.

Laurel's heart banged in her chest. She'd wanted this, and now that she had it, she wasn't entirely certain what to do with it. She had been kissed before, mostly chaste kisses behind the log building that passed for a schoolhouse when she was a child. There had been one notable exception in the barn with a young man who worked for her father. She'd been paralyzed with equal parts anticipation and fear until he thrust his tongue in her mouth. Galvanized into action by the intrusion, she had shoved a knee into his groin with no real concept of the pain she could inflict. She wouldn't have cared even if she'd known. She had been twelve, for goodness' sake, and he had been twenty. He should have known better, even if she hadn't. Not really.

It was different now. When Call's mouth came over hers, she welcomed the humid warmth, and when the tip of his tongue brushed her upper lip, well, she welcomed that, too. It was a tease; perhaps a promise of what was to come because it didn't come right then.

She wondered if he was always so gentle with women or if he was being respectful of her inexperience. Should she be embarrassed if it was the latter? She was twenty-seven. That was a lot of years since twelve.

Call waited for her to kiss him back. She made her mouth available, stayed toe to toe with him, but she didn't quite reciprocate. He changed the slant of his mouth, kissed the corner of hers. He released the hand he'd been holding since he drew her to her feet and cupped her face. He brushed her cheek with his thumb. She hummed. Her lips vibrated against his.

"That's it," he murmured. "Like that." He felt the shape of her lips change. She was smiling. "Yes. Definitely like that." Call kissed her again and her lips parted. She pressed back. The sweep of her tongue across his upper lip felt tentative and he realized she was mirroring him. He slipped his arms under hers and rested his hands at the small of her back. In turn, she slipped her arms over his shoulders and threaded her hands together at the nape of his neck.

"We fit," she whispered. "Did you know we'd fit?"

"Uh-huh."

She nodded. "Kiss me again. I can do better. I *want* to do better." Laurel didn't wait. She stood on tiptoes and brushed her mouth against his. His lips parted and she caught the lower one in her teeth and drew it in. She heard him moan softly, deep in his throat like the purr of a mountain cat. It reminded her that he was dangerous. It was exciting, not frightening.

When his tongue swept the ridge of her teeth, she sucked it into her mouth and twirled her tongue around it. The air around her felt warmer than when she'd gotten to her feet, warmer than when she'd first stood flush against him, but the heat was really only inside her. She whimpered as the tempo of the kiss changed. There was urgency in their touching. His hands moved from her back to the curve of her buttocks. He palmed her cheeks, jerked her closer.

Laurel felt her breasts swell, tighten. She pressed against his chest because it felt so good. She imagined it was the same for him with his groin cradled against her thighs. Laurel thrust her hips forward to make it better than good for both of them.

Call murmured Laurel's name close to her ear and then kissed the sensitive hollow behind it. He kissed her temple, her jaw, pressed his lips in her hair. He came back to her mouth and kissed her hard and long and breathless, just as he had imagined doing almost from the first.

Laurel felt herself start to sag. She held on tighter and willed him to take her down. He didn't do that, though. He held her up, kept her standing when she would have gone to the ground for him.

Breathing a little raggedly, Call lifted his mouth. He pressed his forehead against hers while he steadied himself. "I lost my hat," he said.

"Mm." Laurel gently twirled and tugged at the hair at his nape. "I think I might have knocked it off."

Neither looked for it.

"We should go back," he said.

"All right."

Neither moved.

Call closed his eyes. It was difficult to listen to his conscience for the rushing sound of the falling water. He thought about her clambering up the rocks on a dare and standing on the edge of the precipice. He'd brought her to an edge of a different kind. She hadn't jumped then; he didn't know what she would do now. He lifted his mouth a hairsbreadth from her forehead. "No jumping," he said quietly.

"What?"

He straightened, opened his eyes. It didn't matter if she understood what he meant so he did not repeat himself. His hands slid up her back to her shoulders and then down the length of her arms. He gently disengaged her threaded fingers from behind his neck and held her wrists while he lowered her hands to her sides. "Just a wayward thought," he said. "It's not important."

Laurel nodded her acceptance. She stooped, picked up his hat, and offered it to him after brushing it off.

"Thank you." He took it back but didn't put it on. At the moment it was safer to have one hand occupied. Call pointed over his shoulder to indicate the path behind them. "You want to go first?"

Laurel's gaze shied away from his. "I don't want to go at all."

There was nothing he could say to that. She spoke for him as well.

She laughed softly, uneasily. "I thought I'd be the one with sense enough to call a halt."

He smiled. "I thought the same." Placing a forefinger under her chin, Call gently nudged her to meet his eyes again. "Can I admit I was depending on it?"

"Then I failed you."

"Hardly. It was unfair."

She didn't disagree. "I'm all twisted up inside. You did that."

"It's no different for me."

Laurel wondered if that were true, but to her knowledge he'd never lied to her so perhaps he was speaking the truth now. She wasn't sure why that calmed her skittering heart, but it did. She stepped back.

Call's hand hovered for a moment before he let it fall to his side. He regarded her expectantly, one eyebrow raised.

"This way," she said. "I don't mind leading."

15

As far as Call was concerned, Digger Leary couldn't return to Morrison Station soon enough. It was not in his mind that he should avoid Laurel after the kiss they'd shared at the falls, but apparently she had decided differently, and for the last seventy-two hours she had managed to be anywhere he wasn't. Their interactions were by third party. Work assignments came to him through Rooster. At meals the potatoes could be sitting in front of him and she'd ask Hank to pass them. She asked Dillon to saddle Abby for her even though Dillon was occupied and Call was obviously between tasks.

At first he had been quietly amused, then concerned, and finally annoyed. He was hardly going to pressure her to repeat that intimacy. It was mildly insulting that she seemed to think he would.

"You two have a fight?" asked Hank. He slung Call's saddlebag into place. Artemis stirred but accepted it. "Don't suppose it's my business, but I'm not alone in wondering."

"I figured someone would ask before now," said Call. He looked out through the open barn door. The stage box was empty. Digger and Jed Holloway were still inside the farmhouse. They'd be coming out soon and taking their positions on the stage. Call wanted to leave with them, not give chase.

The driver and shotgun had arrived the evening before,

spent the night in the bunkhouse, and were rested enough to leave this morning. Call had hoped to get Digger alone and hear some answers to his thornier questions, but the man was as skillful at avoiding him as Laurel, although for what Call imagined were better reasons. Digger disappeared into town while Call had been busy, and when he returned, he stumbled into the bunkhouse and passed out. It was an opportunity missed, and rather than corner Digger in what might become a public altercation, Call let it go and began making arrangements to leave.

Laurel stood out in the yard as she always did when a stage was departing. She raised a hand to Jed and Digger, wished them well, and nodded to the passengers looking out of the stage. Call tipped his hat to her as he passed. She stood frozen, unable to return the gesture, unable to smile.

Laurel wondered what he thought about her keeping her distance. She should have explained herself rather than leave it up to him to figure out. Did he think she blamed him? If he considered it for even a moment, he'd know she blamed herself. And this was not merely about responsibility. It was about trust. He'd proven she could trust him, but she sincerely doubted she could trust herself. She had embarrassed herself, kissing him the way she had, wanting more than he was prepared to offer. She didn't know what to do with the discomfort that was inside her. Being around McCall Landry was nearly unbearable.

Rooster sidled up to Laurel and stood shoulder to shoulder, rocking slowly on his heels. "Hell of a thing, boss," he said quietly. "Hell of a thing."

Laurel stared straight ahead. "You'll have to explain that, Rooster. I'm not a mind reader."

"Never took you for a coward. Hell of a thing, that."

Just as if he'd slapped her, Laurel's head snapped sideways. Her lips parted but she had no words. Shock kept her silent.

"Can't figure it out," said Rooster. He stopped rocking and rubbed his chin. "To my way of thinking, Call's a good sort. Fit right in. Worked his share, sometimes more. I reckoned you thought so, too."

"I did. I *do*."

"Uh-huh."

"You don't believe me."

He shrugged his bony shoulders.

"What is it you want to say?" she asked. "Out with it."

"You ain't talked to him above ten words these last three days. You ain't shared the porch with him neither. You walked off with him a few days back, not holdin' hands exactly but near enough, and since you come back, you ain't properly looked at him. Now he's off and you couldn't see your way clear to wish him well. That's not like you. Not like you at all. So, yeah, I'm gettin' the impression of cowardice because you don't seem angry at him. If you don't mind me sayin', you seem scared."

Laurel *did* mind him sayin', but that didn't mean it wasn't true. "What do you think I'm supposed to do?"

"I reckon he's sweet on you. Hank and Dillon think the same."

"If that's what the three of you are talking about, you don't have enough work to occupy you."

Rooster went on as if she hadn't spoken. "And we all think that it's likewise for you."

As uncomfortable as she was with this turn in the conversation, Laurel still did not deny it.

"Yeah," Rooster said. "Figured we were right. So why ain't you sendin' him off like one of those ladies in olden times? Givin' him a hankie or something like that? He's set on clearin' our names. Your name especially. He's fightin' for all of us, but you most of all." He hooked his thumbs in his pockets and began rocking on his heels again. "Guess that's all I got to say."

"I certainly hope so," she said under her breath. She looked off in the direction the stage had gone and then glanced back at the corral, where Abby was walking around the perimeter. She turned once again to Rooster. "How far do you think they've traveled?"

"Jed didn't seem like he was in a hurry. Couldn't be more than a few miles. Why are you interested?"

"You know. I can tell you're smiling."

"Only on the inside."

"Saddle Abby for me, will you?" Laurel didn't wait for a reply. She headed for the house to get her gun. She wasn't planning on shooting anyone, but it defied common sense to be out on her own without a weapon.

Mrs. Lancaster wanted to know where she was going when she came through the kitchen wearing her gun belt and carrying an empty canteen. Laurel didn't give her a satisfactory answer so the cook followed her out to the pump while she filled the canteen.

"I'll be back before the next stage arrives," Laurel told her as she began pumping.

Mrs. Lancaster set her hands on her ample hips. "You're not fooling me. You're going after him."

Laurel held the canteen under the flow of cold water. There was no need to ask who "him" was. "I'm not going *after* him. He's not a criminal."

"Could be he is. Sure enough stole your heart."

Laurel made a sour face. "You realize you sound ridiculous."

"Maybe so. Doesn't make it less true."

"Hmm." Laurel capped the canteen and slung the strap across her shoulders. "I won't be long." Ignoring the cook's deep chuckle, Laurel headed for the barn, where Rooster had Abby saddled and waiting. The Booker brothers were nearby, watching her with identical, knowing grins on their faces. It was disconcerting that everyone knew what she was about, but at least no one would have reason to call her coward again.

"You know what you're going to say?" asked Rooster when Laurel was in the saddle.

"No idea."

He handed Laurel the reins. "You got time to think it over. I figure it'll come to you."

Laurel was not as optimistic as her right-hand man. In

truth, she was hoping that the mere fact of showing up would speak for her. She wanted to believe Call wouldn't require an explanation. She had been struck on more than one occasion by his ability to know her mind, sometimes before she knew it herself. Given that their acquaintance was not much more than a month long, it was remarkable. And if she was being honest, it was also a little frightening.

Clicking her tongue, Laurel turned Abby toward the trail. She didn't look back, but she imagined Rooster was grinning as stupidly as the Booker brothers.

Call rode beside the stage when he was able, ahead of it on the climbs, and hung back during the steep descents. When he and Artemis followed, it was at a distance large enough to keep from eating the coach's dust. Jed Holloway peppered him with questions when he rode alongside, mostly about his experience with Overland, and Call answered those easily. It was when Jed asked what Call thought about the robbery that Call played his cards closer to his vest.

Digger Leary evinced no interest in Call at all. Once again, Call was struck by the shotgun's recovery from his bout of drinking the night before. It was possible that Digger's age accounted for his ability to avoid the consequences of overindulgence. In Call's estimation, the shotgun wasn't more than twenty-five, certainly young enough to throw off the effects of heavy consumption that bedeviled most people.

Call held Artemis back as the stage began another winding descent. The coach's progress was slow enough that he decided to dismount and walk beside his mare for a while. As it happened, it was a good decision because it allowed him to hear the approach of a horse and rider coming up behind.

Hand poised to draw his gun if needed, Call turned to face the rider. "Jesus, Laurel, I might have shot you."

It was not the greeting she had hoped for. "Hardly.

Your gun is still holstered." She thought he might approach, but he stood in place, looking at her without expression now that his initial exasperation had vanished.

"You should be glad I'm cautious."

"Yes. I was depending on that." He didn't move. Neither did she. It was a standoff.

"What are you doing here?"

So much for him knowing her mind. Laurel realized an explanation was in order, an explanation that she did not have at the ready. In spite of the miles traveled, the words had never come. She dismounted and led Abby forward, holding up the mare when they still were ten feet distant. She removed her riding gloves and put them in her saddlebag and then turned to face him again. Her delaying strategy hadn't softened his features. His eyes, the ones she sometimes thought of as translucent as moonlight, were as opaque as a mountain glacier. "Why do you think I'm here?"

"No," he said. "I asked you. Has something happened at the station?"

She shook her head. "Nothing like that."

He waited. "Well?"

Laurel shifted her weight from foot to foot. Beside her, Abby stirred and snuffled. This was not precisely the location for this conversation that she had imagined, but then there was not another private setting like the falls between her station and the next one. She was standing in the middle of a narrow and dusty trail, holding on to her mare's reins as though grasping a rope that was meant to pull her free of quicksand. Six feet to her right the trail was edged by rocks and scraggly pines and nothing else but air. A drop over the side was almost certain death. No more than eight feet to her left, the side of the mountain rose almost vertically. She had only two routes open to her, retreat or forge ahead. Laurel chose the latter.

"Rooster called me a coward," she said. "I suppose I'm here to prove I'm not."

"I'm not sure I understand." Watching her, observing

her discomfort, he amended his previous statement. "No. I take that back. I'm sure I do *not* understand."

Laurel looked down. She chuckled softly, uneasily. "I thought you would, you know."

"Did you?"

"Uh-huh." She stole a glance at him. "I'm here because I haven't been fair to you."

"In what way? Look at me, Laurel. What is it you're wanting to say?"

She did look at him. Holding his gaze just then was harder than it ever had been. "I've treated you badly these last few days, ever since we came back from the falls really. I shouldn't have done that. I behaved like a child, worse actually, because I'm not a child. Avoiding you, not speaking to you, acting as though you didn't exist. When I think back on it, I'm ashamed of myself, but I wasn't at the time. At the time it seemed right. More than that. It seemed necessary." Now it was Laurel who waited for a response and it was a long time coming.

"I know what you did," he said finally, flatly, loath for her to see his hurt. "What I don't know is why."

"You don't?"

Call could give her no quarter. He wasn't ready. After what she had been doing to him, his response seemed justified. "I just said so, didn't I?"

Laurel sucked in a breath. In the back of her mind, she heard Rooster call her a coward, and that more than anything else prompted her to tell him the truth. "I was afraid."

"Of me," he said.

Her eyebrows lifted. "No! Of course not. Of me."

"What?"

"I didn't trust *me* to be around you. I was afraid of making a fool of myself. And I would have, too. There's a reason I'm standing a good ten feet from you now. That's by design. I am done embarrassing myself." She raised a hand, palm out, in the event he thought he should be the one to move.

He stared at her hand for a moment then his remote

eyes returned to her. "You can put that down. You're in no danger from me."

Laurel lowered her hand. "I know that. I'm trying to explain that you're the one in danger."

"Laurel. That's ridiculous."

"You'd think so, wouldn't you? Humor me."

"You said you were done embarrassing yourself. When do you think you did that?"

"You know."

"In case you haven't realized, I'm not in the habit of asking questions that I already know the answer to."

"You're angry."

"I'm annoyed. You followed me to prove to Rooster and maybe to yourself that you're not a coward, but I'm not certain anything you've said demonstrates that. Tell me straight, Laurel. When do you think you embarrassed yourself?"

Laurel pressed her lips together. Her nostrils flared slightly as she breathed deeply through her nose. She emptied her lungs on a long, calming exhale. "At the falls," she said. "What I did with you there . . ."

"I kissed you. You kissed me back."

"Yes."

"How is that embarrassing?"

"I hardly knew what I was doing."

"Did it seem as though I minded?"

"So then you *did* realize how green I was."

"Why is that important? May I point out that you took to it like a mouse to cheese?"

Laurel flushed. "A mouse to cheese?" She tapped the holster at her side. "I'm wearing my gun."

A slim smile touched Call's mouth, the first one since he'd turned and seen her. "Yes. I noticed. What about like a blossom to sunshine?"

Laurel's flush deepened. "Stop it." She nearly put out her hand again before she thought better of it. More softly, said, "Just stop."

"I'm not much for pretty verse. Sorry."

She gave him a withering look.

"Is there anything else?" he asked. Call was more at ease with that withering look than the penitent expression that had initially greeted him. "Anything else embarrassing, that is?"

Although he posed his question innocently enough, Laurel felt challenged. Her spine stiffened and her chin came up. "I wanted more," she said baldly. Was she still flushed? she wondered. Whatever she said would hardly be effective if her face was still pink. She was embarrassed by what she had been thinking then, not by what she was saying now.

"You wanted more," said Call.

"Yes."

"More kissing?"

"That," she said. "And more."

"All right. And that embarrassed you?"

She nodded.

"There's nothing wrong with what you were thinking, maybe even hoping for."

"Maybe not, if it's reciprocated. It wasn't. I'm green, Call, but I'm not ignorant. I knew the direction we were heading. You had other ideas, and I could barely help myself. If you had given me the least encouragement, I would have thrown myself at you. *That* is embarrassing to me."

A clearer picture of the last three days was forming in Call's mind, this time from Laurel's perspective. All of the avoidance, the absurdity of speaking to him through an intermediary when she simply wanted the potatoes passed, was because she was afraid of giving herself away, of doing something that would reveal her mind to a man she thought was not of a similar one.

Now Call was faced with how to respond. The truth had generally served him well so he decided to continue in that vein. "If you'd thrown yourself at me, I would have been flattered, Laurel. Taken aback some, but flattered. I would have welcomed your attention. You were not alone in wanting . . ." He hesitated, searching for the right word, and settled on the one she had used. "*More.* I did. I still do. But my experience counts for something, and I had to use it to call a halt because I was being unfair to you. It occurred to me that I was taking advantage."

"You weren't."

"Hmm. You say that now. The moment's past. You don't know that you'd be thinking that way if the outcome at the falls had been different."

Shaking her head almost imperceptibly, Laurel frowned. "I don't understand you."

"What don't you understand?"

"You grew up in a brothel. Your mother was a—"

"Whore," he finished for her when she snapped her mouth shut. "You can say it. What does that have to do with anything?"

"I don't know. I suppose I thought you wouldn't have, um, wouldn't have—"

"Scruples?"

She nodded. "Something like that. It sounds dreadful when I hear you say it."

"Not as appalling as you thinking it."

"I'm sure."

Call used a forefinger to tip his hat back as he regarded her candidly. "Growing up around whores was not what I think you imagine. Respect for women was bred in my bones. My mother made sure of it, and over the years, there were dozens of women I called aunt who did the same. So, yeah, I have scruples, Laurel. I've been known to take advantage at the card table, take advantage on the draw, take advantage of a cheat, but I never take advantage of a woman."

"That means the women you've known know as much as you."

"I'm not sure I'd put it that way, but that's the gist of it. That's why you're safe around me."

"I bet I wouldn't be if I got some experience."

Call's eyes widened fractionally. He felt as if he'd been gut punched. "What?"

She didn't respond to that. Instead, she asked, "How much experience would I have to get exactly?"

"Laurel."

"I mean it, Call. I'm not interested in you courting me. I'm not looking for a marriage proposal. I don't have a need to be a wife. And there is no danger of falling in love with you. Are you hearing me?"

"Does Rooster know you were going to say all this when you chased me down?" He saw a muscle twitch in her cheek as she clamped her jaw closed. "Yes," he said. "I heard what you said to him."

"Good. I need you to hear this as well. Since meeting you, I've come to realize that I have a hankering to know what I don't know now. I'd rather know it because I'm learning it from you, but if your scruples forbid, then I'll learn it elsewhere. I need you to tell me how much I need to know firsthand so you won't feel as if you're taking advantage. I figured you for my first, but now I'm thinking you'll be last."

"Jesus," Call said under his breath. He lifted his hat, raked his hair with his fingers, and settled the hat back on his head. "Jesus. Who else knows you're a lunatic?"

Disappointed, Laurel asked, "Is that it? Is that all you have to say?"

"I'm catching my breath." Behind him in the distance, Call could hear the faint rumblings of the stagecoach and the echo of Jed Holloway's shouted commands. He didn't hear his name. He doubted they were aware that he was no longer following them. When they figured it out, they would not be returning for him. The stage had a schedule and he was not their responsibility.

Laurel stroked Abby's neck, waiting for Call to say something of consequence. She could have told him that she was catching her breath as well, but it was more important to her that he sit with silence and sort out what she'd said. She was *not* a lunatic.

"We cannot continue this conversation here and now," Call said. He waved an arm to indicate the yawning gulf on one side and the granite wall on the other. "Look at where we are, Laurel."

"I know where we are. I rode Abby hard to get here."

"Take her home," he said. "Take yourself home. I promise you that I'll seriously consider what you've said, and I need to know that you'll do the same. I'm not saying that you don't know your own mind, and I—"

Laurel interrupted, "You said I was out of my mind."

Call took a breath. "I shouldn't have. That was wrong." He observed that she was not particularly placated by his admission, but her mouth flattened and that meant she was going to allow him to finish. "And I have no right to ask you not to act on what you've said, but I'm asking anyway. Maybe you don't believe it, but to my way of thinking, you deserve so much more than what you say you want. That's worthy of a conversation on the porch swing or at the corral or even at the falls, but it's not something for here."

Laurel stopped stroking Abby's neck and lowered her hand. "All right," she said simply.

Relieved, Call nodded. "All right."

She removed her gloves from the saddlebag and put them on before she swung into the saddle. "How long before you reckon you'll be back?"

"A week at the outside."

"I probably can't find anyone inside of seven days to teach me the particulars of what you wouldn't, but give me that eighth day and I'll be lying down with one of the passengers in the hayloft. You think about that." Laurel was not at all unhappy to leave Call standing in the middle of the trail a little more slack-jawed than when she'd come upon him.

16

When Laurel returned to the station, no one asked her if she'd caught up to Call on the Cabin Creek Trail. That was a given. She could see they were curious about the outcome of that encounter, but they remained silent and waited to see if she would say anything. She didn't.

Stages came and went, and Laurel went about the business of operating the station. She hired the preacher's son to lend a hand doing odd jobs and running errands. Jellicoe Palmer, forever known as Jelly, was a gangly youth of fifteen with a cowlick that stood at attention no matter how many times he licked his palm and pressed it down. Laurel gave him an old hat on his second day so she didn't have to bear witness to what had become an unfortunate habit.

Laurel kept herself busy during the daylight hours, purposely avoiding thinking about all the things she'd said to Call. At night, though, there was nothing she could do to keep the conversation from rolling through her mind. Rather than try to force sleep that wouldn't come easily, she got out of bed and made a cup of tea that she drank on the porch swing or went for a walk with starlight as a guide. Sometimes that activity settled her mind.

Sometimes it didn't.

Call had two days yet before the week was up. She hadn't found a candidate to teach her what she wanted to know, and more important, she had no intention of doing so. It had been an idle threat, one of the few things she'd said to Call that she perhaps regretted. She was of two minds about it because the look on his face as she turned to go was satisfying, but that was hard to reconcile with the mean-spirited way she felt when she'd said it, or now, when she thought about it.

Laurel sat sideways on the swing, her back against the arm, one leg stretched out along the seat, the other bent over the side. She used her bare toes to give the swing a gentle push now and again. She'd come outside in her nightgown, a plain white shift with wide straps and a scooped neckline. The hem was rucked up to her knees and fluttered against her legs in response to the intermittent breeze. A light rain was falling. The air was fresh and clean and cool. The skin on her arms prickled but she was too comfortable to bother going inside for a blanket.

Rooster had been right to name her coward for letting Call leave without a reckoning, and so she'd set off to make her apology and lay out the truth of what she felt. What she'd said, though, was a revelation.

To her.

Every word she'd uttered tumbled through her mind now. It was as if she could taste them on her tongue. They were cold and bitter, but did that matter if they were also honest? *I'm not interested in you courting me. I'm not looking for a marriage proposal. I don't have a need to be a wife. And there is no danger of falling in love with you.* For whose benefit had she said those things?

Had she spoken them to ease his mind or her own? McCall Landry had opened a door for her, and she was prepared to step through it and damn the consequences. She wanted what she'd never had, the intimacy of a man's touch, the heat of his body, whispered endearments against her ear. The things that embarrassed also excited. She hadn't fully comprehended that until she stood facing him on the trail. She *would* have thrown herself at him if he'd come too close after their encounter at the falls. She'd been truthful about that. Hearing him say he would have been flattered but also had sense enough not to take advantage was lowering. Call was just that much of a gentleman that he probably thought he was being gallant.

She didn't want gallant. Not now. There was a time when her head would have been turned by a chivalrous, unselfish gesture. Surely she was not the only girl who dreamt of armored knights jousting for her affection or braving the king's wrath to ask for her hand in marriage. But she was not that girl and hadn't been for a very long time. She just hadn't known it.

Call bore some responsibility for her realization. For once she was not taking it all on her shoulders. Whether he'd intended it or not, his presence had provoked an awakening. What she felt was more basic than that. It was a want. Perhaps a need.

It was necessary. How had she not understood that? McCall Landry had uncovered some vital part of her, a part that she'd buried so deeply she'd forgotten its existence. He was no kind of gentleman not to make good use of it.

She would tell him that.

She would make him believe she meant every word of what she'd said. It would be all right, then. He would understand.

Call took off his hat long enough to slap it against his thigh and be rid of the accumulation of raindrops clinging to the brim. It was no longer raining, but the wind was still stirring the trees. As the leaves turned over, heavy drops fell on his hat and the caped shoulders of his duster. He was mostly dry. Occasionally a trickle of water found its way under his collar and slipped down his spine. He could have been annoyed by it, but he chose not to be because it kept him awake.

Earlier, he'd fallen asleep in the saddle and woken when Artemis sensed his inattention and stopped cold. He couldn't even say how long he'd slept. He doubted it was more than a few minutes, but to keep it from happening again, he dismounted and began walking. Artemis deserved relief from the burden of carrying him. She'd been an admirable companion these last five days, standing at the ready whenever he needed her, nearly indefatigable even when their journey went sideways.

Running Digger Leary to ground had never been part of his plan. Call didn't know why he hadn't expected Digger to try to escape. The man had made every effort to avoid him at Morrison Station, and there was no reason to suppose cornering him elsewhere was going to be any easier. Still, Call had been caught unawares, and when Digger disappeared at the last living station before Denver, Call was late discovering it.

The most obvious destination for Digger was Denver, and Call was not at all confident he could find the shotgun rider if he got that far. It didn't come to that. The mount Digger stole from the living station was more horse than he could handle. Digger's skill was shooting, not riding, and when his horse proved reluctant to move off the familiar trail, Digger was forced to stay on the main route and hope that speed, if not strategy, would keep him out of Call's sights.

Call was tempted to shoot the man partly for the aggravation he caused, but mainly for the fact that Digger's run meant Call was that much farther from Morrison Station and the time for returning was growing steadily shorter. Hauling Digger into the offices of Henderson Express on Larimer Street turned out to be a wiser tactic than frog-marching him to the county sheriff. Sheriff Dave Cook had a fair reputation as a law-and-order man. Sam Henderson was only interested in getting the job done.

It took two days, but it got done. Digger Leary held out longer than Call had anticipated, but then the man had quite a bit to lose. There was his share of the payroll money, which he swore he had yet to see, but there was also the matter of finding his neck in a noose, given the fact that he'd stolen a horse from the stage line. The law looked on that as unkindly as Sam Henderson. By the time the sheriff arrived to take custody of Digger, the shotgun rider was visibly shaken, some because he hadn't had a drop of liquor in several days, but more because he saw his fate come to get him.

Call spent another full day in Denver trying to track Josey Pye. The sheriff even spared a few deputies for the search, but it came to nothing. Mr. Pye was in the wind and so was the Stonechurch payroll.

Call led Artemis directly to the barn, where he removed her saddle and rubbed her down. He led the mare to her stall, closed the door, and stroked her nose before he bade her good night. Some of the other mares nickered softly as he passed their stalls on his way out. All was quiet again by the time he slid the barn door closed.

Call had every intention of heading for his bunk, but lamps burning inside the farmhouse caught his eye. Was Laurel still awake, reading perhaps? He was not going to disturb her so he didn't know why he turned toward the house, but he felt an unmistakable draw and answered it. He veered toward the front porch, which was familiar territory, and thought he might take to the swing for what remained of the night and leave his bunkmates undisturbed.

It was only as he approached from the side that he saw the swing was already occupied. Laurel's head lolled to one side, but her back was to him and he couldn't see if she was sleeping. It was a good guess that she was because she'd have seen or at least heard his approach when he and Artemis returned. He couldn't imagine that she wouldn't have made herself known. The way she'd left things, he had no doubt that she still had words for him.

He stepped lightly onto the porch, set his saddlebag down, and eased into a rocker. Call set his boots flat on the floor to keep the rocker from creaking. He removed his hat and let his head fall back and closed his eyes. He could sleep here. Next to her. It would be all right if he could just sleep.

It might have been the movement of the swing that woke

him or the soft metallic shifting of the chains as Laurel rose. He watched from under heavily lidded eyes as she disappeared into the house. In the darkness she was mostly a slender wraith, compliments of her white shift and her grace. She moved so silently that it was easy to imagine that she floated above the floor rather than stepped on it.

He didn't expect to see her again, but he was too tired to move so he stayed where he was. His concession to fatigue and her absence was to stretch his legs and let the rocker groan noisily as he shifted his weight. He was about to nod off when Laurel suddenly appeared with a blanket.

"No," she said. "Don't get up unless you want to. You don't look as if you want to."

"I don't."

Nodding, she unfolded the blanket and covered him with it but stopped short of tucking him in. That, she judged, was a step too close to mothering and not at all how she wanted to be thought of. "Good night, Call."

"Mm."

Laurel smiled and started to leave. She stopped when he caught her hand. "Yes?"

"Don't go."

She eased her fingers out of his and let her hand fall to her side. "You're all but asleep."

"Stay anyway. I'll sleep better. You can have the blanket." He started to raise it, but she gently pushed it back. "Keep it. I'll get another."

Call wasn't sure he trusted her to return and almost said so. Some inkling of good sense kept him from saying it aloud, and he willed himself to stay awake while she was in the house. During his time away, he'd thought a lot about falling asleep lying next to her. This wasn't exactly as he had imagined, but it was a good beginning.

It wasn't long before she was back, more difficult to see now because she was wrapped in a dark wool blanket similar to the one she'd laid over him. She curled up in the same corner of the swing she had vacated earlier.

Call closed his eyes. "What were you doing out here?"

"You should be sleeping, not speaking."

"I might fall asleep before I hear your answer. Humor me."

"It was stuffy in my room. I couldn't open a window because of the rain so I came out on the porch." It was true, just not all of the truth. "I wasn't expecting you to arrive at night."

"But you were expecting me. That's nice." He smiled sleepily. "It's nice to be expected."

"Were you successful?" she asked.

Call required a moment to understand that she was asking what had happened during his absence. "Yes," he said. "And no."

"Do you want to tell me more?"

"Later."

Laurel didn't press. It started to rain again, lightly at first and then harder. Hearing it reminded her of the falls, and she was gently lulled to sleep by sound and memory.

Call woke when there was just a sliver of sunlight breaking through the overcast sky. It looked to be a long day of rain, and as though to confirm his suspicion, thunder rolled from somewhere beyond the mountains.

He groaned softly, stretching, and sat up. He started to throw back the blanket and realized he was covered by two. He looked sideways to where Laurel had been sitting. She was gone but she'd left him with her blanket. He snapped them open one at a time and neatly folded them. Rising to his feet, he dropped them on the swing, picked up his hat and saddlebag, and headed for the bunkhouse.

When Call entered, Rooster stirred but didn't speak. Dillon and Hank were deep under their covers. Call thought it was doubtful they even heard him. Three bodies occupied other bunks. Call recognized a driver and shotgun rider from previous trips. The third fellow was a mere stripling, younger than the Bookers and with even less meat on his bones. He looked vaguely familiar, but Call couldn't place where he'd seen him before and couldn't fathom why he was sleeping in the bunkhouse.

Call dropped his saddlebag on the chest at the foot of his bed and sat on the bunk. He removed his duster and hat, tossed them over the saddlebag, and then lay back. He had perhaps a half hour of shut-eye before everyone would start to rise. He wanted to take advantage of every minute of it.

Call washed up after chores and before breakfast so he came to the table looking less bleary-eyed than he felt. Rooster had introduced him to the new hire while they were moving horses to the corral for exercise, and Jelly Palmer, the preacher's kid, was sitting in what Call thought of as his seat. Call was not amused that after being gone only five days, there was a stripling occupying his chair. Dillon and Hank snickered as he waved the boy to scoot over. Even Rooster smiled. Only Laurel failed to think there was anything humorous about the gesture or Jelly's hasty compliance.

"Don't you sleep in your own bed at night?" Call asked as Jelly passed him a platter of scrambled eggs.

"Mostly."

When he didn't elaborate, Laurel said, "I told him he could bunk with everyone else since it was raining so hard when he was done for the day."

Jelly nodded. "And I was plenty grateful. Still am. Miss Laurel is all kindness. Everyone says so."

It wasn't possible to miss the boy's doe-eyed admiration. Jelly was smitten. If Laurel knew, she didn't attend to it, but the Booker brothers wiggled their eyebrows while exchanging sly grins. Rooster kicked one of them under the table. Call got the other.

"How goes your investigation?" Rooster asked Call as he speared a sausage link. "Learn anything about the money?"

Dillon didn't wait for Call to answer. "What about Josey Pye? You come across his sorry self?"

Call had avoided answering questions while they went about their chores, but there was no putting them off now, and he really didn't want to. Everyone but Jelly had a stake in what he found out. Call looked sideways at the boy, taking his measure. Jelly seemed to understand because he raised a forefinger to his sealed lips and held it there. Call might have laughed if the boy had not been so in earnest.

"I'm not back here with the Stonechurch Mining payroll," said Call.

"That's disappointing," said Hank. "I wagered Dillon that you'd return with it."

Call's smile was wry. "Yes. Disappointing."

"I only meant—"

"I know what you meant," Call said. "I didn't find Josey Pye or come back with Penelope either. Did you have wagers on that?"

"No, sir," said Hank.

"No, sir," said Dillon.

"I did have an interesting conversation with Digger Leary, though. You understand that he was an accomplice in the robbery, don't you?"

Everyone but Laurel regarded him blankly.

Rooster said, "He wasn't riding shotgun on the day of the robbery."

"That's right," Call said. "His absence was the message. It told Josey Pye that the payroll was on board. Mr. Stonechurch was expecting the payroll to be delivered the following day, but because Sam Henderson caught a rumor that some fellows were showing an unnatural interest in the stage, the timing was changed. There were very few people who knew, Brady and Digger being the most important. When Digger claimed the previous night's drinking left him with a hangover that prevented him from riding, Brady went on alone. Even if he had taken on another shotgun, the message would have been the same because Digger was always Brady's partner."

Call bit off the end of a sausage link, chewed, and swallowed. He was aware they were following his every word, but damn, he was hungry. Mrs. Lancaster had come into the dining room with a coffeepot and now she was standing beside Laurel at the table's head simply holding it, hanging on his explanation.

"When Digger didn't arrive, Josey knew it was time to act on their plan. Digger denies it was his idea, but I'm not so sure. At this juncture, it's not what's most important. Recovering the money is."

Hank asked, "How did Josey get at the strongbox? I don't understand that. All of us were around."

"It only required a few minutes of inattention. You had no reason to watch his every move. You were all going about your business. He replaced the strongbox with a nearly identical box with newspaper clippings and a bag of pebbles and stones to add the weight of coins. Miss Morrison and I found the box from the stage in one of the chests in the bunkhouse. Josey didn't hide the strongbox in his own chest, where it might be connected to him. He hid it in one of the other chests. In fact, he used the one at the foot of the bed where Jelly slept last night."

Jelly's wide grin split his face. "Well, ain't I just that much tickled? I never been so close to nefarious goings-on before."

Call and Laurel chuckled while Dillon and Hank rolled their eyes. Rooster shook his head and Mrs. Lancaster clucked her tongue and began pouring coffee.

"You weren't all that close now," said Call. "Digger took the box the last time he was here."

Shoulders slumping, Jelly said, "And here I was all set to get a look at it. How'd you know he made off with it?"

"I checked for it before and after." His gaze circled the table. "Any of you have it?" Call was met by shaking heads all around. "Didn't think so."

Rooster said, "If you're asking us, I reckon that means you didn't find it when you caught up with him."

"You're right. I didn't expect to. If I'm going to be able to put my hands on it, it'll be because that box is still here in Falls Hollow."

Laurel regarded Call over the rim of her coffee cup. "Really?"

Before Call could respond, young Jelly said, "Buried, I bet. Buried deep. That's what pirates do."

"Digger ain't a pirate," said Hank.

Jelly was unperturbed. "Land pirate, then."

Call said, "It's just an empty strongbox, Jelly. There's no treasure in it."

"Oh. Right. I forgot. So where do you think it is?"

Shrugging, Call said, "Around."

"Unfair," said Dillon. "I know you got suspicions."

Behind her cup, Laurel smiled. "I believe he's accusing you of holding out on us."

"I'm playing my cards close," Call said without apology. "I have to for now. I want to be sure."

Laurel nodded, understanding, but Dillon and Hank grumbled under their breath.

Rooster buttered a piece of toast. "You boys got something to say, then say it."

Neither young man spoke up. They ducked their towheads and continued eating.

"Thought so," said Rooster. His attention shifted from his toast to Call. "Digger wouldn't give up Josey?"

"No. If it wasn't so frustrating, I might admire his loyalty."

"Loyalty? That's not a word I'd associate with Digger Leary. Then again, I didn't know him all that well. Came and went, and even when he was here, he was mostly there." Rooster tipped his head in the direction of town. "The man had an appetite for liquor and—" He stopped speaking abruptly and then finished lamely. "For liquor."

Laurel set down her cup. "It's all right, Rooster. I have a good idea where Digger spent his time in town."

Call said, "I no longer think Digger was the drinker he portrayed himself to be. That was a ruse to spend time with Josey Pye and make him seem less capable than he was."

Laurel forked some scrambled eggs and looked at Call. "Is it possible Digger's silence has nothing to do with loyalty? Could he simply be ignorant?"

Hank's head jerked up at this notion. "You mean maybe he doesn't know where Josey is?"

"Yes, Hank. That's what I'm asking Call."

"Oh, right. Guess I'm thinking ignorant suits Digger better than loyal."

Dillon elbowed his brother. "What do you know about it? He hardly spoke to you. To either one of us."

"That's what I'm sayin'. Ignorant."

Laurel cleared her throat and eyed each brother in turn. Whatever Dillon was about to say stayed on the tip of his tongue, and Hank filled his mouth with an entire sausage link and started chewing. Satisfied with their silence, Laurel turned back to Call. "What do you think?"

"It's entirely possible that he doesn't know. Sam Henderson and I talked it over but we concluded that Digger wasn't giving Josey up because he was still hoping he'd get his share of the money. We hadn't yet included the sheriff in our interrogation. Digger believed he was going to get away from us. I think he believes it even now. Can't figure why he's so sure a cell won't hold him except maybe that he thinks Josey Pye is going to break him out."

"Is that likely?" asked Laurel.

"I can't think of a reason that Josey would risk capture and all the money to help Digger escape. Can you?"

She shook her head.

Jelly asked, "How do you know Josey Pye has all the money?"

"I don't," said Call. "I only know that Digger never got his share. I talked to folks at the station and they were able to account for Digger's whereabouts. They were confident that Josey and Digger never met up, and they also swore that Josey never passed through the station. He went off the trail at some point."

"You think he's in Denver?" asked Rooster.

"I think Digger thinks he's in Denver. Sheriff Cook is keeping an eye out along with every member of his Rocky Mountain Detective Association."

Dillon whistled softly. "Never knew there was such a thing."

Call nodded. "It hasn't been around long, but the sheriff believes they're effective as a group. If he's right, Josey Pye won't be a free man forever." Call pushed his plate away and sat back. He picked up his coffee cup. "That's it. You know what I know and about half of what I suspect." His eyes swiveled to Laurel. "I'd like to send a message to Mr. Stonechurch. Let him know about Digger."

Laurel was surprised he hadn't done that from Denver. "Of course. We can do that this morning."

"Thank you." He turned to the rest of the table. "So tell me what I missed while I was away."

17

Laurel tapped out the message that Call dictated. It was short but covered the salient points of his investigation. If Call was unhappy that he did not have better news to deliver, he didn't express it. He also didn't make excuses. Recovering the payroll was always an uncertain outcome, though perhaps he didn't share her opinion.

Turning away from the telegraph machine when Call ended the message, Laurel discovered he was no longer standing beside her desk but seated in her chair behind it. He started to rise when she came toward him, but she waved him back down. It would have been petty to make him vacate her comfortable chair when he'd just spent most of the night in a rocker. She took one of the guest chairs. Pulling her heavy braid forward over her shoulder, she then massaged the back of her neck.

"Crick?" he asked.

Laurel nodded. "You?"

"Shoulders." He rolled them twice to work out the kinks. "I won't be sleeping like that again anytime soon."

Laurel couldn't say the same for herself so she said nothing.

"I met your Mr. Alexander Berry while I was in Denver."

She felt it was incumbent upon her to say that the government man was not *her* Mr. Berry, but after she'd made that clear, she asked, "How did that come about?"

"He stopped in Sam Henderson's office while I was

there. Digger Leary, as luck would have it, was tied to a chair in a back room and insensible of the interruption."

She stared at him. "Do I want to know what you and Sam were doing to Digger?"

"Probably not the particulars. Sam would tell you that we were convincing him to do right by the stage line that had employed him these last five years."

Laurel understood that Sam felt betrayed because she did as well. She could imagine planting her fist in Digger's nose given the opportunity and was not uncomfortable with the thought. "Tell me about Mr. Berry. Was there conversation or merely an introduction?"

"An introduction in Sam's office, but I learned where he was staying and visited his hotel around dinnertime. He graciously offered to share his table."

Laurel nodded. "I wager he wanted to hear about your investigation. Sam probably told him right off that you were working for Mr. Stonechurch."

"He did. Sam's as anxious as you not to have any blame for the robbery attached to him or his business. When I told him I was going to speak to Berry later, he was encouraging. In fact, he gave me a handful of things he thought I should mention."

"Sounds like Sam. Were you able to bring up his points?"

"I think I got around to all of them. Though between discussing the robbery, Stonechurch Mining, and Morrison Station, I might have missed one."

"You discussed the station?"

"Of course. I only had two reasons for seeking him out. One regarded your home station and the second regarded you. If I wasn't able to convince him of your innocence in the theft, then he wasn't listening. He was complimentary about your operation of the station so there wasn't much I could add there without gilding the lily. I got the sense that he's keeping his options open, though. He talked at length about the advantages of an alternate route to Stonechurch. He has a surveyor who's out there now."

Laurel did not try to hide her disappointment. "That doesn't bode well. Did he give you the impression he was open to a bribe?"

Call hesitated.

"Call?"

"Yes," he said finally. "He did."

"I don't suppose he was so indiscreet as to mention an amount."

"No. No amount."

"Did he happen to mention the Hammersmiths? That's the family that would benefit from the alternate route."

"He brought them up when he was talking about the surveyor, but he didn't indicate that there was an offer on the table."

"Perhaps that's reason enough to be hopeful." She smiled faintly. "Thank you for your effort to clear my name. I have to believe he heard you."

"You're welcome, but I got the impression that he was predisposed to hearing what I had to say."

A tiny crease appeared between Laurel's dark eyebrows. "Really? Why do you think that?"

Call supposed he couldn't avoid it forever. "Alex Berry likes you."

"Of course he does. I've never given him any reason to dislike me."

"I'm sure that's true, but you're not hearing my meaning. He *likes* you."

The vertical crease between her eyebrows deepened. "I think you must be mistaken."

"You can believe that if it gives you comfort."

"Of course it gives me comfort. It's a ridiculous notion." She paused and then set her thoughtful gaze on Call. "Or the answer to the niggling problem of finding a proper man to further my education."

Call made a steeple with his fingers and propped his chin on the tips. "And now you know the reason for my earlier hesitation. It didn't take you long to identify the silver lining in Berry's interest."

Unperturbed by his cynicism, Laurel shrugged and said carelessly, "It's only a silver lining if you mean to maintain your scruples. I would happily allow you to take his place."

He stared at her. "You're serious."

"I am."

"Do you understand that Berry could be persuaded to recommend the Cabin Creek Trail for the railroad if you agreed to sleep with him?"

Laurel sat up straight. "What?"

"You don't need money to bribe him, Laurel. He wants you."

She made a face of pure disgust. "That is revolting."

Call actually laughed. "You'll have to explain to me how Berry using you is different than you using Berry."

"It's just different is all."

"Uh-huh."

"Apparently I have scruples."

"You don't seem pleased to learn about it."

"I can't say the same for you. You're smirking."

Call felt the shape of his mouth with his fingertips. "Huh. You're right. That's a smirk."

Laurel waited for his hand to drop away. When he leaned back and folded his arms across his chest, she said, "I haven't changed my mind. I did what you asked me to do. I thought about what I wanted. I thought about it a lot. Nothing's changed. If anything, my mind's more settled."

Every vestige of humor was absent from Call's features now. "You said some things out there on the trail that I've been wondering about."

"Yes?"

"You don't want to be courted."

"It seems unnecessary, don't you think?"

"Maybe." He tilted his head to one side as his eyes rested on her face. Her dark gaze was without guile. She wasn't teasing him. It wasn't in her to play him for a fool. She hadn't asked him for protection, probably would have resisted if it was offered, and yet he couldn't shake the feeling that she was vulnerable. It might have been the light spray of freckles across her nose that made her seem younger than her years and lent the impression of naïveté. Or it could have been the heavy chestnut braid that lay over her shoulder, wisps of hair escaping it at every twist that made him think of a girl just graduated from the school-room.

It was her mouth, though, her perfectly shaped mouth with its full lower lip, that dispelled the impression of innocence, especially when she opened it and sass spilled out. It was perhaps unfortunate for him that he liked her sass.

"You told me you weren't looking for a marriage proposal," he said.

"I'm still not."

"And you had no interest in being a wife."

"You're remembering it all quite well."

"There was one more thing."

Laurel nodded. Against her will, she could feel heat creeping into her cheeks. She might wish he wouldn't repeat it, but she couldn't very well ask him not to. Under no circumstances would she give herself away.

"You said you're in no danger of falling in love with me. Do I have that right?"

"You know you do."

"Hmm. I wonder if during my absence you might have considered what *I* want." When she had no immediate response, he cocked an eyebrow and waited her out.

"I thought those things I said *were* what you wanted. I thought they were holding you back and that it would ease your mind to hear me say them. I asked you once when we were sitting on the porch together if you were courting me."

"I remember. You were teasing."

"Doesn't matter. You almost choked on the notion."

"I was teasing you."

"Really? Because it didn't seem that way."

"All right. Maybe I wasn't teasing, but I've warmed to the idea since."

One of Laurel's eyebrows rose in a perfect arch. "You *want* to court me? I don't believe you."

"Huh. I hadn't anticipated not being believed. Should I pick some flowers and bring them to you? Ask you to walk with me? Maybe we could actually share that porch swing in front of witnesses."

In spite of herself, Laurel's lips twitched. "You've made your point. Please stop. Please."

Call pressed his lips together but only long enough to lull her into thinking he was done. "About that marriage proposal." He ignored her soft groan. "As you indicated, courting generally leads to that end, so I've been thinking about it, and proposing marriage doesn't sound as disagreeable as you made it seem." He put up a hand when he saw she was about to speak. "Doesn't mean you have to say yes. You have to keep that in mind."

She snorted lightly. "Be careful, Call. I might say yes just to see you run for the hills. That'd be a sight."

"I suppose it would, but you shouldn't count on it." He observed that Laurel took him seriously because she sobered. "As for you not wanting to be a wife, well, that's tricky. Marriage makes a woman a wife by definition. Now I don't hold to all the conventions, so if the woman I marry wants to call herself a companion, a friend, a lover, a partner, well, I'm good with that." He paused. "Are you tempted yet?"

Laurel feigned surprise. "Oh, you were talking about me? I thought you were speaking about the woman you marry."

"Amusing," he said in a way that let her know it was not. "As for your last statement about you being in no danger of falling in love with me, well, that struck me as kinda worrisome. I mean it could easily go the other way. You understand what I'm saying?"

"I'm not sure."

"I'm trying to figure out what happens if I fall in love with you."

The arch in Laurel's eyebrow defined cynical. "Have you?" she asked coolly.

A glimmer of a smile touched Call's lips. "Butter doesn't much melt in your mouth, does it?"

"Not much." Laurel was careful to keep her eyes on his and not glance at his smile. That smile stirred her heart in ways that could not possibly be good. "Well, have you?" she asked, repeating her question.

"No," he said, sobering. His smile was a shadow now. "I haven't fallen yet. Tripped some and caught myself before I went head over bucket, but the danger's there. Do you have any ideas about what I should do if it happens? I'm thinking you wouldn't like it."

Laurel didn't know if she'd like it or not. She said the first thing that came to her mind. "It would complicate matters."

"Yeah. Probably."

"You've been in love before. What did you do then?"

"What makes you think I've been in love? Have you?"

Laurel blinked. She wasn't prepared to have the question put to her. "No," she said finally, "but then I'm not—"

Call waited for her to finish her thought, but she shook her head and pressed her lips together. Curious, he prompted gently, "You're not what?"

"You know." She quickly shook her head, remembering what he'd told her about not being in the habit of asking questions he knew the answer to. "I'm sorry. I reckon I meant you *should* know. You're the one who made sure I was aware of your experience."

"All right," he said. "What is it about you that I should know? What is it that you're not?"

Laurel realized he had the bit between his teeth and wasn't going to let go. "I'm not pretty like you. I don't attract bees to my blossom the way you do."

Call sat up. "Wait a minute. Did you just say I was pretty and compare me to a flower?"

"Yeah. I guess I did."

"Huh." He regarded her with interest. "You think I'm pretty?"

Laurel's regard was shrewd. "You know you are."

He shrugged. "What kind of flower?"

She was certain he was enjoying himself just a little too much. She made a pinching motion with her thumb and fingers. "A snapdragon."

"Oh. Something manly, then."

Laurel threw up her hands.

"Are you surrendering?" he asked.

"No. I'm exasperated because you are exasperating."

"No more than you are," he said seriously. "How do you come by the ridiculous notion that I'm prettier than you and that bees don't circle your . . ." He gave her breasts a rakish leer. "Your, um, blossoms? If I didn't know you better, I'd say you were fishing for a compliment, but I'm afraid you believe every word you said."

"I'm not fishing."

"I just said you weren't, didn't I?" Call's lower lip thrust forward as he blew out a breath. "Shall I tell you what I think?"

"Could I stop you?"

He went on as if she hadn't spoken. "I think you wouldn't know a bee unless it stung you. I counted four men crowding around you after Sunday services, and none of them was Rooster or the boys. Jelly trips over his own feet because he's busy watching you."

"Jelly's a baby."

"Trust you to focus on that and not the men hovering around you after church. Did you even notice them?"

"I've known three of them all my life and the other one about half of it. Of course I noticed them. You saw me speaking to them, didn't you?"

"There's speaking to them and then there's giving them the time of day. I don't think you give anyone the latter. With the least encouragement from you, more than one of them would be at your door with flowers and an invitation to go walking. Why don't you encourage them?"

"I told you, I've known them for what seems forever."

"So?"

"So you're mistaken about their interest. It's in the station, not in me."

Call wondered if that could possibly be true or if that's what she told herself to keep would-be suitors at arm's length. "What about Josey Pye?"

"What about him? If you're asking if I noticed him, I did, and I didn't appreciate his attention. I had the impression he thought I was easy pickings. I'm not, you know, in spite of everything I've said to you that points to the contrary."

"I'm clear on that. There is nothing about you that's easy."

Laurel did not mistake that for a compliment. "This station is my life, Call. I don't necessarily like being hard, but I can't afford to be easy."

"Why me, Laurel?"

She understood what he was asking, but she tapped humor to try to avoid answering. "Besides the fact that you're pretty?"

Call didn't smile. "Don't."

Laurel sobered. "All right. You're not long for this place. You're doing a job and then you'll move on. I've never heard you indicate that you want to stay around, and you've never expressed an interest in the station that made me suspicious of your motives."

"Maybe I'm better at hiding it."

"I've thought of that, but you've always impressed me as saying whatever is on your mind. Do you want my station, Call?"

"No. But I envy what you have here. Took me by surprise when I realized it, and I'm not as sure as you that I'll be moving. Not unless you boot me, that is."

"Oh. I didn't realize."

"Yeah. I didn't think you did. It seemed the fair thing to do was to tell you. If I agree to what you want from me, then you should know that there could be complications.

I reckon we'd have jumped right over the courting piece at that point, but that leaves me to wrestle with a proposal, marriage, being your husband, and falling ass over teakettle in love with you."

She simply stared at him.

Call couldn't tell if she was stunned or thinking. He decided it was time to point out what had never been discussed. "There's the matter of maybe being a father that we haven't talked about. I don't have any bastards, leastways not that anyone's ever told me. Being one myself, you can imagine that it doesn't set well with me. I need you to chew on that because everything you think you don't want changes if I put a child in your belly."

Laurel's eyes dropped away from his. Her expression clouded as she pulled in her lower lip and began to worry it. She stopped tugging on her lower lip and looked at him again. "It'd just be the one time," she said carefully.

This was the first Call was hearing of it. He challenged her notion. "Are you certain? You don't sound certain. What if you get a taste for pirooting?"

"Please don't be crude."

"All right, then. What if you enjoy the experience so much that you want to repeat it? Or, and this is more likely, you find your first time doesn't meet your expectations and decide you want another bite of the apple?"

She shook her head. "It'd be the only time and it would be up to you to make it right. You're the one with the experience."

Call said nothing for a moment. He blew out a long breath, raked his hair with his fingers. "Jesus, Laurel, I don't think Lee and Grant dickered this much when they met up at Appomattox."

"Perhaps not, but one of them was surrendering. Neither of us is."

"Truer words," he said under his breath. "Look, Laurel, even if we lie together just the once, there's still a chance you can end up carrying a child."

"You said you don't have any bastards. You must know something about it that I don't."

He sighed. "I might, but then maybe I'm also lucky after a fashion."

"Hmm. Well, I can always ask Mrs. Fry. She's certain to know what to do."

Call almost came out of his chair. "For God's sake, don't do that. The ladies mostly use poisons, and that's after they discover they're pregnant. Preventing is entirely different."

"Maybe that's a bridge we will never have to cross."

Call did not yield gracefully, but he did yield. "Never mind," he said. "I'll take care of it."

"Then . . ."

It was hard for him to reconcile Laurel's dignified demeanor with the hopefulness he heard in her voice. "You're certain this is what you want?"

"I don't know how I could have propositioned you in plainer terms."

"That's just it, Laurel. You're approaching this as if it's a business transaction. It's not." He saw she was about to object and he stopped her. "Don't you *dare* offer to pay for my services."

Her lips parted. She came as close to gaping at him as she ever had. "Services?" she asked when she could speak. "Is that what you think?"

"Don't you? You've made it clear there is no chance of romantic entanglements on your part."

"Well, yes, but that was as much to relieve your mind as my own."

"Then let me decide how much I want to be relieved."

Her brow puckered and the corners of her mouth turned down. "What are you saying?"

"I never saw you as another piece of calico, Laurel. Not from the first. I was honest with you, made my interest clear. I enjoyed sitting with you, teasing and talking, listening to you plan the future of this station. I have respect for you and what you're doing here. I championed your innocence. I don't think it's going to come as a surprise that I like you, leastways most of the time, but maybe you don't know that I bear some affection for you, too." He watched her eyebrows lift a fraction. "That's right," he said. "Affection. You and me, Laurel, whatever it is that exists between us is about to become complicated."

Laurel gave no indication that she didn't doubt that he was right. Her feelings were already compromised, though she believed it was something better left unsaid. "What happens now?" she asked, getting her feet firmly under her.

"Yes," he said dryly. "Back to the particulars."

Laurel would not allow herself to be goaded. She regarded him candidly while she waited him out. He looked comfortable sitting behind her desk, leaning back in her chair. He had picked up her glass paperweight and was rolling it between his palms as he considered his response.

"Is this a clandestine coupling?" he asked, straight-faced. "How important is secrecy to you?"

"Oh, for goodness' sake. Everyone knows everything sooner or later. Why don't you just come to my room?"

"Ah, so you do have some idea of how we should proceed."

"I was thinking of my comfort."

"Of course. Your bedroom. Better than the falls. Not as fragrant as the barn. Perhaps less obvious than the two of us riding off together. I can be stealthy."

She pursed her lips disapprovingly. "No doubt, but it's not necessary."

"What about your reputation?"

"I'm hardly going to be a pariah. This town has had its share of scandals."

He thought she sounded overconfident, perhaps because she was in so deep that she no longer felt she could back down. He would make it a point to be careful even if she believed it wasn't important.

"Well?" she asked.

"Well, what?"

"When can I expect you to come to my room?"

The shadow of a smile crossed his face. He knuckled his beard. "About that, Laurel. I'm thinking it'll be better if I surprise you." With that, he pushed back from her desk and stood, leaving her in no doubt he was done with his side of their conversation.

18

Laurel changed her clothes after church services, relieved to be done with the corset and bustle and stockings and garters, all the things that confined her. She put on a faded blue shirt that was soft against her skin and a pair of well-worn trousers that still fit comfortably after being scrubbed against a washboard dozens of times. She rolled up her shirtsleeves until they were elbow length and slipped an old leather belt around her waist. Her hips mostly kept the trousers in place, but you could never be too careful, and suspenders invariably brought attention to breasts in a way she found more immodest than the deeply scooped bodice of her fanciest gown.

She saddled Abby herself, though Hank and Dillon both offered. She liked taking care of her mare, the quiet time they had together before she swung into the saddle. The boys asked where she was going, but she only gave them a vague answer because she didn't know herself. She felt restless and unsettled and simply needed to be away from the station for a few hours. There was nothing going on that someone else couldn't manage, and they weren't expecting a stage until the following afternoon.

Call was loitering by the corral when she rode by. She nodded to him and he touched the brim of his hat, acknowledging her. They'd had plenty of exchanges in the five days since they'd spoken in her office, but Call had yet to surprise her. Every day, every *night*, that she spent on her own made the next twenty-four hours just that much more fraught with the anxiety of anticipation. For his part, she thought he seemed perfectly untroubled. And why shouldn't he be? She had given him the reins when she should have kept them for herself.

For a while she let Abby wander the property. She passed the boarded-up mine entrances and saw that Call's work was still in place. It made her smile to remember how he'd made light of his own lack of skill with a hammer and nails. Under Rooster's guidance, he'd improved since then, learned how to hold a hammer properly so he could drive a nail in cleanly and mostly miss his thumb.

She remembered the kiss, too. How swift and sweet it had been. He had surprised her with it, and she wouldn't have minded at all if he had surprised her again.

It was inevitable, she supposed, that the wide circle she took around the station would eventually lead her to the falls. Although it seemed that Abby had taken the route on her own, Laurel knew that wasn't so, that without her gentle, almost imperceptible guidance, the mare would have followed a different path entirely.

Laurel didn't dismount immediately. She sat in the saddle for a time, content to watch the falling water and catch rainbows when sunlight illuminated the spray so that prisms appeared. Leaning forward, she patted Abby's neck and spoke to her gently before sliding off her back. Laurel led the mare to a shallow section of the stream away from the falls and let her drink briefly before tethering her to a juniper. Abby rubbed her hindquarters against the bark's red-brown scales, scratching an itch that hadn't seemed to bother her until now.

Lucky Abby, Laurel thought. She also had an itch and had been bothered by it far longer. Rubbing against the juniper trunk wasn't going to take care of it either.

She walked the short distance back to the deep pool at the base of the falls and stood at the edge of the flat slab of rock where she often perched when she was watching her brothers splash and dunk each other. She rarely joined them when they were roughhousing, preferring the safety of her stony seat. When they wore themselves out being idiots, she'd dive in and tug on their ankles, pulling them under. They'd play along for a while and then climb out and let her have the pool to herself. They never left her, though, and she'd never resented their watchfulness. They were good big brothers.

The memory tugged at her heart and she blinked back unexpected, though not unwelcome, tears. Hunkering down on the lip of the rock, Laurel dashed at her eyes. She smiled to herself, a little crookedly, a trifle watery, and began unbuttoning her shirt. When she removed the shirt, she folded it and placed it off to the side and behind her where it was in no danger of getting wet. She tossed her hat beside it and then stood again to remove her boots and belt and trousers. Finally she took off her socks and stuffed them inside her boots.

She didn't hesitate, then. Standing just a couple of feet above the water in her cotton camisole and knickers, she jumped in just as her brothers had taught her, knees clasped close to her chest so she was curled in a ball to make the biggest splash she could. The jump was accompanied by a shout because, well, that's the way it was done. She supposed they'd all hollered in anticipation of the cold that was waiting, but then again, it could have been the sheer joy of the leap and splash and dropping like a stone into the pool.

Laurel allowed herself to sink deeply and then uncurled so her feet touched the bottom and pushed up. She gasped when she resurfaced. The water was colder than she remembered, but then she had been younger and probably hadn't cared. Everything was a good adventure when you were of an age to enjoy it.

Treading water, she gazed up to where water spilled over the rocky ledge above her. She regarded the path she had once climbed to get there and shook her head at the sheer folly of it. She must have frightened George and

Martin near out of their britches when she took up their challenge. Chuckling at the remembrance of them scrambling after her, she breathed in a mouthful of water and sputtered and spit until she cleared her throat. Served her right, she thought, and this time when she chuckled, she was careful not to breathe in water.

The falls poured into the pool with enough force to hold Laurel back when she swam toward it. She dove under and was immersed in froth and bubbles. Holding her breath, she let the power of the falling water push her away. She drifted and reemerged in the relative calm of the middle of the pool. Strands of hair that had escaped her braid fell across her eyes and cheeks. She lowered her head back into the water so they floated away from her face and temporarily plastered themselves to the rest of her hair.

She swiped at her eyes and blinked away water, clearing her vision. What she saw had her wondering if she should dunk her head again or appreciate the view.

McCall Landry was standing on the same slab of stone where she had stood, wearing nothing except a pair of low-slung drawers. "Surprise," he said, and jumped. He didn't curl into a ball or shout or make much of a splash. He entered the water as an arrow might, clean and straight and sharp.

Laurel waited, eyebrows raised, mouth open, to see if his head would break the surface. Certainly he should have been able to push off the bottom and get his head above water even if it was only briefly. He didn't, though. Call stayed under for what she considered an inordinately long time. The fact that he wasn't thrashing about told her that he wasn't panicked. He'd lied to her. He could swim at least well enough to hold his own.

He pushed hair out of his eyes and grinned at her when he came up for air.

"You lied to me," she said. "You can swim."

"No lie. Dillon's a fish. I asked him to teach me a few

things that'll keep me from drowning. Give me a moment." He dropped under the water again.

The water was clear enough that Laurel could see he was wrestling with something at his waist. What in the— She didn't have to finish the thought. He was wrestling with his drawers, which were apparently in danger of getting away from him. He wasn't able to tread water with only his legs so he had to go under while he used his hands on the drawstring.

"Better?" she asked when he surfaced.

"Hmm. Dillon didn't think to mention the drawers would drag."

So they had been skinny-dipping. Laurel didn't want to think about that, at least not about Dillon Booker. She simply nodded her understanding. "How did you know I was here?"

"I didn't. I guess we were of similar minds this afternoon. Sun's hot and high. No breeze. Just seemed right to head out here, maybe get in a little practice keeping my head up."

"Not a good idea by yourself." She looked around. "Unless you're expecting someone. Dillon?"

"Nope. He was dozing in a rocker when I left. I think he had been reading."

"Must be your influence. I've never seen him with a book in his hand."

"Well, this one was lying on the floor so who knows how far he got."

Laurel chuckled. "If we swim closer to where you jumped in, you'll be able to stand on an underwater ledge."

"Really? That devil Dillon never mentioned it."

"Probably because he didn't want you relying on it . . . and because he's a rascal."

Call slipped under the water and swam toward the rocks. He found it easier to move when he was submersed rather than struggling awkwardly to keep his head up. He clutched at the stones until his feet found the ledge and then he stood. Carefully turning around, he faced Laurel.

She was lazily keeping herself afloat by making figure eights with cupped hands. He marveled at her ease.

"Are you frozen through yet?" he asked.

She shook her head. "Used to it already. You?"

"About the same. It feels good." Because he was standing now, he was able to keep his balance and raise a hand. He crooked a finger at her. "Come here."

"I don't think so."

"This won't work if you're not cooperative."

"I thought we agreed you would come to my bed."

He shrugged. "You told me you were thinking of your comfort when you said that. You're comfortable now, aren't you?"

"Yes, but—"

"Well, then, come here."

After a brief hesitation, Laurel sculled the water and moved within an arm's length. He lifted a single dark eyebrow and regarded her sardonically. Laurel was not immune to the challenge and she paddled closer.

"That's better."

Was it? She wasn't so sure.

"Are you getting tired yet?"

"No."

He grinned. "You'd probably let yourself drown rather than admit it. Need I remind you that this was your idea?"

"This? I don't think I ever imagined this. Actually, I'm quite certain I didn't."

Call caught the curve of her waist while she was still talking and pulled her close. "See? It's fine." He settled an arm around her back. "You can rest and I can support you."

Laurel thought she should be sorry that she told him about the ledge, but she wasn't. It was comfortable, the way they fit together, especially now with the water embracing them. His chest was bare and hers might well have been—the flimsy cotton camisole was no barrier at all. The material simply clung to her like a skin she was about to shed.

"Put your arms around my neck," he said.

When she complied, he shifted his hands and cupped her bottom in his palms. Laurel felt herself being lifted effortlessly, and it came to her as completely natural to raise her knees and use them to hug his hips.

"You should probably kiss me," he whispered.

19

Call's smile was charming, Laurel thought. How had she not noticed that before now? Did he hold it back for occasions such as this, when he was single-mindedly bent on seduction? But then how was it seduction if he was asking her to take the lead? She didn't know, but she wasn't opposed to the idea of it.

Laurel bent into the space that separated their mouths and placed her lips against his. She bussed him once. Twice. And then she lingered, her damp mouth moving over his. The edge of her tongue brushed his upper lip. His mouth parted. Hers did the same. His lips were cool from the water but his mouth was warm. She liked the taste of him, the slightly rough pad of his tongue as it circled hers. He pulled her closer. She felt his erection stirring between her thighs. Was she beyond redemption that she wished they had both been skinny-dipping?

Laurel threaded her fingers in his damp hair. At the nape of his neck she twisted it into little curls and then tugged and straightened it. All the while, she kept her mouth on his except for when she had to come up for air. Kissing him was like being underwater. Pressure built inside her, and the urge was there to come to the surface, but she ignored it because there was so much about him that she wanted to explore.

His lips were firm and pliable by turns. Sometimes the slant of his mouth was one way, sometimes the other.

Her tongue darted, licked his lips. She ran it along the ridge of his teeth. He bit down gently and she felt a surge of heat between her legs that rippled all the way to her fingers and toes.

She wanted this. Lord help her, she wanted this.

Laurel cupped his face as she lifted her mouth from his. She rested her forehead against his, catching her breath and calming her racing heart. Laughter bubbled on her lips, but it was an uneasy sort of humor that prompted it.

"Laurel?" His voice was soft, husky. His fingers pressed against her bottom as he lifted her and adjusted his hold. Her thighs tightened against his hips. She wasn't going anywhere, which was good, because it certainly wasn't his intention to let her go. The back of his head was against the rocky side of the pool so he couldn't pull away to search her face. He had to wait for her to lift her forehead. He leaned into her, giving her a gentle nudge.

Laurel raised her head. Her eyes met his searching ones. "I'm all right," she whispered. She could barely hear her voice for the rush of water from the falls, but he must have understood because he nodded. When he looked at her the way he was doing now, it was like bathing in a moonbeam. She barely noticed that the sun was just past its zenith or the heat that was beating down on her shoulders. It might have been translucent silver-blue moonlight on her face.

Call saw that her slim smile was steadier than it had been before, and he observed her eyes darkening as her lips parted. Her hands fell from his face to his shoulders. She kissed the corner of his mouth, his jaw. Her teeth tugged his earlobe and then her mouth moved along his neck.

He returned her attention in equal measure. His mouth hovered above the curve of her shoulder and then sipped her skin along the sensitive cord of her neck. She turned her head to allow him more of the same, and when he obliged her, her hips lifted and slowly rolled against his groin. He doubted that she was mindful of it, but neither did it startle her. What she did came as naturally as drawing a breath, and that was how it should be.

Aware that Laurel had attached herself to him like a burr, Call was able to remove his hands from her bottom. He slid one hand up her back and the other along her thigh. He found the tail of her braid, wrapped it in his fist, and tugged until she lifted her head. He kissed the underside of her jaw and the hollow of her throat. She whimpered and he felt the vibration of it against his lips.

Laurel surprised him then by removing one of her hands from his shoulders and running it along his arm until she came to his hand on her thigh. He offered no resistance as she lifted it, dragged it along her hip to her waist, and then brought it to her breast. She held it there.

"It's all right," he told her. "I've got it."

Laurel was too deep into the sensation of his warm hand cupping her breast to appreciate she was being teased. "You're certain?" she asked.

Call tamped down the urge he had to smile and answered as seriously as she had posed the question. "I'm certain."

Nodding, every one of her features stamped with concentration, she removed her hand from his and let it drift away. Her fingers curled into a fist when Call's thumb passed across her aureole, and the fist tightened when he flicked her nipple on the second pass. He teased the bud. Her wet camisole added an element of delicate abrasiveness that was at once tender and tormenting.

"Hold on," he said.

As soon as Laurel gripped Call's upper arms, he slid the hand that had been moving up and down her spine to her other breast and gave it the same attention as he had the first. He felt her fingers dig into his arms. Her lips parted but he heard nothing. It was as if her breath were lodged in her throat. He buried his face in the curve of her neck and felt her pulse thrum against his lips.

"You're going to have to help," he said in her ear.

"Yes. Whatever you need."

"Put your hands on my shoulders. Lift."

Not knowing what she could expect, she still did as he wanted. Her reward was the hot suck of his mouth on her breast. Laurel gasped as a shudder of pleasure so sharp it was almost painful swept through her. Every part of her tingled with sparks that ignited up and down her skin.

Call slipped a hand between their bodies and fumbled with the opening to his drawers. He felt her give a little start when he released his cock but she didn't try to pull away. He tugged at her knickers, lowering them over her hips before he slid his hand between her open thighs and palmed her mons. Now she did jerk hard, but it was in a way that brought her closer. He slipped one finger inside her and then a second. She came down slowly on his hand as his mouth released her breast.

She met his eyes and said the first thing that came to her mind. "I thought it would be bigger."

Call nearly lost his footing and unseated her for the shout of laughter she provoked. Removing his hand from between her thighs, he took one of hers by the wrist and drew it under the water to his erection. "Go on," he said, folding her fingers around it.

Her eyes widened fractionally.

"Uh-huh." Call couldn't help that he was stupidly satisfied by her reaction. "Slow now." He lifted her hips, tilted them, and urged her to take him in. He found his own way after that, careful as she bit her lower lip and made to accommodate his entry. He wasn't surprised that she was tight, only that she closed like a fist around him when he began to withdraw. The contraction made his blood run hotter. He seemed to swell inside her. The pleasure was intense and he closed his eyes.

Laurel rocked her hips, rising and falling at his direction. The press of his fingers guided her movements. She was in the saddle but he was in control. The initial discomfort was not unexpected and it faded quickly, replaced by a pleasing sense of fullness that was both alien and welcome.

She found his mouth, kissed him deeply, slowly, matching the lazy rhythm of their coupling. When she broke the kiss, she saw he was watching her again. The black center of his eyes was wider but there was no loss of focus. The planes of his face seemed sharper somehow and she wondered if it was the same for her. It felt right, what they were doing. The pleasure felt right. She had wondered if she would feel shame, but she didn't, not even a scintilla of it. The freedom from it made her want to laugh and she thought she might do that later, but just now . . .

Quite without knowing how it happened, the movement of her hips quickened. She felt herself straining, searching. When his hand slipped between their bodies a second time, and he stroked the sensitive and slippery nub of flesh nesting in her nether lips, Laurel understood what it was she had been seeking. A shiver of pleasure made her contract all around him, everywhere. She felt as if she were drowning in it, and she might have if not for Call's steadying presence.

Laurel held on as he continued to move. His features were tight with denial and need, and then he surprised her by lifting her abruptly and holding her away from him. His body jerked; he squeezed his eyes shut. Laurel touched his shoulder as though to offer comfort and he shrugged her off. His breathing was ragged at first, but it slowed and he opened his eyes. He released her altogether and slipped under the water.

Laurel tugged at her knickers as she floated away on her back. The water felt cooler than ever because her skin was so heated. Gooseflesh appeared on her arms, but when she shivered, there was a vestige of pleasure in it that caught her unaware. She thought she was outside Call's reach, but then she felt his fingers circle her ankle. She didn't resist as he slowly pulled her toward him. When the sole of her foot touched his chest, she stopped floating and went vertical in the water. She didn't try to find footing on the same ledge where Call was standing; she treaded water instead.

She watched him push fingers through his wet hair and rub his beard with the back of his hand, removing all evidence of sparkling drops of water.

Call extended his hand, uncertain whether she would take it. She did. Further proof that Laurel Beth Morrison was no coward.

"Are you all right?" he asked.

She nodded. "You?"

"Yes."

She nibbled on her lower lip. "I wasn't sure. When you threw me away . . . well, I wasn't sure."

"Threw you . . . oh, that."

"Yes," she said. "That."

"I needed to withdraw. My back is to the wall. It was easier to put you away from me." It didn't seem to him that his explanation was helpful to her. "Pregnancy," he said. "I was trying to prevent it."

"Oh." She nodded, understanding that he had spilled his seed into the water rather than into her. It seemed impossible now that she had been so naïve. She, who'd spent all her life around animals, had even bred cattle on occasion, had just proven how ignorant she was. "In my defense," she said, "you rendered me senseless."

Call lifted his eyebrows.

"Don't look at me as if you're surprised," she said. "You know very well what you did."

He smiled modestly. "One always hopes for the best."

Laurel gave him a playful push. If he hadn't had the wall of the pool behind him, she would have unbalanced him. It would have been fair, she thought, because he'd unbalanced her. Did he know? She hoped he didn't. She was feeling unexpectedly vulnerable, and that was not comfortable in the least.

"Have you done this before?" she asked.

"I thought we established that days ago on the trail."

"No, I didn't mean *that*. I meant *this*." She waved her free hand just above the surface of the water.

"Oh, *this*," he said wryly, chuckling under his breath. "Making love in the water. No, never done it before. I don't really swim, remember?"

Only one part of what he said gave Laurel pause. "Is that what we did? Made love?"

"Well, you didn't like it when I called it pirooting."

"But we're not in love, are we?"

"That's something best left to answer on our own, don't you think?"

She nodded slowly. "Of course."

"And," he said, "as you insisted this would be just the one time, we really don't need to find other words for it."

Laurel had forgotten that, but he was right. She had said it, had even meant it when she'd said it. He'd teased her about the possibility of getting a taste for it, but then perhaps he hadn't been teasing. She thought she knew herself and what she wanted and should have been able to dismiss that idea out of hand, but now she was fairly certain she'd spoken impulsively. She didn't know if she had gotten a taste for it or if she simply wanted another taste. It probably didn't matter; either was dangerous.

Call pulled her close, kissed her on the mouth, and was careful not to linger. He released her hand and gave her a gentle push.

Feeling bereft, Laurel drifted away. She watched Call turn carefully on the ledge and then find purchase between the rocks. He climbed up, pulled himself out of the water, and grinned at her as he unceremoniously yanked on his sodden drawers to keep them from falling to his ankles. She could have told him that every beautiful part of him was clearly outlined and she didn't care if he stripped to his birthday suit and laid his drawers on a rock to dry. It was what she was going to do once he left. In the meantime, she floated on her back, paddling only when the current pushed her toward the edge of the pool.

Call folded his legs and sat on the warm slab of stone. "Aren't you going to get out?"

"Not just yet."

"You're going to be prickly as a cactus and wrinkled as a prune."

She laughed. "Quite possibly, but it still feels quite lovely so I'm staying put." Laurel arched her spine, dipped her head, and dove under the water backward. She made a complete circle before her head surfaced again, and then she floated for a while longer.

"Can you see when you're underwater?" he asked.

"Yes. Can't you?"

"I didn't open my eyes."

The idea of him swimming blindly under the water made her chuckle. She swallowed some water, sputtered, and spit it out.

"Serves you right," he said.

Laurel stopped floating and went vertical, treading with her legs and one hand while she palmed her face with the other to clear water from her eyes and nose. "It probably does," she said, unperturbed that he had enjoyed her come-uppance. Dipping her hand under to help her tread, she told him, "The water is remarkably clear for the first few feet, then it gets murky. You can still see, especially on a bright day like this, but everything is distorted."

"What's under there?"

"More rock. Grassy things. Sunken treasure."

He grinned. "Uh-huh. Treasure."

"No. Really. There are bits of pottery and drawers from what was probably a china cupboard. My brothers and I figured that some early settler unloaded furniture from a wagon upstream and it eventually was carried here. We never found any money except coins our father tossed in and let us search for."

"Did you always find them?"

"We had to. Coins were too precious to waste. Find them or work to replace their value—that was the deal Pa struck with us."

Call leaned to one side and stretched an arm toward his trousers. He tugged on a leg and pulled it toward him. When he had the denim trousers in his lap, he searched the pockets. He sifted through the coins he found, eliminating the one- and two-cent copper pieces as too difficult to locate underwater. The five-cent coin was better, but he judged it a little on the smallish size. He finally settled on the silver fifty-cent piece. This was at least a prize worth the trouble of diving for it.

"What about this?" he asked, holding the coin up between his thumb and forefinger. "Shiny enough?"

"It is, but don't throw your money away. It's been a very long time since I searched for treasure, and honestly, George or Martin usually found it first."

"I'll chance it." Call flipped the coin into the air and watched its arc until it disappeared under the water beside Laurel's left shoulder. He thought she might make a grab for it, but she accepted the challenge and let it sink. He didn't know if the coin would drift sideways on its way down, but he trusted her to figure that out.

Laurel gave the coin a few moments to settle before she disturbed the water. She waved good-bye to Call, took in a lungful of air, and went under in an effortless dive.

She knew she had been treading water in the deepest part of the pool, but she had forgotten how the pressure would build uncomfortably in her ears as she swam toward the bottom. There wasn't much she could see when her hands touched the rocky basin. If she found the coin, it would be by sheerest luck.

Laurel searched around, patting the smoothly eroded rocks for something that was out of place. If the coin had fallen into a crevice, there was no hope of locating it. She stayed down as long as she dared before she pushed off the bottom and shot to the surface.

Clearing water from her eyes, she saw Call was looking at her expectantly. She shook her head. "It's deeper here than I remember. There's not much I can see. I'm afraid you've lost fifty cents."

He shrugged. "You can work it off."

The way he said it, coupled with a slightly wicked smile, had Laurel sucking in another breath and diving deep. Her ears accepted the pressure better this time around, and she spread her arms to widen her search. She released her air slowly to make herself less buoyant.

When her fingers touched something unfamiliar, she instantly retracted her hand. It wasn't any grassy thing she had found. Her first thought was that it was a snake—and she had no love for the creatures—but on second consideration, she realized the texture was all wrong. Not only that, but what she'd held hadn't wriggled under her touch. With some trepidation, Laurel reached out again, and this time when she found it, she held on.

It was a rope. That was hardly interesting by itself, but the fact that it hadn't floated away meant it was snagged on something. That was a little bit curious, so she tugged. Nothing happened. She tugged harder.

This time the rope gave a little and she had slack to work with. She placed her feet on the rocks and yanked. The rope came free at the same time her lungs were spent. She pushed to the surface and sucked in a great draught of air. When she could breathe properly, she held up the rope. "No coin. But I found this."

Call was standing now. He nodded, but he wasn't looking at what was in her hand. He was looking at what had come to the surface behind her. "That's not all you found."

20

Laurel followed Call's line of sight, turned slowly, and confronted a swollen body bobbing facedown in the water. She didn't scream, but she did swim backward as fast as she could until she was plastered against the pool's stone wall. She stood on the ledge that Call had occupied and caught her breath. That didn't seem to matter because she had no words for what she had discovered. Belatedly she realized she was still holding the rope and flung it away. It drifted toward the edge of the pool before it sank.

"Call?" Laurel craned her head to see him. He was no longer standing where he had been moments earlier. Looking around, she saw him walking toward their horses. "What are you doing?"

He removed the coiled rope attached to the saddle pommel and held it up for her to see. He unwound it as he walked back, looped it, and then passed one end of the rope through the loop. The simple overhand knot created a lasso.

"You don't have to do that," she said. "I can drag the body over here."

Call was firm. "No. Stay where you are or climb out. You've already done the hard work."

Laurel did not argue. "Who do you suppose it is?"

"You're more likely to know than I am." He swung the lasso and let it fly. He missed, dropping the loop on the body's bloated back. He was luckier the second time, catching the body at the head. Call carefully pulled on the lasso until it circled the shoulders. He tightened it and began dragging the body toward him.

Laurel climbed out of the pool before the body reached her. She stood at Call's side, prepared to help him. The literal dead weight would be difficult to pull out. It occurred to her that she should have stayed in the water to assist lifting the body. She edged closer to the lip of the rock. It was as if Call had divined her thoughts because he shook his head and told her to stay where she was.

It was a struggle to lift the body. The muscles in Call's arms and back bunched and strained. At one point, he considered asking Laurel to bring Artemis over to help, but then he managed to heave the body far enough out of the water until he could grasp it under one arm and pull it out the rest of the way.

Call grabbed a fistful of the dead man's trousers and yanked him all the way onto dry land. Breathing raggedly, Call removed the lasso and turned the body over. Several moments passed before he heard Laurel suck in a breath. "I reckon that means you recognize him," he said quietly.

She almost hadn't. The face no longer had any familiar angles; every feature was as puffy as a mushroom head. The open, sightless eyes were clouded over so their color was obscured. Something had nibbled on the bare throat. His coat was unbuttoned. She recognized the water-saturated black leather vest because of the loop of gold chain hanging out of the breast pocket. There would be a timepiece attached to the end. He'd set great store by that watch, claimed it was his father's. Laurel had no reason to doubt him, yet she couldn't deny that she had. She should have listened to her doubts and let him go. None of this would have happened if she'd let him go.

"It's Josiah Pye," she said.

Call nodded. He finished coiling the rope and walked it back to his mare.

"You knew," she called after him.

"I suspected." He attached the rope and then untethered Artemis. He led her over to where Laurel was standing. Her damp undergarments were dripping water on the stones. She had her arms crossed in front of her because, in spite of the heat, she was shivering. He stopped at her neatly folded stack of clothes, picked up her shirt, and handed it to her.

Laurel thanked him and shrugged into it, pulling it closed but not buttoning it. "Should we get the sheriff?"

"I want to examine the body first." He hunkered beside Mr. Pye at the level of his head. He looked first without touching, noting the scratches on the face and the bite mark on the neck. It seemed likely all of those were caused after death. Call pushed his fingers through Pye's wet hair. It didn't take him long to find the deep gash at the back of his head. He turned Pye's face sideways, parted the hair, and pointed out the injury to Laurel. He was so sure she was watching him that he was surprised when she didn't say anything. He looked up and saw her head was averted. "Laurel?"

"I'm all right," she said quietly. She turned to face Call and did not glance at the body. "It's not how I imagined he'd be found. Certainly not how I imagined he'd meet his end."

Call pointed to where Abby was tethered. "Why don't you stand over there? Or would you prefer to ride for the sheriff?"

She nodded slowly but didn't move. "Was he murdered, do you think?"

"There's a big gash at the back of his head, but that could be from hitting the rocks. On the other hand, the rope you found suggested he was tied, and since his body didn't surface on its own, it suggests he was weighed down." Call tugged on Pye's pant legs and saw evidence that pointed to the fact he had been bound. "So, yeah, murdered."

"What about the payroll? Should I search for a saddlebag? He must have carried the money away in something like that."

"No. Let someone else make that their job. I doubt it's there."

"How long do you think he's been in the water?"

"Don't know. Who's the doctor around here?"

"There isn't one, not a real one anyway, not since Mrs. Lancaster's husband died. Nick Buchanan has some doctoring experience, most of it during the war. He owns the feed store and folks are happy to have him suggest remedies if it's not a serious illness or set bones and splints. Leastways he hasn't killed anyone. I'm not sure what you think he can do."

"Probably nothing with his experience. I thought a doc—a real one—might be able to tell us about how long Pye's been in the drink."

"I could wire Mr. Stonechurch. He might send their town's doctor. I know there's one."

"All right. If the doc's willing to travel, that could be helpful." Call hitched his thumb over his shoulder to indicate Artemis. "Why don't you send the message to Stonechurch and ask Rooster to ride for Sheriff Carter? I forgot that it's Sunday afternoon when I suggested that you go. He'll probably be at Mrs. Fry's. Send Dillon here to dive around and see if a saddlebag or a pouch turns up."

"As soon as I'm dry." Laurel plucked her damp camisole away from her body and gathered some of the material in her fist to twist water out of it.

"Sure. Of course. There's no real hurry." Call turned back to examining Pye, running his hands over the man's shoulders, arms, and digging into his pockets. When he darted a look in Laurel's direction, he saw she was watching him.

"What do you suppose happened to Penelope?" she asked.

"Good question. Do you think she would have found her way back to the station if she'd been with him when he was murdered?"

"I don't know. Maybe if she wandered onto the trail,

she might have found us. The trail is what she knew, and the stations, of course."

Call nodded. "I was thinking that if she returned, it might help us narrow the time of Pye's death. If he never left the area as we thought, then Penelope might be around somewhere, but if he did go and circled back, I'm betting he exchanged horses. I doubt he showed up here on foot."

"So there's a horse out there somewhere."

"If no one's come across it and claimed the animal, then yeah."

"Perhaps whoever killed Mr. Pye has it."

"Certainly a possibility." Call looked her over. She stood hipshot, twisting the material of her drawers. "You going to get dressed?" He held up his hands when she gave him the gimlet eye. "Just asking."

Laurel snorted, smoothed her drawers over her hips, and buttoned her shirt. She pulled on her socks and trousers. Damp patches appeared on the thighs of her denim pants. "Better?" she asked with a hint of sarcasm.

"No, not for me. Not at all."

Laurel flattened her mouth to keep her smile in check. Laughter would have been disrespectful, not that Josey Pye would have cared. She turned away from the bloated body as she pulled on her boots and buckled her belt. She'd seen too many dead men in her short life, three of her own family, but Mr. Pye's distorted features, swollen and heavy and waxy gray, were something out of a nightmare. It was not a matter of being uneasy; she was filled with dread.

"I'm going," she said, touching him briefly on the shoulder as she passed. "Dillon won't be long in joining you. If Sheriff Carter's at Mrs. Fry's, it could be a while."

Call told her he'd be fine and waited until she was gone before he dressed. He regarded the climb to the lip of the falls with uncertainty, wondering if he could do it. In his youth, he'd been as nimble as a monkey. He was stronger now but hardly as agile. Still, there was a question in his mind as to whether Josey Pye had been up there at any time before his death. Bound, weighed down, and pushed over the edge, Call thought. Maybe he'd gone over the falls alive and had time to contemplate his own death before he sank to the bottom of the pool.

Curiosity moved him. Call left his socks and boots where he'd taken them off and began to climb. From below the ascent to the top looked to be vertical, but soon after Call started up, he realized the climb was at a slight angle in his favor. He had to secure his hand- and footholds carefully because the water spray made many of the rocks slippery, some with mossy coverings. The closer he got to the top, the more he wondered about how he would make the descent. He believed there had to be another way around, perhaps a path that would lead him on a circuitous route but nonetheless return him to his starting point.

He was pulling himself up the last three feet when he heard someone calling to him from below. He paused but did not look down. The voice came again and he recognized Dillon was shouting his name. Call heaved himself over the edge, lay belly down for a few seconds while his heart calmed, and then got to his feet. He stood, stepped away from the lip, and turned to look at Dillon from what seemed a towering height.

The young man had already dropped his red suspenders and was peeling off his shirt. "You plum crazy, Call?" he shouted over the sound of the rushing water.

Call cupped his hands around his mouth and shouted back. "Might be. I want to look around. How do I get down?"

"Jump!"

"No, seriously. How do I get down?" He could see Dillon's shoulders shaking as the boy had a good laugh at his expense. When Dillon had finally quieted, he made some gestures with his arms that Call guessed were supposed to indicate an alternate route. Call dropped his hands, nodded, and began exploring while Dillon shucked his boots.

The stream that fed the falls was wider than Call had expected. He observed that it narrowed into a funnel as it approached the drop, which gave the falls its force. Following the run of the water, Call could see that the stream bed was shallow in places and rocks broke the surface often enough to provide damp stepping-stones to make a crossing. The water flowed swiftly, but where it wasn't deep, a horse and rider could easily move from one bank to the other.

Call looked for signs that someone had been covering the same ground. Perhaps a more experienced tracker would find disturbances that he couldn't see, but it wasn't as if there was a great deal of vegetation to be trampled or broken. The brush was scattered, leaving plenty of room for someone to pass between the bent and scraggly pines.

Call set his hands on his hips, looked around, and wondered what he thought he might find. It wasn't as if . . . then he saw it out of the corner of his eye. It was the fluttering that caught his attention, and he probably wouldn't have seen it if he hadn't stopped. Turning slowly to the right, away from the stream, Call stared at the bent spindle of a bramble bush that had somehow found fertile ground in a rock crevice. The plant was so young that Call couldn't identify it. That didn't matter.

He could identify the fluttering leaf, which was no leaf at all, but the scrap of a greenback. Call carefully approached the bush, watching his step as he covered stony ground. The greenback, or what was left of it, fluttered again as the air stirred. If the wind took it, Call knew he might never get it back. When he reached the bramble, he hunkered down protectively so his body sheltered it from the breeze, and then plucked the greenback from the thorny stem.

Call held it between his thumb and forefinger while he examined it. It was perhaps a third of the size of a complete legal tender note. The value, shown as a roman numeral V above the engraved portrait of Andrew Jackson, revealed it as a five-dollar bill. He knew from Ramsey Stonechurch that one quarter of the greenbacks in the stolen strongbox would have been five-dollar notes. The faded bill he had in his hand was almost certainly from the robbery, but how it had come to be in this place was still an unanswered question.

Call pocketed the bill and spent another half hour searching the area. He might have spent longer in what was proving to be a fruitless exercise if Laurel had not suddenly appeared on horseback about two hundred feet from where he was standing. Artemis came up over the rise behind her. She tugged on the mare's reins and brought her abreast.

"Where did you come from?" he called, trying to get a look around her.

In answer, she jabbed a thumb over her shoulder and began to approach.

When Laurel was almost upon him, he asked, "How did you get up here?"

"The same way any sensible person would," she said dryly. "On horseback, following the path that shoots diagonally off the Cabin Creek Trail."

"Huh. I reckon I would have found it." He grinned crookedly. "Eventually."

"Sure. You would have had to because I *know* you wouldn't have jumped."

"Right."

She looked him over. He seemed no worse for wear except for his scratched and bleeding feet. "You'll need some salve and bandages for those," she said.

He followed her gaze to his feet. Until now, he hadn't noticed. "I don't suppose you brought my socks and boots?"

"No. I'm sorry. I didn't think of it."

"S'all right." Call took his mare's reins from her and led Artemis to the stream. He waded in and stood there long enough to let the blood wash away before he climbed into the saddle. "Show me the way," he said, coming alongside Laurel.

Call realized that he'd been wrong about the path being circuitous. It wound in a series of S curves, but it didn't bring them back to the pool. They joined the Cabin

Creek Trail some one hundred yards southeast of Morrison Station and about two hundred yards from where the grassy trampled path left the trail and led to the pool.

"Did you and Rooster try that route when you set out to find Josey Pye?"

Laurel shook her head. "Never thought of it. We were following at night and stayed on the main trail. If there was evidence he had gone off that way, we wouldn't have seen it."

"Is there another route down, one that goes toward town?"

"There is, but you'd have to cross the stream up top to find it. It's a less steep incline than what we just traveled and it connects back to the trail about a mile northwest of town. There's not a lot of reason to use it, except if you want to get up to the top of the falls and you don't have a horse. It's an easier climb. Longer, but easier." She swiveled her head to look at him. "Why? What are you thinking?"

Call removed the greenback from his pocket and held it out for her to take. "Better than the scrap we found in the strongbox."

Laurel held it gingerly as she examined it. "You found this up there?"

"Yep. Caught in a bramble bush. Sheerest luck."

"What do you suppose happened to the rest of it? I mean, why isn't it a whole bill?"

"I think someone tore it. Probably meant to tear it in half and missed the mark. I looked around for the missing part but couldn't find it or any other bills."

Laurel returned the bill. "But you think this came from the robbery?"

"It's the only thing that makes sense."

She nodded but she wasn't done. The mere thought of Call making the climb to the top of the falls filled her with real terror, and fear like that made her angry. "You could have killed yourself, you know. Going up there wasn't safe. We talked about that. I'd ask you what you were thinking, but I don't believe you were."

"You won't like it, but I figured I might do myself grievous injury but probably wouldn't die." He chuckled when she muttered something unintelligible under her breath. Better not to ask her to repeat it. "Did you hear back from Mr. Stonechurch?"

Laurel blew out a hot breath and willed herself to calm. "Almost immediately. He's sending Dr. Singer. He's relatively new to Stonechurch. I only met him once when he came through on the stage, but he made a good impression. He lanced a carbuncle on Rooster's neck that was bothering him horribly and didn't charge for the service. Left medicine behind as well. I guess we'll find out what he knows about dead bodies."

"When will he get here?"

"Mr. Stonechurch promised to put him on the next coach. He should be here tomorrow morning." They were passing the station and Laurel asked if Call wanted to stop and attend to his bare feet. He didn't.

"Time enough for that later. Rooster went for the sheriff?"

"Yes. They both should be at the pool by now."

They were. Rooster was standing at the edge of the pool talking to Dillon, who was still in the water. Sheriff Rayleigh Carter was hunkered a few feet back of the body, looking it over.

"You sure this is Josey Pye?" he asked, tipping back his hat and using a forearm to wipe at his brow.

Laurel gave her reins to Call and dismounted. "I'm sure," she said, walking up to him. "Rooster? Any doubt in your mind?"

Rooster turned his head. "No doubt. I said so. Twice."

Carter continued to address Laurel. He was a big man, broad-shouldered and thick-necked, naturally intimidating without making an effort. He would have cast Laurel in his shadow had he stood. He stayed down and gave her what passed for a polite smile but what most people would have called a grimace. "Thought I should hear it from you. I didn't know the man well. Mostly saw him in passing at Sweeny's."

And Mrs. Fry's, Laurel thought. She held her tongue about that.

"We never exchanged more than a few words," said Carter. "Hard to see his features now."

"Yes, I know, but it's Mr. Pye."

"And you found him how exactly?"

Laurel waited until Call joined them. "I was diving. Mr. Landry threw a coin in for me to find." She shrugged carelessly. "Something my brothers and I played at when we were children."

Dillon heard part of this exchange. He held up a hand to show off the coin. "Found it!" he called to them. "You want it back, Call?"

"It's yours now. You find anything else?"

Dillon shook his head, flinging water from his hair. "Sorry."

"You might as well get out," said Call. He turned to Carter. "I asked him to look for Pye's saddlebag in the event it had gone into the pool along with Josey Pye."

Carter raised both wooly eyebrows in surprise. "You think that's likely?"

"I couldn't rule it out."

Before the sheriff could comment or ask another question, Laurel said, "I've been in contact with Mr. Stonechurch. He's sending a doctor to examine the body."

"Really? Looks like a drowning to me."

"When I found him, he was attached to a rope that bound his legs."

Call said, "You can still see the evidence that he was tied in the flesh above his ankles."

Carter stayed hunkered and inched forward. He pulled up one of the pant legs. "Yep. There it is." He stood, shook out stiff legs. "Where's the rope?"

Laurel's expression revealed guilt. "I accidentally unbound his legs when I was tugging on the rope. I brought the rope to the surface and Mr. Pye bobbed up behind me. I'm afraid I tossed the rope away at that point. I'm not sure why. I just did. It's certainly downstream by now. I don't think it serves any point to search for it."

"Probably not." He regarded Call. "Dillon says you're not much of a swimmer, Mr. Landry."

"True. Did he mention he's been teaching me a few tricks to keep my head above water?"

"He did." Carter adjusted the tilt of his hat, bringing the brim lower. "So you were standing around while Laurel Beth was swimming. Do I have that right?"

"Indeed, you do."

"Tossing her coins."

Call held up an index finger. "One coin." He glanced at Laurel. "I wasn't convinced she could find it. Seems I was right."

Laurel heard the teasing in Call's voice that Carter missed. She gave him a reproving look.

The sheriff pointed to the top of the falls. "Dillon said he saw you haul yourself over the top. I wasn't sure I believed him until he pointed out that your socks and boots were here." He didn't wait for Call to confirm. "What were you looking for?"

"Anything that might point to Josey Pye's presence up there."

"And?"

Call shook his head. "Nothing." Out of the corner of his eye, he saw Laurel give a start. He made a quick quelling motion with his fingers to warn her not to say anything about the greenback. "Doesn't mean he wasn't there, just that I didn't find any evidence of it."

"Huh. Almost broke your fool neck for nothing, then."

"I told him the same," said Laurel, relieved that she hadn't spoken out of turn about the greenback in Call's pocket.

Call stepped away and picked up his socks and boots. He found a natural seat among the rocks to sit down and put them on. "What do you suggest we do with the body?

Laurel says it'll be morning before the doc arrives. We can't leave it here or scavengers will get it."

Rooster joined Call on the perch. "I already waved away a few buzzards. Won't be but a few hours before they're circling."

Carter scratched behind his neck. "Could move him to the undertaker, I suppose. Theo Beckley's gonna want to know who's paying for care and preparation."

Laurel started to say that she would, but Call interrupted her. "You tell him I'll pay, but that's on the condition that he doesn't do a damn thing to the body until the doc gets here."

"I guess he can do that."

"He should keep it cool," said Laurel. "I know he's packed ice around bodies before."

"I'll tell him," Carter said. He pointed to Call, who was now leaning back comfortably on his elbows. "You. Help me get Pye on the back of my horse and then you can follow me to Beckley's and tell him about the payment yourself. Knowing Theo, he's probably got something for you to sign."

Call pushed himself upright. Instead of walking over to Carter and the body, he went to the edge of the pool, where Dillon was still treading water, and held out a hand. "C'mon up. You've done your part."

Dillon pushed his toes in a foothold and grasped Call's hand. He practically flew out of the water. Laughing, he shook himself like a puppy, spraying water in every direction. He ducked his head when the sheriff gave him a sour look. The gesture wasn't an apology. He did it to hide his grin.

Call left Dillon's side and joined Carter. "Feet or shoulders?" he asked.

"Feet."

Nodding, Call got behind Pye's head and slid his arms under the dead man's shoulders. He and the sheriff lifted together while Laurel held Carter's animal steady as they put Pye over the saddle. Carter strapped the body down.

Call expected Carter to lead his horse but instead he told Rooster he was taking his mount. There was no opportunity to object.

Thinking of the rheumatism that plagued Rooster's hip, Laurel offered him her horse and said she'd be happy to walk back to the station with Dillon. Rooster hesitated before he accepted. His eyes bore holes through the sheriff's head as the man rode away.

"Just like that," muttered Rooster. "Just like he don't know that *I* know he was trussed about as neatly as a Christmas goose in Miss Mariam's room not above an hour ago."

Laurel and Dillon stared at Rooster. It didn't matter that the sheriff and Call were probably not yet out of earshot. They burst out laughing in spite of it.

21

Laurel made room for Call on the porch swing when he came around the corner of the house and hopped up the steps. Rooster had turned in not long after the sun went down and the brothers were sitting on stools outside the barn taking turns playing their fiddle.

"They're not bad," said Call, sitting beside Laurel as one of the boys struck a tune. He would have taken one of the rockers if her invitation had not been so clear. "This is the first I've heard them play."

"The fiddle belongs to their pa and he doesn't part with it easily. I'm not sure why he allowed them to bring it here this evening. Maybe he thought they needed a distraction from the goings-on today."

"Hank was never at the pool this afternoon. He didn't see the body."

"Doesn't matter. After Dillon finished telling him about it—every gruesome detail—Hank will be seeing it long after his brother's forgotten."

"Dillon has a flair for relating the macabre."

"I blame Edgar Allan Poe."

Call chuckled. There was a pause in the music as the fiddle changed hands and one brother picked up the Stephen Foster tune "Gentle Annie" precisely where the other had left off. "I like this one."

They listened in silence until the last bars were played

and then exchanged grins as the brothers began bickering over what they would play next.

Laurel said, "I swear, if I hadn't hired them when I did, their mother would have paid me to take them off her hands. She couldn't love them any more than she does, but she tells me she wants to knock their heads together within ten minutes of them sitting down to eat."

"They're good boys."

"No doubt." Just then the brothers settled on "Beautiful Dreamer" and the lilting notes drifted toward the porch. "No doubt at all," she said softly.

Call began to gently push the swing. "We haven't talked about what happened this afternoon."

Laurel turned to look at him, a tiny crease between her eyebrows. "It doesn't seem as if we've talked about anything else."

"I wasn't referring to Mr. Pye."

"Oh."

"Uh-huh."

Laurel was quiet a moment, gathering her thoughts. "I'm not certain what there is to say, unless you're looking for accolades. Are you?"

Call had nothing in his mouth but spit and he still almost choked on it.

Laurel leaned over and clapped him on the back. "What happened? Are you all right?"

Call nodded, but he couldn't speak. Not yet. When she withdrew her hand, he leaned against the back of the swing and caught a deep breath, and when he could finally shape coherent words, he asked with a perfectly straight face, "Do you have any accolades?"

"No," she said, adopting his demeanor. "Not a one."

"I reckon I deserve that. I shouldn't have asked, but sometimes you dangle a worm and I can't resist snapping at it."

"You have odd appetites."

"Maybe, but I'll never ask you to truss me like a Christmas goose."

Laurel couldn't help it; she laughed. "How did you

hear about that? You were already riding away when Rooster told us how he found the sheriff."

"Dillon. I asked him what struck the three of you so funny. Carter and I caught your laughter but we didn't speculate as to the cause."

"It's unlikely Rooster would have breathed a word if Carter hadn't been so high-handed about taking his horse. Serves the sheriff right."

Call nodded. "There's an image that won't leave me anytime soon."

"Why didn't you want Sheriff Carter to know about the greenback you found?"

"And just when I thought there wasn't anything left to discuss regarding Josey Pye."

"This is the first time we've been alone since this afternoon. I didn't think you'd appreciate me asking you about it in front of anyone."

"No, you're right." He sighed. "I've got no good reason for it, but Rayleigh Carter doesn't inspire confidence."

"Well, he didn't do much in the way of searching for Mr. Pye, and he gave up far too soon. I put it down to laziness. He doesn't get much opportunity to stretch his law enforcement legs, so they're fairly useless when something important happens."

"I think you're being kind."

"Perhaps. What I know is that no one else in Falls Hollow was interested in the position. There's a vote, of course, but since Carter is generally the only one on the ballot, he wins by default. He became sheriff not long after my father and brothers were killed, maybe about five years ago. Folks have gotten used to him."

"And he's gotten used to having his way, doing or not doing as it pleases him. By any definition, he's merely an officeholder, not a lawman."

Laurel couldn't argue with that. Call was right. The Booker brothers began to play "Jeanie with the Light Brown Hair" and she softly hummed along, sometimes mouthing the words.

Call reached for her hand, gave it a light squeeze. "I need to know that you're all right."

Laurel was lifted from her reverie. It required a moment's thought to understand what he was talking about, but when she did, she blinked. "Ah. We're back to that."

"Yes," he said. "*That.*"

"Well, set your mind at ease. I'm fine." She slipped her hand out from under his. "I told you that when you asked me at the pool. Didn't you believe me?"

"I believed you meant it when you said it, but you've had time to reflect. I wondered if you've had second thoughts."

"No," she said lightly. "No second thoughts." It occurred to her that she should ask the same of him. "You?"

"Some," he admitted. "I wish we'd had time to catch our breath before you found Mr. Pye."

"I thought we had caught our breath. You hauled yourself out of the water almost as quickly as you jumped in."

"That wasn't precisely by choice."

"I don't understand. What do you mean?"

"You set the rules and I aimed to oblige. I needed to put some distance between us."

"Oh. I didn't think about that."

"I'm realizing it now. I keep forgetting how you fail to see your own attraction."

"Ah, yes. That flower and bee nonsense."

Call gave her a quirky grin. "Uh-huh. You brought that up first."

Laurel was not proof against that smile. "I liked what we did, you know," she said impulsively. "And in the water that way, that was something I didn't expect."

He shrugged. "Fish do it."

"Not like we did."

"True."

"And it was brave of you, seeing as how you can hardly swim."

"As long as I had the ledge and you didn't pull me under, I was fine."

"Hmm." He'd been more than fine, but Laurel did not

think he needed to hear that. "You told me at the pool that you came out there to practice swimming. Was that true?"

"Yes. Right up until the moment I saw you. I don't regret that you inspired me."

"Inspired," she said, her lip curling just a tad derisively. "Sure."

"It's up to you whether or not you believe me, but I'm not lying."

She wanted to believe him. It was a new experience to be desired, and certainly that's what he was telling her. She was desired. By him. She considered saying as much, but then she suspected he'd use the opportunity to remind her about the bees, buzzing around her flower, and that she simply hadn't noticed them. She noticed McCall Landry, though. And she'd noticed Josey Pye, too; though not in a way that made her ever want to be with him.

"What is it?" he asked when she fell silent for so long.

"Just thinking."

"Two bits for those thoughts."

"Isn't it generally wise to offer only a penny?"

"Hey," he said gently. "I threw fifty cents away for you this afternoon, and I didn't get anything in return. I figure you owe me."

"All right. I'm going to regret saying this, but you might've been right."

"Oh? About what?"

"That I might get a taste for it."

"But I didn't say that. I asked you what would happen if you *did* get a taste for pirooting."

"I don't like that word, and that's not the point."

"So choose another word and make me understand your point."

Laurel felt as if he'd just put her back to the wall. She set her feet down hard in an attempt to stop the swing. It swayed a little crazily before it stilled. Laurel turned sideways and waited until Call looked at her. One of his eyebrows was raised. Somehow he managed to look amused and challenging at the same time.

"Can we say 'making love' without attaching any special meaning to it?" she asked.

He shrugged. "If you like."

"Well, I do," she said, and almost believed it. "All right. Then my point is that I think you gave me a taste for making love."

"You think? You're not sure?"

She poked him with the toe of her boot. "You *are* looking for praise."

Call rubbed his shin. She hadn't exactly been gentle. Still, he couldn't quite keep the deviltry out of his smile as he asked, "So what happens now?"

Laurel hadn't thought it through and she didn't have an answer. "Don't you know?"

"I don't see us going back to the pool tonight."

Laurel was tempted to kick him again, but she remembered that Jeremy Dodd used to yank on her braids after school and her father told her that was because Jeremy liked her. She didn't want to lend Call the same impression. She regarded him seriously, hoping he would give her question a genuine response.

"There aren't a lot of choices," he said. "You can't come to the bunkhouse and I'd rather not meet in the barn. Out of doors is fine if comfort isn't a consideration, or if comfort is, then you'll want to bring blankets, maybe build a fire if it's chilly. Plus, we'd want to keep the critters away."

"What's wrong with the barn?"

"Besides that it smells of cattle and muck? It's all right for a roll, I suppose, but there's a much better chance that we'll be surprised there, even if we're up in the loft."

"Yes, of course. I should have thought of that."

"I was actually thinking we were fortunate that no one came across us at the falls this afternoon."

So was Laurel, but she understood why she hadn't given it a thought at the time. "I suppose that eliminates all the possibilities save one."

Call thought she sounded more resigned than happy

about it. "You have to be sure, Laurel. Even Jelly's going to figure out where I am at night if I'm not sleeping in the bunkhouse."

She remembered telling him she didn't care about that, that everyone in Falls Hollow found out everything sooner or later, but she'd said all that when she was practically daring him to make love to her. He'd asked her to reflect on it then, and he was asking the same of her now. McCall Landry wanted her honesty, but mostly he wanted her to be honest with herself. He was pointing out the quicksand. He needed to know that she saw it, too.

"I understand," she said at last. "Nevertheless, I'd welcome your company in my bed. What happens after that will happen. People will talk. I can't be responsible for what they think or say."

Call wasn't as certain that word would get around, but he felt the need to remind her that it could. Rooster would cut out his own tongue before he'd talk, and the brothers, for all they were young and titillated by the goings-on at Mrs. Fry's house, they were loyal to Laurel and wouldn't speak out of turn. Jelly was most likely to let the cat out of the bag, but since he didn't often sleep in the bunkhouse, there was a chance to avoid being found out. The one person Call didn't know if he could count on was Mrs. Lancaster. She'd encouraged Laurel to flirt, but bedding down with a man outside of marriage might cross her moral line.

"Tonight?" he asked.

Laurel pressed her lips together. There was a comfortable ache between her thighs and a sense that there was a hollow there waiting to be filled by him. It had to be filled by him. The thought that he might come to her bed this evening made her skin tingle. She felt her breasts swelling, the nipples tightening, and she was flushed with warmth.

"Tonight would be fine," she said. Her voice, for all that she had to swallow hard before she spoke, sounded perfectly normal to her. That was good.

"Jelly's at home," said Call.

She nodded. "Probably better that way."

Call didn't indicate one way or the other that she was right. Dillon and Hank had stopped playing a while ago, but now one of them picked up the fiddle and started "Annie Lisle." The melodic ballad drifted toward them. This time it was Call who hummed.

"Heard a version of this a lot during the war," he said quietly when he realized she was staring at him. "'Course the words were different. 'Ellsworth's Avengers,' it was called. A battle tribute song to the first Union officer killed."

"You don't talk much about the war."

"No."

"Do you ever?"

"Sometimes. I wrote home a lot in the beginning. Told my mother things I probably shouldn't have. I meant to set her mind at ease, but the time between letters was hard for her and then . . ." His voice trailed off and he shrugged.

"No," she said. "Don't do that. You were going to say the letters stopped, weren't you?"

"Yes. They stopped."

Laurel thought about that. "You were captured." He was silent for so long, she didn't think he intended to respond. She made herself wait, let him decide what he was willing to tell her rather than pepper him with questions.

"Yes," he said finally. "Captured in December '62 at Fredericksburg, Virginia. I was an advance scout by that time, serving in the Army of the Potomac under General Burnside. Maybe if you were a Reb, you'd call me a spy, but I never thought of myself that way. I'd already made the river crossing that the men would make later, and if I'd made it back to the camp, I would have advised against an assault on the city. I didn't, though, and they came across without the intelligence I had gathered.

"I learned that they sacked the city later because by then I was being held by Lee's army, well back of the front. General Lee kicked their collective ass—" He caught himself. "Sorry."

"I've heard the word before," she told him, "and heard it said with much less good reason. Go on."

"The victory didn't make the boys in gray any less peeved at me. I'd been hoping they'd rough me up some and send me back to Burnside, but they roughed me up a lot and sent me to Libby Prison." Call understood from Laurel's sharp intake of breath that she'd heard of it. For good reason, he supposed. The Richmond prison was notorious for the crowded conditions and poor care the officers received.

"Were you one of those who escaped?" she asked.

So she knew about that. It was the other reason people remembered Libby. "I was. We dug for weeks. The ground was rock hard. We started in late December and by midnight on February ninth we were ready to go, one man at a time, worming his way through the tunnel. Hell of a thing, that tunnel. We made it without attracting notice, but when over a hundred men vacate the prison, well, even the Libby guards understood something was going on. I heard later that fifty-nine men made it to Union lines. A couple of fellas drowned. The rest of us were recaptured. Later that month, we were moved south."

Laurel slowly shook her head as she brought her hand to her mouth and spoke from behind it. "Oh, no. Please tell me you did not end up in Andersonville."

Rather than lie, Call remained silent.

Laurel lowered her hand, as she understood what he was saying when he said nothing. Libby's deplorable conditions were exceeded by only one other place, the Camp Sumter Prison Camp, known better as Andersonville Prison. "I never heard about escapes from Andersonville," she said quietly.

"Because there weren't any, at least not that I ever heard. Guards in towers shot if you got too close to the line. The dead line, we called it. I knew men who skirted it as if it were a game to see if they could provoke the guards to shoot. They usually did, and their aim was true.

For some it wasn't a game, just a way to end a life when they believed suicide was a sin they'd carry forever."

"You were there until the end of the war, then."

Call drew in a breath and let it out slowly. He nodded. "Made my way back mostly on my own. Traveling with others made even two or three of us seem threatening. And we looked like hell, emaciated, wearing filthy rags, lice-ridden. You'd have barred the door if you saw us coming. Folks did until we figured out that alone was better. After that, people were mostly kind. They shared food if they had any, sometimes liquor. One woman took fresh-washed clothes off her line and gave them to me. A barber stepped out of his shop as I was walking by and handed me a comb to pick nits out of my beard and hair." Call's faint smile was rueful. "He didn't invite me inside, though."

Laurel mirrored Call's sheepish smile. "I suppose even a kindhearted barber has his limits."

"For good reason. I caught a look at myself in his window front and didn't know the man looking back at me. The generosity of people still suffering from their own losses was humbling. I wouldn't have made it home without their help. I know it and I'm grateful."

"So am I," said Laurel. She stood and held out her hand to him.

Call did not take it immediately. He stared at it and then at her.

Laurel smiled. "Go on. Take it. Have you noticed the boys stopped playing? That means they're heading to bed now. I figure we should do the same."

22

Call waited at the foot of the stairs while Laurel extinguished the lamps burning in the parlor and her office. She merely turned back the one in the dining room, leaving it to flicker at the window to mark the entrance to the station house, and carried another with her. She didn't take his hand again as she climbed the stairs to the second floor, but she did look over her shoulder once to make certain he was following. He was. Oddly, his mouth was dry and his eyes were damp. Damn, if he wasn't in love with this woman.

It wasn't precisely an epiphany. He'd known his feelings were moving in that direction for a while, but tonight the current of emotion carried him right to where he was now. He rarely spoke about Libby, and only once about Andersonville, and yet he'd told her about both. Laurel Beth Morrison was someone to him, someone important, someone who could bear knowing about the wounds he carried and was as grateful as he that he had survived them.

So am I, she said and offered him her hand. He'd almost told her then. It's why he hesitated. By accepting her hand and the invitation inherent in the gesture, he was agreeing to her terms. She was the one who did not want to attach meaning to making love and he made a conscious decision to honor that. It was only as he reached the landing that he wondered if he'd been wrong.

Laurel passed three closed rooms before she stopped

at a door at the end of the hall. She set her hand on the knob and looked at Call. "This is my room," she said for want of something to say. She held the lamp away from her, hoping he wouldn't notice that she was embarrassed by her unnecessary comment. If he thought she was nervous, if he doubted her sincerity, he would walk away. She was sure of that, and it was the last thing she wanted.

Laurel opened the door, let it swing wide, and led the way into her bedroom. She set the lamp on the bedside table between a short stack of Beadle's Dime Novels and a pair of gold-rimmed spectacles. She turned to face him, arms at her sides, and was mindful of not shifting her weight or curling and uncurling her fingers.

"Maybe you should close the door," she said.

Call had stopped just over the threshold. He pulled on the doorknob so it swung toward him and then tapped it closed with the heel of his boot. He walked to the room's only window and looked out. Laurel's room faced the barn and the corral. The bunkhouse was off to the left at a hard angle. The chicken coop and smokehouse weren't visible. He released the tabs that held the curtains closed and waited until they fell in place before he closed the short distance separating him from Laurel.

"I didn't know you wore spectacles," he said.

Surprised, Laurel blinked widely. "What?"

"Your spectacles. They're on the table behind you. I didn't know you wore them."

"For reading sometimes. Mostly Beadle's. The print is small."

"Put them on."

She frowned slightly and didn't move.

"No, really. Put them on. I want to see you in them."

Laurel didn't turn. She reached behind her instead and felt around on the table until she found them. Unfolding the stems, she slipped on the spectacles and pushed them up the bridge of her nose. She tilted her head and regarded Call over the rims. "Well?" she said.

Call placed a forefinger under her chin and tipped her

face toward him. He was unsmiling as he studied her. "I was right," he said eventually. "You can't help but look lovely."

Laurel huffed a laugh and brushed his hand away. When she realized he still wasn't smiling, her eyebrows folded. "You're serious."

"Yes."

"And ridiculous."

"Frequently," he said, "but not about this."

Shaking her head, Laurel removed the spectacles and put them behind her. Without quite knowing how he'd done it, Laurel realized he'd set her at ease. She appreciated that because now that she had him here, she wasn't sure what to do about it. "You could take off your hat," she said.

Call removed it, tossing it toward a painted ladder-back chair. It caught one of the white spindles and hung there.

Laurel watched the hat's flight and looked at him suspiciously when it landed. "You got lucky."

He grinned, pushing his fingers through his hair. "I did. I *am*."

The gleam in his eye made her think she'd gotten lucky as well. Not for the first time in her life, Laurel took the bull by the horns and curled her fingers in his leather vest. She pulled him closer, stood on tiptoes, and sought his mouth with hers.

The kiss started out hungry and just got hungrier. She didn't know how much she needed this, needed him, until she felt his mouth against hers. His lips were dry. She licked them with the damp edge of her tongue and heard him groan softly at the back of his throat. He kissed her deeply as she fumbled with the buttons of his vest and pushed it over his shoulders. It fell to the floor and he kicked it away. His mouth never left hers.

Their tongues tangled. Laurel breathed in the earthy scent of him and found she liked it. At the pool there'd been no fragrance. The clean, crisp scent of the water overwhelmed the man. Now she recognized what the heady combination of the faint odors of sweat and horses and whiskey could do to her. McCall Landry overwhelmed her.

Laurel tugged on his shirttail, pulling it out of his trousers. Reaching under it, she unfastened his belt and then set to work unbuttoning his shirt. Her fingers were clumsy. It was his mouth, she thought. The kiss clouded her mind, made her fingers fumble. She was no longer wearing her shirt, and she had no idea when that had happened. He was holding it crumpled in his fist at the small of her back. She felt, rather than saw, him pitch it over his shoulder and had no idea where it landed.

Laurel opened his shirt and slipped her hands inside. He was wearing a loose cotton undershirt. She plucked at the material, lifted it, and laid her palms flat against his skin. He was warm. His flat belly retracted when she touched him because he sucked in a breath. It was the first time his mouth left hers.

She found him again, lightly bit his lower lip, nibbled it. She ran her tongue along the ridge of his teeth and along the sensitive underside of his upper lip. She kissed the corner of his mouth, touched his jaw, rubbed her cheek against his beard.

One strap of Laurel's camisole fell over her shoulder. Before she could even think of righting it, Call's mouth was at the curve of her neck. He sucked on her flesh and she felt the pulse of it all the way to her toes.

Laurel's palms climbed his smooth back; her fingers traced the length of his spine. Her nails settled at his nape and dug in ever so lightly. She twisted his hair with her fingertips, ruffled the ends. He made her moan when he drew his lips along her collarbone. His hands lifted her camisole and cupped her breasts. His thumbs made a pass across her nipples and she arched into him, cradling his erection with her thighs.

Call ground his hips against her, but it wasn't enough. It wasn't nearly enough. His lips were at her ear when he told her what he wanted in language so rough it was like gravel in his throat. She didn't pull away or take him to task. What she did was shiver.

Laurel grasped the hem of her camisole, pulled it over her head, and let it sail. Call shrugged out of his shirt, undershirt, and yanked on his belt. They sat on the bed at the same time and shucked their boots. Call got out of his first and knelt on the floor at Laurel's feet to help her with her second one. He tossed it to the side and removed her socks. She wiggled her toes. Call set his hands on her knees and looked up at her. He said nothing, merely looked at her while she stared back. Her pupils widened. His desire was mirrored in her eyes and she would see the same in him.

His hands slid up her thighs and parted her legs. He stood between them, took her by the wrists, and brought her hands to the buttons of his fly. Call waited to see what she would do, but he needn't have asked himself the question. Laurel handled these buttons with a deftness that was missing when she unfastened his shirt. She slipped her hand inside his trousers and cupped his balls through his drawers. He caught her by the wrist and held her hand there, pushing back against the pressure of her palm.

Now she asked, "What do you want me to do?"

"Nothing," he said, closing his eyes. "Nothing." After a moment, and before he came out of his skin, Call stepped back and drew Laurel to her feet. He stripped her out of her trousers and drawers and shed his own while she stood naked at the bedside watching him. "I appreciate your interest," he whispered, pulling back the covers, "but I want you here more." He gave her a little push just below the hollow of her throat and she toppled back without complaint.

Laurel twisted and rolled to make room for Call, and when he was beside her, she tugged on the top sheet to cover them. Call immediately tossed it aside. "For later," he said. "We've got nothing to hide, and I missed this at the falls. I regret I wasn't able to see you like this."

Laurel's skin prickled. He did that with his talk; he did

it with the way he looked at her. She remembered Call as he was when she first met him. He'd been a little green around the edges from the journey, but he'd looked at her then as he was looking at her now. She had been fully clothed and he didn't undress her; it wasn't that kind of interest he showed. He regarded her with respect and something like reverence. He'd liked her then, but she hadn't understood, hadn't recognized the signs of a man's admiration.

She had come to know those signs, for he was certainly admiring her. His darkening eyes told her that. The silver-blue rings had narrowed around his widening pupils, and the color was less like moonlight and more like smoke. She wondered about her own eyes because she was shamelessly admiring him. What color would they be if not merely brown? As dark as coffee grounds? Lighter like cinnamon? What would he see as she studied the slope of his shoulders, his tapered waist, the gentle concave curve of his hip?

Laurel had been with him in the full light of day, but she hadn't seen him like this. The lamplight was a steady muted glow, casting Call in dim golden light and shadow where the light could not reach.

"You're beautiful," she whispered. When his lip curled and he looked away, she asked, "Are you blushing? I can't tell." She laid her fingertips against his cheek in the event she could feel rising warmth.

Call circled her wrist and removed her hand. "I am *not* blushing."

"Oh, so you've grown accustomed to the compliment. Is that it?"

"That is *not* it. Where do you come by these absurd assumptions?"

"I don't know." She shrugged a bit defensively. "They simply occur to me."

"Well, put it out of your mind. I don't blush." Because he was still holding her wrist, he lifted her hand to his ear. "Go on," he said. "Touch the tip. Feel that?"

Laurel brushed aside his hair and traced the outer shell of his ear with her fingers. She nodded. "It's warm."

"That's because the tips of my ears are red. Like I said, I don't blush."

Laurel's quiet laughter ended when she leaned toward Call. Her mouth hovered a hairsbreadth above his. "Whatever you say." Then she kissed him.

Call rolled onto his back and hauled her in. She laid her bent knee across his thighs. One of his palms cupped her rounded buttock. He told her she was a perfect handful and she slipped her hand between their bodies, found his cock, and huskily declared that so was he.

Mere seconds passed and she discovered the truth. He was more than a handful. She moaned softly against his lips when his hand slid to the small of her back and his fingers walked up her spine. They returned to their starting point and then dipped lower, drawing another sweet whimper from her.

He showed her how to move her hand along the length of his erection, promised that she wouldn't hurt him, and when she proved to be adept at it, Call dug his heels into the mattress, bucked, and threw her off him before he came. He gave her no time to ask questions or adapt to suddenly being under him. He moved swiftly, parting her knees and lifting them so when he was between her legs, she was hugging him. Call didn't know if she was ready for him, and some part of him understood he was being careless by not making certain, but she had brought him to this point where he could do nothing else but what he was doing.

Call pushed himself forward and then pushed into her. Laurel cried out once at the hard thrust of his entry and then was quiet. She clutched him with her knees, her arms, and where he'd filled her so abruptly and intimately, well, she clutched him there, too.

Call groaned, pressed his face into the curve of her neck. He mouthed words of apology that were hardly coherent, and it was borne home to him that she either understood or did not care because her fingers fluttered in his hair and she stroked the back of his neck. She whispered something in return and her hips lifted and fell, lifted and fell again.

Call pushed himself up on his forearms and accepted the rhythm that she established. Laurel had seized the moment and Call knew himself to be well and truly caught in it. His thrust pushed her toward the head of the bed. She yanked the pillow out from under her head and flung it away. She arched her throat, digging the back of her head into the mattress to find purchase.

The long stem of her neck was an invitation. Call dipped his head and brushed his lips against the pulse beating there. He wanted to do more and couldn't. He closed his eyes against temptation and put his concentration where it needed to be. Laurel was tugging on every thread that made up the sharp sensations holding him together. He knew what would happen if he let her have her way, and as much as he wanted to, he couldn't allow that.

She resisted when he needed to leave her, tightening her grip everywhere. Her knees pressed more deeply against him. Her fingers clasped behind his back. And where he felt the fine, razor-sharp edge of pleasure most keenly, her slick walls contracted around him.

Call gave a shout as he heaved himself away from her, shuddered, and spilled his seed across the flat of her belly. Sucking in a deep breath, he rolled onto his back and lay still. Beside him, Laurel slowly lowered her knees and then lay as quiet as he did. She stared at the ceiling, dry-eyed and a little bewildered. He stared at her profile.

Laurel stirred first. As Call watched, she lifted one hand and touched the milky seed on her belly with a forefinger. She raised the finger so it was in her line of sight and inspected the tip. She rubbed the semen between her thumb and forefinger, introducing herself to the texture and viscosity. From Call's perspective, her examination looked thorough, but then she brought the finger to her

lips and touched it with the tip of her tongue and he realized he had been wrong.

"It's warm," she said, lowering her arm. "A little salty.
Just a hint of sweet. I didn't expect that."

"I didn't expect you," he said.

Laurel had no reply to that. She wasn't certain what he
meant by it, yet she was oddly pleased that he'd said so.
"Have you ever tasted it?" she asked, turning her head to
look at him.

"Yes."

"Huh."

"I was curious," he said. "Like you."

Laurel sat up and put her legs over the side of the bed.
"I wouldn't have it as a condiment, though," she said,
glancing at Call over her shoulder. His appreciative laughter warmed her, but when he stretched an arm to reach
her, she eluded him by standing up.

"Where are you going?" he asked.

"To wash." She caught one corner of the sheet, which
had been pushed to the foot of the bed, and loosely fastened it around her. Stepping over and around the clothes
that littered the floor, Laurel reached the washstand and
poured water into the basin from a large porcelain pitcher.
She made a three-quarters turn away from Call when she
saw he had rolled on his side to face her. She wondered
about her modesty and why she should be overwhelmed
by it all of a sudden when Call did not seem bothered in
the least. He was still lying on the bed uncovered, completely at his ease, while she was wearing a sheet like a
Roman senator and keeping her back to him.

Laurel soaked a washcloth, wrung it out, and wiped
her belly. Bending her knees slightly, she washed between
her legs. Had she been alone, she might have lingered
there to relieve the quiver of pleasure that touching herself
there had provoked. Instead, she threw the bunched-up
washcloth in the basin as though it were a hot potato. Water sloshed over the rim of the basin and splashed her. She

used one corner of the sheet to dry her face before she tucked it securely around her.

When she turned around, Call was still stretched out on the bed, though perhaps as a concession to her reserve, he had pulled the log cabin quilt to his waist. Laurel looked around at the clothing scattered on the floor. She picked up his shirt and tossed it to him. Rather than catching it, which he could have easily done, he batted it away so that it fell at the foot of the bedside table.

"Why did you do that?" she asked.

"Why did you throw it to me?"

"I thought you might want to put it on."

"Nope. I'm fine."

"Yes. I'm sure you are right now, but you can't go back to the bunkhouse wearing that quilt."

"Who said I'm going back to the bunkhouse?"

"I think I just heard me say it."

Call rubbed the underside of his chin with the back of his hand. "Must be you've taken another absurd assumption into your head."

Laurel hitched the sheet fractionally higher. "No, really, you need to return to the bunkhouse."

Both of Call's eyebrows rose. "Oh, no. We're not done here."

"We're not?"

"No," he said, shaking his head. The glimmer of the smile that curved his mouth reached his eyes. "No, we're not."

23

"C"ome here," he said.

She didn't move. "So help me, Call, if you crook a finger at me, I'll break it."

"I believe you. It wasn't my intention."

Laurel eyed him as if she could divine precisely what his intentions were. When he merely continued to regard her patiently, she moved toward the bed. At the point where he could have reached her, he made no attempt. "What do you mean, we're not done?"

"One of us isn't satisfied, and I'm not satisfied with that."

She blinked. "I'm not sure what you mean."

"Liar. I wasn't kind to you. Or fair. I want to make amends. I want to please you."

"You did. It was, um, nice."

"Nice," he said. "Damned by faint praise."

"Well, it *was* nice," she said defensively.

"I think I need to be blunt here. Did you come? This afternoon at the falls you came. You had an orgasm. I want to give you another."

Laurel felt as though her knees would sag. She sat on the edge of the bed before that happened.

"In fact," said Call, "you should demand it."

Laurel stared at him, struck by the idea. She lifted her chin. "Maybe you're right. I should."

Call welcomed the thrust of her chin. It was like greeting an old friend. He took her hand, squeezed it gently. "I think I hurt you," he said. "Did I?"

Her astonishment was not forced. "No. No, you didn't. Why do you think that?"

"I got ahead of myself. I was needy and I was rough."

"Do you think I'm fragile?"

"God, no."

"Then there's your answer." She drew a breath and averted her eyes before she thought better of it. "I didn't want you to put me away like you did at the falls. I wanted to keep you in me."

"I know. You were almost successful." He brushed the heart of her palm with his thumb. "You haven't forgotten why I have to do that, have you?"

"No. I remember. I just don't like it."

"Neither do I." He pushed himself toward the middle of the bed, tugging on her hand as he moved. She didn't resist, stretching out in the depression he had occupied. The awkwardness of their handclasp finally forced them to release it. Call propped himself up on an elbow. "I'll see if I can get my hands on some French letters," he said.

"French letters?"

"Preventatives. It's a sheath, animal skin of some kind, usually sheep or goat, that fits over the penis. We used them during the war; at least some of us did, mainly to prevent disease. If they don't break or tear or have pin-prick holes to begin with, they can prevent pregnancy."

"Why are you only telling me about this now?"

"Because they break and tear and sometimes have pin-prick holes. And they're not cheap. Three dollars for a dozen the last time I bought some."

Laurel did not trouble herself to hide her interest. "When was that?"

"Before I was captured."

"So long ago. What about since then?"

"Since then I've been careful."

"There's still disease or don't you consort with women of a public character?"

Call chuckled at the expression. "That's how my grandmother referred to her daughter. My mother had become a woman of a public character. Not surprisingly, Mother preferred 'whore.'"

"You speak of it all so casually. Were you never bothered by it?"

"Grandmother did her best to make me ashamed of my mother, and it's her deepest regret that she was unable to make it happen. I love my mother; I love all the women I called aunts while I was living at the brothel. They came and went and had a hand in raising me, and I like to think I was better for their attention. I didn't attend school until I tried college so I didn't experience much in the way of name-calling and slurs. Mother schooled me. Some of my aunts couldn't read so we learned together. There were other women who knew history or geography or mathematics and tutored me. Aunt Estella read the philosophers and championed John Locke. She was impressive."

"They all sound impressive. Who tutored you in—" She hesitated.

"Say it," said Call. "It will come to you more easily if you start saying it."

"All right. Who tutored you in pirooting?"

He laughed. "I learned something about making love from every one of the whores I lived with. They taught me to respect women, to treat them with dignity, to care for their tender feelings and never make the mistake of thinking them the weaker sex. As for the physical aspects, I never bedded any of the women in my mother's brothel."

"I believe you had an excellent education," she said. "In all things." Laurel warmed to his soft and tender smile and loosened the knot that held her sheet closed. She didn't part it. She let him do that. His fingertips brushed her skin as lightly as a butterfly's wing against her ear. He didn't look at what his fingers were doing. He looked at her. It was infinitely better that way.

Lowering his head, he kissed her on the mouth, moving slowly over it and then down. He kissed her chin, her throat, and then made a trail to the gentle hollow between her breasts. He felt her breathing quicken as her heart stuttered. His mouth moved to her nipple and he rolled it between his lips, laved it with his tongue. He heard her start to say something, but whatever it was ended on a little gasp that was wholly satisfying. He pressed a smile against her skin.

Laurel threaded her fingers in his hair. She wanted him to linger, and he did for a time, but eventually he slid sideways and gave his full attention to her other breast. She held her breath in anticipation of his mouth closing over her areola, and when it did, she realized she still had room in her lungs to suck in another gulp of air.

He lifted his mouth and rose above her. Without prompting, Laurel raised her knees and Call moved between them, but how he accepted her invitation was entirely different than before. He let her see his perfectly wicked smile before he dipped his head, placed his lips between her breasts a second time, and then made a damp trail between her ribs and down her abdomen.

"What are you—" She didn't finish her question. She raised a hand and dragged her fingertips through Call's hair. Whether she intended to keep him close or push him away was unclear even to her, and Call, if he noticed, was not troubled by motive. He breathed in the musky scent of her and separated her slick and swollen lips with his tongue, flicking the tip of it along the kernel of flesh between them.

Laurel's breath caught. It wasn't possible to fill her lungs; she sipped the air instead. Pleasure unwound in tiny increments, slipping under her skin until all of her was flush with it. She thought she wouldn't be able to tolerate it. She wanted it to be over and she wanted it to go on forever.

Clearly, Call knew her mind better than she did because he kept going, licking, laving, and loving her in this most intimate way. Laurel's fingernails pressed white crescents into her palms before she grasped the sheet and bunched it in her hands. She arched her neck and her heels dug deep. She closed her eyes, squeezed them shut really. A small keening cry rose from her throat before she could call it back, and almost immediately the long muscles of her arms and legs contracted.

Laurel felt as if her body had shattered and she was flung in so many directions, she would never recover the pieces. Of course that wasn't the case. Not at all. Not only was she all of a piece when her breathing slowed and her heart resumed its normal rhythm, she was whole.

"Oh, God," she whispered. "That was . . . that was . . . there are no words."

Call levered himself over her. "There are, but you probably shouldn't strain yourself to come up with them."

Laurel put a hand to the side of his face and gently pushed him away. He flopped on his back beside her.

"Are you smiling?" she asked.

"You can't see?"

"I'd have to turn my head. Right now that seems like too much work." It wasn't much of an exaggeration. She couldn't recall another instance when she'd known such lethargy or felt so replete.

"Then I'm not smiling," he said, smiling.

"Liar." She said it not unkindly. "What you did to me . . . someone taught you that."

"Uh-huh. And a few other things besides."

"Not now," she said, though she wondered about those things. "Maybe another time."

Call's chest shook when he laughed.

"Why are you laughing?"

"Because you sound so damn determined. Do you have a list you're checking off?"

"Now how could I have a list when I'm just learning about these things?" she asked in practical tones. "I'm *creating* a list that I can refer to at some later date."

"Later date?"

"After you're gone."

Call couldn't tell if she was being deliberately provocative or perfectly serious. "Who said I'm going anywhere? We talked about this. I told you then that you're surer about me moving on than I am. I like it here, and not just because I like you." Call paused, expecting her to say something. "What? You're getting used to the idea?"

"Hmm. Getting used to it *and* comforted by it. Surprises me some, but then I like you, too."

"There's a relief."

Laurel poked him with her elbow. "That's no reason to mock me. You know very well I wouldn't have propositioned or invited you into this bed if I didn't like you."

Call turned on his side. She appeared serene in profile, not at all like a women who had just poked him in the arm. She hid the impish side of her quite well. "Laurel. You told me in no uncertain terms that if I didn't do what you wanted, you would find someone who would. As I recall, liking the gentleman of your choosing wasn't a consideration."

"Oh, that."

"Yes," he said. "That."

"I meant it when I said it," she said quietly, sparing him a guilty glance. "Sort of. It was mostly a threat, though I can't very well swallow the words now, can I?"

Call said nothing, waited for her to continue.

"And as it turned out, I couldn't act on it. I reckon that liking the fella had something to do with it after all. I narrowed the field in my mind, gave it consideration as an exercise in examining the possibilities, but I pretty much knew that only you would do."

"Why am I not flattered? Tell me about this narrowed field. Exactly how narrow was it?"

"You're not going to let this go, are you?"

"Not a chance."

Laurel sighed. "Very well. There were three remaining."

"Oh, no. You can't leave it there. Who were they?"

"I don't think anything good can come of you knowing."

"Tell me and we'll see."

Trying to decide how serious he was, Laurel hesitated before surrendering. She sighed. "The only one you know is Rayleigh Carter." She turned her head to gauge his reaction and was immediately suspicious. "Are you trying not to choke on your laughter? Stop it. You look apoplectic."

Call buried his face in his pillow. His shoulders shook.

"So help me, Call, if you smother yourself, I'll feed you to the hogs."

Lifting his face, Call gasped once for air and steadied himself. Biting the inside of his cheek helped. "Go on," he said. His voice had a quaver in it, but he managed to set his features gravely.

"Jack Friendly. You might have seen him at church services. Beanpole tall and just about as skinny, but he's a kind and gentle soul. He's a second-generation farmer." Laurel observed that Call had no urge to laugh now. He was thinking, obviously trying to place Jack. She knew the moment he did because a gleam crept into his eye.

"He's more than twice your age."

"So?"

Call pressed his lips together and avoided going face-down in his pillow. "Yes, you're right," he said after a moment. "He's a kind and gentle soul."

"His first two wives thought so."

"Dear God," he said under his breath. He briefly closed his eyes, rubbed above them with a thumb and forefinger. "And the third man?"

"Sweeny."

Now Call's eyes opened wide. "Sweeny? Sweeny's Saloon Sweeny?"

"No. His nephew Malcolm. He's a lawyer. His practice is in Stonechurch but he comes to Falls Hollow a couple of times a month to see folks who need his help. You probably saw him getting on or off the stage here and didn't pay him any mind. He's about your age so you can't find fault there, and he's fit and fine looking. I am not alone in that opinion."

"Does he carry a leather case? Wear a brown bowler with a little feather on the side? Talk like someone has him by the—"

"All right," she said, interrupting. "You know who he is."

"Yeah, I do. Why wasn't he acceptable?"

"He talks like someone has him by the balls. Would you want that voice whispering in your ear?"

Call leaned over and whispered, "No."

She pushed him back in spite of the little burst of pleasure she felt when his breath touched her cheek. "Satisfied?" she asked.

"Hmm," he murmured, giving her a most significant look. "I could be. I reckon that depends on you."

Laurel's eyes widened a fraction and her lips parted. Her voice came so softly, she barely heard her own question. "Again?"

Call nodded, raised a brow, and leaned in. This time she did not push him away.

24

Laurel stirred, rousing herself enough to open one heavily lidded eye and lift her head a fraction above the pillow. Almost immediately, her head sank back. She managed to keep the eye open, though, and that was good enough to see that Call was sitting in the chair and pulling on his boots. The bedside lamp had a fingernail of light at the end of its wick and was on the verge of dying. The curtains were still drawn. Laurel could not make out if it was the middle of the night or if dawn was approaching.

"You're leaving," she said drowsily.

"You asked me to."

"I did, but you didn't listen to me then."

"I wasn't ready. I'm ready now."

"Oh. All right."

He chuckled. She was agreeably composed and he decided to appreciate it rather than bring it to her attention.

Reading his mind, Laurel said, "Don't get used to it."

Grinning, he stood, covered the distance to the bed in a couple of long strides, and bent so he could kiss her cheek. She turned her head to greet him and they clumsily bumped noses. "Sorry." He pressed a quick kiss to her forehead when she covered her nose with her palm. "Go back to sleep. You have a few hours yet."

Laurel dutifully closed her eyes and listened to Call leaving the bedroom. She was asleep before she heard him leave the house.

* * *

Call expected questions come morning from the brothers, but it was Rooster who cornered him in the barn while they were grooming horses in preparation of the morning stage.

"You came in pretty late last night," said Rooster. "That's kinda unusual, ain't it?"

"Suppose it is. I didn't think about it except for trying to be quiet. I guess I wasn't very good at it."

"No, on the whole you were as stealthy as a thief until you dropped one of your boots. Thumped me right awake."

"Sorry." Call continued to run a curry comb over Willow's back. The mare tossed her head, apparently satisfied with the attention she was getting.

Rooster finished caring for Mary Ann and stepped to the next stall to groom Sylvia. He stroked the white diamond on the mare's nose. "Yes, you're a good girl," he said, showing her the curry brush in his other hand. "I guess finding Josey Pye yesterday probably made it hard to shut your eyes."

Call straightened and looked at Rooster over Willow's back. "Are you talking to me?"

"Well, Sylvia here didn't find Josey Pye, so I musta meant you to hear me."

"What is it you want to know, Rooster?" Call asked bluntly.

"I'm not going to ask you where you were before you came to the bunkhouse 'cause it ain't my business and I don't want to hear a lie even if it's meant well, so I'm just gonna say that you better treat her right, Call. She deserves that. I've never asked myself if she knew what she was doing before, but the question's come to me now. I figure it's up to you to make certain she doesn't have regrets."

Call wasn't sure why he felt as if he'd been taken to the woodshed, but he was tempted to check his backside for welts. "What will set your mind at ease?"

"Don't rightly know. Maybe if you was to move on

before there's been too much hurt done, or maybe if you was to go the other way and say you're staying put after this Josey Pye business is over, I reckon either one of those would ease my mind some."

"You think I should ease your mind before I ease hers?"

Rooster considered that. "Guess not."

"Look, Rooster, I appreciate that you want the best for Laurel. You've been at her side for a lot of years so it's natural that you'd be looking out for her whether or not she thinks she needs looking after. I'm telling you that you're talking to the wrong person. You should be putting your concerns to her."

Rooster's jaw went slack and he shook his head emphatically. "You're plum loco, you know that?"

"Maybe," Call said carelessly. "And maybe you're afraid to speak your mind to her. You know, you bear some responsibility for whatever you think is happening between Laurel and me."

Frowning, Rooster busied himself currying Sylvia. "What do you mean?"

"You recall telling her she was a coward?"

"I might've said something like that."

"Uh-huh. That was the catalyst."

"Catalyst?"

"The thing that lit a fire under her."

"Oh. Didn't realize what would come of it when she set off the way she did. I reckon she needed to prove something to herself."

"I reckon she did," Call said quietly. "Are we done here, Rooster?"

"Except for the animals, yeah, we're done."

Call nodded, satisfied they would not be talking about Laurel again. Ever.

The second time Laurel woke, the sun was higher in the frame of her bedroom window than it usually was when she rolled out of bed. She hadn't remembered Call opening the curtains before he left, but maybe he had. She had slept like the dead.

Laurel washed at the basin, cleaned her teeth, and dressed in yesterday's denim trousers and a fresh but faded blue cotton shirt. She rolled up the sleeves to three-quarter length before she dropped to the upholstered stool in front of the vanity. She usually groomed the horses with more care than she showed for her hair, but today was different, and in spite of the late hour, Laurel took her time pulling her mother's old brush through her hair and pulling it into a smooth tail instead of plaiting it. She secured it with a blue ribbon that was almost as faded as her shirt and wondered at the sudden urge she had to visit the mercantile for new ribbons and maybe material to make something new.

The old vanity mirror was cracked, darker at the bottom than it was at the top, and there were little bubbles in the glass, but Laurel valued it for its history because it was one of the precious items her mother brought with her from the East. Now she twisted her head this way and that to find the best reflection, and when she finally found it, she mocked the effort with a short laugh. Really, she thought, she had lost her mind.

Laurel jumped off the stool and hurried out of the bedroom. She stole a heel of bread from the loaf Mrs. Lancaster was slicing, ducked the playful swipe the cook took at her, and headed for the privy. She was washing her hands at the pump when Jelly sidled up to her and waited his turn to do the same. When she stepped back from the pump, she caught him staring.

"What is it, Jelly?" She swiped self-consciously at her cheek with the back of a damp hand. "Is it gone?"

"Is what gone, Miss Laurel?"

"Whatever it was that you were staring at."

He grinned toothily. "Nope. Still there."

She started to lift her hand again and stopped when she realized he was talking about her. "Does your father know what a devil you are?"

"Yes, ma'am. He remarks on it regularly, but it wouldn't

be right not telling you that you are looking especially fine this morning."

Laurel glanced to her right and left and then over her shoulder before she rested her gaze on Jelly again. A flush was beginning to creep under his fair skin. Still, Laurel was suspicious. "Who put you up to saying that?"

He shook his head earnestly. "No one. I swear. Cross my heart. It came to my mind on its own. One of those vagrant thoughts that trips off my tongue before my better self can stop it. Did I offend you, Miss Laurel? That surely was not my intention."

Laurel judged his distress was sincere and knew a pang of guilt that she had assumed it was someone else's mischief that had provoked his declaration. She put a hand on his shoulder. "You did *not* offend me, Jelly. You surprised me, is all. It was a lovely compliment and I should have accepted it graciously. You were kind to say so."

Jelly looked at her hand on his shoulder and then back at her. His lopsided smile was a trifle giddy and swallowing hard didn't alter it.

Laurel removed her hand and let it fall to her side. She smiled gently before she turned and walked toward the house. "How long ago did I hire Jelly?" she asked the cook.

"Been at least a week now." She frowned in disapproval as Laurel spun a chair away from the table and straddled it. "That's no way for you to sit, Miss Laurel. I'm never going to get used to your boyish ways."

Laurel set her forearms along the back of the chair. It was not the first time she'd heard Mrs. Lancaster's criticism and she merely grinned.

"Why'd you want to know about Jelly?" the cook asked.

"Oh, he just said something to me that made me wonder if he might have a bit of a case of calf-love."

"Good Lord, Miss Laurel. Are you only getting around to noticing that now? Me and Rooster remarked on it the second day the boy was here. You gave him that hat on account of him always trying to squash his cowlick. He was already a gone goose but that just about did him in."

"I had no idea."

"If you'll pardon me for saying so, you'd notice one of the mares limping at a hundred yards before you'd see a man making eyes at you at arm's length."

"I noticed Mr. Pye," she said dryly. "I didn't like it."

Mrs. Lancaster snorted derisively. "Not the kind of eyes I'm talking about. I saw how he looked at you and you were smart to keep him at a distance. That man had no good thinking on his mind, and I'm not talking about his thievery."

"Why didn't you say anything to me about that?"

"Because you kept him in your sights all the time you were avoiding him. I figured you for handling him on your own."

"I don't know, Mrs. Lancaster, you made a point of telling me you don't like the way I'm sitting in this chair and yet you kept your counsel about Josey Pye. That doesn't make a lot of sense to me."

"I'm talking about a *good* man making eyes at you. And forget about the darn chair. That ain't what's important. As for Josey Pye, anyone could see the man was so bent, he could swallow nails and spit out corkscrews."

"I didn't see *that*," said Laurel. "I wouldn't have hired him if I'd seen that."

"Well, maybe I didn't either, truth be told," Mrs. Lancaster admitted grudgingly.

"And Jelly's a child, so why you think I should have noticed him right off, I don't know. I think it's better that I didn't."

Exasperated, the cook huffed. "I ain't talking about Jelly." She tapped her long-handled wooden spoon against the table. Every beat was a staccato, a snap to attention. "I'm. Talking. About. McCall. Landry."

Laurel's eyebrows rose. She held her tongue for a long moment, collecting herself. Keeping her voice neutral, she said carefully, "You think Mr. Landry likes me?"

"That's what I'm saying." She thumped the spoon again

for emphasis. "You should do something about it, Miss Laurel."

Laurel could have told the cook that she already had, but she realized she wanted to keep it to herself for a while longer. "Like what?" she asked.

"Like making an effort to smile more when he's around."

"I smile."

"When he's around," Mrs. Lancaster repeated. "You gotta do it when he's around and it's got to be for him. It's no good when you only smile at Rooster and the brothers and leave him out. I got eyes in my head. I see how it is at the table. He looks at you and you look everywhere else. That's not encouraging. You're a ripe piece of fruit, Miss Laurel, and maybe it's time for you to think about getting plucked."

Laurel frowned deeply. "What did you say?"

"I said *plucked*." She made disapproving noises. "As if I'd ever say the other. What gets into your mind, I'll never know."

Laurel knew exactly what had gotten into her mind. She had been well and truly plucked last night. There was no chance of her withering on the vine now. "I'll think about it," she said.

"Well, while you're thinking about that, maybe you should consider saying his name. There's Rooster, Hank, Dillon, and now Jelly, but *he's* Mr. Landry."

"You're Mrs. Lancaster."

The cook gave Laurel a smart tap on the forearm with her spoon. "That's not the same. Not the same at all and you know it."

Laurel removed her arms from the tabletop and eyed the cook's spoon warily. "That stung."

"It was supposed to. It was supposed to wake you up."

"I'm awake. I swear to you that I'm awake."

"Prove it."

Laurel didn't hear a challenge in the older woman's words. Mrs. Lancaster said the words gently. It was how

Laurel imagined her mother would have spoken to her. "Mr. Landry—Call—is just passing through," she said, adopting the cook's quiet tone. "When this business with the stolen payroll is concluded, he'll be on his way."

"Maybe so, maybe not. I'm not as certain of that as you seem to be. He talks like he'd want to stick, at least that's what I hear him saying. Look, Miss Laurel, I don't want to see you get your heart broken, but maybe you should test the waters."

Laurel chuckled humorlessly. "I tested the waters yesterday and you know what happened. I found Mr. Pye."

"I didn't mean it literal." She sighed heavily. "I swear, you are trying my patience this morning. Next time I find you sleeping in, I'm going to shake you awake."

That startled Laurel. "You were in my room?"

"Sure. When you didn't come down, I went up to check on you. I can't remember the last time you slept so soundly. I picked up the mess of clothes you left on the floor and opened the curtains so maybe you'd wake gentle like, but you didn't stir. I reckon all that nasty business yesterday—and on the Lord's Sabbath no less—must've left you plum tuckered. Me? I hardly slept a wink and I only know what Dillon told me."

"I'm sure he was descriptive."

"Right down to the fish nibbles on the man's neck and the waxy gray skin." She shivered. "See that? Now I got it in my mind again."

Laurel's cheeks puffed as she blew out a breath. "I think I've heard enough." She stood, spun the chair around, and pushed it under the table. "I'm going to my office. If someone needs me, that's where I'll be."

"Won't be long before the stage arrives," said the cook. "Call says he's expecting a doctor from Stonechurch."

Laurel had forgotten. Her conversation with Mrs. Lancaster must have rattled her. It was an unfamiliar feeling and it had nothing at all to do with finding Mr. Pye or being reminded of his appearance.

He talks like he wants to stick.

Laurel had heard words to that effect from Call, but she hadn't wanted to believe them. The fact that Mrs. Lancaster had heard the same made her think that she'd been wrong to dismiss them.

He talks like he wants to stick.

They were tempting words, and she was tempted.

25

Call was exercising one of the mares in the corral when Laurel came over and perched herself on the uppermost rail. She waved him on when he and Mary Ann approached her and closely watched the mare's awkward gait. "She's looking a little puddin' footed. Did you check her shoes?"

"I did. I had Rooster give them a look, too. Picked them clean. I thought I'd give her a chance to work it out. It might not be the shoes at all."

Laurel nodded. "She can't make an exchange this morning. Not today."

"Rooster and I decided to let the paint take Mary Ann's place."

"The paint? Oh, you mean Marigold."

"Right. She's rested and in good form."

"Good. Do you mind if I have a look at Mary Ann?"

"No. More eyes can't hurt."

"Not right now," she said when he started to bring the mare over. "Later this afternoon. The stage from Stonechurch will be here soon."

"Is that what you came to tell me?"

She shook her head. "I couldn't spend another minute looking at the accounts. I figured fresh air was what I needed so I came over here."

"Glad you did."

"Where are the boys?"

Call pointed to the barn loft. "Pitching hay. Jelly's with them and I suspect he's doing most of the work. He's at an age where he still thinks it's fun. Hank and Dillon are taking advantage of that."

"Rascals," she said.

"Rooster's in the kitchen snapping beans for Mrs. Lancaster," he said without being asked. Call looped Mary Ann's leading rope over her back and patted her flank to move her along without him. He leaned a shoulder against the rail beside Laurel and looked up at her. In spite of the fact that there was no one around to hear him, he asked quietly, "How are you?"

"Fine," she said. "I'm fine." She hesitated. "I have marks on my skin."

"Love licks."

"I don't know about that. More like I've been branded."

A faint smile flickered across Call's lips. "I'm not sorry. In fact, I kind of like it. Did I hurt you?"

"No." There was an ache between her thighs that she couldn't quite describe to herself, let alone tell him about. She thought of it more as an emptiness, a vague reminder of the use he'd made of her body. Of the use she'd allowed him to make of her body, she corrected. Nothing, not a solitary thing he had done to her, had been without her permission. Even when she didn't quite know what she was asking for, the response was always what she wanted. "You didn't hurt me at all. I'm just a little . . ." Her voice trailed off as she backed away from explaining.

"Tender?" he asked.

She nodded.

"I was too rough, then. I don't mean it as an excuse, but I lost my head last night."

"Really?" It was hard to fathom. He'd seemed so controlled.

"Believe it," he said and pointed a finger at her. "You bear some responsibility for that. I'm not saying it's all on you because I know better, but knowing better doesn't necessarily mean doing better."

"Truly," she said, moving his pointer aside. "I don't know how you could have done any better."

Call gave a shout of laughter that startled Mary Ann into bolting to the other end of the corral. "Look at her go. Did you see that? She doesn't look a bit puddin' footed to me."

"I saw," said Laurel. "I think she was faking. Craving your attention."

"Well, it worked." He set his hand on Laurel's knee and squeezed. "And, no, you don't have to limp to get me to notice you."

Laurel gently put his hand aside, and looked back at the house to see if anyone had noticed. "Rest her today anyway. I don't want to risk her coming up lame on the trail."

"Of course."

Laurel looked down at his hand and wished she could have let him keep it on her knee. "Do I smile enough at you?"

Call arched an eyebrow. The question had come out of nowhere. "Define 'enough.'"

"Mrs. Lancaster says I smile at Rooster and the boys more often than I do you, especially when you're around. Do I? Because I never noticed."

"I'd have to agree with her. I figured you were doing it on purpose, you know, to make it seem as if you don't care when in actual fact you do, trying to throw me off the scent."

"I would never—"

"Maybe not on purpose," he said, changing his mind. "It could be something that was going on in your mind that you didn't know about. I figure you were born with feminine wiles same as any other woman. I like your hair, by the way. Real pretty. It curls a little at the end and swings when you walk."

Laurel forgot what she had been going to say. "How do you know it swings? Or has a curl for that matter? It's behind me and I was walking toward you."

"I saw you at the pump earlier, talking to Jelly. And, you know, the mannerly thing to do is say thank you when you get a compliment, not question its veracity like you're the prosecution cornering a defendant."

It didn't matter that Laurel knew he was right; she didn't appreciate being chastised. Flatly, she said, "Thank you."

"Good," he said. "It'd be better if you smiled when you said it."

"No one else is around. I don't have to smile."

"Right."

"And about those feminine wiles . . . you're wrong, I don't think I was born with any."

"I don't know why I thought I could distract you from that. If you weren't born with them, you've acquired them and you use them to great effect. You can argue the point, but since I'm on the receiving end, your opinion is going to have about as much impact on me as water on a duck's back."

"Then there is no reason to waste my breath, is there?"

"None at all."

Now she smiled. "I like dickering with you."

Call tipped his head back and stared at the sky.

"Are you looking for guidance?" she asked.

"For a lightning strike."

Laurel laughed. "You're good to be so patient with me."

Call regarded her narrowly. "As long as you realize my patience is not infinite."

"You could have just said thank you."

"Thank you."

"Good," she said. "It'd be better if you kissed me when you said it."

"Uh-huh. What you just did there, that'd be a feminine wile."

"Not a successful one."

"Don't tempt me, Laurel. A little bit ago you removed my hand from your knee because someone might see and now you're talking about kissing. You can't keep me twisting in the wind."

Laurel pressed her lips together and nodded shortly. He was right.

"You should know that Rooster heard me come in last night and he had some words for me this morning."

"What kind of words?"

"Just what you'd anticipate from a man who cares about you. If he was your father, he'd have likely got out his shotgun, but since he's less than that and more than a friend, he wanted reassurances that I was either going to leave quickly or stay in place."

Laurel felt her heart hammer once and then resume beating a little faster than before. "What did you say?"

"I asked him if he expected me to ease his mind before I eased yours."

"My mind's easy."

"Is it?" He shrugged. "Then I'll tell him that when it comes up again."

Laurel would have kicked herself if she could have managed her balance at the same time. Why had she said her mind was easy? It wasn't true. It was so far from being true, it would take a week on horseback to reach it. "What if my mind wasn't easy?" she asked. "What would you say then?"

"Hypotheticals unsettle me. Kind of like an itch I can't reach to scratch. You said your mind is easy. I take you at your word."

Now Laurel wanted to kick *him*. Why was he choosing to believe her when she was lying? Did he really not know? Of course he did, she realized, and at any other time he'd have called her on it, except now he was punishing her for lying to him, but mostly for lying to herself. She could either dig in her heels or tell the truth. It shouldn't have been a difficult choice.

"Mrs. Lancaster says you talk like you want to stick," she said, walking the tightrope between digging in and fessing up.

"Odd, isn't it, her saying something like that to you?"

"Not so odd. Not so different than Rooster speaking to

you, except she doesn't know where you spent most of last night."

"Doesn't she?"

"No. She came into my room this morning when I was late getting up. She let me sleep, figured it was yesterday's excitement that left me tuckered out. I let her think it. She picked up my scattered clothes and opened—"

Listening to her, Call had been rubbing thoughtfully behind one ear. He stopped to make a casual observation. "I bet she found the sock I couldn't."

Laurel sat up straight and nearly unseated herself. "What?"

Ignoring the question, Call went on. "Do you think I should ask her about it or wait for her to give it to me?"

"Stop. That's not funny."

"You know, I wouldn't be surprised if it just shows up in my laundry. Lucky for me she'll be collecting it today and I'll get it back tomorrow."

"You're an evil man, McCall Landry."

He crossed his heart. "I swear it's true."

Laurel's shoulders slumped as she sagged in place. "Then she knew all along," she said. "I'm not sure why she called you a good man."

"She said that? Maybe you should believe her."

"I'm not feeling kindly toward you just now."

Call said nothing, merely watched her.

"My mind isn't easy," she said suddenly, as if the words were torn from her against her will.

"Oh?"

"I didn't think it would matter to me if anyone found out about us, but I didn't know enough to understand that it does. Rooster and Mrs. Lancaster, they both mean well, and even though I don't want them looking out for me, they're doing it because they don't think I can look out for myself. In this particular situation, with you, I'm realizing they might be right."

"So what is it you want to know?"

"I guess I want to know what you intend to do after your investigation is done?"

"After settling up with Mr. Stonechurch?"

"Yes, after that."

Call's eyes narrowed a fraction as he studied her face. "I wonder if you're prepared to believe me," he said. "You haven't before."

"You never said it straight out."

"I thought I did."

Laurel tried to remember. Had she been so concerned with protecting herself that she hadn't been able to hear him? "I'm prepared to hear you now," she said.

He stood rooted, tension in the line of his shoulders, in the curled fists at his sides, and said in a clear, steady voice so there could be no mistaking that he was serious, "I'm not going anywhere."

Just like that, she thought. Simply put. Sincerely meant.

"Well?" he asked. "Do you believe me?"

Did she? She wanted to. Lord knew, she wanted to. Why was it so hard to lay herself open? The answer, when she found it, came from her guarded heart. "I believe you believe it."

Call blinked. As though from a blow, he rocked back on his heels. "Jesus, Laurel, I don't know if your aim could be any more true. That's the last time you're going to get the drop on me." Turning, he began walking away.

"Wait," she called after him. "I'm—"

Call glanced over his shoulder. "Go to hell," he said quietly.

Simply put, she thought. And sincerely meant. She watched him walk away.

26

Laurel left her office to meet the stage. She was wearing her spectacles, not because she had been poring over the accounts again, but because she had been crying and they were in aid of disguising that. She had to reach back years to recall the last time she'd wept, and it hadn't been in the immediate aftermath of the death of her father and brothers. No, she'd been stoic then, putting one foot in front of the other, managing the day-to-day operations because she expected it of herself and believed it was what the dead expected of her as well. It was months later, perhaps as many as six, before she confronted the reality of being alone. Not on her own. That was different. She had Rooster and the other hires to help her with the station, and Mrs. Lancaster was with her by then. They shared the burden and benefits, so she never felt completely on her own even though she was solely responsible.

The hard, salty tears came when she reckoned with being alone. Her family was gone and her heart was empty. Men came calling, wanting her time, her attention, but mostly wanting the station. She appreciated the ones who said it straight out; however, they were in the minority. She'd warmed to a couple of them, flattered by their consideration and courtesy, by the words they used that she believed were for her ears alone. That was before she realized those words had been rehearsed, and before she came to her senses and remembered these callers hadn't given her notice when she still had her family around. Maybe her father and brothers had driven them off, kept them from pursuing her, but she didn't think that was the case.

No, she wasn't wanted for who she was but what she had.

She'd never moved past that epiphany. She was well and truly stuck, and admitting it was what brought on the ache behind her eyes and caused a hard lump to form in her throat. The tears came after that, and they ran so quickly that she had to slam the ledger closed for fear of smearing the entries.

She couldn't indulge in tears long. Someone shouted that the stage was coming, and it was the cue she needed to blink back tears and swallow the next sob. Standing, she'd wiped her face with the tail of her shirt and tucked it back in place before she started out. At the last moment, she thought of her glasses and put them back on. Now she stood ready to greet the passengers, a carefully crafted smile on her lips.

Out of the corner of her eye, she saw that Call was helping Hank with the animals hitched to the stage. Rooster and Dillon were bringing out the fresh team. Jelly was loping along after them.

She had a warm welcome for the passengers as they disembarked, but the man carrying a black leather physician's bag was the only one to receive an animated greeting. When he thrust his hand forward, Laurel took it in both of hers.

"Thank you for coming," she said. "I am Laurel Morrison."

"Yes, of course you are. Mr. Stonechurch described you very well."

Laurel released his hand. "I'm sure he was too kind, whatever he told you, but I'm afraid he said nothing at all about you except that you'd be on the stage. If you weren't carrying that bag, I wouldn't know you as the doctor."

"David Singer," he said, tipping his bowler. He was a man without distinguishing characteristics. Average height. Medium build. In his middle years. His eyes were remarkable only for the fact that they had the same dark brown coloring as his hair. He wore a buttoned-up black jacket and trousers that were a little long in the inseam. His features became lively when he grinned. He had an open and kind smile that crinkled the corner of his eyes and lifted his cheeks. "I'm not sure Mr. Stonechurch knew my name before he had a personal need for my services. I understand you have a body for me to examine."

"Not here, Doctor. Mr. Pye is at the undertaker's. But please, won't you have something to eat first? If not that, perhaps you want to avail yourself of the facilities. The pump and privy are around back. I'll take you to Mr. Beckley's after the passengers return to the stage."

"Pump and privy it is. I wouldn't mind a meal after I make my examination. Settles better then."

"Of course. Would you like me to take your bag while you wash up?"

"Thank you."

Laurel hugged it to her chest when he gave it over. "Come around to the front of the house when you're done. Coffee? Tea?"

"Tea."

"I'll have some waiting for you." Laurel waved Jelly over to show Dr. Singer the way and chuckled to herself when the boy began to pepper him with questions immediately after hello. She watched them walk away and then headed into the house to attend to her other guests.

Call was waiting for the doctor when he came back around the house. He waved Jelly off and put out his hand to introduce himself. "McCall Landry," he said. "I'm—"

"Mr. Stonechurch's man. Yes, I was told you'd be meeting me, although being welcomed by the lovely Miss Morrison was quite refreshing after being cooped in that stage. I'm David Singer." He dropped Call's hand. "I understand you're the one that found the body."

Call shook his head. "Did Mr. Stonechurch tell you that? It was Miss Morrison who discovered it."

"Perhaps I misunderstood. You can tell me all about it in a bit. Right now, I believe there is a cup of tea waiting for me inside. Will you join me?"

"No, not right now. I have work to do, but when you're ready to examine the body, I'll take you there."

"Miss Morrison already offered to escort me to the undertaker's."

This was news to Call, but hardly surprising given Laurel's curious nature. "She did?"

Singer nodded. "I believe I heard her correctly."

"Then we'll both accompany you."

"Very good. You don't think she'll want to see the autopsy?"

"I have no idea. Why?"

"Because it is not for the faint of heart."

Call's short laugh was without humor. "There is nothing faint about Miss Morrison heart." He was aware that the doctor was looking at him oddly. "If you don't want her in the room, then you'll have to tell her. I have no sway there."

"I see." But he didn't. "Well, I do like to have a witness when I can, someone to take notes as I work. I don't perform many autopsies because death is usually straightforward in these parts, but when I do, my wife assists me."

"And she's not faint of heart?"

"I met her in medical school. She was my partner on the cadaver dissection. I'm Jewish. She's a woman. No one wanted to work with us."

"Not a traditional courtship, then."

Singer chuckled. "Not in any way, but I learned that my future wife had a cast-iron stomach and nerves of steel."

"Admirable qualities."

"Indeed. And she's lovely as well." The doctor looked past Call's shoulder to the porch as Laurel approached with a cup in her hand. "Ah. Here's my tea."

Call turned and saw Laurel. He stepped to the side to

allow Singer to pass. "The buckboard will be ready for you when you want to leave."

"Thank you. It's been a pleasure."

Nodding, Call headed to the barn.

Laurel felt the lump forming in her throat again as she watched him go. Aware of the doctor's observation, she forced a smile and gave him her full attention. "Come around to the steps," she said. "You can have your tea on the porch or inside if you'd prefer that."

"The porch is perfect."

She met him with the cup when he reached her. "The rockers are comfortable, but then so is the swing."

Singer took the cup and chose one of the rockers. "Will you join me?"

"I have the guests to attend. A fresh team's in place so they'll be leaving soon." Laurel refused his offer to pay for his tea before she went inside. She had every intention of rejoining the passengers at the dining table, but her steps took her into her office, where she sat behind her desk and carefully removed her spectacles. She stared straight ahead until the view beyond the front window blurred, then she closed her eyes and sank back in her chair, wishing without hope of it coming true that she could begin this day over.

Call and Laurel climbed aboard the buckboard from opposite sides and reached for the reins at the same time. Dr. Singer was already seated between them and neither wanted to initiate a tug of war or have words in front of him. They simultaneously deferred to the other, which was nearly as awkward. After a brief hesitation, Call sat back and gave Laurel leave to handle the reins.

"Riding shotgun, are you?" the doctor asked when they started to move.

"It's what I know best," said Call.

"Mr. Stonechurch indicated you had that job with Overland at one time."

"That's right."

"And you, Miss Morrison, how long have you been operating the station?"

"I was born here so I don't really know anything else."

"You know, my wife and I came through your station about eight years back. We were answering a call for a doctor in Stonechurch. Liked it well enough to stay. I mention that because I don't remember seeing you at the station then."

"My brother George greeted the stage in those days. I did kitchen work, cooking, setting the table, washing up. Do you remember biscuits as tough as hardtack?"

He said carefully, "I have that recollection, yes."

"I made those." There was no apology or embarrassment in her tone. She offered the truth proudly. "The passengers had to put up with those biscuits for six whole months before my father realized I belonged anywhere but in the kitchen. Martin, my other brother, took over my chores and I worked with the horses."

Singer chuckled. "Excellent strategy on your part."

"I thought so."

Call reckoned the tension on the buckboard bench must be more palpable than he realized since the doctor was trying his best to cut through it. Problem was, the man needed a sharper scalpel. Call decided they all would be better served by going to the root of what brought them together.

"What information do you need about Josey Pye before you perform your autopsy?" he asked. The abrupt change in conversational tone was met with silence. The buckboard creaked and groaned as it bounced along.

"Mr. Landry has to move his investigation on," said Laurel.

Call expected her to add something about him moving on as well. She didn't, though, and that left him feeling unsettled. In some ways it was better when she was predictable.

"Of course," said Singer. "Perfectly understandable. I

don't need to know many particulars. It's better if I draw my conclusions from the evidence rather than what either of you say that might sway my judgment. Does that make sense?"

"Yes," said Call.

Laurel nodded. "We passed the path to the falls a little ways back. Would it be helpful for you to see where we found him? I can turn around."

"Actually, that would be helpful. Thank you."

Laurel guided the pair of roans to make the wide turn and take them back to the trampled path leading to the falls. She offered to stay with the buckboard while Call escorted the doctor.

"They'll be fine," said Call, looking over the team. "You made the discovery. Go on. Toss me the reins and I'll hitch them to that willow over there before I follow. Doc? You want to leave your bag here?"

"No. It goes where I do. It's too valuable to be where I can't reach it."

Call nodded and watched the doctor fall in step behind Laurel before he led the team over to the willow and looped the reins around a branch. He purposely did not try to catch up to Laurel and the doctor to give them an opportunity to talk alone. Laurel was telling Dr. Singer about the falls when Call came upon them.

"It's mostly rocky ground above," she said, pointing to the lip of the horsetail waterfall. "Mr. Landry found some evidence that suggests Mr. Pye was up there at one point." When she saw the doctor look up and his expression turn doubtful, she explained there were alternate routes to reaching the top other than the one she'd used in her youth.

"I don't have the excuse of youth to explain why I made that climb," said Call.

Singer raised both dark eyebrows, whistled softly, but otherwise kept his thoughts to himself. He asked Laurel to point out where she'd found the body.

Laurel walked to the edge of the flat rock that was her

usual perch and pointed to the middle of the pool. "I didn't know that I'd found anything except a rope. Mr. Pye came up behind me. Mr. Landry saw him first."

"Pye was tangled somehow?"

"Seemed as if he was," said Laurel. "I had to yank hard on the rope to free it."

"You pulled him out, Mr. Landry?"

"Yes. Lassoed him. Laid him over here." He pointed to the ground a few feet to the left of where he was standing.

"On his side? On his back?"

"Both. On his side briefly, and then we left him on his back for the sheriff to see. Is it important?"

"Might be. You used a wagon to transport the body to the undertakers?"

"No. Slung him over the back of one of the horses."

Dr. Singer sighed and nodded. "All right. Tell me what's under the water. More rocks, I presume, but what about animal life and vegetation?"

Laurel answered. "It's not a good fishing hole. That's better downstream, but there's always a few circling in the pool, especially deeper where the current isn't as strong. Some turtles call it home. I used to see them sunning themselves on the rocks, but not so much anymore. I think the children who come out here to swim have scared them away or carried them off. I don't know about the vegetation. Dead leaves if you stir the bottom and things I can't identify."

"It's all right. Doubtful that it matters."

"Anything else?" asked Call.

"No. We can go back."

Laurel took up the reins again once they were on board. Theo Beckley was sitting on a stool outside his business smoking a thin cigar when they arrived. Call took care of the team while Laurel introduced the doctor and the undertaker.

In appearance, Mr. Beckley was nothing at all like the men of his profession portrayed in Gothic novels. He was squat, stout, and rosy-cheeked. When his services were engaged, he wore black. When they were not in use, he often wore colorfully checked trousers, usually yellow and black so he resembled nothing so much as a bumble-bee. He was genial in his public presentation, shrewd in matters of business. The first thing he did after introductions were completed was verify that Mr. Stonechurch would indeed pay for the storage, service, and burial of Mr. Josiah Pye.

"I have your money right here," said Call, producing the bills from his pocket. "All your expenses are covered as promised."

Theo Beckley led the way to his workroom in the back. "This is where I make the coffins," he explained, pointing to the wood shavings and carpentry tools. He cleared the table. "I could use your help bringing the body up from the cellar," he said to Call. For the doctor's benefit, he went on, "We put the deceased down there where it's cooler. I built this house over a natural hollow in the rock for storing fruit and vegetables and canned goods, but it's been helpful on the few occasions I have to keep a body."

"Excellent notion," said Singer. "Could I work down there?"

"Not nearly enough light."

"I see. Then by all means, bring Mr. Pye to me."

Call thought the doctor could have been a tad less enthusiastic about his work, but he supposed what Singer was about to do was not at all macabre to a man of medicine. He waited for Mr. Beckley to light a lamp and then followed him down the stairs. The undertaker's girth almost filled the narrow passage and blocked most of the light. Call treaded carefully.

Beckley set the lamp on a shelf crowded with jars of jelly, tomatoes, pickled beets, and something that looked like a human hand but Call hoped was some sort of sea creature, though why either of those things should be in Mr. Beckley's cellar was outside his imagination.

"Head or feet?" asked Call.

"Feet, if you don't mind."

Call didn't mind at all. Mr. Pye was lying exactly as he and the sheriff had left him. Mr. Beckley had fetched a stretcher to move the body and now it and Mr. Pye rested on the table in the middle of the room. Call turned around so he could grasp the stretcher's handles and lift Pye behind him. There was some fumbling as the undertaker struggled with his end, but they managed to coordinate their steps by the time they began to climb.

Beckley directed Call to set the stretcher on the table. "I'm going to get the lamp I left behind. Feel free to light the lamps in here."

Singer nodded absently. He was already looking over the body. "Would you do that, Miss Morrison? Open the curtains, too, please. Is there a stool around here, something to set my bag on?"

Call found Beckley's work stool in a corner and set it beside the doctor while Laurel dealt with the lamps.

Singer set his bag down, opened it, and removed a pair of scissors. He used them with deft efficiency to cut away Josey Pye's clothes, all of which were still damp and clammy. He only hesitated when he was ready to take the scissors to Pye's union suit. His attention strayed to Laurel long enough to cock an eyebrow and ask, "Are you certain you want to be here? I cannot attend to your modesty."

"Yes," she said. "I'm staying. All I ask is that you treat him respectfully."

"Always." He cut away the union suit, made a cursory examination of Pye's genitals and then used the man's shirt to cover them. "Which one of you is going to take notes?"

Laurel looked to Call and shook her head. "I don't have my reading spectacles."

"All right, but God knows if it will be legible. Mr. Beckley! Paper and pencil, please."

Beckley was standing just outside the room, well away from the doctor's activity. "There's a drawer in the worktable, right where Dr. Singer is standing. You'll find both there."

Singer stepped aside and gave Call access. He immediately went back to work, describing Pye's visible injuries and then carefully examining the man's skull by sifting through his hair. "Three-inch gash on the left temporal area approximately two inches from the central body line. Perhaps made by a rock, though whether above water or below is impossible to know. Other scratches and bites evident on the scalp. Miss Morrison mentioned turtles. They are the likely culprits."

Call was scribbling as fast as he could, attempting both accuracy and legibility. He was glad when the doctor straightened, and stretched his lower back, as it gave Call time to catch up.

Singer took a scalpel from his bag and made a Y-shaped incision on Pye's torso. He was expecting the noxious gases that the incision released, but Call and Laurel were not. They both took a step back. "You can open a window," the doctor said.

Laurel moved immediately to do that and breathed deeply of the fresh air that wafted in. When she turned, she noticed that Mr. Beckley was now farther away from the entrance. He was an odd one, she thought, even for an undertaker.

Call was writing furiously again as Singer described the condition of the heart and lungs. "No water in the lungs," said Singer. "He was dead when he went under. Oh, dear. What's this?"

"What?" asked Laurel, leaning a bit toward the table. "What do you see?"

Singer didn't answer. He set the scalpel aside and chose a probe from his bag. He used it to examine something that had caught his eye in Pye's left pectoral muscle. It was only after pulling back the muscle that he had a glimpse of it. He probed the area, separating the smooth filaments to search for what he'd seen. "Tweezers," he said to no one in particular and held out a hand with the full expectation that the instrument would be placed in it.

Laurel met that expectation since Call's hands were occupied with paper and pencil.

Singer kept the muscle filaments separated with the probe and used the tweezers in his other hand to extract a bullet. He held it up so Call could get a look at it. "Isn't this a minié ball?"

Call stepped forward and stared at it narrowly. "It is. Battlefields in the East are littered with them. I carried a Springfield rifle that used a minié. It was standard issue on both sides."

"I don't understand," said Laurel. "Why isn't there evidence of a wound in Mr. Pye's chest?"

"Because, Miss Morrison, Mr. Pye was shot in the back."

27

Dr. Singer swept away the shirt covering Mr. Pye's privates and held it up for Laurel. He pulled the material taut so the back of the shirt could be inspected. The tattered hole was clearly visible now. "*Mea culpa*," he said. "My fault. I should have examined his clothing at the outset." He replaced the shirt and lifted Josey Pye by the shoulder, turning him just enough to see the lead ball's entry. "There you are." He pointed to the puckered tissue with his probe. "The minié ball entered here"—Singer lowered Pye so he was once again lying flat on the table and carefully ran his probe along the rib closest to where he'd located the bullet—"and nicked this rib right here, which slowed it down and changed the trajectory, and then lodged in the pectoral muscle."

"Not a fatal wound, surely," said Laurel. "The bullet missed his heart and lungs."

"With proper care, Mr. Pye might have survived. It's hard to say. I've known men who survived far worse, but there was no intention of saving Mr. Pye. The shooter meant for him to die, perhaps even thought he had." He wiped off his scalpel and returned it to his bag before he addressed Call. "You said you were up above the falls."

Call stopped writing and put the pencil behind his ear. "That's right."

"Did you see evidence of blood?"

"No. We've had enough rain since Mr. Pye's disappearance to wash it away. Why? What are you thinking?"

Singer snapped the shirt and laid it over Pye's body. He used his probe to outline the faint bloodstain that had blossomed on the back. "The force of the bullet should have made him fall forward, but this stain suggests that at some point he turned on his back, perhaps on his own, perhaps with help. However it occurred, the position contributed to his death through blood loss." The doctor used his probe again to indicate the discoloration around Pye's wrists and ankles. "He was bound hands and feet. The bruising suggests he struggled, so he was still alive at that point, though I doubt he had long. That evidence that Miss Morrison said you found . . . it wasn't a pair of socks and boots, was it?"

Call shook his head. "No."

Laurel frowned. "Why did you ask—" She stopped, realizing the obvious and feeling foolish she hadn't thought about it earlier. "Oh. Mr. Pye wouldn't have marks on his ankles if he'd been bound wearing his boots."

"Precisely," said Singer.

Call said, "So the killer took them. If they were a good pair, maybe he's wearing them now."

"I don't think we should pin our hopes on that," said Laurel. "We can ask Rooster and the boys about Mr. Pye's boots, but isn't it more likely they were taken to discard?"

"Pitched over the falls?" asked the doctor.

"Doubtful," said Call. "They would have turned up before Pye's body, and he wasn't meant to be discovered. Can you tell us how long he'd been in the drink?"

"Time of death? No. The best I can tell you is that it's been weeks, not days."

"So it could have happened soon after the robbery," said Laurel. "Pye might never have left the area. Rooster and I took the trail after him, and it never occurred to me that he might still be around. As for the path that goes to the top of the falls, I didn't realize he knew it existed."

Call could see Laurel was working up to blaming herself. Before their conversation at the corral, he would have said something to reassure her. Now he remained silent. "Is there anything else you can tell us, Dr. Singer?"

He shook his head. "I'm about done here. Can you tell me about the evidence you found at the top of the falls?"

Call glanced over his shoulder to where Theo Beckley was still loitering in the hallway. The undertaker might not have been interested in the doctor's procedure, but he was certainly interested in the conversation. Call shook his head and had to hope that Laurel would not speak up.

She did, but not in a way that undermined Call. "Perhaps at another time. When this business is concluded."

Singer accepted that. "I understand that Mr. Pye left the station in the middle of the night. Correct?" When Call and Laurel nodded, he went on. "I'm assuming you both understand that it was daylight when Mr. Pye was shot. Depending on the shooter's skill, the Springfield rifle loaded with a minié ball is accurate up to three hundred yards."

"Four hundred," said Call.

"Four hundred," the doctor repeated. "I yield to your expertise. My point is that no one shoots at a target like Mr. Pye at night. Daybreak, yes, with only a light wind."

Call nodded. Knowing about the bullet meant he could go back to the top of the falls and confidently widen his search. He couldn't say what he would be looking for, not precisely, but it seemed likely the killer left some trace of his passing. Another proverbial needle in a haystack, but with patience and some luck, even a needle could occasionally be found.

Dr. Singer addressed the undertaker. "We're done here, Mr. Beckley. Thank you for the use of your workshop. We'll leave you to it now." He returned the probe to his bag. "Is there somewhere I can wash my hands?"

"There's a pump in the kitchen." He pointed the way.

"I'll only be a minute," Singer said.

Laurel shut the window where she'd been standing and closed the curtains. "I'll send one of the Booker boys around with clothes for Mr. Pye. You can't bury him in what's been cut away."

"No, Miss Morrison," said Beckley. "Wouldn't be right or respectful." His gaze shifted to Call. "I guess you'll be talking to the sheriff now."

"Why would you say that?"

Beckley shrugged. "I thought I heard him say that he wanted to know what the doctor learned."

"Did he say that?" Call frowned as though thinking back to yesterday's conversation with the sheriff. "I don't recollect that he showed much interest."

"You don't know him like I do. He hasn't had something like this to sink his teeth into for a long time. A robbery. Now a murder. He's interested. Just real quiet about it."

"Real quiet" was not how Call would have described Rayleigh Carter's demeanor. To his way of thinking, "indifferent" and "unresponsive" were more accurate. Both of those were telling of the sheriff's confidence in job security. "Then I'll be sure to speak to him."

Satisfied, Beckley nodded. "You'll send one of your boys right around, Miss Morrison? I want to get Mr. Pye in the ground today."

Laurel grimaced slightly but answered that he would have clothes for Mr. Pye that afternoon. She was grateful for the doctor's return just then and walked past Mr. Beckley to join Singer. "Mr. Landry? Are you ready to go?"

Call didn't hesitate. He wanted to leave before the undertaker asked for assistance with the coffin and digging the grave. Beckley had no shame. The money Call had already provided was plenty enough for the undertaker to hire help with both those things. He plucked the pencil from behind his ear and gave it and the notebook to the doctor. "Good day, Mr. Beckley. We'll show ourselves out."

Laurel handed over the reins to Call when she climbed in. "Your turn. You know what you want to do."

He did. It was bewildering to him how Laurel could know his mind about some things and be so completely thickheaded about others. Shaking his head at the puzzle of it, he took the reins without a word.

"Why are we going back this way?" Singer asked when Call turned the buckboard onto a side street and then down the alley behind the buildings on the main street.

It was Laurel who answered. "Mr. Landry wants to avoid the sheriff's office. If Sheriff Carter saw us on our way to Mr. Beckley's, he wasn't moved to cross the street to hear what you had to say, but now that we're leaving, he might very well stop us."

"Let him hear it from Beckley," said Call. "The undertaker was hanging on your every word."

"Why wouldn't the sheriff want to hear everything directly from the horse's mouth as it were?"

"The kindest way to put it," said Laurel, "is that he's indolent. I told Mr. Landry early on that no one really wanted the position when it became available. He ran unopposed and no one's expressed interest in running against him."

"Maybe I will," said Call.

Laurel leaned forward on the bench so she could see past the doctor and get a good look at Call. His profile told her nothing at all about how serious he was. She sat back, frustrated.

Call said, "Since we left Beckley, I've been thinking there might be another reason for Carter's lack of involvement besides laziness."

"Oh?" asked Singer. "And what is that?"

Call shook his head. "It's premature. And only conjecture. I'd rather not say."

"Mr. Stonechurch told me you would play your cards close."

Chuckling, Call said, "So he asked you to find out about my progress. Why am I not surprised?"

"He's a careful man. He wants this resolved with as little notice as possible."

"I understand. The robbery's made the company vulnerable. I imagine it's no different for him since he *is* the company. Assure him that I have been as discreet as it's possible to be and that is why I haven't communicated more. Maybe that will set his mind at ease. You don't have to be convinced, Doctor. You just have to do it."

Singer nodded. "I will, of course. I will also inform him that you've taken great risks in your pursuit of recovering the stolen payroll." When Call looked at him with one eyebrow cocked in question, he said, "That insane climb you made to the top of the falls."

"Oh, that."

"Yes, that."

"I don't think Mr. Stonechurch needs to know about that," said Laurel. "It won't necessarily make him more confident about hiring Mr. Landry."

In spite of himself, Call grinned. "She's right, Doctor. Probably better left unsaid."

Dr. Singer reluctantly agreed. He changed the subject. "I'm going to want to go over the notes you took to make certain I can read them. I like to keep good records."

"Of course."

When they reached the station, Call stopped in front of the house to allow the doctor and Laurel to climb down. He drove the buckboard to the barn and began to unhitch the team. He was almost finished when he was aware that Laurel had come to stand on the opposite side of the buckboard.

"If you're looking for one of the boys, they're both out back in the garden."

"I know. I told Mrs. Lancaster to send Dillon to the mercantile to purchase clothes and take them to Mr. Beckley. I came here looking for you."

"You found me." He turned his back on her to hang up the tack.

"I want to go with you," she said.

"Oh? Where am I going?"

Laurel waited until he'd finished with the tack and turned around. She refused to say another word to his back. "You're going to the top of the falls again. You think there might be something there that will tell you about Mr. Pye's killer. I'm volunteering to help. Two pairs of eyes are better than one."

"What makes you think I'm going up there?"

"Because you went up before with nothing but a gut feeling motivating you. Now you know that Mr. Pye died up there and you know how he was killed. You have to go."

"I do. You don't."

"But—"

"I'm not arguing with you. I'm going to review Singer's notes and then I'm leaving while I still have plenty of daylight." Turning his back on Laurel a second time, Call headed for the house.

28

Dr. Singer was pleased with Call's documentation and made only a few corrections for clarification. It required but a half hour of Call's time before he was able to saddle Artemis and leave the station. Mrs. Lancaster packed a sack of food for him when he told her where he was going. He'd laughed when she thrust it at him because the sack was heavy enough to feed him and his horse. She had merely smiled in return.

Call remembered that sweet but slightly forced smile as he crested the last few yards of the steep slope leading up to the falls. He thought she hadn't cared for his joke. Perhaps she hadn't, but it wasn't the reason for her frozen smile. No, she knew something he didn't and was honor bound not to tell him.

The secret Mrs. Lancaster held back revealed itself when he came over the top. Laurel was waiting for him.

There was no point ignoring her. He urged Artemis forward and came abreast of her and Abby under the broad boughs of a ponderosa. Without preamble, he said, "Can you fathom how much I do not want to be around you right now?"

"You've made that clear, yes."

"And yet here you are."

"To keep you from cutting off your nose to spite your face. You know you can use the help."

"If I thought that, I could have asked Rooster."

"Not without my permission," she said. "He wouldn't have come, and you would have tied yourself in knots before you asked me to let him go." Abby stirred under her, a reminder to Laurel to steady herself. "I'm here, Call, and I'm staying. You may as well take advantage of it. Where do you want me to begin?"

Call held her gaze a moment longer. It hurt to look at her. "We have to go on foot," he said, dismounting. He tethered Artemis to the cinnamon-colored trunk of the pine. The bark released a vanilla scent when the leather reins rubbed against it. "Start about a hundred yards from the water and make a semicircular path. When you're done, go out ten or twenty yards more and do it again. And again. It will be tedious. You can quit anytime."

Laurel joined him at the tree and looped Abby's reins around the trunk. She didn't snap at the bait he dangled in front of her. "Is there anything specific I should be looking for?"

"Anything that doesn't belong." He raised an arm and pointed northwest. "See that rocky rise over that way? Where the limber pines are?" The short trees were gnarled, shaped by the wind, and grew in places the mightier pines disdained. "That's the kind of ground where I'd lie in wait if I were looking to make someone my target. Lots of good places where a person can stay low and keep a Springfield steady."

"The wind's stronger up there," she said doubtfully. "Dr. Singer mentioned a light wind for accuracy."

"Do you think the good doctor's ever fired a rifle? No? Well, I have, and I know it can be done. I'm going to start there."

Laurel nodded and started walking in the direction of the stream. She stopped at a place she judged to be a hundred yards out and marked it by turning a few rocks over so their darker undersides were visible. She covered the ground carefully, occasionally looking up to see Call's progress as he headed for the rise. It was slower going for him to reach the point where he wanted to begin. He had to scale large rocky outcroppings or climb around them. His journey was as much up as it was long.

Laurel was aware he had given her the easier route to walk. Her path included large grassy areas where her only obstacle was scrub brush. There wasn't a lot of cover where a sharpshooter could hide, and she assumed, as Call did, that Mr. Pye was unaware that he was a target.

She considered what that meant. Exactly how many people were involved in the robbery? Pye, of course, and they knew Digger Leary had helped. Digger rode shotgun so perhaps he had sniper skill with a rifle. If Digger was the killer, then there must have been some arrangement to meet after the robbery, when he and Pye would split the payroll. But if that were true, why would Digger shoot Pye at such a distance and risk missing his target? Surely Digger would choose to take his partner unaware at close range.

Laurel shook her head to clear the thoughts distracting her from her assignment. When she looked up to find Call, it was just in time to see him disappear over the rise. She wished him better luck than she was having. He was right about one thing. The search was tedious.

In the few instances when something caught her eye, Laurel bent and dragged her fingers through the grass to sift and separate it. For her efforts she found a few smooth white stones and the broken shell of a bird's egg.

When she'd finished her first route, she moved out fifteen yards and started again. She never sighted Call and finally stopped looking for him. She was thirty yards out when she spied something fluttering in a thicket. She carefully plucked it free. It was not immediately apparent what it was, though by the size of it she suspected it was a greenback. This specimen was bleached from the sun and rain so it was virtually colorless. Turning it this way and that, and with a little squinting to compensate for not having her spectacles, Laurel was finally able to identify it as a ten-dollar bill.

She pocketed her prize and took the blue ribbon from

her hair to mark the thicket. Satisfied that she would be able point out the spot to Call, she went on, trying to imagine all the while what had happened that allowed money to escape. Had Pye been showing the money to someone, perhaps opening his saddlebag to prove he had the bills? She supposed he could have been counting the money, but if she had taken the risk to steal the Stonechurch payroll, Laurel was sure she'd have made a better job of holding on to it.

Working with her head down, she got a crick in her neck, which she stopped to massage away. She also lost track of how much time had elapsed since she and Call parted ways. It was only when her stomach rumbled that she realized several hours had passed. She knew that Call had a sack of food in his saddlebag because she'd asked Mrs. Lancaster to provide him with one. She was mightily tempted to wander over to where the horses were tethered and help herself, but she resisted because she wanted to be invited to the meal that was meant for both of them.

"Laurel!"

Hearing her name, she sprang up, straightened, and looked toward the rise. Call was standing on a large slab of rock, legs parted, one hand on his hip. In his other hand, he was holding a pair of reins.

"Look who I found!"

Laurel saw Call take up the slack on the reins and thought her heart would stop when Penelope clambered over the rise to stand at his side. She sucked in a breath and covered her open mouth with her hand, too astonished at first to do more than stare. Her frozen stance lasted mere seconds and then she was running. She stumbled twice, caught herself both times just before she fell, and only stopped her mad dash when she reached the base of the rise. She would have started to climb if Call hadn't shouted at her to stay where she was. It was all she could do not to dance in place as Call led the mare down the rough slope. Penelope balked several times and forced Call to find a less treacherous route.

Laurel frowned as the mare picked her way around the rocks. There was hesitation in her step. Gone was the sure-footed lady who was the natural leader of any team. "Has she thrown a shoe?" she called up.

Call was close enough now that he only had to nod. He continued to watch his step and the mare's until he reached Laurel. He held on to Penelope's bridle as Laurel ran her hands along the horse's neck and flank and spoke in dulcet tones meant to ease herself and the mare.

"Oh, sweet girl. You've had a time of it, haven't you? Where have you been? And so roughly used. You're safe now. Everything will be fine." Recognizing a familiar voice, Penelope rubbed her nose against Laurel's shoulder. "That's it, girl. You know me, don't you?"

Call let the reunion go on awhile longer before he spoke up. "She lost the left shoe on her forefoot."

Laurel bent and gingerly ran her hand down Penelope's foreleg. The mare let her raise the hoof. "This needs filing and cleaning. Poor thing." She stood, sifted the mare's black mane with her fingers. "Burrs and thistles." She pulled out several twigs and tossed them aside. "Where did you find her?"

"About half a mile from where I started. I heard her first and I walked on to investigate. I had no idea what I'd find. She got her reins caught in a limber pine. Twisted. Looped. And finally knotted. I don't how she managed it, but she hurt herself trying to get free. The girth straps cut into her. I had to right the saddle because it'd slipped, but I didn't want to take it off until we got back to the barn. She was pretty spooked and it took a while for me to be able to calm her enough so I could touch her."

Laurel thought she might weep. She gently rubbed the mare's neck and nose. "Surely she wasn't trapped the whole time she's been missing. She'd be—"

Call didn't let her finish. "No, she wasn't caught this whole time. I figure she wandered for a while. She'd have had water from the stream and grasses down here, but she made the climb and then got herself in trouble. She was probably nosing around the pine looking for food when she trapped herself. I'm going to take her over to the water and let her drink a little. Look in my saddlebag and see if Mrs. Lancaster put anything in the sack that we can give to Penelope. Maybe a couple of carrots or some dried apples."

Nodding, Laurel let him take Penelope away. She'd have to let Sam Henderson know they'd found his mare and hope she could convince him that it would be a while before Penelope could make another stage run. The girl deserved some rest and pampering.

When Call returned to where their horses were tethered, Laurel had some dried apple slices ready. She held them one at a time in the flat of her hand while Penelope sniffed and then gobbled. "More later," she said when the last of them was gone. She looked at Call. "Do you think we can trust her not to wander far if we don't tie her?"

"I think she'll stay put. She knows you." He pointed to his saddlebag. "What else is in there?"

Laurel opened the bag and took out the sack. "Ham sandwiches. Hard-boiled eggs. A couple slices of cherry pie."

"Two of everything, I bet."

"Mm. Seems that way."

He took the sack from her, peeked inside, and then gave Laurel a knowing look. "This was your doing, wasn't it?"

She didn't pretend she didn't know what he meant. "Yes."

"Then I suppose I'm meant to share."

"I hoped you would."

"I'm not even talking to you, Laurel."

All evidence to the contrary, but Laurel understood. She placed one hand over her belly as her stomach rumbled. Maybe it was the noise that decided him, but he gestured her to walk with him and found a place on a thick bed of pine needles to sit down. She crossed her legs and sat. He took out a sandwich and then handed her the sack to get her own. She opened her mouth to thank him but he shook his head and she closed it again. The implication was obvious. He didn't want to hear anything from her.

She took small bites simply so she could linger. Call had eaten his egg and was eyeing the cherry pie when she was just finishing her sandwich. She brushed crumbs off her hands before she reached for the egg. She hesitated, and rather than cracking the shell, she held it out to Call.

"It's yours," he said, shaking his head.

"Mrs. Lancaster knows I don't really like boiled eggs."

Call was suspicious, but he took it. He cracked it against the scaly bark of the ponderosa and eyed Laurel as he peeled it. She wasn't staring at the egg as if she regretted giving it to him so he ate it in three bites instead of two quick ones. "Maybe you should have held back some of the dried apples for yourself," he said, handing her one of the pie slices.

She shrugged and carefully unwrapped the pie. Her mouth watered, but she waited for Call to take his first bite. "Dr. Singer is leaving tomorrow on the afternoon stage."

"Yes, he told me."

"I invited him to take a room in the house tonight."

"You didn't need to tell me. You don't have to worry that I'll run into him."

Laurel inhaled sharply. "You are determined to be cold."

Call didn't deny it.

"Very well," she said after a moment. The pie did not look as tempting as it had when she unwrapped it, but Laurel would have eaten it if it were a prairie pancake and made the same effort to pretend she enjoyed it.

Call finished first and wiped his mouth with the gingham towel the pie had been wrapped in. He opened the canteen at his side and drank deeply before he offered it to Laurel. When she shook her head, he closed it, leaned back against the trunk behind him, and closed his eyes.

Laurel wondered if he could actually fall asleep. He looked perfectly comfortable. In contrast, her stomach was in knots. The silver lining, she supposed, was that it was no longer rumbling.

"Did you find anything?" asked Call.

Laurel noticed he didn't trouble himself to open his eyes. "A faded ten-dollar tender note. Not a scrap like you found. It's a whole greenback."

"Red seal?"

"Yes. More pink than red, but it's still evident."

"What about the serial number? Those notes have serial numbers. Could you see it?"

"I didn't look." She started to retrieve it, but he stopped her, and she realized his eyes were not quite as closed as they seemed. He was watching her from beneath the fan of dark lashes.

"When we get back," he said. "We'll look at it under your magnifying glass."

"Why is it important?"

"The red seal series has serial numbers to track legal tender notes. It discouraged counterfeiters during the war. The Denver bank uses those notes for the Stonechurch payroll and records the serial numbers of the bills they release. We'll be able to trace the bill back to the payroll that was on the stage."

"I had no idea."

"Neither did Mr. Pye. Most people don't pay attention to the money they pass. Shopkeepers and banks do, of course. Counterfeiting is a profitable business."

"If this note is from the robbery and the money never left Falls Hollow, isn't it possible that some of the notes have been spent?"

"That's two big 'ifs,' but yes, it's possible."

"Then isn't it possible that one or two or more of them have gone through Mrs. Booker's hands at the mercantile or Sweeny's hands at the saloon or Mr. Higgenbotham's hands at the bank?"

Call sat up and stared at her. "Also possible," he said, nodding slowly as he thought it over. "Likely, in fact. You know, Laurel, if I wasn't still so peeved at you, I'd undoubtedly want to kiss you senseless right about now."

"Oh. Then it's probably just as well that you don't, you being peevish and all."

He didn't want to smile, but something about the way she spoke so matter-of-factly proved he was capable of it. "Dammit," he said under his breath.

Laurel heard him swear but was fairly confident it wasn't directed at her. She didn't think long on why that made her feel better. It simply did. She finished the cherry pie, neatly folded the gingham napkin, and returned it to the sack. She did the same with Call's.

"What about you?" asked Laurel when Call showed no indication that he was prepared to leave. "Did you find anything besides Penelope?"

"I found what I think was the sniper's nest. The distance and elevation are about right. There's room to lie down in relative comfort. It's a location where a man could rest himself and his rifle. I was searching for a spent cartridge when I heard Penelope."

"You need to go back, then."

He nodded. "But you can return to the station with Penelope. You've done plenty already to advance the investigation."

Laurel looked at Penelope. The mare certainly needed tending but she was reluctant to leave Call to finish exploring on his own. "I'd like to stay," she said. "Penelope is reacquainting herself with Abby. She won't fare any worse for a few hours' delay, and I want to know that you return safely after climbing all over that rise."

"Nothing's going to come of arguing with you, is it?"

"Probably not, no."

Call released a heavy sigh. "All right. But you stay here. If you want to continue to look around, fine, but don't follow me."

That Call didn't want her coming after him was a good indication that the climb was more dangerous than it appeared at first glance. "I've never been up there," she told him. "There was never any reason to stray that far."

"There still isn't," he said. "Not for you."

She held up both hands in a declaration of surrender. "I'll be right here when you get back."

Call got up, brushed his hands on his trousers, and adjusted the tilt of his hat. "I won't be long. It's probably better if you don't watch."

But of course, she did.

29

It was dusk by the time Laurel and Call returned to the station. Laurel was amazed when Call showed her the paper cartridge he'd found wedged between the rocks. It was burnt at the edges but mostly intact. By all rights it should have ignited after firing. She was tempted to call his discovery a miracle except she knew it was sheer doggedness that had produced the find. When she mentioned his tenacity, he shrugged it off, but she could tell that he was secretly pleased with himself and not unhappy that she'd noticed.

Laurel insisted on caring for Penelope herself. The mare's arrival caused a stir and everyone came out to see her. Mrs. Lancaster declared herself so excited that she left a pot of chicken stock simmering on the stove to visit the barn.

Call stayed behind when the others went back to their respective duties. His offer to help had been rebuffed earlier and he didn't bring it up again. Looking around, he chose a bench a few feet from where Laurel was washing Penelope and sat. As was his custom, he removed his hat and leaned back against the wall. He stretched his legs and crossed his ankles.

"Comfortable?" asked Laurel.

"Hmm." He set his hat beside him on the bench and folded his arms across his chest. "Hey!" he said when droplets of sudsy water splashed his beard and the front of his shirt. "You did that on purpose."

"Did I? I think you're mistaken." She ducked her head to hide her smile and continued scrubbing. "You haven't said anything about the sniper's identity. I don't suppose that finding the cartridge can help with that."

"No. No, it can't. But the cartridge and the minié point to a Springfield rifle, probably a war issue, and maybe there's a possibility of finding that."

"There are two in my gun cabinet," she said. "You don't have to look all that far."

"Your brothers' guns?"

"Yes."

"Then it's in your favor that you're not a suspect. Who else in Falls Hollow served in the war? Either side."

"Why do you think it's someone local?"

"I have to start somewhere."

"All right." She dipped the brush in the bucket of water and applied it to Penelope's hindquarters. "There weren't all that many, but you'll also want to ask Dillon and Hank. Their father served. So did their older brother."

"Mr. Booker? Really? I wouldn't have guessed that."

"Talks about everything except the war. Digger Leary was gone for a while. I know he's not from Falls Hollow, but you're already aware he was an accomplice in the robbery."

"Right. Who else?"

"Magnus Clutterbuck. He's a frequent overnight guest of the jail because he starts paintin' his nose at Sweeny's in the afternoon. His drinking got a lot worse after he got back. His fiancée married someone else while he was gone."

"Lots of stories like that," said Call.

She nodded. "Oh, and there's Jelly's father. He wasn't always the preacher here. Folks say he found God during the fighting."

"Lots of men did that, too. What did he do before?"

"Barbering."

"Huh."

"Jeremy Dodd. He's one of the ones that left and came back. He's married with children and works the family farm, but he used to yank my braids in the schoolyard. He wasn't mean."

"He probably liked you."

"That's what my father said. I don't see him for something like this."

Neither did Call. "Anyone else?"

"There's the sheriff and Bobber Jordan. Bobber serves as Carter's deputy from time to time. I think Theo Beckley might have gone off, but it couldn't have been for long. There was a rumor back then that he was a deserter. I don't know how the gossip started because no one gave it much credence."

"That's interesting. He was standing around when we were discussing the minié ball and he never mentioned his experience. Then again, maybe he wasn't in the army long enough to be issued a Springfield. It'd be worth asking him about."

Laurel straightened, dropped the brush in the water, and stretched her back. "I can't think of anyone else offhand. As I said, you'll want to ask the boys about their recollections."

"Maybe Mrs. Booker would be better. Mrs. Lancaster, too."

"Of course." She ran her fingers through Penelope's mane. "It's going to take me a while to comb out her mane and tail. There's no reason for you to stay when supper'll be ready soon."

"I'm good here."

She shrugged. "Suit yourself." Laurel felt his eyes on her as she worked and wondered if the bees were circling her blossoms. It made her smile. Later, when she worked up the nerve to look his way and catch him out, she saw not only that he had closed his eyes but also that he was sleeping. Served her right, she decided, for getting a little too full of herself. She kept the laughter bubbling inside to herself and went on working.

When Call woke, he required a minute to orient himself and take inventory of his aches. He was alone except for the horses, and when he looked at the open barn door, he saw that full dark was almost upon him. His neck and back were stiff. He sat up and stretched, massaged his nape, and plowed his fingers through his hair. No hat. He felt along the bench, found it, but didn't put it on.

Standing, he stretched again. The horses stirred and nickered as he made his way out of the barn. He stopped long enough to stroke Penelope's nose before he stepped out. His intention was to go to the bunkhouse and collapse, but the light coming from the kitchen beckoned him and he remembered that Mrs. Lancaster had been making soup. He went to the pump and washed his face, neck, and hands, and feeling more awake if not exactly alert, he went off in the direction of the kitchen.

Mrs. Lancaster turned from blacking the stove when the door opened. "And there you are," she said. "Come. Come. Sit. Soup's still hot and the bread's warm. I'll get it for you right now."

Laurel had also looked up when Call entered. Her spoon hovered in the air halfway between her bowl and her mouth. She slid a forearm protectively around her bowl and bread as if she expected he might snatch them from her. "I just got here myself," she said. "And I did try to wake you."

"Hmm. Evidently not hard enough." He hung his hat on a hook by the door before he took a chair at a right angle to Laurel and sat. Mrs. Lancaster set a bowl of chicken and dumpling soup in front of him and he thanked her. His nostrils flared as he breathed deeply of the aroma, and when she added a heel of warm bread, his mouth watered.

"I didn't shake you, if that's what you mean, but I said your name several times."

At the stove, Mrs. Lancaster chuckled. "Maybe a kiss would have served," she said. "Like Sleeping Beauty."

One of Call's eyebrows kicked up as he regarded the pink creeping into Laurel's cheeks. He pretended to give the cook's suggestion serious consideration. "That might've done the trick," he said.

Laurel's mouth flattened in disapproval.

"Guess not," Call said to Mrs. Lancaster. "She didn't care for your idea. In her defense, I can't say that I would have been receptive."

Mrs. Lancaster stopped blacking the stovetop long enough to look at Call over her shoulder. "Why's that? What's wrong with you?"

"Not a thing. We had a little setback."

"Well, set it back to right." Confident that she had the final word on the matter, Mrs. Lancaster returned to her work.

Call grinned at Laurel, who was looking fit to be tied. He saw her open her mouth as if she intended to retort, and he gave her a quick shake of his head. Better to let it rest for now because there was no chance that the cook would not continue to weigh in with her opinion.

"Excellent soup," he told Mrs. Lancaster. "And I don't know that I've ever had better dumplings."

"You haven't," Mrs. Lancaster said, perfectly certain she spoke the truth.

"Do you have time to answer some questions that would help me with my investigation?"

"I do if you don't mind my back to you. I've neglected this stove for too many evenings."

"Whatever you like," he said. "I already asked Laurel for names of men from Falls Hollow who served on either side during the war. I thought you might be able to add to her list."

"Names, eh? Am I right that you don't want names of the men who didn't come back?"

"Yes. Only the men who returned."

The first five names the cook rattled off were all among those Laurel had given him. Then she mentioned Jack Friendly. Call knew he'd heard the name somewhere then he remembered that Jack was one of the men Laurel had considered taking to her bed if he hadn't been willing.

"Right," said Laurel. "I forgot about Jack. Should you be writing these down, Mr. Landry?"

"I will." He tapped his temple. "I have them right here for now."

Mrs. Lancaster ticked off three more names and repeated the same rumor Laurel had about the undertaker. "That's all I can recollect. There were days and months it seemed as if most all of the men were gone." Her voice dropped to a whisper. "Hard times."

"Indeed," he said quietly. "Thank you, Mrs. Lancaster. You've been helpful."

"May I ask what all this was in aid of? I know you said it was for your investigation but in what way?"

"I'm afraid I can't speak to that."

"Doesn't surprise me," she said, taking his answer in stride. "Thought I should ask anyway."

Call got up from the table and went over to the stove. He put an arm around her shoulders and gave her a squeeze. "Thank you," he said again. "I mean it."

"Ah, go on with you." She blinked rapidly and pointed to the stockpot. "There's plenty more soup. Help yourself."

Chuckling, he produced his bowl from behind his back and helped himself.

Dr. Singer left the station on the afternoon stage carrying correspondence from Call for Mr. Stonechurch. Call communicated his latest findings in terms that were cautiously optimistic in regard to identifying the remaining person or persons involved in the robbery. He was less confident about recovering the payroll. Given the fact that he and Laurel had located pieces of it at the falls, it was already impossible that all of it could be reclaimed.

Call found Laurel in her office poring over the accounts. Her spectacles were resting on the tip of her nose, and she had one pencil in her fingertips and another poking out of the knot of hair at the back of her head. Her lips moved ever so slightly as she added numbers on the page. He was loath to disturb her and he waited until she wrote down a sum and finally turned to acknowledge his presence. Her eyebrows lifted in question.

"I'm going to visit Mrs. Booker at the mercantile and ask her who might have been passing ten-dollar legal tender notes. Is there anything I can get for you while I'm there?"

"Not that I can think of. Do you need the note I found yesterday?"

"No." They had examined the greenback under Laurel's magnifying glass after they ate. Call recorded the serial number as well as the names of the men Laurel and Mrs. Lancaster had given him. That information was now in his pocket. He had also included the serial number in his letter to Mr. Stonechurch as proof of his progress. "Where did you put it?"

Laurel pointed to the small safe tucked under the bookshelf. "I still have that scrap of a bill you found in the strongbox. I decided to keep it under the glass rather than put it in the safe. I thought it might get lost in there."

Call glanced up at the shelf where the overturned glass was still covering the first evidence he'd found. "It's good where it is."

She tapped her pencil against the desktop as she regarded him curiously. "You're leaving now?"

"Yes. I'll let you know what I learn."

Nodding absently, Laurel returned to studying her accounts. When she looked up again, Call was gone.

Call was still jawing with Mr. Booker outside the mercantile when Laurel arrived. She hitched Abby to a post and stepped up on the boardwalk. Her smile encompassed both men as she passed them on her way into the store.

Mrs. Booker placed her hands on her ample hips as soon as she saw Laurel. "What have they done?" she asked, leaving no doubt as to whom she was referring.

Laurel laughed, shook her head. "Nothing. They haven't done a thing." She noticed that the mother of the boys did not look especially relieved. "I mean they haven't been a bother. They were both working hard when I left them."

"Hmm."

"They're good boys," said Laurel.

"Oh, and I know it." Mrs. Booker dropped her militant stance. Her arms rested at her sides. "I worry that they'll turn shiftless." Her dark eyes glanced toward the front window, where she could see her husband sitting in his usual place. Her face clouded, but she would bite off her tongue before she'd say a word against him. "That's Mr. Landry out there, isn't it?"

"Uh-huh. I couldn't think of anything I needed when he said he was going into town, but then I remembered that I wanted some ribbons so here I am." She wandered over to the shelves of bolts of fabric and notions. "Ribbons aren't the sort of thing someone else can pick out for you, are they?"

"No man that I know," said Mrs. Booker. "Do you have a particular color in mind? Is it for trimming a bonnet or a dress?"

"No. Just something pretty for my hair." Laurel felt awkward as soon as she'd said it. "I haven't bought anything for a—"

"Lord, Laurel Beth, you don't have to explain yourself to me. You look it all over and choose whatever strikes your fancy. Clarice would help you but she's home with the baby today. I'll just be over by the counter when you're ready. Take your time."

Glad that Mrs. Booker was not going to hover, Laurel thanked her. There was a veritable rainbow of ribbons to choose from and in a variety of fabrics. Grosgrain. Satin. Lace. Sateen. Velvet. Laurel fingered them to test the textures. Idly, she asked, "Would you be able to make change for a ten-dollar note?"

"A ten-dollar note?" asked Mrs. Booker. "It *has* been

a long time since you've been in. Always sending Rooster or one of the boys like you do, you're forgetting you have credit here."

"Oh, no. I remembered. I just didn't want this on my account, so I was wondering if you could make change."

Mrs. Booker opened her cash drawer and examined the contents. "Depends on how many ribbons you purchase, but I should be able to. I've been trying to keep smaller bills and coins handy because I've been getting some larger notes lately. I had to send Calvin to the bank a week past to make change for Mrs. Fry. Now there's a woman who knows about notions. Ostrich feathers. Mother-of-pearl buttons. Satin trimming. She comes in to look at my catalogs and fashion magazines once a week. Always has something particular in mind and somehow manages to find it. I hardly understand it myself, but I appreciate her business even if I don't appreciate her *business*. If you take my meaning."

Laurel smiled. "I believe I do." She looked out the window and saw Call was no longer standing. Mr. Booker must have invited him to sit. "You said you've been getting some larger notes lately. Is that because of Mrs. Fry?"

Mrs. Booker sat on a stool behind the counter. "Mostly her, I reckon, since she's a frequent customer, but a couple of others, too." She chuckled. "I'm recalling Bobber Jordan came in flashing a ten-dollar note he won playing poker at Sweeny's. I thought for sure he'd have spent it all at the saloon, but he bought a saw, a hammer, two boxes of nails, and some sundries for his wife and left here a happy man."

"Good for him."

"And for me. It's a pleasure when sales are brisk."

"I'm sure it is."

"You know," said Mrs. Booker, "you got me thinking. I had a note from Magnus Clutterbuck of all people. Can you imagine? Magnus Clutterbuck. I was glad for it since I don't extend him credit anymore, not with him spending so much of his time sleeping off his drink in a jail cell."

"Did you ask him where he got it? You must have suspected it could have been counterfeit."

"I sure did. He told me Sweeny gave it to him for leaving the saloon while he was still on his feet. Seemed incredible to me so I asked Sweeny and he said it was true. Apparently it was worth it to him to get Magnus out before he started breaking things up."

"Truly? I had no idea that Mr. Clutterbuck was so disorderly."

"Same here. It gives me pause, though, and I thank the Lord my man never took to serious drinking. None of my sons either."

"Certainly not Hank or Dillon," Laurel said. "I've made my selections, Mrs. Booker."

"Bring the spools here and I'll measure and cut them for you."

Laurel carried them over. "Eighteen inches each, please."

"I especially like this cornflower blue grosgrain." Mrs. Booker measured, snipped, and wrapped all three ribbons in a brown paper envelope that she tied off with string. "That'll be one dollar twenty cents."

Laurel's hand went to the pocket of her trousers and stopped before she reached inside. "You know, if it's all the same, I think I'll put it on my credit."

"That's fine." She got out her pad and flipped through it until she came to Laurel's name. She wrote down the purchase and the amount. "Anything else?"

"No. I'm good. Thank you."

"See you at services, then." She jabbed her index finger at the front window. "And if you expect to get a lick of work from Mr. Landry today, you best pry him away from my husband."

Laurel grinned. "My plan exactly."

30

I didn't require rescuing," said Call when he and Laurel were out of Mr. Booker's hearing. "He's an interesting fellow. I was enjoying myself."

"I'm sure. But did you learn anything you came to town to find out?"

"Not a thing, but when I saw you go into the mercantile, I knew my presence inside was unnecessary. Why are you here anyway? And where are we going?"

"I'm here because I wanted to purchase some ribbons." She showed him her packet. "We're going to the bank. I learned that Mrs. Booker took ten-dollar notes from Mrs. Fry, Bobber Jordan, and Magnus Clutterbuck. Mrs. Fry gave her more than one over the last few weeks. Bobber won his note playing poker. Sweeny paid Mr. Clutterbuck to leave the saloon before he destroyed property, and I reckon we know where and how Mrs. Fry came by her legal tender."

"Where and how," said Call, "but we don't know who gave them to her. I doubt she'd be forthcoming if I asked. Maybe I can find out who was at the poker table with Bobber Jordan. Did Mrs. Booker wonder why you were asking about the notes?"

"She didn't seem to." Laurel told him how she had come by the information.

"Clever. I knew I was right to leave you in there with her."

"Yet you didn't invite me to accompany you."

"You were busy. And you didn't mention ribbons."

Laurel let it go, mostly because they'd reached the bank. Call held the door open for her and she waited for him to accompany her to the teller's cage. "I'd like to see Mr. Higgenbotham. Is he in?"

The man behind the cage offered a perfunctory smile. "He is, but allow me to tell him you're here, Miss Morrison." He looked at Call. "Mr. Landry. Another withdrawal?"

"Not today," said Call. "I'm here on Mr. Ramsey Stonechurch's behalf."

"Of course."

When the teller disappeared into the office behind him, Laurel spoke to Call in hushed and faintly accusing tones. "He knew you."

"Sure. I took Mr. Stonechurch's money out of my boot a long while back. It was damned uncomfortable."

"No longer a legal tenderfoot, is that it?"

He groaned softly. "It was awful when I said it. Don't remind me."

The teller returned and ushered them into the bank manager's office. Mr. James Higgenbotham was a man of fleshy physical consequence. He carried most of his extra weight in his belly, some of which rested on his lap, but there was enough left to fill out a second chin. His fingers were as plump as sausages, and when he smiled, his round and rosy cheeks lifted until his eyes were mere slits.

"Welcome. Welcome." Higgenbotham heaved himself out of his chair and came around the desk to greet Laurel warmly. He took her hand in his and shook it. "Close the door, Simms," he said to the teller. "No disturbances."

"Of course." Simms backed out and shut the door.

Call extended his hand. "McCall Landry."

"I remember you, Mr. Landry. You've hardly used the account Mr. Stonechurch set up for you. Is everything not satisfactory?"

"On the contrary. My expenses are modest."

"Please. Where are my manners? Sit. Sit." He indicated the chairs in front of his desk and waited for Call and Laurel to take their seats before he returned to his. He lowered himself carefully into his chair, sat back, and rested his folded hands on his belly. "What can I do for you?" His gaze wandered from Laurel to Call and back to Laurel.

"We're here on the same matter," said Laurel. "Strictest confidence, naturally."

"Naturally," said the banker. "Confidence is essential to banking."

Call said, "We are aware there are some legal tender notes in circulation, specifically ten-dollar notes. Issued eighteen sixty-two and later, with the red seal and serial numbers. Mrs. Booker received several at her mercantile and she would have deposited them here. Do you still have them or have they gone back into circulation?"

"We have some," Higgenbotham said. "I can't say they are the ones Mrs. Booker deposited."

"We'd like to see them."

The banker blanched a little. "Do you suspect counterfeiting?"

"No. We have no reason to think that."

Marginally relieved, Higgenbotham said, "Well, it's highly unusual."

"Mr. Stonechurch will hear from me about your cooperation."

Higgenbotham pretended to consider the request so as not to appear to be swayed by Call's statement. "I suppose it would be all right since Mr. Stonechurch would approve."

"Yes. Absolutely."

"I have to open the safe." He rolled his chair to the large rectangular Morse safe situated against the wall six feet away and turned his chair so it blocked the view of his guests. "It will only take a moment."

It took several because Higgenbotham kept going past one of the numbers in the combination and had to start again. When he finally pulled the door open, he removed a short stack of ten-dollar notes. "You'll have to look at them here," he said, shutting the door and spinning the lock. "I would prefer to be present."

"That's fine," said Call. "Count them first, please."

Higgenbotham did and passed twenty bills to Laurel. She gave them to Call, who fanned them out and removed the ones they knew they weren't interested in.

"Six," he said, handing the others back to the banker. "Paper? Pencil?"

Higgenbotham took both out of his desk drawer and held them out.

Laurel took them. Not having her spectacles put her at a disadvantage reading the serial numbers on the greenbacks. It was easier to take the numbers down as Call read them. With the pencil poised over the paper, she waited for Call to begin. He read out the numbers slowly and clearly and checked them once she had finished transcribing.

"That's all," he said, returning the sixty dollars to Higgenbotham.

"And you're certain they're not counterfeit."

"Certain, but feel free to examine them for yourself. Are there any more? In the tellers' drawers, for instance."

"We don't keep the bigger notes out there. No reason for it."

"All right." He stood. "Thank you."

Laurel got to her feet and also thanked the bank manager. "Strictest confidence," she said again.

"Absolutely." He was still scratching his head when they left him alone.

Call and Laurel waited until they were outside before they spoke. "I noticed the serial numbers weren't consecutive," said Laurel.

"I didn't expect them to be," Call told her. "If they're in the range of the bills that the bank in Denver sent out, that's plenty good enough. We'll know that at least one person in town is passing the money."

"I'll send a message to the bank when we get back."

"Send it to Sheriff Cook. He'll investigate for me and he already has Digger Leary in custody. Digger might have more to say once he knows Pye is dead and the money is in someone else's hands."

Laurel nodded. They were approaching their horses when she saw Sheriff Carter leaving his office. She nudged Call with her elbow.

"I see him," he said. "Keep walking. We can't assume he's interested in talking to us." The words were barely out of Call's mouth when Carter shouted at him to hold up. Call stopped, turned, and waited for the sheriff to cross the street. Out of the side of his mouth, he told Laurel to keep going. There was no time to express his surprise as Carter was upon him. Call nodded in greeting. "Sheriff. What can I do for you?"

Carter jerked his chin in Laurel's direction. "Where is Miss Morrison going?"

"Back to the station. Did you need her? You only called for me."

"No. No, you'll do." He looked Call over. "Theo Beckley told me you were at his place yesterday. With the doctor."

"That's right." Call had an urge to step back to an arm's length distance from the sheriff, but he held his ground because he figured Carter wasn't used to that. The man's size put him at an immediate advantage in most situations. "Is there a problem?"

"You tell me." He rubbed the back of his bull neck as though he were thinking on it. "Guess I'm wondering why you didn't stop before or after your visit. I like to be kept informed of the goings-on. Mr. Stonechurch might have hired you to look into the robbery for him, but I'm still the law here. I've got a right to know what you've learned."

"Of course."

Carter waited a few beats, and when Call didn't elaborate, he said, "Well?"

Call maintained a pleasant demeanor in spite of his annoyance. "It wasn't my intention to keep you in the dark. Honestly, I didn't think of stopping by to tell you we were on our way to Beckley's because I figured if you were in your office, you'd see us and come on over. And on the way out, the doc and I were anxious to get Miss Morrison back to the station as she was feeling out of sorts after what she witnessed."

"Lots of women I know wouldn't have been in the room."

"Maybe so, but she insisted."

"Mind of her own, that one." He looked past Call's shoulder to where Laurel sat patiently waiting on her horse. "Are you and she . . ." His voice trailed off, leaving the question hanging.

Call was not going to let the sheriff off so easily. "Are she and I what?"

"I know you're working for her some, but are you, um, calling on her?"

Call hadn't expected the sheriff to put it quite so delicately. Physically he was more bull in a china shop than dainty dancer. Call had to be careful not to smile. "No," he said. "Not calling on her."

Carter nodded thoughtfully. "Right." Then he was back to business. "So what did the doc have to say?"

"Didn't Mr. Beckley report all that? He was present throughout the autopsy."

"I want to hear it from you. I'd rather not have to ask Miss Morrison."

There was a threat there that Call did not care for. He told the sheriff what Dr. Singer had learned, all of which he was certain Theo Beckley had already reported.

"So he was murdered, tied, and pitched over the falls. Is that what we're supposed to believe?"

"He was shot and allowed to bleed to death. As for getting trussed, that could've happened before or after he died, but he was never thrown over the falls. His injuries would have been more substantial. He was transported to the pool, weighed down with a rock, and dropped in to sink to the bottom."

"Huh. Seems a lot of work. Pushing him over the falls makes more sense."

"There'd be no guarantee that he'd stay under. A rock hitched to him up above wouldn't likely stay hitched on the way down."

"Maybe so. Still, seems like an awful lot of trouble to go to. Could've left his body up there and it might not have been recovered yet."

"I was up there," Call said. "I would have found it days earlier."

"Yeah, I heard you climbed the rocks. Stonechurch must be paying you a lot of money to take fool chances like that."

Call didn't respond.

Carter's wooly eyebrows made a thick black line across his brow as he took Call's measure through narrowed eyes. "You been up there since to look around?"

"Yes. Yesterday afternoon, in fact."

"So after you got back from Beckley's."

"That's right."

"Find anything?"

"Penelope."

Carter frowned. "How's that again?"

"Penelope. She's the horse that Pye stole from the Morrison Station. Miss Morrison has names for all the mares that go through the station."

"Now that's downright peculiar."

"You probably shouldn't mention it to her."

"No. I won't. Still, it's peculiar to my way of thinking. A work animal like that. Suits her, though."

Call wasn't sure if he was saying Penelope was suited to her name or peculiar suited Laurel. He didn't ask. Instead, he told Carter about the mare's condition when she was found and how she was recovering.

"You find anything else up there?" asked Carter.

"Nope."

Rayleigh Carter was in full considering mode. He rubbed behind his neck again as he thought. "What made you think Pye was shot up top of the falls? Why'd you go up there the first time, and if you didn't find anything then, why'd you go up again?"

So the sheriff was not quite as dull-witted as he appeared at times. Call realized he would do well to remember that. "A gut feeling," he said. He was not going to mention the greenback scrap he'd found after his initial climb that had prompted his return. "Can't say it was any more than that."

"Huh. Sometimes you have to trust your gut, is that it?"

"Yes."

"I was thinking that maybe I'd have a look up there myself. Could be there's something you overlooked. I mean that mare could've gotten up that way on her own. There's no proof that Pye rode her up there or that he was shot there. That's right, isn't it?"

Call admitted to the sheriff that he was right.

"Seems like you're making some assumptions, Mr. Landry."

"Seems like. Good to know you have my back."

The sheriff shook his head. "Not yours. Miss Morrison's. I don't give a good goddamn what happens to you. I want to make sure her name and reputation remains in the clear."

"Is there some reason you think it won't?"

"Other than the fact that I don't trust you?"

"Other than that, I guess."

"You're just passin' through and got no stake in this town. I don't like that. Makes you something of a wild card."

"A wild card, huh? That's a good thing to keep in mind, Carter, because I'm going to run for sheriff next election."

Carter stared at him, making no effort to hide his incredulity. That lasted only a few seconds. The sheriff threw back his head and laughed hard enough to startle the horses.

Laurel settled Abby and reached for Artemis's reins to reassure the mare.

Carter got hold of himself long enough to apologize to Laurel and took out a handkerchief to dab at his eyes. He was still shaking his head and occasionally snorting as he walked away.

Call watched him cross the street and only went for his horse when Carter had disappeared into his office.

"What was that about?" Laurel asked as Call took up the reins.

Call shrugged. "Your sheriff finds me amusing."

"Maybe I would, too, if you'd tell me."

"I doubt it. I doubt you'd believe me."

"Call. Don't do that."

He said nothing until they were out of town and Laurel didn't press. He was glad of that, and it was what decided him to tell her. "I informed Carter that my name would be on the ballot opposite his in the next election."

"Ah. Well, I'd vote for you. If I could vote, that is."

"Maybe you'll feel different when I tell you that the sheriff is sweet on you."

"I can't vote for him either, so I don't know that it's important. And what made you say it anyway? There are some suspicions you need to keep to yourself."

"Not a suspicion. A fact. He asked me if I was calling on you, and he definitely left me with the impression that he'd like to."

"He did? That's disturbing."

"Why? You told me you considered him as a candidate to take to your bed if I didn't accept your offer."

Laurel waved a hand dismissively. "Forget about that."

Call's eyebrows climbed his forehead. "Really? You think I can do that?"

"Why not? I have. Or I would if you didn't bring it up."

"How did this become my fault?"

"That's rhetorical, isn't it? I mean you don't expect me to answer."

He had, but in light of her question decided against it. "I told him that I wasn't calling on you, so you should be prepared for flowers and maybe an invitation to walk in the moonlight."

"I doubt it. He's had plenty of time before now to express an interest and he never has."

"Maybe because he didn't think there was competition and he had plenty of time to pursue you."

Laurel made a face. "But you told him there is no competition. You're *not* calling on me."

"I told him. I didn't say he believed me."

"I'll worry about it if he shows up at my front door and not a moment before. What else did you talk about? I know that conversation wasn't just about me."

Call went over it with her. "I didn't mention the money."

"I wouldn't have either. Did you ask him if he owned a Springfield rifle?"

"No. It wasn't the right time. I'll find some excuse to visit the jail and look around."

"Maybe I could do that."

"What? And encourage him? I don't think that's a good idea."

It probably wasn't, but Laurel was fairly certain she'd be greeted with less suspicion than Call. "So he's going to look around at the top of the falls?"

"He says he is."

"Is there anything left for him to discover?"

"Maybe he'll find another greenback, but I don't think we'll ever know. I'm not at all confident that he'd mention it."

"I think he'd like to show you up to Mr. Stonechurch. Solve this himself."

"If that were true, why didn't he try harder to find Mr. Pye?"

"He didn't know about the robbery when I went to him. I only reported Mr. Pye as a horse thief."

"He knew everything later and still didn't do much. He took a deputy with him and didn't form a posse. Didn't that ever strike you as odd?"

"I chalked it up to Carter being out of practice and generally unmotivated. Why? Why do you think he hung back?"

"Self-preservation, Laurel. I think the sheriff of Falls Hollow is up to his neck in this thing."

31

Over the course of the next week, Laurel thought a lot about what Call had told her. The investigation stalled again while Call casually asked folks around town about their war experiences and managed to raise the topic of Springfield rifles. Most of his inquiries were done in Sweeny's, sometimes after a few drinks, sometimes during a game of cards. It wasn't unusual for both to be involved. Laurel wondered how he squeezed information from men known not to talk about the war, but when she asked him, he merely shrugged, not dismissively, but as if he didn't know.

Rooster tagged along on a couple of occasions, and Laurel put the same question to him. "He's got a way about him," said Rooster. "Puts folks at ease, though I know him well enough now to see that he isn't easy himself. He talks about Libby Prison and Andersonville sometimes. Doesn't say much, but men respect him for it. They tell him things they'd never tell their mothers, wives, or sweethearts. Not sure they realize they're telling him."

Laurel took in what Rooster told her and hugged it to her heart. Through no intentional avoidance on her part, she didn't see much of Call except at meals. Everyone at the station was working their routine during the day, feeding, watering, grooming the horses, weeding and picking vegetables in the garden, gathering eggs, milking the cows, providing slops for the hogs, butchering, smoking, repairing, cooking, baking, washing, and welcoming every stage passing through.

In the evenings, Laurel sat on the porch alone. Sometimes she read until it was too dark to see; sometimes she only pretended to read. Call rarely returned from town while she was sitting outside, and when he did, he only raised a hand in passing and went straight to the bunkhouse. They never spoke of him returning to her bedroom. With deep regret, Laurel came to realize they were rarely speaking at all.

She didn't like it. She simply didn't know how to fix it.

Rayleigh Carter never showed up at her door bearing flowers or asking her to walk with him. She had suspected all along that Call had been pulling her leg and the sheriff's lack of attention seemed to be proof of that. She was relieved that it had only been a tease, especially now that she knew about Call's suspicions.

As far as Laurel knew, Carter was the only person on Call's list that he hadn't spoken to about the rifle. Call had also talked to a number of men who weren't on the list, but that was in aid of providing cover. She supposed he had his reasons for excluding the sheriff, but other than his suspicion that Carter was involved, he hadn't told her what they were. She tended to go at a thing straight on. Call practiced circling his prey.

"Well, don't you look fine today," Mrs. Lancaster said when Laurel walked into the kitchen. "And it not being a Sunday, I have to wonder what's going on in that busy, busy mind of yours."

Laurel smoothed the midriff of her bodice and plucked at her skirt to make it fuller. She was wearing a modest cherry-red-and-ivory-striped dress with three-quarter-length sleeves and a buttoned-up neckline. "You approve?"

"Of the dress, yes. What you're going to do in it, well, I'm reserving judgment."

"I haven't worn this in an age," Laurel said. "It was in the back of my wardrobe. I'd forgotten about it. Probably because it requires lacing my corset so tight I can barely breathe. Can you tell?"

Mrs. Lancaster pursed her lips and looked Laurel over. "You seem to be breathing just fine. Leastways the corset hasn't interfered with your talking." The cook punched the puffy ball of dough on the table, folded and turned it, and then dug in with the heels of her hands. "What I surely can tell is that you're avoiding my question."

"You haven't really asked one, have you?" When Mrs. Lancaster merely gave her the eye, she relented. "Very well. I'm going to visit the sheriff."

Mrs. Lancaster's eyebrows rose halfway to her hairline. "Now why are you going to do that?"

"I have some questions to put to him."

"Well, I reckon you're dressed to get some answers."

Laurel nodded but her smile was suddenly uncertain. "Maybe I should change."

"That'd be up to you, but it seems a shame to waste that dress on the sheriff. Promise me you'll make sure Call sees you in it before you go."

Since Call was the one who hitched the buckboard for her, he had a long good look before he helped her up onto the bench. "Is that a new ribbon?" he asked, pointing to her hair.

Self-conscious, Laurel's hand went immediately to the ribbon securing her heavy tail of dark hair. "Yes."

"Pretty."

Laurel said nothing because her throat was suddenly dry. Smiling weakly, she took the reins when he handed them to her and gave them a shake. The buckboard rattled off and she didn't look back. If she had, she would have seen that Call had removed his hat and was pushing his hand through his hair.

Go bother someone else," Mrs. Lancaster said, flicking flour at Call as he entered the kitchen by the back door. "I'm busy."

Ignoring her, he asked, "What's she up to?"

"I guess you're talking about our Miss Morrison."

"You know I am. Give."

"Did you ask her?"

"No. I didn't want her to lie to me."

The cook's mouth twisted disapprovingly. "Now you don't know that she would have done that."

"Oh, I think I do. Maybe she lied to you."

"I'm sure she didn't," she said smugly. That slightly superior smile faded when she realized she had given Laurel up. "All right. She's going into town."

"Obviously. To do what?"

"She's, um, she's going to visit the sheriff."

"No," he said, shaking his head. "She's not."

Mrs. Lancaster did not take offense. It was obvious from Call's tone that he believed her and didn't want to.

"I told her not to do that," said Call.

"I'm sure she took that into account."

"And did as she damn well pleased."

"Yes, well, taking it into account isn't the same as doing what you wanted, now is it?" Mrs. Lancaster shaped her dough into a loaf and placed it in a pan. "Open the oven door for me, please." When Call did, she slipped the pan inside and stood back. "She's got a good head on her shoulders, Call. Look at all that she's done here and continues to do. If you're still worried, then maybe you should go after her. I don't know why she wanted to speak to Sheriff Carter, but it seems to me that you do."

"You're right." Call sighed. "She won't thank me for it."

"Then I reckon you have to decide how important that is."

He nodded. "She looked real fine in that dress."

"Uh-huh. Did you tell her?"

"I asked her about the hair ribbon. Told her it was pretty."

Now it was the cook who sighed. "You're a real sweet talker, aren't you?"

Call smiled wanly. "Leaving now."

"And me without my foot in your behind," she said dryly. "Will wonders never cease?"

Laurel was studying wanted notices when Call entered the sheriff's office. The chair behind Carter's desk was vacant. There was a shot glass on the blotter and a bottle of coffin varnish beside it. The whiskey bottle was less than half full.

Laurel turned, acknowledged his presence by putting a finger to her lips, and tipped her head sideways to indicate the rear of the building, where the cells were. Call listened and heard snoring. He nodded and was quiet until he was beside her.

"Is it Carter back there?" he whispered.

She nodded. "He's alone."

"Fine. Let's go."

Laurel didn't move. "I suppose Mrs. Lancaster gave me up."

"I threatened her."

"You did not."

"No, but I thought about it." He glanced sideways at the door that separated the office from the cells. If Laurel knew Carter was alone, it meant she had gone back there. "You didn't speak to him, did you?"

"No. He doesn't know I'm here."

"Good. We can go then. No harm done."

Laurel bristled a little at that. "I had no intention of doing harm. Give me some credit."

"Please, save your annoyance with me for later. I promise I will give it all the attention it deserves."

"Ha. You think I don't know what that means."

"Can we go?"

"In a moment. Did you notice the gun rack on the opposite wall?"

He had to admit he hadn't. Besides the shot glass and whiskey and Carter's empty chair, he'd only had eyes for her. He wished he'd never seen the glass, bottle, or vacant chair, then he could have said truthfully that he'd only had eyes for her. On the other hand, even though she looked as lovely as she did, Call wouldn't put it past her to poke him in the ribs for spewing romantic twaddle.

"I'm going to examine the guns," he said.

"Mm. I thought you might want to do that." Laurel continued to examine the notices while Call went to the other side of the room. She was tempted to remove Mr. Pye's wanted notice, which was front and center of the lot. She'd have thought that Carter would have taken it down by now, but for reasons beyond her understanding, he'd left it up. Was he even lazier than she'd reckoned? She looked over her shoulder at Carter's desk. He was obviously feeling secure in his position because he hadn't bothered to put away the proof that he'd been drinking.

Shaking her head, Laurel turned away from the wall and went to join Call. "I'm relieved you're going to run for sheriff," she said. "Otherwise I might have to do it and I don't know how I'd find the time."

Frowning, Call gave her a sideways glance before he resumed examining the rifle in his hands. "What are you talking about?"

"You. Running for sheriff. You're serious about it, aren't you? I hope you didn't tell Sheriff Carter that simply to goad him."

"If you recall, my announcement only goaded him to laughter. If I was a more prideful man, I believe that would have stung."

"Would you please answer my question?"

"Yes, Laurel, I'm serious. I told you I was thinking about it before I ever told Carter. Go back to being relieved and stop planning your campaign." He thrust the Springfield he was holding at her. "Here. Take this."

Her mouth snapped shut as she grasped the rifle in both hands, which, she supposed, was his point in pushing it at her.

Call took down a second rifle and pointed out the government stamp on the steel lock plate. "You're holding the eighteen sixty-one model. This is an Enfield, produced in England. Put yours up to your shoulder." When she did, he said, "Feel how that stock is curved so it sits well against your shoulder. That's one of the features that adds to its accuracy as a long-range weapon."

"What about the one you have?" she asked, lowering the gun.

"It's a good rifle. Used by both sides, but primarily by the South because England would sell to them. I saw a lot of these when I was in Andersonville. Most of the guards carried an Enfield. I wasn't expecting the sheriff to have one of these."

"What does it mean?" She returned the Springfield to the rack.

"Probably nothing. He could have picked it up on the battlefield or been issued it. After the Springfield, the Enfield was the most popular rifle."

"Can you tell the difference between a minié fired from one rifle compared to the other?"

"Wouldn't that be a fine thing, but no."

"I thought every man in Falls Hollow fought for the Union, but maybe Carter didn't. It could be how he came by the Enfield."

"Maybe, but I don't think it matters to Josey Pye which rifle killed him." He set the Enfield back on the rack. "We need to go now. I think we've pushed our luck far enough."

Nodding, Laurel preceded him out the door. Neither noticed that the rifles had not been returned to their original positions on the rack.

Carter did, though. The first thing to catch the sheriff's eye when he returned to his office was that his glass and bottle were still sitting out. He didn't recall leaving them there, but what the hell. He poured himself a drink and indulged in the hair of the dog as he sat back—and came bolt upright when his gaze shifted to the gun rack. He swore under his breath, and then because it didn't make him feel one whit better, he threw the shot glass at the far wall, where it shattered in a satisfying manner.

32

Call hitched Artemis to the back of the buckboard and sat beside Laurel on the way back to the station. "Just to make sure you go straight home," he said, and he was only half kidding.

"Why did you follow me?"

"I didn't as much follow as go after you. You see the difference?" As far as he was concerned, he was not splitting hairs. "I didn't know what trouble you were going to get yourself into, especially in that getup."

"Getup? Did you truly just say that?"

"I did." He paused, sensing he'd stepped into deep water. "Does it matter that I regretted it as soon as the words were out of my mouth?"

She snorted. "Not much."

"It bothered me some that you made yourself up so fine for the likes of him."

"When you're in a hole, Call, the first thing you need to do is stop digging."

"Right."

"I wasn't looking for trouble," she said. "I was looking for that Springfield. I didn't think you'd talked to the sheriff yet so I made it my business."

"Even after I told you not to do that."

Laurel made a show of breathing in and expelling that air slowly so he couldn't possibly miss the fact that she was out of sorts with him. "Even after that. Maybe you hadn't noticed, but I have a mind of my own."

"Oh, I noticed. Hard not to. You take a thing in your head and marry it for life."

Frowning, Laurel looked at him sideways. "What is that supposed to mean?"

"You know damn well."

And she did. She couldn't very well take back the words she'd said to him when he told her he intended to stick. *I believe you believe it.* She had cut him bone deep and the wound hadn't healed. "I meant it at the time, Call."

"I know. Unlike you, Laurel, I take you at your word."

"Do you intend to keep throwing everything I say back at me?"

"I think I do, yes."

His honesty stung, but she took it on the chin as deserved. "When I said I meant it at the time, you were supposed to understand that I don't think the same way now. Contrary to what you believe, I don't always marry an idea for life. Didn't I say I'd vote for you for sheriff if I could? I thought you'd hear that as acknowledgment that I believed you were going to stay around. What did you hear if you didn't hear that?"

"It's not the same as you saying it straight out."

She nodded slowly, thoughtfully. Her fingernails pressed white crescents into her palms. She took a steadying breath. "No, of course it isn't. You're right. You shouldn't have to interpret or guess. So here it is straight out. I love you. My heart aches so fierce at times that I want to curse you. Sometimes I do. There's not much that frightens me, but I've been scared to death for a long time now, some about this twisting, aching feeling that I can't shake, but mostly about something happening to you. I think Sheriff Carter would as soon shoot you as look at you, so yes, I made it my business to see him in this getup and keep you out of his sights."

It was a lot to take in and Call didn't say anything for

a time. The buckboard creaked and rumbled. Behind him, Artemis nickered. Grasses shifted in the breeze. Laurel was staring straight ahead and Call could only see her in profile. A muscle jumped in her cheek as she clenched her jaw. It made him smile. She was always so determined. It was one of the many things he loved about her.

"That achy, twisted feeling you have? I have it, too."

Laurel risked a quick look in his direction. "You do?"

"Uh-huh."

"Are we both afflicted, you reckon?"

"Seems as if we might be."

She nodded. "It ought not to make a body feel so unsettled."

"Skittish, too, like a cockroach on a hot griddle."

Now Laurel stared at him, eyes wide, jaw a little slack.

"I know," he said, deadpan. "Mrs. Lancaster says I'm not much for sweet talk."

"To say the least."

He reached for her hand, put his over hers, and pulled up on the reins. The buckboard rattled to a stop. Artemis came forward and nudged Call's shoulder with her nose. He shrugged her off. "Laurel."

Her eyes shifted from the hand covering hers to his face. "Hmm?"

"I love you," he said. "I wanted you to hear it straight so you can't mistake my feelings. It's been in me for a long time, but I didn't trust what you would do with it."

Laurel felt pressure building behind her eyes. She blinked. Tears came anyway, unbidden, unwelcome. They hovered, blurring her vision, but they didn't fall, and she shut her eyes. Call's thumb made a pass across her spiky lashes, erasing her tears. She gave him a watery smile. "I'm sorry," she said, her voice a mere whisper. "You were right not to trust me. I've been horrible."

"You've been afraid."

"Yes. Since you showed up at the station."

"First or second time?"

"Second time," she said, and then because there was a

gleam in his eyes, she added, "I didn't give you much thought when you were only passing through."

Call studied her face. "Liar. You were probably scared then, too. Scared you'd never see me again."

There was some truth in what he said, not that she was going to admit to it just now. "You don't think much of yourself, do you?"

He chuckled. "You'll always keep me on my toes and in my place."

"In your place? Where do you think that is?"

"With you," he said simply. "It will always be with you."

She was going to say that maybe he did know something about sweet talk after all, but then he was kissing her and it seemed best to say nothing.

It wasn't a perfunctory kiss, no quick stamp as if he meant to seal a promise. No, he took off his hat and tossed it in the back of the buckboard. It was a sure sign that he meant this kiss to be sweet and slow and serious. He lingered, tasting and teasing just a little. The reins slipped out of her hand and dropped to her feet. The horses shifted but didn't move forward. Laurel gripped the bench to steady herself in the event they changed their mind. It was not a satisfactory solution, not when Call steadied her so much better. She raised her hands to his shoulders, holding him as she held on.

He lifted his head a fraction so their lips were only a hairsbreadth away, and he murmured her name. She heard longing and need and something like satisfaction. That was all right, then, because she was satisfied as well. This man—and only this man—had become necessary to her, essential to a life fully lived.

Call changed the slant of his mouth, swept her damp upper lip with the tip of his tongue. Her fingers tightened on his shoulders while his curved around her waist. He pulled her closer. When she raised her head to catch her breath, he took advantage of her exposed throat and nipped at the slender cord in her neck.

"You're all buttoned up," he whispered.

Laurel laughed low and deep in her throat. "Of course I am."

"Hmm." Call raised one hand to her modest neckline and deftly undid the uppermost button. Encouraged because she didn't slap his hand away, he unfastened another. Then another. His fingertips lightly brushed her skin.

She shivered, and when he dipped his head to touch the hollow of her throat with his lips, Laurel held him there, her fingers threading deeply in his hair. If he had invited her to lie down in the buckboard, she might have taken him up on it, but she opened her eyes just then and saw Artemis was preparing to shove her nose against Call's back.

"Your lady's jealous," she said, batting Artemis away. Call groaned softly, which made her smile, and he sat up. "She's not happy with you."

"The feeling is mutual," he said wryly. Turning, Call stroked the mare's nose and spoke nonsense to her before he pushed her away. He leaned over the bench seat and stretched to reach his hat. By the time he put it on and faced Laurel again, she was buttoned up and had the reins in her hands. "This isn't over."

Laurel offered up a slightly wicked grin. "I sincerely hope not."

33

Laurel accepted the stack of plates Mrs. Lancaster gave her so she could begin setting the table.

"You've come undone," said the cook.

Laurel *had* come undone, but she didn't think it showed. How did Mrs. Lancaster know? "What do you mean?"

The cook wiggled a finger at the bodice of Laurel's dress. "Your buttons."

Looking down at herself, Laurel saw that although she'd buttoned up, she had missed one. There was a gap where a button should have been. She set down the plates and fixed the problem. "Thank you."

"Makes a body wonder." Mrs. Lancaster gave her a significant, knowing look. "You were secure as a vault when you left here. I would have noticed different, you going to visit the sheriff, and all."

"If you think unbuttoning was in aid of tempting Sheriff Carter, then you have another think coming. I didn't even see him. Well, I did, but he'd been drinking and was sleeping it off in one of the cells. Did you know he was a morning drinker?"

"Oh, no. I won't be put off as easily as that. I know Call went after you and I saw the two of you arriving together. As I said, it makes a body wonder."

Laurel pursed her lips and said primly, "You just keep on wondering." Picking up the plates, she headed to the dining room.

Mrs. Lancaster called after her, "And you tell that man to pick up his own socks the next time he beds down with you."

That stopped Laurel in her tracks so abruptly, she almost lost the plates. She thought she should probably be more embarrassed than she was, but if her face was flaming, it was because she was considering murdering McCall Landry. The cook was still talking at her from the kitchen and she was trying not to listen.

"It's your job to train him right from the beginning. You start out as you mean to go on."

A slow, painful death.

It was only much later that she considered Mrs. Lancaster's reaction and found it remarkable. No censure. No questions about her intentions or his. In fact, the cook's comments were edged with amusement as if she were just that much pleased. It made a body wonder.

Laurel was back in her work clothes by the time supper was served. Only Jelly mentioned it. "You still look right fine, though," he added quickly lest she take offense.

"Thank you, Jelly." Hank and Dillon received one of her pointed, narrow-eyed stares when they snickered. "You two could learn a thing or two about complimenting a woman, you know."

"But you're our boss," said Hank. Beside him, Dillon nodded earnestly.

"Not me," she said. "*Any* woman. Your sisters or your mother, for instance."

The brothers wrinkled their noses.

Mrs. Lancaster set a basket of hot biscuits on the table. "As long as you don't apply to Call here for instruction."

"Hey," said Call, taking umbrage. "I know how to give a pretty compliment." He helped himself to one of the biscuits and held it under his nose, sniffing deeply. "This, for instance, is pure ambrosia. Food of the gods. You, Mrs. Lancaster, are surely an angel for setting it in front of us, undeserving sinners that we are."

Pleased, the cook dimpled. "Ah, go on with you."

Call sat back, grinning. "That's how it's done, boys." Enjoying himself, he took a big bite of biscuit and almost choked on it when Laurel kicked him under the table. "What was that for?"

"Because you really are an undeserving sinner," she said. "Pass the basket."

The next time Laurel saw Call, he was rounding the house to the porch carrying a fistful of wildflowers. She smiled, genuinely delighted with his offering as he held it out to her. Laurel didn't immediately accept the bouquet. She bent her head toward it and breathed in the fragrance of his Rocky Mountain tribute. Call had found blue columbine and mixed it with the tiny white petals of bittercress and the lavender, bell-shaped flowers of the harebell. She knew where all these flowers grew, but she imagined it had taken some effort on his part to come upon them.

She took the bouquet from him before he squeezed the stems beyond recovery. "They're lovely. Thank you." Standing, she said, "I'm going in to put them in water."

"You don't need to fuss with them," he said a shade diffidently. "They're only wildflowers."

Laurel realized he hadn't been at all confident as to how she would receive his gift. "Of course I need to fuss," she said quietly. "I've never had flowers I didn't pick for myself." Standing on tiptoes, she kissed him on the cheek.

Call watched her disappear into the house and waited for her to return before he sat beside her on the swing. He gave the swing a gentle push. "I saw a patch of the blue ones when I found Penelope. I had to search some to find the others."

"I wondered about that. The blue ones are columbine." She moved closer and leaned her shoulder against his. He lifted his arm and put it around her. The fit was even better now. She told him the names of the other two flowers in the bunch. "What made you think of it?"

"Besides shirking barn work?"

Laurel's chuckle stayed deep in her throat. "Besides that."

"I suppose it was what Mrs. Lancaster said about not making pretty compliments. That stung some. Jelly does it better than I do."

"I hurt you terribly," she said. "I didn't deserve pretty words. The way I'm remembering it, you didn't think I deserved any words at all. I didn't like that."

"I didn't either, but it was safer than what I wanted to do."

"Oh?"

"Shake the living daylights out of you."

"Have you ever done anything like that?"

"No."

"I didn't think so. You have a cold temper, I think. Not a hot one."

"I'm not sure one's better than the other."

"I was contemplating a slow death for you earlier today," she said. "In case you didn't notice, I blow hot, not cold."

"I noticed," he said dryly. "What did I do that left you considering murder?"

"Left a sock in my bedroom."

"I told you I did."

"I thought you were trying to get a rise out of me."

"Nope. That was a side benefit, not the purpose."

She gave him a little poke with her elbow. "Well, Mrs. Lancaster finally got around to telling me she found it."

"I wondered about that. She passed it right back to me with my clean laundry. Never said a word, though."

"I'm only fooling myself thinking I could have secrets."

"What did she say?

"No sermon. No admonishment. I don't think she's unhappy about it. Oh, but she did say I should tell you to pick up after yourself. Begin the way you mean to go on, she told me. Apparently, it's my responsibility to train you."

"We can start tonight," he said, "unless you have some objection."

"Not a one, but I'd rather we didn't attend to the socks."

"Fine with me. I bought some French letters."

"Can I see one?"

"Later. I don't have one on me. I put them in my foot locker."

"How many did you buy?"

"A dozen. They come a dozen to a packet."

Laurel nodded sagely. "Enough for one night, then."

Call's shout of laughter jostled the swing. He put his heels down to set it still but it continued to bounce in time with his shoulders. He required a full minute to get himself under control. "Sorry," he said, knuckling his eyes to dash the tears. "I appreciate your confidence, but unless you're inviting a garrison to your bed, there will be plenty left for another night." He studied her face when his vision finally cleared. She looked disappointed. "You knew that, right? You were pulling my leg." When she didn't say anything, he frowned. "Laurel? You *were* pulling my leg, weren't you?"

The laughter she had been suppressing broke free. "Yes, I know," she said between taking in gulps of air. "You looked so worried there for a moment. It was—it was—oh, I don't know what it was except funny. Twelve times in one night. Would we even be able to walk, do you think?" She sobered a little thinking on that and had an urge to cross her legs that she did not give in to. "It feels good to laugh, doesn't it? It's been too long."

He nodded. "I reckon laughing requires exercise like any other part."

"Mm." Laurel rested her head in the curve of his shoulder. She felt his lips brush her hair and then kiss the crown of her head. She closed her eyes.

Call waited until he was certain she'd fallen asleep before he eased his arm from around her. He wanted to shake it out, but he couldn't do it without jostling her so he let the limb return to life slowly, pins and needles pricking his skin as it woke. Nightfall blanketed them and still he didn't move. It was comfortable sitting with her like this; it always had been even when he was relegated to the safe distance of the rocker. This was where he wanted to be. He remembered asking his mother how he would know when he met the girl he was meant to marry. She'd given it a great deal of thought before she answered. After all, he'd been only seven at the time and didn't fully understand the breadth of the question he was asking.

She'd said, "You'll know because there will be times when she's out of your sight and it will feel as if you can't quite catch your breath, and when you see her, you'll feel exactly the same."

"It's like that with Mary Louise Emberly sometimes," he'd told her.

"Only sometimes? Then she's probably not the one."

His mother had been right. Over the years he'd used her measure to gauge his feelings toward a woman. Until Laurel, it was always sometimes, never always. Call had known when he left Morrison Station the very first time that he would be going back eventually. Working for Mr. Stonechurch made it easier for him to return, but he would have found a way sooner or later. He hadn't been able to catch his breath since he'd met her.

"Hey, sleepyhead," he said, nudging her. "You might want to think about heading to bed."

She stirred but didn't lift her head. "Fine here."

"You're going to have a stiff neck."

"Mm."

"Do you want me to carry you?" As he'd anticipated, that suggestion had a predictable reaction. She sat straight up.

"Don't be ridiculous." Laurel blinked, rubbed her eyes. "It's dark."

"It's late."

She covered a yawn with the back of her hand. "Oh, my."

Call chuckled. "Indeed." He slid a hand behind her back and gave her a gentle push as he held the swing still. "Go on."

Laurel nodded and slowly got to her feet. Once she was

steady, she leaned over Call and kissed him on the cheek. "You're coming, aren't you?"

"Shortly."

"Right," she whispered. "French letters."

He smiled. She was almost asleep on her feet and didn't know it. Call watched her disappear into the house and then stood in the doorway to make sure she made it up the stairs. When he heard the door to her bedroom close, he figured he'd done as much as he could, or at least as much as she'd let him. He walked from room to room, extinguishing all but one of the lamps, and then he left by the kitchen door and headed for the bunkhouse.

Laurel was sound asleep when he let himself into her room, but she was lying on the far side of the bed as though she meant to leave space for him. Call set the lamp he was carrying on the bedside table beside her spectacles and sat down on the ladder-back chair to remove his boots. Remembering Mrs. Lancaster's advice, he rolled his socks and put them inside his boots. He didn't mind if the cook wanted to believe Laurel was training him as long as Laurel didn't think she had him on a leash.

Call stood and placed his hat on the caned seat before he stripped down to his drawers. He didn't fold his clothes, but he did lay them neatly over the back of the chair. Laurel's things were lying willy-nilly on the floor. Amused, he stepped around them on his way to the bed and turned back the lamp. Raising the sheet, Call slipped under it and lay down. He was only halfway to turning on his side when Laurel rolled to the middle of the bed and sought his warmth. He whispered her name, but as he suspected, she was sound asleep. At the moment, that was fine with him. He'd forgotten about the French letters. They were still tucked in his hatband, where they would do neither of them any good.

34
❧

Laurel stretched, turned, and rolled right into Call's chest. She didn't know it was Call's chest until he grunted. She recognized that sound. "Sorry," she whispered.

"That's your fist in my belly."

She unfolded her fingers and laid her open palm against his skin. "You're toasty."

"Not toasty," he said quietly. "Hot." He circled her wrist and drew her hand down to where his cock was straining against the front of his drawers. "I've been awake longer than you have."

She lifted her head just enough to see past his shoulder to the window. The bedside lamp had been extinguished. The curtains were drawn but a sliver of moonlight was visible at the edges. "Did you just get here?" she asked, walking back her fingers and plumping the pillow under head.

"Hours ago."

"I didn't hear you. Why did you let me sleep?"

"There's nothing wrong with you and I using a bed for sleeping."

"Maybe when we've been together for fifty years. Where are those French letters?"

Laughter rumbled in his throat. "Tucked in my hatband."

At any other time she would have taken a moment to comment on his choice to carry them there, but right now she was feeling fairly warm herself. "And your hat is . . ."

Call grimaced. "On the chair."

"I don't suppose you pulled the chair closer to the bed?"

"Nope."

"We could do without them, I suppose. You managed before."

"Not again. Not until we're married."

"Married? You only just brought me flowers." When he didn't respond, she cast him a sideways glance. He was staring at the ceiling, his jaw set. She thought a muscle might have ticked in his cheek, but she couldn't be sure. "Never mind. I'll get them." She crawled over him and slid out of bed on the other side. She stumbled once when her toes struck one of her shoes, but it was her only misstep. Unsure of what she was looking for, Laurel didn't search for the French letters. She carried Call's hat back to him and handed it over. "Should I light the lamp?"

"Please."

She opened the drawer in the bedside table and felt around for the box of matches. She warned him she was going to light the match before she struck it. They both squinted against the flare. She lit the wick, replaced the globe, and waved the match until it was extinguished. Call made room for her to sit on the edge of the bed.

"How many did you bring?" she asked.

"Not all twelve." He held up two fingers and turned the hat over. "I was probably being hopeful anyway. It'll be morning soon." He removed one of the flat packet squares. The manufacturer's trademark was in bold red lettering.

"Can you use that more than once?"

"Only if I'm prepared to father a bastard," he said bluntly. "I'm not."

"Call. That wasn't kind."

"I love you, Laurel, but I don't always feel kind toward you."

"Why? Because I won't allow you to use marriage as a trump card? I wanted to make love to you and I thought you wanted the same and then you toss out marriage as a condition to do it without one of those. I could be carrying

your child already, you know. You said your method wasn't
certain."

"Which is why I don't want to risk it again." He dropped
his hat on the floor and held out the packet to her.

"Keep it," she said. "I'm no longer interested in using it."

Call didn't argue. He set it on the table and didn't say
a word as Laurel crawled back over him and lay down. He
was encouraged that she hadn't left the room. He turned
on his side, raised his head on his elbow, and looked at
her. She was staring at the ceiling. His body shielded her
features from the light. There was no hint in her face as to
what she was thinking.

"I can make a better proposal," he said at last.

"You'll have to."

"Do you have some thoughts about what you'd like to
hear or how you'd like to hear it?"

"No. I never imagined it."

"All right. Bended knee or standing?"

"Standing. I don't think I could bear seeing you on your
knees."

"It'd only be the one knee."

"Doesn't make it any better."

"Standing, then. Flowers?"

"Yes. Like the ones you brought me this evening."

"Of course. Indoors? Outdoors?"

"Outdoors, please."

"Public or private?"

"You know the answer to that. Private."

"Just making certain. Promises?"

"All of them, I suppose. I want you to promise me
everything."

"I can do that."

She nodded. "What do you want from me?"

"I want you to say yes."

Laurel smiled faintly as she turned her head toward
him. "I can do that," she whispered. "I promise you I can
do that."

Call took her at her word and it settled his thoughts, his

heart, and hers, too, it seemed, because she edged closer and took his hand.

"Like that," she said. "Touch me there."

He did.

"And your mouth, too. Yes. Just like that. Mm. You can't know . . ." Her voice trailed away as he tugged on threads of pleasure.

No, he didn't know, but he could guess. Her fingers curled as they traveled the length of his spine. He felt her knuckles pressing against his skin. It sent a shudder through him. Groaning softly, he buried his face in the curve of her neck. She stretched, giving him everything he wanted.

"Ahh. Are you biting me?"

"Nipping."

"That's all right, then." She moaned softly as he suckled flesh. There would be marks on her skin come morning to remind her he had done this thing and she'd let him. Right now she would let him do anything. Her hands slipped under his drawers and drew a line around his waist from back to front. They slid lower and she cupped his balls.

"Yes," he whispered against her ear. He was hot and heavy in her hands, and when she circled his erection, he caught his breath. "Yes," he said. "Like that."

She stroked him, tentatively at first. It required assurance from him that she wasn't hurting him for her to be firm and deliberate.

"Wait," he said, gripping her hand. "I can't . . . you can't . . . I have to . . ." He sat up suddenly and leaned toward the table. He patted the top, felt around the lamp, knocked Laurel's spectacles onto the floor, and couldn't find what he wanted. "What did you do with it?"

"What?" It wasn't right that he should make her all muzzy-headed and noodle-limbed and then expect her to answer questions. "Oh. That."

"Yes. That. What did you do with it?"

"Nothing. You had it last. Maybe it fell in the drawer."

He found the knob, pulled the drawer open, and blindly searched for the French letter packet.

"There are matches in there," she said helpfully.

"I know. I found them."

"Maybe you should use one."

When he grunted something unintelligible, Laurel also sat up and leaned around him so she could reach the table. Her hand joined his in the drawer, but her search was for the matches. She found the packet first and gave it to him then her fingers closed over the matches.

"What are you doing?" he asked. "I have what I need."

"I want to see."

"Of course you do," he said dryly, but then his cock stirred and he admitted to himself that it wasn't the worst idea in the world. "Well, light the lamp, for God's sake."

Laurel smothered her laughter against his shoulder before she inched closer to the edge of the bed so she could use both hands. When she finally lit the lamp and blew out the match, she was still smiling, albeit a little wickedly. "I'm watching," she said, rising to her knees for a better view. "Show me."

"Your curiosity is oddly arousing."

"Huh. Well, that's good, I think." She watched him carefully open the packet, remove the French letter, and carefully unfold it. It was so thin as to be almost transparent and so delicate that she feared he would tear it before it served its purpose. Most astonishing, it wasn't much bigger than his thumb. "That won't work," she told him. "It's too tiny, and you're enormous."

"Oddly flattering, too," he said to himself. "It stretches."

"Oh. Like a sausage casing."

"I swear, Laurel, if you don't shut up, we're never going to get to it."

But they did get to it. Neither could help the laughter that bubbled up from time to time. It was release of a different sort and it made them playful and attentive to the needs of the other in a new way. He learned she was ticklish at the back of her knees. She discovered that touching the dimples at the base of his spine made him shiver. His beard was delightfully abrasive against her breasts, and her hair, when it was finally free, made a silky cascade for him to sift with his fingers.

She raised her knees and hugged his hips when he pushed himself into her. She pressed her lips together, closed her eyes, and allowed herself the simple joy of feeling. It took her a moment to realize he wasn't moving. She looked up at him and saw it was the same for him. That made her smile, not wickedly now, lovingly. Her hands left his arms and cupped his face. She brushed his mouth with her thumb. "I love your mouth," she whispered. His lips parted and he bit down gently. Her skin quivered and her womb contracted. She arched and he thrust more deeply. It was exactly what she wanted and her small cry of satisfaction told him that.

He was a long time loving her, at least it felt that way. Laurel teetered on the edge of pleasure so often that she no longer knew when or if she could expect to find release, and when it finally happened, when she felt herself falling as though from a great height, she pressed the back of one hand to her mouth to muffle her shout that was both surprise and relief.

He wasn't very far behind her. It had only taken her stifled shout to toss him to the wind. A few short, shallow strokes and he was joining her. The long muscles in his arms and legs contracted and then rippled as a shudder went through him. With an effort, he lifted himself off Laurel and slipped onto his side.

"Move over," he said, nudging her. "I'm going to fall off the bed."

"It would serve you right," she said when she could catch her breath. "You're a horrible man." She slid six inches to her right to make room for him. She frowned when he sat up and put his legs over the side of the bed instead of moving over. "What are you—oh, you're taking it off, aren't you?"

"I am." He was also examining it for tears but he didn't mention that. After judging that it was still intact, Call returned it to the envelope it came in. Disposing of a French letter wasn't generally a problem, but here he had Mrs. Lancaster's keen eye to consider. He thought he might have to bury the damn thing, and he wasn't sure he was kidding. Standing, he went to the washstand and poured water in the basin. He cleaned himself, aware that Laurel was watching him with her usual unabashed interest. Settling his drawers over his hips again, he returned to the bed and slipped under the covers she held up for him. "Why am I a horrible man?" he asked.

"You tortured me."

"Did I?"

"Didn't you hear me scream?"

"It was more of a shout and you covered it up."

"In my head I was screaming."

"Next time, let it out so I'll know."

"Even if it brings Rooster and the boys?"

"As long as it doesn't bring Jelly from the far end of town, it'll be okay."

Laughter bubbled on Laurel's lips. "I think you'll be safe." She swiveled her head to look at him and said seriously, "I feel well and truly loved."

"I hope so. You about killed me."

"I don't mean what you did or what I did or what we just did. I mean I feel—"

Call put a finger to her lips. "I know what you mean. You *are* loved, Laurel. I know because I love you."

"I'm maddening," she said when his finger dropped away.

"I know it."

"And stubborn."

"That, too."

"I have opinions."

"That's not a revelation."

"And you love me anyway. I can think of a lot more reasons why you shouldn't."

"Laurel. I don't love you in spite of those things. I love you because of them. I don't relish arguing with you, but I don't go out of my way to avoid it either."

"I noticed."

"You hold your own. I do the same. Somehow we work it out. I think it's better to know that now."

She nodded. "You're right about a lot of things. Most things, actually. It's annoying. I figured I should tell you in case no one else has."

"I've had it brought to my attention. My mother said it was disturbing. I think I was about ten the first time she pointed it out."

"Not only disturbing," said Laurel. "Unnatural."

He chuckled. "Probably." Call turned over, extinguished the lamp, and then lay on his back. "It'd be a good idea to get some sleep now."

She moved closer and tucked her head against his shoulder. "Do you mind?"

"Not at all."

Laurel closed her eyes. "What are you going to do with that . . . with that . . . *thing*?"

"The French letter? I'm thinking about burying it."

"No. Really."

"Let me worry about that." He tipped his head and kissed the top of hers. "I took care of the socks. I'll manage this, too."

35

Laurel had a vague memory of Call leaving when she woke and found him gone. She looked around her room to be certain that he had taken everything with him. It didn't matter that their affair was common knowledge; Laurel decided that she could at least preserve the secret of his coming and going. Mrs. Lancaster didn't need to know everything.

Laurel washed, dressed, and passed through the kitchen on her way to feed the chickens. Mrs. Lancaster hadn't yet arrived, which in some ways was a relief. The brush burns from Call's closely trimmed beard might disappear by the time the cook took over the kitchen. His little love bites weren't visible, but she couldn't quite hide the marks where he'd nuzzled her neck. Turning up the collar of her shirt only brought attention to her throat. She would simply have to brazen it out.

Lord, she hoped he was getting that proposal into an acceptable state.

Laurel spread chicken feed and fed the pigs. She put on gloves to gather eggs because two of her best layers were viciously protective. When she carried them into the kitchen, she heard Mrs. Lancaster coming in the front door. Laurel put the eggs in a bowl on the table and hurried out. She was almost sprinting by the time she reached the barn.

"Whoa there, Miss Laurel," Rooster said, looking up

from where he was filing one of Sylvia's hooves. "Something on fire?"

Laurel ground to a halt and smiled weakly. "No fire."

"Oh. Well, that's good." He went back to filing without further comment.

"I thought I'd give Abby a good brushing. She's been neglected."

"Uh-huh. And I'm my favorite aunt's tea trolley."

Chuckling, Laurel waved off his comment. "I'm going to take care of her anyway. Chickens and hogs are fed. Eggs gathered and in the kitchen."

Dillon and Hank appeared in tandem from empty stalls. They held up shovels. "Mucking's underway," said Hank. "You go on and take care of Abby."

"Thank you for your permission," she said grandly. "Where's Jelly? I thought for sure you'd foist that job on him."

Dillon made a face and pointed up to the loft. "Call got to him first. Cat had kittens. They'll get around to pitchin' hay here in a little while. You'd think they never saw the like before."

Laurel was tempted to climb the ladder and look for herself, but Jelly was certain to say something that would set her off balance. She elected to stay her course and see to her mare. She went to Abby's stall and let the animal out to the corral, gathering a brush, currycomb, soap, and a bucket along the way. Laurel let Abby roam inside the fencing while she went to fill the bucket.

She was carrying it back to the corral when a horse and rider coming off the trail caught her attention. They veered away from the house when the rider spotted her. Laurel was so unused to seeing Rayleigh Carter outside of his office that she didn't trouble herself to hide her surprise. His hat was pulled low over his broad forehead, and he was wearing a jacket that hid the star he always wore on his vest. She set the bucket on the ground and lifted her head to greet him since he made no effort to get down from his horse.

"Good morning, Sheriff. This is unexpected. What can I do for you?"

"Morning," he said. His response was perfunctory, not friendly. "Thought I'd ride out and hear what you've got to say for yourself."

"About?"

"I'm not really of a mind to be led around by the nose, Miss Laurel. I know you were in my office yesterday. I want to know why."

"I don't much care for your tone. Are you accusing me of something?"

"I'm not sure. I reckon that depends on what you're going to tell me."

"Sure, but why don't you get down and come inside for a cup of coffee? We can talk in the kitchen. I'm getting a crick in my neck." She watched Carter hesitate and thought he was on the verge of accepting her invitation when Rooster stepped out of the barn.

"Everything all right?" he asked, wiping his hands on a rag and looking from Carter to Laurel.

"Just fine," said Laurel.

"Social call," said Carter.

Rooster chewed on that some before he finally nodded. "I'll be getting back to my work, then."

"Looks like I interrupted what you were doing," Carter said after Rooster had disappeared into the barn. "Forget the coffee. Go on about your work. Never knew a woman who couldn't talk and work at the same time. I bet that's true for you, too."

Smiling wanly, Laurel picked up the water bucket and headed for the corral. Carter followed her and only dismounted once she was inside the fencing. Abby came right over to her. "Good girl," she said, rubbing the mare's neck. She dipped the brush in the water, made a lather with the soap, and began washing down the animal's coat with long strokes in the direction that Abby's hair grew.

Laurel looked over her shoulder at the sheriff. He was leaning against the corral, his forearms resting on the top rail. It struck her as odd that he hadn't prompted her to answer his question because he was looking a mite anxious. Or perhaps it was just that he needed a drink. "I paid you a visit to ask if you'd learned anything new about the robbery or Mr. Pye's murder."

"Since I saw you last? It wasn't that long ago. You were with that man of yours, remember?"

"Of course I remember." Laurel's fingers tightened on the brush. "You spoke at length to Mr. Landry, and he told me you were thinking about going up to the top of the falls and having a look around. You said that, didn't you?"

"I did."

"And?"

Carter shrugged his wide shoulders. "And so I did."

Laurel realized he was going to make her drag it out of him. He was no longer looking anxious. It was pure ornery smugness that was shaping his features. "Well?" she asked. "Did you find anything?"

"Nope. I would have come here straightaway if I had."

She very much doubted that but refrained from telling him so. "I guess that's that, then."

"Not quite."

Laurel stopped washing Abby. She held the brush loosely at her side. "What else is there?"

Carter took his time answering. He looked Laurel over head to toe, nodding to himself as his eyes roamed. His gaze was appreciative and lingered just that little bit longer where her damp shirt clung to her breasts. It was his opinion that a more modest woman would have put up an arm to cover herself or turned a quarter away from him. Not Laurel Beth Morrison, though. She stared straight at him as if she was daring him to take his fill. So he did.

"You're a handsome woman, Miss Laurel," he said. "Always thought so. Never had it in my mind that you were much interested in men, though. Not that I thought you hankered after women. Just thought you weren't interested in anyone. Then that Landry feller comes along and I see how you look at him and that gets me thinking that maybe I should have called on you a long time ago. Is it too late?"

Laurel lost her capacity for speech. Eyes widening fractionally, she could only stare at him.

The sheriff smiled. "Maybe not. I understand you were looking mighty fine when you came calling the other day. Theo told me you were wearing your Sunday best. I sure would have liked to have seen that."

"Then you should have been awake," she said sharply.

"Maybe so, but I was feeling poorly, and not so much happens in this town that a man can't treat himself to drink when the urge is upon him."

Laurel wasn't certain that he was sober now, which would explain why he kept some distance between them. "That's all I care to hear from you, Rayleigh. I answered your question. You answered mine. You need to leave."

Carter didn't move or show any indication that he was thinking about it. "I saw him, you know. Up there above the falls. I saw him."

Laurel didn't understand. "You're not making sense. Who did you see?"

"Him. Your man Landry. Pickin' posies. Did he give them to you?" When Laurel didn't respond, he went on. "Oh, did I misspeak? Maybe they were intended for some other woman. Desiree, perhaps. He's spent time with her. I know it for a fact because she told me. She doesn't like him. I don't know that flowers would change that, but then a gift sometimes warms a woman."

"Leave," Laurel said. Beside her, Abby shifted her weight, sensing her mistress's agitation. She laid a hand on the mare's back to reassure her.

Carter straightened. "Not before I talk to Landry. I came here to see him, too."

Laurel regarded him with narrowed eyes. "Have you been drinking?"

Carter ignored the question. "Where is he? In the barn? The bunkhouse?"

Call put down his pitchfork and stepped into the corral from the barn. "I'm right here." He didn't feel the need to mention that he'd been standing in earshot ever since

Rooster told him who'd come calling. There had been several occasions when he'd wanted to interrupt, but Laurel seemed to be holding her own. She hadn't thrown the brush or the bucket of sudsy water and Call counted that a good thing. He didn't know if he would have shown as much control in her place. "Something I can help you with, Sheriff?"

Carter got right to the point. "What's made you so all-fired curious about my rifles that you'd take them off the rack without asking me first?" The sheriff put up a hand to stop Call from replying right away. "In case you're fixin' to unravel a yarn for me, think before you speak. I know you were in my office same as Miss Laurel. It looked to Theo like you might've followed her since you arrived on horseback and she had the buckboard. Now Theo couldn't see what the two of you were doing in there, but he told me it accounted for a good ten minutes of his day. A little longer for Miss Laurel since she got there first."

"You couldn't go wrong hiring Mr. Beckley as your deputy, what with him living and working right across the street the way he does."

"Then I'd have to pay him. Right now, his information comes free."

"That's practical."

"So tell me about the rifles."

"I saw a lot of Springfields during the war. Not near as many of the Enfields except when I was a prisoner in Georgia." Call saw that raised the sheriff's eyebrows. He didn't think the man's surprise was feigned and that meant Carter didn't know about his conversations with veterans in town. No one had placed any particular importance on them, certainly not enough to mention them to the sheriff even casually. "I guess you've heard of Andersonville."

Carter nodded. "You own a Springfield?"

"No. Sold it after the war. That money helped get me home."

"Huh. You looking to buy one now?"

Call lied without compunction. "I got to thinking about

it when I saw yours. It's a good rifle, that Springfield. How'd you come by it?"

"Same way you got yours, I expect. Army put it in my hands and told me to shoot the Grays."

"What about the Enfield? I never heard of the army giving out two rifles to a soldier."

"That rifle belonged to the last Johnny Reb I killed. I took it out of his hands before he was cold on the ground. I guess he could have stuck me with his bayonet but he didn't have any fight left in him. I stayed beside him until he passed. It just struck me as the right thing to do before I left the battlefield."

Laurel did not give herself time to wonder what part, if any, of what Carter said was true. She spoke up. "Is the Enfield for sale? I have my brothers' Springfields, but I liked the other rifle. I'm the one who took them down."

The sheriff spared her a glance. "Then you should have returned them to the same place."

Would that she had, Laurel thought. Carter wouldn't have known anyone visited his office while he was sleeping if she hadn't been careless. He wouldn't have asked Mr. Beckley about visitors, and Mr. Beckley might never have mentioned they were there. After all, the undertaker didn't know the sheriff was sleeping in a cell. It took considerable strength of will not to cast a guilty look in Call's direction.

"I apologize," she said. "You're right, I should have returned them properly, or better still, not touched them at all." Carter grunted something that she supposed was acceptance of her apology. "Is it for sale?" she asked again.

Carter responded curtly. "No."

"What about the Springfield?" asked Call.

"I might part with it for the right price."

"Think about it. Get back to me when you're certain."

Carter nodded. "Guess I'll be going, then."

Finally, Laurel thought, and tried not to let it show in her expression. "Good day, Sheriff."

Carter pushed away from the corral and tipped his hat. "Good day, Miss Laurel. Mr. Landry."

Call and Laurel watched him mount and ride away. He was well off the property when they spoke. Laurel leaned a shoulder against Abby while she recovered her bearings.

"Awful man," she said.

"Hmm. Should I have made my presence known earlier?"

She shook her head. "No. I think he'd been drinking before he came. He was annoying but essentially harmless."

Call wasn't as confident about the harmless part. "I didn't know he saw me picking flowers."

"Oh, you heard that part. Why do you think he didn't show himself to you?"

"I imagine he wanted to see what else I was going to do up there. I'm afraid I disappointed him. I was only after the flowers. We already had what we needed."

"I wonder if he found anything. He said he didn't, but I don't know that I trust him."

"I know I don't," said Call, "but even he probably tells the truth from time to time."

"Did you give me all the flowers you picked?"

He frowned, regarding Laurel narrowly. "Yes. Why in the world would you think—" Call stopped because he divined the source of her suspicions. "Wait. You just told me you're not sure you can trust Carter and yet because of what he said, you're wondering whether any of the flowers I picked went to Desiree?"

"Oh, you heard that, too."

He spoke as if she hadn't. "Laurel, I could make a convincing argument in front of a jury that you're downright loco, and I'm no kind of lawyer."

She smiled. "And my defense is that you made me that way."

Call saw there was nothing to be gained by advancing his argument so he advanced on her. She peeled herself away from Abby and tried to duck out of his reach. He caught her easily, spun her around, and pulled her flush to his chest. His arms settled around her; his hands folded into a fist at the small of her back. She looked up at him, grinning.

"I love you," she said.

He kissed her. He didn't think about where they were, who might be watching, or what they might think. She obviously didn't either because she didn't try to wriggle out of his arms or rear back and push him away. She kissed him back with all the enthusiasm he had come to expect. If she was loco, then so was he, and there was no point in not reveling in it.

The clapping came to him distantly at first. Call opened one eye and saw Mrs. Lancaster standing on the back porch holding a cured ham under one arm so her hands were free to applaud. "Oh, Lord," he whispered against Laurel's mouth. Then he heard clapping coming from behind him, this ovation louder and slightly out of sync indicating it was the admiration from more than one individual. He felt Laurel nod and tasted the bubble of laughter on her lips. She'd heard what he had and she didn't care.

He would have dropped to one knee and proposed right there, but she had been clear about what she wanted. No knees. No public proposal. Besides, he didn't have flowers or all the promises worked out. It would have to wait.

The kiss lingered a couple of mutual heartbeats longer before Call took her by the upper arms and steadied her while he stepped back. He gently turned her to face their audience, first Mrs. Lancaster and then the rowdy bunch loitering at the barn's open doorway. He made a courtly bow and Laurel, her cheeks tinged with a becoming pink, did the same. No simpering curtsy for the woman he was going to marry. No, she bowed with the confidence of a stage actor after a great performance, the star of the show.

And she was.

36

Desiree removed a stocking from the back of her overstuffed armchair and flung it at the bed. It landed at
Rayleigh Carter's feet. He was stretched out on her quilt,
his hands cradling his head. He didn't give the stocking any
attention, nor did he trouble himself to look in Desiree's
direction when she flopped onto the chair cushion and
adopted a most unladylike posture by hooking one leg over
the wide arm.

"You should straighten up this room, Desi," said Carter.
"How do you find anything?"

"I found your cock, didn't I?"

"And serviced it admirably."

"Cover yourself," she said, not bothering to hide her
disgust. "It looks like a slug trying to crawl out of your
trousers."

Carter raised his head only that degree necessary to
get a look. Desiree wasn't wrong. He tucked his sluggish
cock inside his trousers and drawers and lay back again.
He wished he'd taken the time to get out of his boots, but
he was already so randy by the time he reached Mrs. Fry's
that he thought he'd come when Desiree took his hand
and led him up the stairs.

"Help me out of my boots, will you?"

Desiree merely stared at him. She idly toyed with the
ruffle on her knickers, smoothing it between her fingertips. "I want to leave," she said.

"Go. Send someone up who'll help me with my boots."

"I meant I want to leave this town."

"I know what you meant. Go."

"I need money."

"God almighty. I just paid Mrs. Fry for your time. See her."

"What she gives me won't be enough to get me half-way to Denver."

He turned his head slightly so he could see her and troubled himself enough to raise an eyebrow. "What the hell do you spend your money on? I know what I pay for you, know how many men you entertain in a week, and know how long you've been in Falls Hollow. You should be almost as rich as Stonechurch by now and you never had to pick up a shovel."

"Go to hell."

"Probably." He twisted onto his side, raised himself on an elbow, and regarded her frankly. "Now's not a good time."

"You always say that."

"And it's always true. Why are you so bent on getting to Denver? Digger Leary is sitting in a cell there. Landry told me when we were on our way to Beckley's place with Pye's body."

Agitated, Desiree began to swing the leg she'd thrown over the arm of the chair. "You should have told me. This isn't your first visit since Josey was found."

"Slipped my mind. I'm thinking about other things when I'm here."

"Laurel Beth Morrison. That's sick, Carter. You're sick. A nice lady like her wouldn't have you, but I guess you know that. I can't think of another reason you never called on her."

"I figured she wasn't interested in men."

"Because she never flirted with you? That's not a good yardstick."

"And I say it is. Young women and widows sashay by

my window at all hours of the day. All of them respectable. Don't forget, Laurel Beth had nothing to do with Pye either, and women liked him, too. You sure did."

Desiree's leg stopped swinging. "Shut up."

Carter shrugged. "I think she's got her eye on Landry. I can't decide if he's pokin' her or not. I'm pretty sure he wants to."

"What do you know about it?"

"Got a feelin', that's all. I was out at the Morrison Station this morning."

Well, that explained his cockstand when he came through the door. She kept that to herself. "What provoked you to go out there?"

"The two of them—him and her—visited my office yesterday. I was out," he said. It was true after a fashion. He *was* out. Out cold. There was no reason for Desiree to know that. She was already out of sorts with him. "When I came around, I noticed a couple of things were out of place. Looked for a note, but there wasn't one. I went over to Theo's and asked him if he'd seen anything."

"There's a man who likes to watch."

Carter's eyebrows kicked up as he realized Desiree's comment had another meaning. "Really?"

"Uh-huh. That's what he pays for. No touching, just watching."

"I'll be darned. You never know what a person gets up to."

"So I take it he saw Miss Morrison and Landry."

"Right. She came into town on her buckboard. He followed later on horseback. My sense is that he was coming after her, but I still don't know what she was up to. Theo described what she was wearing right down to the white bows on her red leather shoes."

"Fancy," said Desiree. "Did she have other business in town?"

"What are you saying? You don't think she was dressing up just for me?"

"Forget it."

"As it happens," said Carter, "she didn't have other business. I asked."

"What did she say when you asked her why she was there?"

"Just what I expected. She said she came by to ask me if I'd learned anything new about Pye's murder. I didn't believe her but I let it sit. It bothers some that she thinks I don't know better, but I figure I can use it. Landry was around. Seemed to me that when he showed himself, it was to protect her."

"A regular hero."

Carter's eyes narrowed as he regarded Desiree with more consideration than he usually did. "You don't like him, do you?"

"He rubbed me wrong the first time I met him." McCall Landry saw too much. She never felt so naked as she did when she sat with him. That did not endear him to her.

"Hmm. Hard to know what Stonechurch saw that prompted him to hire Landry. As far as I know, they only met the one time."

"Maybe that's exactly the reason Landry got the job. He's an outsider. He's had to learn everything for himself. No old notions to sway him one way or the other."

"Could be. He asked after my rifles. Struck me as odd, but then Laurel Beth said she'd like to buy my Enfield so he might have been looking it over for her. When I told her it wasn't for sale, Landry asked about the Springfield. I agreed to think about it."

"Is that a good idea?"

"No harm thinking about it." When he saw her lip curl, he said, "Of course I'm not going to sell it. He as good as said he doesn't need it so I figure it's one more way he's up to something. You know what I saw him doing when I was up top of the falls?" Since she didn't appear to want to guess, he went on. "Picking wildflowers. Can you believe it? He was picking posies." He shook his head as if he still couldn't believe it and chuckled under his breath. "It was a sight, I can tell you."

"And you didn't shoot him. Wonders abound."

"Thought about it, but I wasn't outfitted properly. I only had my Peacemaker with me. Anyway, I'd already had a look around and there was nothing to find to point to Pye's killer."

There was nothing Desiree wanted to say, know, or listen to regarding Josey Pye. She glanced at the clock on the mantel. "Don't you have anywhere else you're supposed be?" she asked. "It's not Sunday, you know."

"How about another go?"

"Show me your money first. I have to make a living."

"Damn, but you're a hard woman." Carter sat up and put his legs over the side of the bed. He stretched his arms wide and arched his back. Standing, he pulled his pockets out to show her they were empty. "I handed over what I had to Mrs. Fry."

"That's too bad because I don't do credit."

"That's not what Pye told me."

"Get out, Carter." She pointed to the door. "We're not done, not by a long chalk, but I can't stand the sight of you right now. Respect that, will you?"

Carter looked her over. "Never really occurred to me that you had feelings for him. I thought for sure you were using him, same as you use every other man who gets a hankering for what's between your legs."

Desiree set her jaw and kept her finger pointed at the door while Carter put on his gun belt and jacket. He took his sweet time for no other reason than he could and she waited him out. It wasn't until the door clicked into place that she allowed herself the luxury of tears.

37

The afternoon stage from Denver carried four passengers, a mailbag, and a short stack of papers from the *Rocky Mountain News*. Brady was the whip again and he was glad to give up his seat to the station's last driver as his lumbago was bothering him worse than a hot poker stuck in his back. He emptied his mailbag on Laurel's desk before he went to join the passengers and his shotgun at the dining table.

He eased himself into a chair and let Mrs. Lancaster fuss over him when she realized he was in pain. "You're a good woman, Mrs. Lancaster. I surely appreciate you."

She blushed a pretty pink and set a cup of coffee in front of him. "I'm going to get you a packet of powders that will ease your back some. No laudanum. I know how you feel about that. And I have a bag that I can fill with hot water. You put that up against your spine when you lie down and you'll be at peace long enough to get some sleep."

Laurel's attention was elsewhere but she heard enough snippets of their exchange to be intrigued. Perhaps she could give the cook a taste of her own meddling medicine and see how that went down. Smiling to herself, she nodded in response to Alexander Berry's query about the Cabin Creek Trail.

The government man's arrival was a surprise to everyone. Laurel was a bit annoyed with Sam Henderson for not wiring her that Berry was on one of his stages. She would have appreciated having a little notice so she could prepare.

"I have plans for improvements to the station after you approve this route," she told him. "I'm going to add a restaurant that can accommodate the number of railway passengers we can expect to pass through. I want to increase the size of our garden, raise a larger variety of vegetables to meet people's tastes, and add to our livestock. You should know that I've heard talk about a hotel in town for folks who want to stay over a day or two. I'm also willing to put up a water tower for the railroad's use. This would be a fully functional station."

"A water tower?" Berry nodded thoughtfully. "You have been thinking about this."

"Of course." Laurel held his gaze, careful not to look away. Alexander Berry had a shadowed stare because of his deeply set eyes. His brow was high and wide, and ever since she'd known him, his sandy brown eyebrows appeared perpetually raised as if he were in a state of constant curiosity or mild surprise. He had a friendly smile, one that seemed authentic, not practiced. Laurel remembered what Call had told her about Berry's personal interest in her and wondered why she had never noticed it herself. It was difficult to see because he seemed genuinely interested in what she had to say, and she found that to be an attractive quality. Perhaps Call had mistaken the matter.

"The railroad can't follow the trail through town as the stage does," Berry said. "Have you considered the best route around Falls Hollow? You must know the Hammersmiths have no such problem. The countryside is wide open. If there's going to be a town, it'll grow up around the railroad."

Laurel did not show her alarm. Her voice remained soft, carefully modulated. "Falls Hollow can contribute labor to the effort. The railroad will have easy access to a food supply for the laborers. We have an excellent water source for the tower the engines require. Proximity to Falls Hollow is not a liability for the railroad. It benefits both parties. I hope you are considering that in your determination."

"I'm considering everything."

She nodded. "As for the route that needs to skirt the town, I believe it would be better to put down rails immediately south of Falls Hollow. Trains would stop here at the station and then cut a diagonal that would take them behind the town and through the valley. I'm no surveyor, but I've ridden that way dozens of times and it's an easier grade back out of the valley. I can show you, if you like." She saw he was considering it. "Perhaps on your return from Stonechurch."

"I'm not going to Stonechurch. This is the end point of my journey. I came here to speak to you."

"Oh."

"I know Mr. Stonechurch's views. He's been openly in favor of the rails passing this way. I wanted another opportunity to hear what you had to say. That gentleman working for Mr. Stonechurch—"

"Mr. Landry."

"Yes. Mr. Landry. Did you know he sought me out in Denver?"

"I learned about it after the fact. I hope you don't think I asked him to do that."

"Not at all." Berry added coffee to his cup and took a tentative sip. "Mm. That's fine coffee."

"We'll be serving that in our restaurant."

Berry chuckled and set his cup down. "You're not one to miss an opportunity, Miss Morrison."

"I hope not."

"Mr. Landry shares that opinion. He had several persuasive arguments as to why the railroad should come this way, but chief among them was you and what you've accomplished here. You have advocates. Sam Henderson is also one of them."

"They're very kind."

"I specifically asked Sam not to let you know I was coming. It seemed a better test of how things run if I don't announce myself. That was certainly true when I visited the Hammersmith family."

Laurel wondered what Berry saw at the Hammersmiths', but it seemed he was not disposed to tell her, and good manners dictated that she not inquire. "We are pleased to have you here anytime. We do what we do, rain or shine, visitors or no."

"That's been my observation all along. I'd like to send another surveyor out to look at that route you're talking about. Property rights will require investigating if we go that way."

"You should know that I own a fair tract of the land I'm talking about. There'd be some who might think that what I'm suggesting makes it a conflict of interest, but I'd deal with the railroad fairly and expect the same in return. You'd have the same concern with the Hammersmiths when it came time to buy up some of their land."

Berry didn't comment on whether he saw a conflict or not. He said, "Do you have time to show me that land now?"

"Yes. Yes, of course. Do you ride, Mr. Berry?"

"Please," he said. "It's Alex."

Laurel could have kicked herself for addressing him as Mr. Berry. He invariably corrected her. She smiled, acknowledging his request, but didn't respond in kind. "Do you ride? We can take the buckboard but it will be rough going."

"I ride," he said.

Laurel wondered if he'd been insulted by her question. There'd been an undercurrent of defensiveness in his brief answer, but she figured he would have plenty of opportunity to prove himself. You never could tell if a city fellow—a government man, to boot—had any horse skills. "Since there's no stage going through here today for Denver, I'm assuming you're spending at least one night with us. Do you want me to arrange a room for you at one of the wayside homes in town or would you like to bunk with the men?"

"Actually, Miss Morrison, I was hoping I could rely on your splendid hospitality and that you'd put me up here for the night."

Berry's suggestion took Laurel aback. She wondered how much of her surprise showed in her expression. It wasn't unheard of for her to put up a passenger in her home for a night or two. Desiree had been one who'd stayed in her home. She had even taken in a family on occasion, provided they were willing to accept relatively crowded accommodations. But except for Dr. Singer, who was at the station at her request, she had never made the offer to a man traveling on his own, and no man had ever suggested it. The more she thought about it, the more astonished she was by Alexander Berry's proposal.

Laurel shot a quick glance around the table. The other diners were finishing their meal. Plates and utensils clattered as they were passed to Mrs. Lancaster along with the gratitude of the passengers. No one was looking her way or showed any curiosity about her conversation with Mr. Berry. She was as sure as she could be that he hadn't been overheard and doubly relieved that Call was far out of earshot, taking care of the horses.

"I'm afraid that isn't possible," she said. She let that stand alone and hoped he wouldn't make her explain herself.

Berry smiled, nodded. "That was a test," he said. "You passed beautifully."

"A test?"

"Yes. Of your moral character. The railroad expressed concerns regarding a woman operating one of their stations on her own. I'm sure you understand."

Laurel felt herself flinch. "Actually, I don't. As a test of my moral character, it is deeply insulting."

"I hope you will accept my apology, Miss Morrison. I am only doing as I was directed."

For all that he sounded sincere, Laurel didn't trust that he was following anyone's direction save for his own. She managed a brief smile. "Of course," she said, getting to her feet as the other diners began to rise and head for the door. "I'll speak to Rooster about showing you the property. He knows it as well as I do. I'll try to join you later after I've arranged a room for you at one of the wayside homes. You'll be more comfortable there than in the bunkhouse."

Alex Berry came to his feet slowly. He was a full head taller than Laurel, but he had the good sense not to crowd her. "I don't mind waiting for you," he said.

Laurel felt trapped. "Very well. Do you have a valise?"

"Still on the stage."

"Let me find someone to take it off for you." She looked out the window at the coach. "The boys are done with the exchange so someone will be free. I won't be long." Excusing herself with a murmur, Laurel left the dining room with none of the haste that was her preference. Behind her, she heard Mrs. Lancaster ask Berry somewhat impatiently if he was finished with his meal. The cook's tone was so out of character when put to a guest that Laurel wondered what Mrs. Lancaster might have overheard above the din of dishes and conversation.

Laurel ran into Dillon when he came around the coach on his way to the barn. "Hold up," she said before he bowled her over. "I need you to take Mr. Berry's bag out of the carryall and set it in the front hall, then I want you to go into town and make arrangements for him to stay at one of the wayside homes. Start with the Kinsey house. I've heard they have the most comfortable accommodations. It's only for the one night."

Dillon swept back a lock of tawny hair that fell over his forehead when he nodded vigorously. "Bag. Front Hall. Kinsey house."

"That's it. You can take one of the horses."

That pleased him. "Thanks."

Laurel left him to get Berry's bag while she wished her exiting guests safe travels. She waved good-bye to Holloway and his shotgun and then headed for the barn. Call, Jelly, and Hank were caring for the horses that had just been exchanged, washing them down and checking them for injuries. Rooster was sitting on a bench, looking disgruntled, and Laurel suspected he was there against his will. It made her wonder if his hip was plaguing him more than usual.

Everyone but Call stopped working and looked her way when she spoke. "I'm taking Mr. Berry on a property inspection. I'll need Abby saddled along with a horse for Mr. Berry. Even-tempered and responsive to a rider with limited skills, I think. Jelly? Would you accompany me?"

Jelly came up on his toes and jabbed himself in the chest with a forefinger. "Me? You mean me?"

Laurel almost laughed. "Yes, Jelly. I'd be pleased to have you ride along. You can spare him, can't you, Rooster?"

"Sure. He can go with you. Where will you be riding?" It was a measure of Rooster's discomfort that he didn't offer to accompany her himself.

"I offered to show Mr. Berry the tract of land that runs behind the town. I've suggested it as a good place to lay down rails."

Now Call looked up. "He's made his decision, then?"

"No. At least he hasn't indicated to me that he's firm on it. He'll be our guest for a while, as long as he wants to look around."

Call's eyebrows lifted, but then so did Rooster's, Hank's, and Jelly's.

"Dillon's arranging for him to spend the night in town," she said, answering the question no one dared to ask aloud, and then added with a touch of sarcasm, "In case you were wondering." She heard someone approaching from behind, looked over her shoulder, and saw it was Dillon. "I told him he could take a horse," she said to the others. "Thank you. I'm going to collect Mr. Berry."

She heard them murmuring in their huddle as she left.

38

Mr. Berry was waiting for Laurel on the porch when she returned to the house. "They're saddling our horses now," she said. "You haven't changed your mind about taking the buckboard, have you?"

"No. You said yourself it would be a rough ride." He pointed back toward the front hall. "One of your young men put my bag inside."

She nodded. "He'll be on his way shortly to arrange your accommodations. I've asked my youngest stage tender to ride with us."

Berry frowned slightly. "Oh? Why is that?"

"He needs the opportunity to get in the saddle. His father's the preacher, and there's never been much reason for him to learn to ride so he's doing it here."

"He's green, then."

Laurel smiled, nodded. "As green as a new shoot, but he's a hard worker and eager to learn." Movement out of the corner of her eye caught her attention. "Here he comes. They've saddled Sylvia for you. She's the one with the white star on her nose." Laurel introduced Mr. Berry to Jelly and then to his horse. She watched him climb into the saddle before she mounted in the event he required assistance, but he managed it competently, if not comfortably.

She started out with Berry riding abreast and Jelly lagging behind. She hadn't told Jelly where she wanted him, but he had either figured it out on his own or Call had told him where to position himself.

The tract of land that lay behind the town was a lush green extension of the Morrison Station. It was decent grazing land, and Laurel allowed the locals to use it for family-owned cattle and sheep just as her father had before her. Sheep clustered in a wooly blanket on the hillside, and a few cows gathered near the stream that was fed by the falls.

Laurel pointed out where she thought the tracks could be laid with a minimum of disturbance to the land. For the most part, the tract was fairly flat with only an occasional rise and fall that would be no challenge to level. She took him beyond her property boundary and showed him the climb an engine would have to make to leave the valley. It was not an impossible grade for the engineers to manage, but the Hammersmith property had no such impediment and that remained the largest obstacle to being awarded the contract.

Berry studied the depth and width of the rolling stream as they picked their way across it. "Flooding?" he asked.

"Not in all the years I've lived here, and that's been all of my life. There's a pool at the base of the falls that rises above its rocky banks during heavy rains. Water floods the plain around it but doesn't much affect this stream. Still, even that is rare."

Berry nodded and glanced up at the sky as a cloud moved to block the sun. A dark shadow swept the valley and the sheep began to seek shelter. "Speaking of rain . . ."

Laurel followed his gaze. The undersides of the approaching clouds were gray and vaguely threatening. She heard the rumble of thunder in the distance. "Have you seen everything you wanted to see?" she asked. "We should be heading back. That's a fast-moving storm."

Alex Berry was philosophical about it. "It may be providential. In exchange for a soaking, I'll see firsthand whether or not there's flooding." The words were no sooner out of his mouth than lightning flashed above the mountaintop.

Laurel prepared herself and Abby for the clap of thunder that followed. Still, it was loud enough to cause her to flinch and Abby to startle. Jelly and Mr. Berry were in no way ready for the boom that echoed through the valley. Their horses bolted. Berry, whose command of his animal was tentative at best, was thrown almost immediately. Laurel had no thought for the government man's welfare as she gave Abby a swift kick and urged her to run hard after Jelly.

There was another jagged lightning strike, this one close by, and the following thunder rolled and rumbled and shook the ground they were pounding. Laurel leaned forward in her saddle. There was a second crack of thunder from a bolt of lightning that she never saw. Her hat flew from her head and she felt the sting of the first fat raindrops on her face.

The rain came hard and fast then, but it was not so blinding that Laurel couldn't see Jelly's terrified face when she and Abby drew alongside. It took her two tries to grab the reins and then a hard yank to get them out of Jelly's white-knuckled grip. Abby's presence was a significant help as Laurel managed the reins and Jelly. When she had them both under control, she dismounted, putting herself between the animals and setting a hand on Jelly's knee.

"She might bolt again," said Laurel. "Why don't you get down and walk her back? That way you won't get hurt if she runs."

Jelly's brow furrowed. He looked back at where the government man was sitting up and pouring water from the brim of his bowler. "What about him? You might need my help."

"I'll look after Mr. Berry. You go on back."

He nodded but the knit in his brow did not ease. "You lost your hat."

"I'll get it."

Jelly dismounted and looked toward the station. "Hey! It's Rooster."

"There. You see? I have all the help I need." Laurel gave his shoulder a nudge and he started off. She shielded her eyes from the rain as Rooster came upon her. "Glad you're here. Mr. Berry took a spill."

"I see. Where's your hat?"

"Lost it when I was chasing down Jelly. I'll get it."

"*I'll* get it. And Mr. Berry, too. You're soaked through. Better you go back with Jelly and make sure no harm comes to him."

Laurel was too grateful for Rooster's arrival to argue with him. Berry would be in better hands with Rooster than he would be with her anyway. She'd had enough of grinning and bearing him through their tour. The unexpected rainstorm provided timely relief. "See you when you get back." Because she was already wringing wet, Laurel elected to walk beside Abby. They caught up to Jelly and arrived at the station together. Laurel sent Abby to the barn to be cared for while she went to the house to change. By the time she'd returned downstairs, the rainstorm had ended and there was a suggestion of sunshine between the passing clouds.

Laurel was prepared to leave the house when she heard Mrs. Lancaster hurrying toward her from the kitchen.

"I showed Mr. Berry to one of the spare rooms," the cook said, wiping her damp hands on her apron. "I didn't know what else to do. He was wet through and his suit was soiled. I told him I'd clean it as best I could. He has a change of clothes."

"That's fine." It wasn't fine, but then Mrs. Lancaster hadn't had any other options.

"He's not staying here tonight, is he? I heard him suggest it, but I didn't catch your reply. Am I right that you were properly insulted?"

"Indeed," she said dryly. "Dillon was making arrangements for Mr. Berry to room in town. I'm going to see if he's returned yet. Keep our guest here while I'm in the barn and don't let him in my office."

"You better lock the door, then."

Laurel agreed that was a good idea and took care of it while Mrs. Lancaster stood watch. "I won't be overlong," she promised and hurried out before Mr. Berry appeared at the top of the stairs.

When she arrived in the barn, the men were gathered in a circle, their heads bent as though they were studying something. Rooster appeared to have whatever it was they were looking at in his hands, but Laurel couldn't see past their tight ring to know what it was.

"What do you have there?" she asked as she came upon them. Since Jelly was the shortest member of the circle, she peered over his shoulder. Rooster wasn't quick enough to hide what he held, although that certainly seemed to be what he had in mind. It got caught between him and Call as he tried to shield it from her. "Rooster? That's my hat. Let me have it."

Jelly and Dillon turned sideways to make room for Laurel to join the circle. She held out her hand and gestured to Rooster to give it over. He did so but with considerable reluctance. Laurel barely gave it a glance. She was more concerned that Jelly was still dripping.

"Rain's stopped, Jelly. Go on home and get dry. You're done for the day, and all and all, I'd say you did well."

"But—"

Laurel pointed to the open barn door. "Go."

Jelly went, hanging his head and dragging his feet. "You'll tell them how I stayed in the saddle?"

"I will." She was a little surprised he hadn't already told the tale. Wondering what had kept him quiet on that score, Laurel looked at her hat again, lifting it for a better view. She turned it slowly. A small vertical crease appeared between her eyebrows as she realized she was the only one breathing. "What in the world—" Squinting, she jabbed her index finger through a hole in the crown of her hat. "Is this what I think it is?" Without waiting for an answer, she turned the hat one hundred eighty degrees and found another hole on the other side of the crown. Fury kept her knees from buckling.

"Does Mr. Berry know about this?"

Rooster shook his head. "I didn't tell him because I

didn't notice it when I picked it up. Call saw it when I brought it back."

"I had no idea," she said. "I never heard a shot."

Call spoke slowly, carefully, but his thoughts were already leaping ahead of his words. "With that thunder, you wouldn't have. Tell us what happened."

Laurel described the race to catch Jelly and how she leaned forward to urge Abby to a faster pace. "That's about the time I lost the hat. I didn't think anything of it except to figure it was the wind." Her dark eyes darted around the circle, looking each man in the eye, not accusingly but wonderingly. "I don't understand. Who would do this? Who wants me dead?" When no one spoke, she said, "That was surely the intent, wasn't it? That shot was meant to kill me, not merely frighten me."

"I'm afraid so," said Call. Contrary to the calm in his voice, his hands were curling and uncurling into fists at his sides.

"But who—? Why?" She frowned deeply. "Besides all of you, who knew I was showing Berry the back property?" Laurel watched all eyes turn to Dillon. Beside her, the young man hunched his shoulders and stared at the floor. "Dillon? It seems as if you know something."

He nodded, swallowed hard, and still couldn't speak. Neither could he look at Laurel.

Rooster jabbed him with an elbow. "Go on. Tell her. Ain't none of it your fault. She'll know that."

Standing next to Laurel, Dillon spoke quietly. He'd already told the others what had happened so now his explanation was for Laurel alone. "I spoke to the Kinseys about a room for Mr. Berry and was on my way back. It hadn't started raining yet so I was taking my time. Chatted some with my pa about nothing to do with anything. You know how he is."

Laurel nodded. She was anxious for him to get to the point but knew him well enough to let him find his way.

"So shortly after I left him, I see the sheriff stepping kinda lively out of Mrs. Fry's place. I waved to him, polite and all, even though I think he's a humbug with a badge. He waved me over, which I didn't expect, so I went. He asked how things were at the station, and I didn't see the harm in telling him that the government man was visiting. He was real interested in that on account of what it could mean for Falls Hollow. That's what he said. So I told him about you taking Mr. Berry over the ground behind the town, how you thought it'd be a good tract to lay down rails. He was impressed. I could tell he was, but then he waved me off real abrupt and headed to his office like someone lit a fire under him."

"You're certain you didn't speak to anyone else about where I was going?"

"I'm certain, ma'am."

"Look at me, Dillon." She waited him out and he finally lifted his head and met her eyes squarely. "You didn't do anything wrong. Do you hear me? I never told you to keep where I was going a secret. It *wasn't* a secret. Are you listening? It wasn't a secret."

"Yes, ma'am."

Sighing, Laurel turned to Rooster. "You talk some sense into him later." She addressed the group. "Are all of you thinking it was Rayleigh Carter who took a shot at me?"

Call said, "We are. I told them what we know about Josey Pye's murder and about Carter's Springfield rifle. They made the connections you're making now."

"But why would he do it? Even if he killed Mr. Pye, that was about the payroll. Why would I be a target?"

"Maybe it's never been about the money," said Call. "Or not only about the money. Rooster thinks it's about the station, the railroad, and the government contract. I'm inclined to agree with him."

"That doesn't make sense. The Hammersmiths are the competition for the route. Mr. Berry confirmed that again while we were speaking earlier. He was careful not to say how we compared, but I had the impression that his surprise visit to their property a while back did not meet his expectations."

No one said anything in response. They let her hear her own words, play them out in her mind, and waited for her to come to the obvious conclusion.

It came at her hard. Laurel set one hand against her stomach as it turned over. Acid burned in her throat and she swallowed it back.

"Water?" asked Hank. "You're as pale as salt, Miss Laurel."

"Get it for her," said Call. "And give her some space. She can't talk just yet."

Hank raced off. When he got back, Laurel was sitting on a bench with her head lowered but not quite between her knees. Rooster was beside her, the flat of his hand at her back.

"She went down," he told Dillon, taking the water glass. "Never seen her do that before. Call caught her just like he was prepared for it. Never seen a fella move so fast." Rooster took Laurel's hand and pressed the glass into it. "Drink."

Laurel's fingers curled around the glass and she sat up. "That was unexpected," she said with a wry, sheepish grin. She took a few sips of water and then passed the glass back to Rooster. "It's enough. I'm all right."

Call asked, "How well do you know the Hammersmiths, Laurel?"

"Not well at all. I've never met them. What I know, or think I know, is through the grapevine and bits and pieces from Mr. Berry."

"Have you ever suspected that Carter is kin to the family?"

She shook her head. "Never. Rooster?"

"No," said Rooster. "I already told Call that. Carter's been around here years before the Hammersmiths settled on their land. Best I can figure is that he's just working for them."

Laurel leaned back against the wall and looked up at Call. His features were set gravely. It was the glacial sharpness of his eyes that spoke of something other than concern. She wasn't certain she wanted to know what he was thinking. "What an awful turn."

"Beautifully understated," said Call, surprising even himself with the lack of feeling in his tone. "How many years has Carter been sheriff?"

It was Hank who answered. "Five. I remember because it was right around my fourteenth birthday and my ma was despairing that no one was stepping in to challenge him. Pa considered it just so Ma would quiet down, but she came close to braining him with a skillet for saying so. Election was in May."

Call considered that. "So a few years before the Union Pacific and Central Pacific Railroads met in Utah."

Hank didn't know why that crossed Call's mind, but he nevertheless confirmed it.

Call asked Laurel, "When did you receive notice about rails coming out this way?"

"Official notice didn't come until a year or so later, but Sam Henderson met with me long before then. It might even have been before the spike was driven at Promontory. He told me the writing was on the wall and the time of the express stages would be coming to an end. He promised the coach line would continue runs for as long as it was profitable because of Stonechurch Mining, but he expected tracks to come through sooner rather than later. If the government responded as quickly as Sam did, the trains would already be running."

Nodding, Call said, "And the Hammersmiths were already settled here by then."

"Yes."

"So it's entirely possible they were as perceptive as Sam Henderson and began their campaign to secure the route and contract around the same time you did."

"I have no knowledge of that, but it's possible."

"They might have had Carter in their pocket for a long time."

Rooster said, "You could have it backwards. That snake Carter might've approached them. The man never did much as sheriff—never had to—but he always had his ear to the ground, I'll give him that. Could be he heard the Hammersmiths were interested in the government contract same as Laurel Beth. It'd tickle him to pull the wool over her eyes."

Laurel blinked and sat up straight. "Why would that tickle him? You make it sound as if he has something against me."

"He thinks you're uppity," Rooster said bluntly.

Rather than taking umbrage, Laurel was thoughtful. She said to Call, "I reckon you were wrong about him having a sincere interest in me. More like he wanted to play me for a fool."

Call started to respond, but Rooster interrupted him. "Oh, never doubt that Carter has a sincere interest in you, Miss Laurel. He just can't muster the courage to act on it. Probably why he says you're uppity. Easier to say something's not right with you than own up to being a coward."

"How do you come by this, Rooster?"

"Sweeny's," he said, shrugging. "Fellas talk."

"Lord," she said, closing her eyes briefly as she rubbed her temple. "That might be more disturbing than our sheriff trying to kill me." She cast a look around. "Is there a plan? What do we do now? Carter knows he missed me. If I had mounted Abby instead of walking her back to the station, he would have had a clear shot. She shielded me."

Call was very much aware that Laurel's decision to walk had saved her life. His gut churned every time his eyes strayed to her hat. "I'm going to pay Carter a visit," he said.

"You can't go to the jail," said Laurel. "He'll toss you in a cell."

"I doubt that, but in any event, I'm not going to see him there."

"I don't understand."

"He went to his office to get his Springfield, but he didn't try to shoot you from there. Think about where you were when you lost your hat and then consider where the jail is in relation to that spot."

Laurel did think about it. "He wouldn't have been able to get a good sighting out of either of the jail cell windows. He'd have needed some height so he could see where I was."

"Right."

"The brothel," Laurel said. "That's it, isn't it? He took his shot from Mrs. Fry's."

"Right. It's the only building on that side of the street with a second floor that he could access without question. The women would take their cue from Mrs. Fry, and she certainly wouldn't stop him."

Laurel offered her agreement reluctantly, not because she didn't believe him but because she knew there was nothing she could say that would stop Call from confronting Rayleigh.

"I'm leaving," he said.

Rooster said, "I'm going with you."

Call hesitated. "All right. Dillon. Hank. You keep an eye on Miss Laurel. See that she stays put."

Laurel wanted to roll her eyes, but resisted because the brothers might think she was disparaging their abilities. "I'm going to stay in the house with Mr. Berry. He's probably wondering what's become of me. What can I tell him about what happened?"

"Nothing at all would be best. He should hear it from Carter. If you can get him to talk about the Hammersmiths, that could be helpful."

"Be careful." Laurel took Rooster's hand and squeezed it. "Look out for each other."

"You know we will." He followed Call out of the barn to get his gun.

39

Y ou're completely mad," said Desiree. The rain had
stopped and she was sitting on the padded seat beside
the open window. The air was fresh and cooler than it had
been before the thunderstorm. She'd had to wring out the
curtains that framed the window because they'd been swept
outside when Carter pushed through the opening to sight
his target. Desiree didn't know what he was aiming at until
after he'd fired and then withdrew. It wasn't difficult to
make out that he'd missed because of the sharp string of
curses that followed his effort, but he wasn't forthcoming
about what he shot at until he tossed the Springfield on her
bed and flopped down beside it. That was when she got up
and went to the open window to see what she could see.
She could hardly draw a breath when she realized the truth.
Still, she asked him what he'd done, and never doubted that
he told her honestly. There was only one reason for con-
firming her suspicions, and it wasn't because he trusted her.
It was because he didn't, and he wanted an accomplice,
someone who would share the burden of blame if it came
his way.

"Not mad," said Carter. "Not like you mean. Mad I
missed, that's true. The rain didn't help. I had that shot
and then she bent over the damn horse."

"You need to get out of here."

"Why?"

"I don't want you here. I don't want to be any part of this."

"You're part of nothing. Who's going to know?"

"Everyone who watched you march in here with a rifle."

"You were in this room when I fired it. Did you hear it go off?"

Desiree had to admit she hadn't. "You got lucky with the thunder."

"Luck? I *timed* that shot to follow the lightning."

"Then I bow to your expert marksmanship," she said sarcastically as she turned to look out the window again. "You miss the war, don't you? Miss picking off the enemy from your hidey-hole. Miss the recognition from your commanders. I bet you count those years as a sniper as the best years you ever had."

"I never shot from a hidey-hole," he said mildly.

"You know what I mean." She waved a hand dismissively. "Rain's letting up."

"That's what I was waiting for." In spite of his words, he didn't move.

"They're all gone now," she said. "No one looked up this way. Maybe your luck is holding."

Carter pushed himself into a sitting position and leaned back against the headboard. He closed his eyes. "Did you see anyone pick up her hat?"

"That skinny fella. Rooster? Is that his name?"

"That's him. He musta come along after. He wasn't around when I was taking aim."

"What's important about her hat?"

"I blew it right off her head."

"Jesus, Mary, and Joseph," she said under her breath. Drawing her knees close to her chest, Desiree hugged them. "Why? I don't understand why you wanted to kill her. You like her. I know you do."

"Like has nothing to do with it. It's the job."

"What job? You mean as sheriff?"

"Leave it, Desi. It's got nothing to do with you."

"You're in my room. I'd say you're wrong there." When he didn't reply or show any inclination to remove himself, she said, "Maybe I don't want to know why you shot at her, but you could tell me why you haven't shot at *him*."

"Who? Alex Berry? No sense in it. Or maybe you meant the preacher's boy. That sure would have got the town talkin'."

"Dammit, Carter. I know you're not a fool. Don't act as if you are. Wouldn't we all be better off if you took care of Landry?"

He chuckled humorlessly. "Took care of? You mean kill. I know you're not squeamish. Don't talk as if you are."

Desiree didn't care for having her words more or less repeated back to her. "All right. Kill. He's the real fly in the ointment. You said as much when he tracked down Digger and turned him over in Denver."

Carter shrugged. "Digger's no threat. He knows what he knows, which ain't all that much. What's Landry going to do with anything Digger told him? Pye's a dead end, so to speak." He opened one eye and spared Desiree a glance before he closed it again. Predictably, she was making a face. His pun did not set well with her. She didn't like it when he mentioned Josey Pye. "Cheer up. You'll get your money soon enough."

"I don't understand why I don't have it already."

"You got some."

"Not enough. Not nearly what we agreed to."

"I didn't agree to it. That was your agreement with Pye. He thought he could cross me and, well, you know what happened."

"You took his saddlebag."

"So? I gave you some money then for your trouble and your loss and I took the bag."

"Then why can't I have my share now?"

"Because I don't have it anymore. I helped myself to some greenbacks and turned over the rest."

Desiree eyed the Springfield lying next to Carter and wished she knew how to use it. Wouldn't he be surprised to open his goddamn eyes and find himself squarely in the sight of his own weapon?

"Put it out of your mind, Desi," he said as if he could read hers.

She gave a little start. Lord, she despised this man. "What do you mean you turned the money over? Who has it if you don't?"

"The money. The bag. It's not important who has it now. Not to you. I told you that you'd get yours."

Desiree wasn't certain she liked the sound of that. She let it go without comment.

"You're better off not knowing everything. You should be thanking me."

"Maybe I will someday. I think it hangs on you leaving now."

Carter sighed heavily, rubbed his eyes with the heels of his hands before he opened them. He stared at the Springfield and his expression was regretful, not remorseful. The rifle had failed him. It had been a long time since that had happened, and he did not want to repeat it. Next time he would use the Enfield.

He scooted to the edge of the bed and set his feet down, and then he picked up his rifle and set it across his lap. "I don't suppose you'd let me leave this here?"

"No. That's a stupid idea."

"Yeah. Probably was." He stood. "Leaving."

Desiree nodded.

"I promise I'll have your money for you soon."

She wanted to believe him, but she suspected she was never going to get out of Falls Hollow. "Just go."

"Desi," he said softly. When she didn't look at him, he left.

40

<hr>

"Ah, there you are," Berry said when Laurel joined him in the parlor. "The cook said you went to the barn, but I looked out once and didn't see you or anyone else." He folded the newspaper he'd been reading and set it on the side table.

"Please. Don't stop reading on my account."

"Old news," he said. "I read it when it was released in Denver."

"Of course." She took a seat in an armchair catty-cornered to where he was sitting on the sofa. "I was taking care of my horse."

"Surely that's what you have stage tenders to do."

"I like to look after Abby myself. And the tenders had other horses to see to."

"I see. Forgive me. I'm woefully ignorant about caring for the animals. I've never owned a horse."

"Most of the horses here belong to Henderson Express."

"What will happen to them if the train comes this way?"

"I imagine it will be the end of their trail days if the train doesn't pass through here. Sam will sell off what mares he can and either pay me to care for the ones that are left or tell me to shoot them."

Berry blinked. "Could you do that?"

"No, but Sam doesn't know I can't. I'll board them for free for as long as I can. There won't be much for any of us to do if . . ." Laurel looked away and couldn't finish her sentence. Instead she said, "When do you plan to make your decision?"

"Soon."

She looked at him again, studying his face, trying to discern the thoughts at the back of his dark, deep-set eyes. When she couldn't, she asked baldly, "Are you in anticipation of a bribe?"

Of all the things he could have done just then, he did the least expected. He laughed, genuinely and with obvious humor. He removed a handkerchief from his pocket and dabbed at his eyes. "Forgive me," he said. "My only excuse is that it was so astonishing. Usually the offer is put to me with the assumption that I'll accept it. You're the first person who's ever asked me straight." He tucked the handkerchief back into his pocket. "What sort of bribe did you have in mind?"

"I'm not offering."

"And I'm not accepting. More curious than anything else."

Laurel took a breath and spoke quickly before she lost her nerve. "When you asked me if I'd put you up for the night here, I thought . . ."

"I'm sorry for that. Truly. I had to know that you were unimpeachable. It was expected of me. The railroad could not be swayed from having an answer."

"You hinted that you were open to that particular favor when Mr. Landry had dinner with you in Denver."

"I'm not surprised he told you. I hoped he would. I needed to plant the seed and I thought I recognized fertile ground there. Mr. Landry was complimentary of you. It seemed that there might be something behind those compliments."

Laurel thought it best not to confirm or deny what Berry supposed was the truth. "What have the Hammersmiths offered you?"

Berry's sandy brown eyebrows lifted. "You know about that?"

"I do now."

His smile saluted her. "Well done. They offered me money. Quite a lot of it. I didn't accept, Miss Morrison. I was carefully selected for this assignment because I *don't* take bribes. My behavior to the contrary, I am happily married *and* financially comfortable. More to the point, taking a bribe goes against my grain. Everything cannot be bought."

"Oh."

"Yes. Do you have money, Miss Morrison?"

"No. If you were open to bribery, you'd be insulted by how little I have to offer."

He chuckled. "Well, it's safely yours."

"Why haven't you made your decision yet?" she asked. "I don't believe for a moment that it's dependent on getting a surveyor out here to look at the land I showed you. I think you know that it's satisfactory. So what is it, Mr. Berry?" She paused. "Alex."

Alex Berry nodded approvingly at her use of his name. He judged her to be comfortable in his presence. Finally. "It's the matter of the payroll," he said. "It went somewhere, Miss Morrison, and I have cause to believe it's supporting this station or the Hammersmiths. I aim to know which it is."

Laurel frowned deeply as she leaned forward. "Who *are* you?"

He smiled faintly. "What do you mean?"

"You're no ordinary government man."

"No matter how you intended it, I'm accepting that as a compliment."

"You were appointed to look for the best rail route before the payroll was ever stolen. You and I met back then. I imagine you also met with the Hammersmith family. So what was that all about?"

"Just what it seemed. The best rail route."

"No," she said, shaking her head. "It was something else." She sat up, straightened her shoulders, and said in a tone somewhere between accusation and epiphany,

"Stonechurch Mining. You were investigating Stone-church Mining."

Berry simply held her gaze.

"I don't expect you to tell me if I'm right. I feel sure I am. I don't know why you were looking into the mine or what you hoped or didn't hope to find, but I need to know that your business with Morrison Station is legitimate. I need to know that there will be tracks laid and that you are truly empowered to decide the route. If you're not, I need to know that, too. My life was nearly forfeited this afternoon because of the competition for your approval."

Now Alexander Berry came to attention and moved to the edge of the sofa. "What are you talking about? What happened?"

"Someone took a shot at me while we were out."

He shook his head. "I was there. I didn't hear—"

"It must be lowering for a Pinkerton man such as yourself to have something like that happen almost under your nose and not be aware of it."

"I'm not a—oh, never mind that. Tell me."

"You took that ignominious fall and I went after Jelly. You were probably still on the ground when the shot took off my hat. You didn't hear it because of the thunder. I didn't hear it either if that makes you feel any better."

"It doesn't. You're all right, though?"

She nodded. "I didn't get shaky until I saw the holes in my hat, but I'm over that. Now I'm just angry."

"Do you know where the shot came from?"

"Probably Mrs. Fry's place. Sorry. The brothel. Least-ways that's what Rooster and Mr. Landry figure."

"And who do they figure did the shooting? Unless I've completely overestimated Mr. Landry's competencies, he certainly has some idea about that."

"He does. He's on his way to confront the sheriff right now."

Alex Berry jumped to his feet. "Give me directions."

"It will be easier if I show you."

It spoke eloquently of his urgency that he didn't argue.

* * *

Call and Rooster were on their way up the stairs as Carter was on his way down. Having no reason to suspect he was going to confront resistance, the sheriff was boldly carrying his rifle.

"Out of my way," said Carter, fully prepared to push between them if they didn't part for him. Neither man moved and the sheriff took a step down. "Out."

"Up," said Call, jerking his chin toward the landing.

Carter closed the distance that separated him from the others and shoved a shoulder between theirs. His effort was rebuffed when they were able to hold fast. He retreated a step and swung his rifle up and around so that the polished stock was aimed at their shoulders. "I have business," Carter said.

"So do we."

Carter wasted no time jabbing the rifle's butt. Call and Rooster saw it coming and created a space between them so the rifle struck air, not flesh and bone. The sheriff nearly lost his balance and needed to place one hand on the banister to stay upright.

Call easily wrested the rifle from Carter's one-handed grip. "Up," he said, jerking the Springfield in that direction.

Carter didn't move. "Mrs. Fry!"

"I'm standing right here," said the madam from below. She had adopted a militant stance, hands on hips, jaw set. Four of her unattended women were standing in a protective semicircle around her. "What do you think I can do? Send for the law?"

Struck by her sarcasm, Carter's complexion took on a ruddy hue. "This is still your place."

"And I don't want it shot up. I suggest you do what Mr. Landry wants."

Desiree appeared at the landing and braced her arms against the railing. "This way, gentlemen. Whatever your disagreement, I'm confident it can be settled peacefully."

When no one moved, she added, "But probably not on the stairs."

Carter didn't like turning his back on Call Landry, but neither did he want to give the impression of retreating by backing up the steps. He chose the lesser of two evils, pivoted, and started to climb.

Desiree opened the door to her room and indicated the men should precede her. When they filed in, she followed. Carter told her to close the door. She did, except she put herself on the other side of it. Desiree heard Carter yell to her to come back, but she ignored him. She figured that Landry and Rooster would not let him go after her, but she hurried down the stairs anyway. "We should probably just go," she told Mrs. Fry and the others.

Mrs. Fry was doubtful and it showed in her expression. Desiree took her on. "Who are you going to apply to for help?" she asked. "Sheriff's in there already, and I don't think he's going to fare well." If Desiree's logic was not sufficient to move the madam toward the front door, the crash of furniture toppling and the subsequent thud was.

"Let us retire to the porch, ladies," Mrs. Fry said, hustling them out.

Desiree looked up once and then she followed.

"Get up, Carter." Call's voice was calm, his stance loose and easy. The sheriff's attempt to go after Desiree had earned him a bruising roundhouse punch to the jaw. Call had to shake out his knuckles but Carter had to shake out the cobwebs. Call reckoned a few swollen knuckles made it worthwhile.

The stool that had tripped Carter up was upended beside him. He picked it up and flung it hard across the room. It bounced harmlessly against the padded window seat and dropped to the floor. Carter used the overturned writing desk to help him rise before he shoved it aside. It grated noisily against the bare hardwood floor.

Carter worked his jaw from side to side. "You did it," he said to Call. "Finally did something I can arrest you for. I don't know about where you're from, but here in Falls Hollow you can't hit the law with impunity."

Call eyed the rifle that he'd tossed to Rooster before laying Carter out. "What if I just shoot you? How about that?"

Carter's gaze narrowed. His right hand hovered above the butt of his revolver. "Suppose you tell me what this is about."

Call kept his eyes on the sheriff but spoke to Rooster, "Check the rifle."

"Did that while he was the floor," Rooster said. "Sure enough, it's been fired. Barrel's still a little warm to the touch."

Now Call addressed Carter. "You want to explain that?"

The sheriff's broad shoulders relaxed and he lowered the hand that had been prepared to draw on Call. "You could have just asked me if I fired it. I would have told you. You got some reason for questioning me about it? I have a right, you know."

"I suppose it's a practice of yours to carry your Springfield in here."

"Not a practice, but not unusual. Desiree should be here. She'd tell you. So will any of the others when you ask them."

"Hmm. I bet they will."

Carter pointed to Desiree's window, which was still open. "Have a look. It's nothing but valley back there. Good for target shooting if the cows and sheep don't get in the way. A man needs to practice from time to time or else he gets tight and rusty."

"You avoid the cattle and target folks instead, is that it?"

"What the hell are you talking about?" Carter's eyebrows pulled together and his mouth curled to one side. "Are you accusing me of something? Maybe you better say what's on your mind."

"Who are you working for, Carter?"

"That's what's on your mind? Tell him, Rooster. I work for the goddamn town."

"Falls Hollow needs the railroad," said Call. "No one here directed you to kill Miss Morrison. So who did?"

"What? Laurel Beth's dead?"

"You know the answer."

"But I don't. Maybe you hit me harder than I thought because you're making no kind of sense."

"Don't make me shoot you, Carter. Right now that's pretty much all I'm thinking about."

"Are you threatening me?"

Call sighed. "You don't know the answer to that either? I swear I'm wondering what you have under that hat besides hair. Yes, I'm threatening you. Rooster, didn't it sound like a threat to you?"

"Yeah, it sure did."

"There," said Call. "You have a witness. Oh, for God's sake, Carter, put your hand back down. You don't want to draw on me. You're real sharp with a rifle, but I'm betting that revolver at your side is mostly for show."

"You don't want to test me, Landry."

"I'm not entirely against it, but I'm looking for answers first. How about you unstrapping that gun belt and tossing it over here?"

"When hell freezes."

"How about now? Cold enough for you?"

Carter blinked. He was staring at the business end of Call's Colt with no blessed idea of how he'd been drawn on. A muscle jumped in his jaw.

"Kinda unexpected, isn't it?" said Call. "I've seen that expression before. Unfortunately for you, looks can't kill. Now, about that gun belt. Nice and easy."

Carter raised his hands slowly. His eyes never left Call's steely gaze. He unbuckled the gun belt and dropped it on the floor at his feet.

"Kick it this way," said Call. When Carter hesitated, Call added, "Now."

Carter kicked it but directed it sideways so it slid under

Desiree's bed. It disturbed something on its way to disappearing, creating a metallic clunk that made his eyebrows furrow but cleared Call Landry's expression.

"Damn," Call said softly, shaking his head. "You have a hard time following instructions, don't you? Just as well, I reckon. Rooster. Look under the bed and see what the sheriff's gun belt disturbed."

Rooster bent, whistled softly, and then used the barrel of Carter's rifle to swipe at the object and slide it clear of the bed. "Bet you figured it for what it is," he said to Call. "Did you?"

Call spared a glance for the strongbox and shrugged modestly. Everything he knew told him it was empty, but he asked Rooster to check anyway. Sadly, he was right again. He waited for Rooster to resume his position against the door before he spoke to Carter. "How much did you keep for yourself? Did the Hammersmiths suspect you couldn't be trusted when they hired you? I'm imagining they were pretty riled when you didn't deliver the whole of the Stonechurch payroll."

"You imagine whatever you like. Ain't none of it gospel."

Call ignored him. "What are you going to tell them when they hear that not only is Miss Morrison still walking among the living, but also that she's been awarded the government contract? You were supposed to stop that from happening. I bet you've been a real disappointment."

"Who the hell are these Hammersmith folks you're talking about?"

"Try not to be dumb as a stump, Carter, or pretend that I am. I never met anyone in Falls Hollow who has an interest in the railroad not knowing who the Hammersmiths are."

Carter didn't have a response to that. He shifted his weight between his feet.

"So let's start with that as a given," said Call. "You know the Hammersmiths. Ephraim Hammersmith is the head of the family so he probably hired you, though I'll concede that it could have been one of his brothers. Doesn't matter if you approached them or they approached you, in the end you struck a deal that was mutually satisfying." He deliberately paused before he added, "That means you both liked it."

Carter gritted his teeth and didn't comment.

"You arrived at a plan to place the Morrison Station under suspicion and hired Josey Pye to steal the Stonechurch payroll with Digger Leary's help."

"Yeah? And how did I do that when I hardly ever saw the pair of them?"

"Desiree," said Call.

"What about Desi?"

"She was your go-between." Call observed the subtle deflation of the sheriff's chest. The star on his vest actually seemed to sag. To Call, it was a clear sign that he'd mistaken none of it. Not so bad for telling only one lie. He didn't know for certain that the railroad would lay rails past Morrison Station and Laurel would be awarded the contract, but after he had Carter's confession, he was confident of that outcome.

Carter looked past Call's shoulder toward the door. "Desi should be here. She'll tell you that you don't know what you're talking about."

"Maybe. Maybe not."

The sheriff jerked his chin at the door. "Go on. Get her. Ask her."

Rooster took a sideways step to block access to the door in the event Carter foolishly chose to charge it.

Call holstered his revolver. "You know, Carter, it was a mistake to kill Josey Pye. I can't think why you felt the need to do that except maybe you thought he was going to cross you and take off with the payroll. He could have done that in the beginning, but since he didn't, I'm guessing he returned to give Desiree her share. You found out about their plan to meet at the top of the falls and killed him. I found your cartridge in the spot you chose to lay in wait. Found some of the greenbacks that got away from Pye and Desiree when you shot him. I also tracked the legal tender you spread around town. Spending some of that money wasn't a good idea."

"You don't know anything."

"Serial numbers," said Call. "That's what Laurel and I were doing at the bank when you came across us in town. We were identifying the serial numbers of the money you passed to Mrs. Fry, Magnus Clutterbuck, and Bobber Jordan. They spent their money at the mercantile. Mrs. Booker was helpful. So was the bank manager. Finding the money and tracing it back to you is how I know you didn't turn over all of it to Ephraim Hammersmith. I'm thinking the man knew to the penny how much he was expecting. It'd be the amount he offered to Alexander Berry as a bribe."

"I don't know anything about a bribe, Alexander Berry, or Ephraim Hammersmith. You just keep wasting your breath, Landry. It doesn't bother me none."

But Call knew that wasn't true. He started to say as much and stopped when he heard a shout from downstairs. He recognized Mrs. Fry's strident voice calling up to them.

"Company's coming!"

41

Call did not find it a particularly helpful announcement as the madam did not identify the company. The sheriff, he noted, looked hopeful. Call risked a glance back at Rooster, whose expression was as uncertain as Call's own.

"Your deputy?" Call asked Carter. Footsteps could be heard pounding up the stairs. Call supposed it was possible the madam had sent someone for Bobber Jordan. Mrs. Fry had a long and lucrative relationship with the sheriff. Call realized he should have taken that into account.

"Let him in," Call told Rooster. "And get his gun."

Rooster opened the door wide enough to look out and kept his foot jammed against the bottom in the event the intruder was unwelcome. "Well, I'll be darned," he said when he saw who stepped onto the landing. "It's Miss Laurel and Mr. Berry. And they're packin' iron."

Call swore under his breath. By the time he thought of telling Rooster to keep them out, it was too late. Rooster had already stepped aside, thrown open the door, and was ushering them in. Call took a step sideways so he was no longer squarely in Carter's path. His position in the room was necessitated by his desire to keep an eye on the visitors at the same time he was observing the sheriff for sudden movement. Disarming the man did not mean he was no longer dangerous.

"What are you doing here?" asked Call. He directed his question to Alex Berry.

"I want to avert bloodshed. Miss Morrison told me what happened while we were out riding, and she said you were here to confront Sheriff Carter. I aim to make sure 'confront' isn't a euphemism for 'kill.'"

"He's a Pinkerton detective," Laurel said as if it explained everything.

Call addressed Berry again just as if Laurel hadn't spoken. He was imagining throttling her and couldn't talk to her just yet. "Why did you bring her along?"

"Could you have stopped her?" asked Berry. "It wasn't a choice."

Call grunted something unintelligible. "You can see for yourself that Carter's still standing." Not only was he standing, but he had also inched toward the bed in those brief moments when Call was speaking to Berry. Call gave him a look that stopped the sheriff in his tracks and then pointed to the spot on the floor where he wanted him to return.

Carter did as directed and appealed to Berry. "Are you really a Pinkerton man?"

"I am."

He jerked his thumb at Call. "So you can arrest him."

"Maybe."

"He's making all kinds of false accusations and he slugged me. Caught me unawares. Assaulting a lawman. That's a jailing offense."

"Hmm. You know you're whining."

Carter's mouth snapped shut. He winced because his jaw still hurt.

"Perhaps this will help you, Sheriff. Miss Morrison and I had an instructive conversation with Miss Desiree before we came up here. Miss Desiree was forthcoming about her role in the robbery, and therefore most helpful in identifying your part. Do you understand what I'm saying? We know everything."

The sheriff shook his head. "Desi is a liar. You can't trust anything she says."

Laurel said quietly, "That's simply not true." Her eyes

fell on the metal strongbox lying on the floor at the foot of Desiree's bed. She asked Call, "Is that the box we found and Digger took away from the bunkhouse?"

"The very same," he said. "Closes the circle between Pye, Digger, Desiree, and this miscreant with a badge."

Laurel shook her head slowly as she regarded Rayleigh Carter. "Do you even comprehend your mistake?" She didn't wait for him to reply. "Desiree was in love with Mr. Pye. I can't speak to whether the reverse was true, but she believed it was. She told us that they had plans to leave Falls Hollow separately and meet up in Denver. You made sure they couldn't do that when you murdered Mr. Pye."

"They were going to split the money and cut me out."

No one spoke. No one moved. They all stared at Carter in the aftermath of his confession.

Carter frowned. "What are you looking at me like that for? That's what you all think, isn't it? That's the yarn Landry's been unraveling before you got here, Laurel Beth. I ain't admitting to nothing."

Laurel was more disappointed than surprised. "You always were strong-headed." She glanced at the rifle Rooster was still cradling in his arms. "Is that the Springfield you used to try to kill me?"

The sheriff did not respond.

"It's a real shame about my hat, Carter." Laurel swept it off her head and poked her finger through one of the holes. "I never realized you hated me so much."

Call said, "It was just business to him."

Laurel nodded. She watched the sheriff's complexion turn ruddy. Was he actually embarrassed? "I don't know if that's better or worse."

"Desiree gave you up, Carter. Mr. Berry is taking you in."

Carter squared his shoulders. "No, he's not."

"Afraid so," said Berry. "You first, then I have business with Ephraim Hammersmith and his family. You could perhaps buy yourself some goodwill by clearing your conscience about their involvement."

Call observed the sheriff subtly shifting his weight again. He only noticed because he was looking for it. The man's hands were curling at his sides and the faint tic in his jaw was back.

"Where is your gun, Sheriff?" asked Berry.

Rooster answered when Carter remained mutinously tight-lipped. "His belt's under the bed."

"All right," said Berry. "We have your rifle, your gun's out of your reach, so how about you coming along without a Peacemaker poking you in your back. Miss Morrison tells me you're familiar with sleeping in a cell. You'll be fine."

Call had been wondering which one of them Carter was going to charge when he finally lost his mind. To Call's way of thinking, the danger was imminent. Berry was the likeliest target since he'd been speaking and his gun wasn't easily drawn as it was partially covered by his jacket. But then Berry had been talking about something Laurel had told him, and that couldn't have set well with the sheriff, so perhaps she was a better mark, especially taking into account her willowy frame.

Call drummed his fingers against his leather holster, hoping to pull Carter's attention in his direction and remind the man of the threat of bloodshed. It didn't work.

Carter drove forward on the balls of his feet, leading with his bent head like a charging bull. No one but Call was prepared for it, and even Call was a beat too late to stop Carter from ramming his head into Rooster's chest. The older man toppled backward against the wall and the door, and the knob pressed hard into his rheumatic hip. He gave a pained cry and lost his grip on the Springfield as soon as Carter laid hands on it. Rooster's hip gave way and he slid to the floor.

Carter stepped clear of Rooster's feet and swung the butt of the rifle hard at Berry's head. The Pinkerton detective went down to his knees and slumped to the floor. The blow's recoil barely slowed Carter down. He swung the rifle over his head and brought the stock in hard contact with Laurel's shoulder. The pain radiated all the way down her arm to her fingertips. She dropped the gun she was drawing as her knees buckled.

Call ducked as the sheriff continued to wield the rifle butt above his head like a whirligig. When he missed connecting with Call, it set him slightly off balance. He staggered sideways but held fast to the rifle and brought it around again, this time narrowly missing Call's chin when he reared back.

Call didn't announce his intention to shoot. He didn't shout a warning or bring attention to the Colt in his hand. He fired once. The sheriff staggered but didn't fall or stop swinging. He came at Call again, this time aiming for the Colt. Call easily avoided the blow but it influenced his aim. Instead of catching Carter in the thigh, the bullet hit the sheriff squarely in the chest.

The momentum of the swinging rifle and the impact of the bullet pushed the sheriff off his feet. He fell back against the bed. It shook and shifted but ultimately provided Carter with a softer landing than he had given his opponents. Call appreciated the irony even if the sheriff couldn't.

"Dead," Call said softly. He holstered his weapon and held out a hand to Laurel. She shook out her fingers and then put her hand in his and let him help her to her feet.

"You're sure?" she asked, looking past Call's shoulder to the bed.

"Sure," he said. "Rooster? You okay?"

"Bruised some. That'd be my pride I'm talking about."

Laurel smiled because he meant her to. She left Call's side to see to her mentor and friend. She hunkered beside him. "Can you stand? Here, put your arm around my shoulders."

Call let them struggle to their feet. It seemed important just then that they manage on their own, and when he was certain they were up and steady, he went to Berry's side and bent over the man. Berry's eyes were still closed, but he was breathing with a regular, if shallow, rhythm. Call cast a sideways look at Laurel.

"Is he really Pinkerton?"

Berry groaned but didn't open his eyes. "I really am."

"Huh. You ready to get up?"

"Maybe in a hundred years."

"There's no chance anyone here is kissing you, Sleeping Beauty."

"Damn," he said under his breath. "All right." He put out a hand to stop Call from assisting him. "I can do this on my own." Opening his eyes, he pushed himself into a sitting position. He remained there for more than a minute, getting his bearings and pressing a palm to the side of his head. "Damn, that hurt. Still does."

Laurel asked, "How is your vision? Are you seeing double?"

"No. I'm good." He got to his knees, then rose to his feet and stared at Carter's body lying crossways on the bed. "Did you do that, Mr. Landry?"

"Call. Please. Yeah, I did that. Didn't plan to kill him, though. He struck me and it changed my aim. I shot him in the arm first, but I'm not sure he felt it. Meant to hit him in the thigh the second time. You can see that didn't work out."

Berry nodded. "What did you get out of him before Miss Morrison and I got here?"

"Not as much as I would have liked. He denied everything. The closest he came to a confession was when he told all of us that Pye and Desiree were going to split the money and cut him out. You heard how he took that back."

"Did I?" asked Berry. He touched his temple. "That blow to my head. My memory's a little vague on that count. I remember the confession, but after that . . ." He shrugged. "No. Nothing's coming to me."

"It's odd," said Laurel, "but I'm not recalling what the sheriff said after his confession either."

"Same here," Rooster said. "Darndest thing."

Call felt their expectant gazes settle on him. He knew what they wanted. He wanted it, too. "Huh," he said after a while. "Maybe I got it wrong."

Berry asked, "Do we know where the money is?"

Laurel answered. "Call and I think that Carter turned most of it over to the Hammersmiths."

"The money they offered as a bribe. Yes, that makes sense."

Call said, "I made that claim to Carter. He didn't bite."

"Well, we know he murdered Pye," said Berry. "Miss Desiree turned on him. The sheriff's second mistake where she was concerned was not giving her what she felt she was owed. She would have been on a stage to Denver if he had. Instead, she couldn't wait to tell us what she knew."

"Are you going to arrest her?" asked Call.

Rooster added, "Seems a shame, if you care a lick for my opinion."

"She's culpable," said Berry. "She was an accomplice. She admitted that she helped Josey Pye by cutting strips the size of legal tender from the newspaper."

"You heard her say that?" Call asked Laurel.

She nodded. "You were right about her part in this." Laurel looked at Berry, her eyes pleading. "She did it for love. Doesn't that matter?"

Call pressed his knuckles to his mouth and coughed to smother his laugh. *She did it for love.* Of all the things Laurel might have said in defense of Desiree, to Call's mind, that was the least predictable. From Berry's slightly openmouthed expression, the Pinkerton detective shared his opinion.

"I doubt it will matter to Mr. Stonechurch," Berry said dryly, "but I'll be sure to ask him."

Laurel was not amused. "You're going to recover the money from the Hammersmiths, aren't you?"

Berry cocked an eyebrow and looked at Call. "Am I? As I understand it, that's why Mr. Stonechurch hired you."

"A little help wouldn't come amiss."

"That's what I hoped you'd say." He turned to Laurel. "Yes, we're going to recover the payroll, or what's left of it."

"I'll make up the difference," she said.

"You don't have to do that."

"No. I want to. The robbery happened at my station. I know I wasn't the cause of it, but I want to do something anyway."

"Perhaps I haven't been clear," said Berry. "The government hired me to make a recommendation, and I'm recommending that the railroad use the Cabin Creek Trail. Tracks will be laid down past Morrison Station. I'll be sending a surveyor to look over the land you showed me today, but I saw enough to believe it will prove satisfactory. There's nothing you need to do to improve your standing with Washington or the railroad. The contract will be yours."

Call watched Laurel's chin come up in a way that was at once familiar and splendidly unwavering. He smiled, waiting.

She said, "What I offered has nothing at all to do with improving my standing with the railroad. I have to live with myself, Mr. Berry, and this is where I stand."

42

Laurel tugged on the strap of her camisole, which had slipped over her shoulder. The sun was warm on the back of her neck. She stood above the blue-green water's edge wriggling her bare toes as she anticipated the leap she was about to make. It was the hand pressed to the base of her spine that decided her. She made a shallow dive into the pool, turned over, and surfaced on her back. She blinked water out of her eyes and grinned up at Call, who was still standing on the lip of the same rock that she had just abandoned. "C'mon in. I dare you."

"There used to be a body in there, Laurel."

"You are unexpectedly squeamish about some things."

"And I make no apology for it."

Laurel's grin disappeared and she said earnestly, "I should hope not. It's easily one of your most oddly appealing qualities."

Call chuckled and tightened the string on his drawers. "All right. I'm coming in." He jumped, drawing his knees up to his chest so he displaced as much water as possible and rocked Laurel's peaceful sculling. He came up sputtering and still managed to catch her by the ankle before she drifted away.

"You have me," she said. "Now what are you going to do?"

Call turned on his side and swam to the rocky wall, where he knew he could find the ledge. He pulled Laurel along with him and only released her ankle when she remained in easy reach.

Laurel dropped to vertical and began treading lazily. She dipped her head to clear strands of hair that had fallen across her cheeks. Her heavy braid slipped over her shoulder and floated behind her. "This is nice, isn't it? I'm glad you're back."

"It's very nice, and I'm glad to be back. Alex Berry wasn't a terrible companion, but he wasn't you."

Call had been gone six days, putting the investigation to rest, and arrived at Morrison Station only to have Rooster remind him it was Sunday and Laurel was at services. He gave Artemis to Rooster to care for and began walking toward town. It was never his intention to join Laurel in the tent. He found a comfortable spot to lie in wait at the footpath that led to the falls. He hadn't counted on falling asleep, but he did, so it was Laurel who found him. It was not a bad way to wake up, he remembered. He would be happily contented the rest of his life if she woke him with kisses.

"Tell me what happened," she said, flicking water at Call when she saw his thoughts drifting. "You must have recovered the money or you wouldn't be here."

"We did. Most of it. If you're serious about making up the difference, you owe Mr. Stonechurch fifty dollars."

She blew out a short breath. "I was afraid it might be more. Evidently the Hammersmiths saved what Sheriff Carter gave them for their bribe."

"You know Stonechurch isn't going to accept your money."

"We'll see," she said, preferring not to argue. "So Mr. Berry is returning the payroll to him? I thought you'd want to do that."

"The payroll is safely in the Denver bank. Berry and I took it with us when we were escorting Ephraim Hammersmith to jail. He wouldn't give up his brothers, although we suspect they were very much part of the scheme. Ezekiel, in particular, seemed to want to confess."

"Ezekiel? Ephraim's brother is named Ezekiel?"

"Mm-hmm. And there's Enoch, too. We learned that Enoch briefly worked for Sam Henderson. That's how he met Digger Leary. The way Berry and I figure it is that Ephraim planned the robbery but Enoch was either too scared or too smart to have any real part of it. He approached Digger after Ephraim had Carter in his pocket."

"How does Mr. Pye come into it?"

"Hard to know with certainty. Ephraim says it was Carter who arranged details with Pye, but it could have been Enoch working with Digger who came up with the idea. What we know for sure is that Pye didn't come to the station with robbery in mind. He didn't take a job at your station for that purpose." Call watched relief wash over Laurel's features.

"Thank you. You knew I was wondering."

"I suspected. How could you not? Anyway, Berry will be spending more time with Digger and Ephraim in Dave Cook's jail. I think he'll get to the truth. It won't be astonishing if Enoch and Ezekiel eventually join their older brother." Call tilted his head as he regarded Laurel warmly, wonderingly. "Berry told me you asked him straight out if he was open to a bribe. He said no one had ever put the question to him so baldly before."

"He told me the same thing."

Call nodded. "If only one of the Hammersmiths had thought to ask, they could have spared themselves a great deal of grief. Money doesn't tempt Berry."

"Neither do I."

"Uh-huh. He told me about that. I didn't like it. The only reason I didn't knock him out of his saddle was because I knew you'd have already stepped on him hard." He paused. "You did, didn't you?"

Laurel got a mouthful of water when she laughed. She spit it out in a spout that nearly reached him. "Yes, I stepped on him. Perhaps not hard enough at first because I was still wary of riding out with him alone."

"Good thinking to take Jelly with you."

"I could depend on him to champion me without laying a hand on Alex Berry. I didn't trust any of the rest of you. We all know now that Berry is entirely honorable so we can put that behind us."

"Hmm. Wouldn't have minded pushing him out of his saddle, though."

"I'm sure." Laurel offered up her most patronizing smile and dropped underwater, laughing, as he reached out to dunk her. When she came up, she was right in front of him and she was no longer laughing or even smiling. "Has Berry decided what he's going to do about Desiree? I don't think he was persuaded by my she-did-it-for-love argument."

Straight-faced, Call said, "Perhaps not, but I was moved."

"To laughter. I saw you trying to suck it in." Her deeply brown eyes dared him to deny it. He wisely remained silent. "So what did he decide?"

"He didn't. He wired Mr. Stonechurch, gave him the information, and left it up to him. Stonechurch telegraphed back and told Berry to let her be. Desiree assisted Pye in only a minor way, and she didn't profit from the robbery. She met Pye above the falls as planned to take possession of her share of the money, but Carter found out about the meeting, shot Pye, and took his saddlebag from her. There was nowhere for her to go to turn him in and she was afraid for herself. Can you imagine how it galled her when he paid for her services with money from the robbery?"

Laurel could imagine it. "Will she leave town, do you think?"

"I believe she will once she comes into a little of the reward."

"Reward money? Isn't that yours?"

"I was paid fairly in advance for my work. I figure Desiree deserves something for trapping Carter in her bedroom with Rooster and me. Carter wanted her inside and she most definitely wanted to be on the other side. It was a good plan."

Laurel agreed. "She did have a lot to say to Mr. Berry and me when we arrived. At first I thought she was trying to keep us from you, but then I realized she just needed to unburden herself. I'm glad she'll have money."

"Yes."

There was nothing more to say. Call watched Laurel drift away on the current and then scull toward him again. She lifted her damp face to the sun. Her complexion glistened and tiny prisms of color appeared in the mist around her dark hair.

Laurel looked at him, smiled. "I have lovely memories of this particular spot."

"Mm. So do I."

"We're outdoors," she said, trying to sound casual about the observation.

"Indeed we are."

"You're standing."

"Your powers of observation have no equal."

"They really don't," she said. "I notice you don't have any flowers."

"Sadly, no. They're all around, though. You could take that into consideration."

"I could. I suppose that depends."

"On what?"

"The promises you make. You are going to make them, aren't you?"

"I said I would."

She waited, but he remained silent. "Well?"

"Oh. You want to hear them now."

"I could drown you, you know. And I'd make a better job of seeing you stayed on the bottom than Carter did with Mr. Pye."

Call made a face and feigned a shiver. "Don't remind me."

Laurel lightly pressed her fist against his hard belly. "And don't make me laugh."

"All right," he said, covering her fist and raising it higher so it rested against his heart. Her fingers splayed under his hand. "Come here." He placed his free hand on her bottom and urged her to wrap her legs around him. When she was comfortably settled, he said, "You know I love you."

"Mm. I know."

"That's forever, Laurel. I promise that's forever."

She felt herself tearing up and didn't try to hide it. She gave him a watery smile instead.

"I promise that there will be occasions when you'll find me unbearable."

Laurel nodded. "It's difficult living with someone who thinks he's always right."

"Who *knows* he's right. You see the difference?"

"I do," she whispered. She kissed him on the mouth. "Unbearable."

"We'll argue," he said.

"Is *that* a promise?"

"Not exactly. More like stating the inevitable."

"Oh."

"We're both stubborn, sometimes more than a little unreasonable, but I promise you that there is nothing that we can't resolve even if it means we agree to disagree. I promise that I will always have your back. I admire your strength, your fierce independence, and if you ever think I'm standing in your way, you have to tell me because the view from here is that I'm protecting you. I promise to take you seriously. I promise to respect you. I promise to be at your side when you want a partner and at your back when you want a push. Laurel, I promise there will be times you'll catch me smiling and you won't know why, so I'm telling you now there's no help for it because it feels just that good to be with you. I promise . . ." Call stopped. "Suppose you tell me why you're crying."

"There's no help for it. I'm just that happy."

He used his thumb to erase the tear tracks on her cheeks. "You're hard to figure sometimes."

She sniffed a bit inelegantly. "I hope so. You like puzzles."

"I do." He cupped her face so her eyes were steady on his. "Do you have an answer for me, Laurel?"

"I haven't heard a question."

"Right."

When he didn't say more, Laurel frowned slightly, trying to divine why he was hesitating. "Are you feeling a mite squeamish about this, Call? Because no matter what I said before, I'm not finding it endearing."

He laughed then. The sound came up from deep in his chest, and it was born of amusement and adoration, and when he'd caught his breath, he kissed her hard. "You can't possibly know how much I love you," he said when he'd caught his breath a second time. "I couldn't have imagined anyone like you ever coming into my life, and now I can't imagine ever having a life without you. Laurel Beth Morrison, will you marry me?"

"Yes," she said softly, with no hesitation. Then more loudly, "Yes." And again, this time shouting it so it could be heard above the rush of falling water, "Yes!"

He didn't mind it when she threw her arms around him and dragged him under. She kissed him hard and deeply, and when they'd surfaced, they each had breath to catch.

"Here?" he asked. "Or there?" Call pointed to the sun-baked slabs of stone.

"Here," she said, reaching for the opening in his drawers. "Up there is warm but also hard." She curled her fingers around his erection. Feigning surprise, her eyes widened. "Oh. It's the same down here."

"Mm-hmm." He hummed his response against her mouth. "Go on," he said. "Take me."

And so she did. She was ready for him, had been since she'd spotted him lying in the grass. He'd been waiting for her. It didn't matter that he'd fallen asleep; she knew he'd set himself on the path to intercept her. Fatigue had been his enemy. Even sunshine couldn't erase the faint shadows beneath his eyes. He must have ridden hard to reach home. To reach her.

He was easy with her. That was all right, she thought.

They would be easy with each other. Slow would make this homecoming last. She hugged him with her thighs and cupped his face in her palms. She kissed him tenderly and felt their bodies hum with gentle pleasure. She told him she loved him, told him how she'd ached while he was away.

"Promise you won't leave again," she said. "Not without me. Never without me."

It was the promise that he'd left unsaid earlier when he saw her tears. The words had been resting in his heart and now he made them his solemn vow. "I promise," he said. "Never without you."

They didn't speak again until they climbed out of the water. Call gave Laurel a boost before he pulled himself up. She started to wring out her undergarments but gave up quickly. She dropped to the flat stone, stretched on her back as sinuously as a sleek mountain cat, and generously patted the warm, dry space beside her.

Call did not require any more encouragement than that. He shook himself off, flinging water droplets with abandon, and sat down at her side.

Laurel shaded her eyes with her hand to look up at him. "Don't you want to lie down?"

"In a bit. I already had a nap."

"Not much of one, I'm thinking."

"Go on," he said. "Close your eyes. I won't be long joining you."

Laurel murmured drowsy agreement and let her hand fall away from her eyes as she closed them. She had no intention of falling asleep, but it wasn't really up to her. Replete, she allowed sleep to come in its own time, as natural and necessary as breathing, and when she woke, the sun was significantly lower in the sky and Call was sleeping deeply beside her. He looked as if he was smiling and Laurel wondered at it, wondered if it was merely her imagination because she so dearly loved his smile, but then she sat up and saw the blue and pink and yellow and violet wildflowers scattered all over and around her, and knew it was his doing and that his satisfied smile was no part of her imagination. She plucked a blue columbine from among the flowers in her lap and leaned over Call to tuck it behind his ear.

"Don't you dare," he said.

"How do you know what I was going to do? You haven't even opened your eyes."

"I just know," he said. "Some things I just know. Come here."

She scooted over, crushing flowers as she went, and laid her head in the curve of his shoulder. "It's not so bad you knowing. I thought it would be, but it's not. You gave me flowers because you knew. It was a lovely gesture."

"You're welcome."

"I love you." She said it easily, without hesitation, and once again felt remarkably lighter for saying it aloud. It struck her then that loving Call was a life sentence without fetters. Had she understood that sooner, she would have proposed to him and was on the point of telling him that when she felt him shift and press his lips against her hair.

Call breathed in the fragrance of the wildflower crown Laurel didn't yet realize she was wearing and smiled to himself. "Tell me," he said. "Do you know what I'm going to do?"

Laurel tipped her head to look at him. She could have told him that he had no secrets when he spoke in that husky, gentle yet rough voice of his, but she found it endearing that he thought he did. "I think I know," she said, angling her body against his. "I hope I'm right."

And she was.

Turn the page for a preview of Jo Goodman's

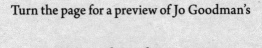

A Touch of Forever

Available now from Berkley

Lily Salt did not raise her voice when her older boy attempted to make a stealthy entrance into the kitchen. Neither did she turn around from the stove, where she was stirring a pot of chili. "Clay Bryant Salt."

"Yes, ma'am. I'm going to oil that hinge first thing tomorrow."

"Won't help you. I suppose I know when my son's been wandering and when he's home."

"Chili smells good." He sidled up to the stove and bumped her affectionately. "Better than good, I'm thinking. Might be excellent."

"I am not mollified. Not even a little." But she bumped him back while she continued to stir. "Go tell your sister it's time to set the table and then you wash your hands. Help Ham and Lizzie, too."

When Clay took a step sideways but didn't leave the kitchen, Lily was immediately suspicious. She swiveled her head in his direction. He was tall now, as tall as she was, and she hadn't quite gotten used to it. It pained her some to look him in the eye. He had his father's eyes and coloring, though in every other way he was nothing at all like his father. Still, the eyes. "What is it?" she asked.

Clay pointed to the kitchen door, where Roen Shepard stood framed in the opening.

"I beg your pardon, Mrs. Salt," Roen said, removing his hat and holding it in front of him like a penitent. "I wanted to see your son home safely. I'm Roen Shepard, the engineering surveyor employed by Northeast Rail."

Lily indicated that Clay should take the long-handled wooden spoon. "Stir," she said. She thought he was glad to have the spoon in his hand and not hers, though she had never once raised it against him. There were memories of his father not easily erased. "I know who you are, Mr. Shepard." She crossed a few feet to the table and rested one hand on the back of a chair. She did not close the distance between them.

Roen did not inch into the room, nor did he back away. Lily Salt was regarding him warily, with the innate stillness of a rabbit in the wild sensing something feral in her midst. In deference to what he perceived as distress, he remained rooted where he stood.

It was in the back pew of the Presbyterian Church that Clay's mother had made her first impression on Roen Shepard. He'd been sitting five pews ahead on the aisle when a cloth ball rolled between his feet. He picked it up, looked around for the owner, and passed it back to a harried mother with a child set to squall on her lap. The squalling was averted, and he was grateful for that, but more grateful that his backward search had afforded him a glimpse of the woman who later became known to him as Lily Salt.

She looked to him as composed and serene as any Madonna rendered in oils by the great artists of the Renaissance. That she was flanked by two boys and two girls, who could only be her children, made her calm seem preternatural. She had the smile of the *Mona Lisa*, which was to say it was more a smile of imagination than it was of reality, but when he turned away, that perception of her smile lingered.

She wore a wide-brimmed straw sailor hat trimmed with a black ribbon and tilted forward as was the fashion. Her hair, what he could see of it then, was rust red, but her older daughter had hair like a flame and made him suspect that this was Lily's color in her youth.

When he caught sight of her escaping the church with her children in tow, Roen knew himself to be mildly intrigued. He was saved from expressing any measure of curiosity by Mrs. Springer's account of the congregation, their lineage, their talents, and their foibles. Amanda Springer was a wellspring of information, most of which, he later learned from the minister, could be taken as gospel.

So here he was facing Lily Salt, age thirty-four, a widow whose husband had perished in a fire almost two years earlier, mother of four children, seamstress employed in the dress shop owned by Mrs. Fish, and doing well enough on her own that she had no interest in inviting a man into her life, though according to Mrs. Springer, a number of men had tried.

This last was rather more than Roen had expected or even wanted to hear, since he had no interest in such an invitation, but Amanda Springer, once sprung, said what was on her mind. All of it. Her husband, an affable man who tended bar at the Songbird Saloon, seized on the opportunity to disengage her at the first sign she was winding down. Later, Roen rewarded Jim Springer's strategy by buying him a drink at the saloon, though he never explained the reason for his generosity.

At the risk of Lily Salt turning tail and fleeing her own kitchen, Roen offered a slim, apologetic smile. "Your boy was a help to me," he said. At the stove, Clay glanced over his shoulder and gave Roen an appreciative eyeful. Roen ignored him. "Thought it was the least I could do to see him home."

Lily's slim hand, the one that curved over the back of a chair, tightened so her knuckles stood out in stark white relief. Her chin came up. "I reckon Clay knows the lay of the land a mite better than you do even with all of your fancy instruments."

Clay stopped stirring and stared openmouthed at his mother. "Ma!"

Roen thought Lily appeared more surprised by her temerity than she was regretful of it. Her lips parted but she had no words. It fell to Roen to supply them. "You're correct, Mrs. Salt. Clay was a better escort to me than I was to him, and I'll be taking my leave now."

"Ma!" This time Clay's cry was plaintive. "I invited Mr. Shepard to take supper with us."

"Did you now?" she asked without taking her eyes off Clay's guest.

"I did. He's been taking his meals regular at the hotel and I figured home-cooked food would do him right." He jerked his chin in Roen's direction. "You can see for yourself that some meat on his bones wouldn't come amiss."

Lily's eyes did not stray from Roen Shepard's angular face, but it was impossible not to note that her son was correct. The man standing in her doorway probably filled out a black coat and tails just fine, even excellently, but his blue chambray shirt drooped some at the shoulders. The butternut leather vest was loose across the chest, and his denim trousers looked as if they would benefit from a belt *and* suspenders. Someone needed to take him in hand. That thought flitted uncomfortably through her mind, but what she said was, "The Butterworth serves excellent food."

She stepped back to the stove, took the spoon from Clay, and set it aside. "Go do what I asked you to do."

Uncertain, Clay nonetheless hurried from the kitchen.

When he was gone, Lily pointed to the pegs to the left of the door. "You can hang your hat there."

Roen did as he was told and closed the door behind him. Lily was already turned back to the stove when he was done. Her thick hair was neatly arranged in a braided coil at the back of her head. His eyes settled on the fragile nape of her neck as she bent to her work. "What decided you?" he asked.

"It's the least I can do to make amends for my son pestering you."

"Oh, but he didn't."

Lily picked up a folded towel and used it to open the oven door. She removed a pan of cornbread, but not before she gave Roen Shepard a jaundiced look that said she knew her son as well as her son knew the lay of the land. It was gratifying that he accepted that silent reprimand and said nothing in return.

The warm fragrance of cornbread was wafting through the kitchen as Hannah came rushing in from the hallway. She skidded to a halt, closely followed by her younger sister, Lizzie, and the pair of them held up their hands to show they'd been washed clean. Droplets of water flew from their fingertips as they shook them out. Whatever admonishment Lily meant to say when she opened her mouth to speak came to nothing as Hannah interrupted her mother.

"So you *are* here!" she said, addressing Roen Shepard. "Clay said you were but I didn't know if I could believe him. He likes to play tricks. Say hello, Lizzie, to Mr. Shepard."

Lizzie, at five, was a practiced coquette. She gave Roen a sidelong glance and a sweet smile while tilting her head just so. Her curls, the color of sunshine, swung to and fro when she righted her head. "Hello." Then she sidled closer to her sister, where she sought the protection of Hannah's gingham skirt.

"Hello, Lizzie. Hannah. What a pleasure it is to see you again."

Lily set the pan of cornbread on a warming plate on top of the stove. "Set the table, Hannah. Bowls and spoons. Lizzie, take your seat." To Roen, she said, "How do my girls know you?"

Hannah answered before Roen could. "We see him in church, Ma. Same as everyone."

Lily recognized the truth in that, but she also recognized there was something left unsaid. "I was speaking to Mr. Shepard."

Roen hadn't moved more than two feet into the kitchen. His place at the table was not clear to him, and he waited to be invited to sit or asked to help. "They introduced themselves when we were in Hennepin's mercantile."

Lizzie plopped herself into her chair and swung her feet under the table. "He bought us a bag of licorice whips and horehound drops."

Lily frowned deeply. "Why would you do that? No, Lizzie, I don't want to hear from you. I want to hear from Mr. Shepard."

Lizzie clamped her lips closed and regarded Roen sorrowfully. She had told the truth but her mother's expression led her to believe it wasn't the right answer.

Without the least regret, Roen said, "It appears I overstepped, and that certainly was not my intention. Indeed, my intention was to move them along. As I'm sure you're aware, Mr. Hennepin has a large selection of candy and your girls could not decide between the peppermint, the butterscotch, or the horehound drops. It was amusing at first, and then it was painful. I had an appointment, you see, and needed to be on my way, and Mr. Hennepin was giving the girls their due, as a good shopkeeper should. I chose the horehound candies for them and added the licorice whips because I wanted one myself. And that's how it came to pass. They were grateful and I was on time for my meeting with the town council."

He thought he saw Lily's lips twitch, but whether she was amused or skeptical, he couldn't say. After a moment she nodded once and the subject was closed. Lizzie's sigh of relief was audible and Hannah actually winked at him. If Lily noticed either girl's reaction, she did not comment.

"Can I help?" Roen asked as Hannah set bowls on the table.

Lily pointed out a chair. "You can sit yourself there. Ham will sit beside you. The girls opposite. Hannah. See what's keeping your brothers."

He assumed from the position of the chairs that it meant Clay sat at one end and Lily at the other. Roen went around the table but stood behind his chair rather than sit down.

Lily cut the cornbread and placed the warm pan on a trivet on the table. As she ladled chili into the bowls, Hannah reappeared with her brothers on her heels. The boys held up their hands for inspection, and when Lily pronounced them fit, they moved to the table.

Unlike his whip-thin older brother, Ham was a sturdy

boy with a cherub's face and deviltry in his eyes. Roen noticed he wasn't wearing shoes and his hands were considerably cleaner than his feet. As soon as Ham sat, he leaned over to the empty chair designated for Roen and patted the seat. "This is you here, Mr. Shepard. Beside me." With the unaffected aplomb of a six-year-old, he held out his hand and announced, "I'm Hamilton Salt, by the way, and I am glad to make your acquaintance."

Lily regarded her younger son with suspicion and then her gaze slid sideways to Clay. He made a show of shrugging just as if he hadn't been helping Ham master that introduction.

Roen solemnly extended his hand and shook Hamilton's. "It's a pleasure."

"You can sit now," said Ham.

"I am waiting for your mother."

"Oh." His mouth screwed up to one side while he considered this as Lily returned the chili pot to the stove.

Roen skirted the table and held out Lily's chair for her. She stared at it and then at him. A vertical frown line appeared between her eyebrows. She sat slowly, hesitantly, almost as if she anticipated the chair being pulled out from under her. That didn't happen. Roen pushed the chair closer to the table.

Ham watched this all with naked curiosity. "She'll just get up again," he said. "She always does."

"Hush," Lily whispered, and under the table, Hannah kicked him.

"Ow!" He glared at his sister. "Why'd you do that?"

"Because Lizzie's legs are too short."

It was true, but it was hardly the answer Ham was looking for. He settled into his seat and tucked his legs under him. He was quiet until Roen took his seat and then he announced, "We pray now," and bent his head over dimpled hands folded into a single fist.

Roen bowed his head. The prayer was familiar, one he had learned as a child, but he chose to mouth the words rather than give voice to them with the rest of the family.

As soon as every "amen" was said, Ham reached for the pan of cornbread. Lily lightly tapped him on the back of his hand with the bowl of her spoon. "I should let you burn your fingers. We serve our guest first." She slipped a turner into the pan and removed a square of cornbread. Roen raised his chili bowl toward her and she set the bread neatly on the lip. She did the same for Ham and herself and then let Hannah serve Lizzie and Clay.

"Go on," Lily said, tipping her head in Roen's direction. "Tuck in." She saw him nod, but she also noticed he did not take his first bite until she had. She acquitted him of suspecting that she was trying to poison him. His reticence was born of good manners, and while she was grateful for what he was demonstrating to her children, it made her distinctly uncomfortable. She wasn't used to this deference and doubted that she deserved it.

Lily's throat felt thick. She choked down the first mouthful of chili and was grateful that no one noticed her distress. It faded with the second bite and was nothing at all by the third.

"There's plenty more," she told Ham as he shoveled chili and cornbread into his mouth. "Slow down."

"It's good, Ma. Real good."

"I'm happy to hear it. Now slow down."

Out of the corner of his eye, Roen saw Ham dutifully slow the lift of his spoon to his mouth but not the size of his bite. Aware that Lily Salt was watching him now, Roen took care not to smile. Amusement would not have been appreciated just then.

"Your chili is excellent," he said. "A family recipe?"

"No. Mrs. Butterworth's. If you take your meals at the hotel, you've met her."

He nodded. "Ah, yes. Ellie. The owner's wife."

Clay spoke around a mouthful of cornbread. "She's the sheriff's mother. Did you know that?"

"I believe she mentioned that," he said, his voice a tad dry. "Several times."

"Well, she's that proud," said Lily. "And no one faults her for it. Sheriff Ben is good people."

"I've had the pleasure." Roen guided another spoonful of chili to his mouth. The aroma teased his senses. "He welcomed me, took me around to meet the shopkeepers and the gentlemen who manage the land office."

"Dave and Ed Saunders."

"Yes. The brothers. They've been helpful providing me with maps and plotting boundaries."

Clay said, "Mr. Shepard was looking at Double H land this afternoon, but I told him that Ol' Harrison Hardy isn't going to fool with the railroad."

Lily raised a single eyebrow and regarded her son with a seriously set mien. "Maybe. Maybe not. That's business between Mr. Hardy and Mr. Shepard."

As a reprimand, Roen thought it was a mild one, but nevertheless Clay ducked his head and nodded.

Lily served another square of cornbread to Roen. "How long will you be staying in Frost Falls, Mr. Shepard?"

For all that the question was politely posed and made with an offering of sweet cornbread, Roen had the sense that if his answer was more than a few more days, it would be too long. Unless she was anticipating that he would be a frequent dinner guest, Roen couldn't imagine why it mattered. "It's never clear this early," he said, hedging. "It's hard to project a timeline at this juncture, and Northeast Rail has hired me on to see this through."

"But roughly," said Lily.

"I'll know better inside of six weeks."

"Oh."

Roen could see nothing in the placid composition of her delicate features to indicate that she was aggrieved; yet he couldn't shake the feeling that she was. Her children, on the other hand, appeared to be delighted.

Hannah said, "So you'll hardly be a visitor to Frost Falls. More like regular folk."

"I suppose that's true."

"Oh, it is. Especially since you're staying in Sheriff Ben's house, or what used to be his house, and not taking a room at the Butterworth."

Lily frowned at her daughter. "And just how do you know so much about it?"

Hannah shrugged. "It's like you say. Everyone here knows everything."

Lily felt her cheeks warm. It was her own voice she heard in Hannah's ironic tones. Her daughter was a perfect mimic. "Yes, well, you don't have to repeat everything you hear."

"No, ma'am."

Roen said, "Northeast Rail is renting the sheriff's house for the duration of my stay. I spend a lot of time in hotels and railroad cars, so this is a welcome change."

Clay said, "Sheriff Ben likes having someone living in the house. He told me. I work for him sometimes. Me and my friend Frankie Fuller. Odd jobs mostly. I'm real good at a lot of things. So is Frankie." He tilted his head to the side as he regarded his guest. "You ever have a need for an odd jobber?"

"Clay." Lily said his name quietly, without inflection, but he nevertheless sat back in his chair as though pushed. "This is supper, and Mr. Shepard is your guest. You can talk business after over cigars and port when the rest of us retire to the front room."

Her response was so unexpected that Clay's jaw went slack. Hannah stared at her mother. Lizzie and Ham looked at each other with identical frowns. For his part, Roen threw back his head and gave a shout of laughter.

Lily took this all in, nodded faintly, satisfied, and smiled in a way that suggested she had swallowed a secret.